TO DANCE WITH THE DEVIL

Tor Paranormal Romance Books
by C. T. Adams and Cathy Clamp

THE SAZI

Hunter's Moon
Moon's Web
Captive Moon
Howling Moon
Moon's Fury
Timeless Moon
Cold Moon Rising
Serpent Moon

THE THRALL

Touch of Evil
Touch of Madness
Touch of Darkness

WRITING AS CAT ADAMS

Magic's Design
Blood Song
Siren Song
Demon Song
The Isis Collar
The Eldritch Conspiracy
To Dance with the Devil

CAT ADAMS

TO DANCE WITH THE DEVIL

A Tom Doherty Associates Book

New York

This is a work of fiction. All of the characters, organizations, and events portrayed in this novel are either products of the authors' imaginations or are used fictitiously.

TO DANCE WITH THE DEVIL

A Tor Book
Published by Tom Doherty Associates, LLC
175 Fifth Avenue
New York, NY 10010

www.tor-forge.com

Library of Congress Cataloging-in-Publication Data

Adams, Cat.
To Dance with the Devil / Cat Adams.—1st ed.
p. cm. (Blood Singer)
ISBN 978-0-7653-2875-5 (trade paperback)
ISBN 978-1-4668-3420-0 (e-book)
1. Shapeshifting—Fiction. 2. Vampires—Fiction. 3. Demonology—Fiction. 4. Vendetta—Fiction. I. Title.
PS3601.D3697T63 2013
813'.6—dc23

2013023855

Tor books may be purchased for educational, business, or promotional use. For information on bulk purchases, please contact Macmillan Corporate and Premium Sales Department at 1-800-221-7945, extension 5442, or write specialmarkets@macmillan.com.

First Edition: November 2013

Printed in the United States of America

0 9 8 7 6 5 4 3 2

First, and always, we dedicate this book to our families, particularly Cathy's husband, Don, and Cie's son, James. But during the writing of this book, Cie's father, also James, died. So this book is especially dedicated to him, and to Cie's mother, Mary Frances, for her love and care for the family in good times and bad, in sickness and in health. Cie says, "I love you both, always and forever, and am more grateful than I can say for the privilege of having been brought up by you."

ACKNOWLEDGMENTS

Every book is a major endeavor and involves the efforts of a group of talented people working behind the scenes to bring it from an idea in the author's head to the product you see on the page or screen. We thank our team, including our agents, Lucienne Diver of The Knight Agency and Merrilee Heifetz of Writers House, our brilliant editor, Melissa Ann Singer, and the amazing staff at Tor/Forge. You guys rock, and make us look good in the process. We appreciate it.

AUTHORS' NOTE

Happy families make for happy writers but fairly boring characters (in our opinion). So we have saddled Celia with a formidable amount of family misery that (thankfully) neither of us had to endure. So in the interest of a better book, these happy writers will once again drag our poor character into the fray.

If you dance with the devil,
you're bound to get burned.
—proverb

feud (fyüd) *n* 1. also called **blood feud**, a bitter, aggressive hostility, esp. between two families, clans, etc., often lasting for many years or generations 2. a war of revenge or rivalry

TO DANCE WITH THE DEVIL

1

I dressed carefully for the meeting. The setting was casual; since we were currently officeless, Dawna had agreed to meet Ms. Abigail Andrews, a potential client, for lunch at La Cocina. Unfortunately for me, my business partner had bailed on the meeting at the last possible moment, with what seemed to me to be a fairly flimsy excuse. This was just one of a whole number of things we were going to have to have a serious talk about in the very near future. I get that Dawna's busy getting ready for her wedding. I understand that she's distracted. But to not even have done the basic research on Ms. Andrews or filled out a client intake form was just sloppy. Dawna is better than that. She was better than that the first week she had started as my receptionist, years ago.

Graves Personal Protection was the company I'd formed shortly out of college. I am a bodyguard, and a good one. Until very recently I'd run a one-woman operation out of the top floor of an old Victorian mansion in downtown Santa Maria de Luna. Now that building was gone—long story—and I'd been forced to decide whether to expand the business or lose it altogether. I'd chosen to expand, but we were definitely experiencing growing pains.

Dawna Han Long and I have been friends practically since the moment we met, when she came to work for me. She's smart, beautiful, hardworking, efficient, and one of the most ambitious people I've ever known. I'd thought that offering her a piece of the action and partnership in the business would make her even more committed to its success. Thus far, not so much. I reminded myself, yet again, that we've been through worse than this, more than once, and made it through just fine.

Still, no matter what I was feeling, I was about to take a business meeting. I needed to smile (but not show fang) and look pleasant, cordial, and ever so competent. With that in mind I'd decided to wear a purple silk shell over black jeans, with my standard black suit jacket. Black and purple are among the few colors that really look good with my paler-than-pale skin tone, gray eyes, and naturally blonde hair. I had to work very hard to find ways to look good—but not too good. Bodyguards are never, ever, supposed to outshine their clients. It's a rule. Unwritten, but a rule nonetheless.

I was armed to the teeth. No, I did not think Ms. Andrews was going to attack me. But a few months ago some quasi-religious extremists had declared "war" on sirens, and while I'd helped take out the top of their hierarchy, there were still a few stray nut jobs on the loose with an axe to grind. So I don't go anywhere unarmed—ever. Today I was wearing my Colt in an underarm holster and a new Derringer on my ankle, and carrying an assortment of spell disks. I also had on wrist sheaths that held a pair of very special knives. Made for me by a top mage, they are spelled heavily enough to be considered major magical artifacts. They're worth more than my car, possibly more than my house. Five years in the making, they are my most prized possessions. Last, but not least, there is a garrote hidden in the collar of my jacket. I've never had occasion to use it, but it's there nonetheless.

Most people think they should be able to tell if someone is a walking armory. Sometimes that's true. Fortunately for me, my jackets are well tailored and have enough magical spells on them to make them hang perfectly, concealing everything. Still, I don't look completely nonthreatening, and that's just as well. After all, a touch of intimidation is part of the service.

La Cocina is a tiny family-run Mexican restaurant tucked up against the college campus. When I was an undergrad, my friends and I hung out there all the time, and we'd continued the pattern long after graduating. Barbara and Pablo, who run the place, feel like my aunt and uncle. When they found out that I'd been bitten by a vampire and partially turned, Pablo made it his mission to come up with something nutritious that I could actually digest—no easy task since solids were impossible for me. He more than succeeded, creating one of my favorite things ever. It's called a Sunset Smoothie, and it's made with cooked cow's blood, spices, and melted cheese, all blended together and liquid enough that I can actually eat it.

I made my way to the back of the restaurant, where there was an area that was fairly quiet and private. Barbara came over as I took a seat with my back to the wall and a good view of the door and proceeded to wait for my potential client.

I didn't have to wait long. She came a little early, a small, dark-haired, middle-aged woman with bright blue eyes. One side of her face was flawless. The other half didn't quite match and bore faint scars that were slick and smooth. She'd had major reconstructive surgery at some point. Her medical team had done a great job, but it wasn't perfect. My guess, the damage had been too severe. There's only so much even the best doctors and mages can do.

I assumed her use of a motorized wheelchair could be attributed to whatever had led to the reconstruction. She steered the chair through the restaurant carefully but without hesitation, coming straight toward me. No real surprise that she knew what Celia Graves, bodyguard, looked like, considering how often I've been on the news in the past couple of years. She wore a traditional navy suit, her blouse a paler blue that exactly matched the color of her eyes.

I scooted a chair away from the table, making room for her. She slid smoothly into the space.

"Ms. Graves."

"Ms. Andrews. It's a pleasure to meet you." I extended my hand. She shook it, her grip firm but not too tight. Her eyes raked me up and down, taking my measure. I could understand that. Hell, most clients do the same. But there was something irritating in the way she did it. Her attitude was just a teeny bit rude. I forced myself to smile politely, but I knew already that this was going to be difficult.

It was the siren thing.

I am part siren. It wasn't really an issue until the vampire tried to turn me. Somehow the magic he used activated the latent siren abilities in my bloodline. My awakened heritage brought me in contact with family I never knew I had, which is a good thing. But there's a definite downside to that lineage. One of the primary reasons I asked Dawna to take any meeting with a female client was that, unless the client was wearing a charm, was infertile, or was gay, she'd pretty much hate me on sight.

Ms. Andrews wasn't wearing a charm.

"I'd recommend the quesadillas, they're quite good." I smiled so hard my cheeks hurt, trying hard to radiate bonhomie and goodwill.

"Is that what you'll be having?" The words were polite, but her tone of voice and body language were just short of hostile.

"No, I'm afraid I don't eat solids." I smiled, flashing just a hint of fang. It probably wasn't polite, but she was pushing me, deliberately provoking me under an oh-so-polite façade. I'd take it in the interests of business, but only for so long without pushing back a little.

"Oh? I'd heard you'd made some progress in that department."

Really? Where on earth had she heard that? It was true. I was now able to swallow most baby food, something I would never have dreamed possible right after the bite. But it wasn't the kind of information that had been passed on to the general public. I was very curious how Ms. Andrews had found out.

I gave her a noncommittal smile as Barbara arrived with water glasses and a menu for my guest.

Ms. Andrews wasted no time ordering, asking for quesas and iced tea. I ordered a smoothie, in part to be social but also because I'm less inclined to have issues with my vampire nature on a full stomach. Abigail Andrews was irritating the hell out of me, but I was not about to let her get to me to the point where I scared a restaurant full of customers.

"So," I said as Barbara disappeared toward the kitchen, "shall we get to it? What exactly do you want to hire me to do?"

"I want you to protect my daughter."

"Why?"

She blinked at me, as if I had asked the most stupid question in the world. I didn't grit my teeth and I kept my voice even and pleasant as I said, "What does your daughter need protection from?"

"Not what, who."

I raised my eyebrows and gestured for her to continue.

"I adopted my daughter when her birth mother, my sister, was murdered by her husband. He is scheduled to get out of prison two days from now. He is a terrible man—a vicious, violent killer." She gestured to her chair. "*He* did this to me."

"What's his name?" I interrupted her. Yes, it's rude, but she was gearing up for a tirade. And while her emotion was real, the speech itself seemed a little too pat, as if she'd rehearsed it in front of a mirror. I've run into that before, usually when clients are lying or hiding something I really need to know. They rehearse the BS they plan to feed me so that they won't say what they shouldn't.

Unfortunately, it's what clients feel they shouldn't say that is most likely to bite me in the ass. If I rattle them, I can sometimes get the straight scoop. Temperamental as Ms. Andrews was, this might cost me the job. But I'd rather lose a potential client than get myself or my people killed by walking blind into a dangerous situation.

Abigail sat straighter in her chair, her expression shifting swiftly from startled to annoyed. But she answered, her voice crisp and precise. "Harry Jacobs."

"Which prison?"

"Excuse me?"

It seemed like a simple enough question to me, but I repeated it. "Which prison is he getting out of?"

"Why do you need to know—"

"If I'm going to be protecting your daughter from someone, it's generally a good idea to keep an eye on him. That way I can be ahead of the game instead of constantly reacting." Okay, I was making that up. But now that I said it, it seemed like a good idea. Assuming I had the manpower—which I was working on. If I actually hired one of the people I'd be interviewing tomorrow, I could sic him or her on Harry, if there actually was a Harry.

"Oh." She was somewhat mollified by the explanation, but she shook her head. "I don't know."

Now that was weird. She knew he was being released but didn't know from where? That made zero sense. My expression must have shown how dubious I was.

"I don't," she repeated with a bit more heat. "I got an anonymous call telling me he was getting out. So I called the parole board. I got the runaround for a bit, but eventually they told me that he was not being paroled but was being released early for good behavior. I didn't think to ask which facility he'd been in."

Okay, I still didn't buy that, but I decided to move on. "How long was he in?"

"A little over twenty-two years. I don't see why—" She stopped speaking in midsentence. She was obviously angry now. Red spots had appeared on both cheeks; her breathing was rapid and a little ragged. The overreaction told me I was right. Something was amiss. She'd intended to keep me off balance, maintain control. She wanted her daughter protected, but she didn't want me to know from what. Not acceptable. If I'm going to put my life on the line, I want to know *all* the details. It can make the difference between success and failure, or success with a major hospital stay.

"This isn't going to work," she said grimly as she rolled away from the table and turned to leave.

She was right about that. "I'm sorry you feel that way," I said. I was lying. I wasn't sorry at all. "Before you go, can I give you a bit of advice?"

She turned her head, giving me an unfriendly look over her shoulder.

"If you hire someone ethical, he or she will maintain confidentiality. But we all have to know what we're up against. Tell the truth. All of it."

She gave me a long narrow-eyed glare before setting her chair in motion. She motored smoothly past Barbara, who was heading for our table carrying a pitcher of iced tea. Barbara watched her go, lips compressed in a thin line. Turning to me, she said, "I take it I should cancel her order?"

"Yep. And bring me a margarita if you would." It was a little early, but all things considered, I figured I deserved a drink. While I was waiting, I pulled out my phone and dialed Emma's number from memory. She answered on the first ring. "Hey, girlfriend," I said, "you got any plans for the day?"

"None I can't change. What's up?"

"You know all those boxes cluttering up my house?"

"The ones from when your gran moved?"

"And the ones Dottie sent over before the office blew up, and the ones with Vicki's stuff from Birchwoods . . ." I tried to think if there were any others.

"You still haven't gone through Vicki's stuff?"

Vicki had been my best friend. She'd died a couple of years ago, the same night I was attacked and partially changed by the vampire. She'd stuck around as a ghost for a little while but eventually had moved on to her final reward. I still miss her every single day. Until just recently I simply hadn't had the heart to go through her stuff and sift through those memories.

"Not yet. You know how she was about pictures." Emma laughed. I'm sure that, like me, she was remembering all the times Vicki had pointed a camera at us, or had someone else photograph the three of us together. "I'm thinking there should be some good shots of all of us."

"I'd be happy to help. Will Dawna be coming?"

"Nope. She's busy."

If Emma heard the irritation in my voice, she chose to ignore it. "Her loss. See you at your place in an hour. I'll bring the wine."

"Sounds like a plan."

2

All right, spill it." Emma plopped down into the armchair, mock-glaring at me. "You're upset about something. I can tell." Emma is petite and pretty, with naturally blonde hair and blue eyes. A former gymnast, she's built rock solid. Today she was wearing shorts and a T-shirt, but even dressed for sorting through boxes, she looked pressed and neat. I wonder sometimes how she does it.

I sighed in response to her question. She knows me so well. Being with Matty has relaxed her a little, but only a little. Ah, Matteo DeLuca, he is the love of her life and the brother of my current love, Bruno DeLuca. Matty is currently working on getting a transfer out of one of the militant orders of the priesthood to the regular branch, so that he and Emma can get married. It's funny, I would never have thought to put the two of them together romantically, but it works.

I was glad I'd invited Emma over to help. Being around happy people always cheers me up. Emma was radiantly happy, and it showed. Of course, she's in love, and Matty loves her just as deeply. I took a second to be thankful that the two of them found each other. Life is crazy at the best of times. Love should never be taken for granted.

I forced my mind back to the topic at hand. "It's Dawna. She bailed on a meeting with a client. A *female* client."

"Seriously?" Emma shook her head. "Crap."

"She said she had to take Chris's mom to the airport," I explained.

"Isn't that what cabs are for?"

"Thank you," I said with vigor. "That's *exactly* what I said."

"And?"

I shook my head. Dawna hadn't given me a further explanation, so I had nothing to share. "She hadn't even done the preliminary paperwork. If she had, we would never have made the appointment. It was a complete waste of time. The woman was lying through her teeth and it would have been evident with even a simple examination."

"Ouch."

I took a deep breath. "It'll be fine."

"Uh-huh." Emma packed a lot of skepticism into two little sounds.

I sighed. "I'm scared. I think . . ." I paused, trying to find the right words. "Okay, maybe I'm nuts, and I don't have any proof, but ever since our office building was blown up, Chris has been pushing Dawna to quit. She told him no before, but I think she may give in to him after all."

Emma's expression grew pained enough that I had the sinking feeling I'd hit the nail on the head . . . hard. Crap. I must have looked curious, because she blushed and frowned.

"I can't talk about it," she said. I wondered if Dawna had said something to her or if Emma's clairvoyance had picked something up. In either case, she wouldn't tell me what she knew. If it was Dawna, Emma wouldn't break a confidence, and if it was her magic, well, Emma and I both knew that sometimes talking about a vision of the future could make it come to pass. Or not. Either way, it was usually a good idea to say nothing.

I gave Emma a look that spoke volumes, then went into the kitchen to get us some drinks.

I poured Emma a glass of the wine she had brought, but I was in the mood for something different. *Let it go*, I told myself as I rummaged in the freezer for one of those pouches of premixed frozen cocktails. Available at the grocery store, you just stick 'em in the freezer for a half hour and they're ready to go. Tasty, too. I found what I was looking for, salted the rim of a glass, and poured myself a margarita before heading back into the living room. I passed Emma her glass and raised mine.

"*L'chaim!*"

"To life!" Emma agreed, clinking her glass with mine before taking a long pull. "So, I understand you've put some ads out and are hiring. Are you looking for anything specific? Maybe someone male, and a mage?" She put a teasing note in her voice, but she was at least partly serious.

I shook my head. "No. Bruno made it very clear. He wants to work at the university. Besides, I couldn't afford him."

Bruno DeLuca: my fiancé in college, now my lover, my friend, and one of my favorite human beings on earth. He's got power—he'd made those amazing knives of mine—plus brains and money. He's sexy as hell. He can raise my pulse rate just walking into a room, even after all these years. You'd think I'd jump at the chance of bringing him into the company. Other people certainly do. I've seen some of the offers that have come his way from really major players.

It was her turn to give me a narrow-eyed look. "Uh-huh, like he wouldn't change his mind if you asked him. That's not why you're not doing it."

Ouch, that stung—probably because it was the truth. Bruno did want to work as a professor, to get out of the rat race in the private sector. I respected that. He'd made a ton of money making artifacts, but he'd wound up having no control over who used them or for what purposes. He didn't like the idea of something he made being used for evil, but more than that, my honey is all about control.

That's one of the main reasons I didn't want him as a business partner. He's a take-charge kind of guy, and I wanted to be the one in charge of the company. I'd already dealt once with a man who wasn't able to follow my lead in a crisis. The results had been spectacularly ugly. I wasn't going through that again. No way.

"Fine," I admitted. "You win. I want to run the company and I don't think he'd follow orders any better than John did. Been there. Done that. Wasn't fun."

Emma didn't even try to argue. Instead, she stared across the room, her eyes growing just a little vacant. She could have been looking at the future—she's a clairvoyant, after all. Or it could have been just a reaction to the alcohol.

I didn't ask. If she wanted me to know something, she'd tell me. Instead, I put my empty glass down on top of a magazine on the coffee table and reached for a box.

There were a lot of boxes. I've been living in the same place for several years now, and for a while I'd cleaned up once or twice a year by throwing anything I wasn't immediately using into a carton. Add that to Vicki's boxes, and Gran's, and the ones from my office—before and after the bombing—and there were plenty of boxes to go through. I didn't expect we'd crack more than a few today.

The box I grabbed wasn't a packing carton. It was smaller

and flatter and clearly marked with the logo and image of the VCR it had once held. It was also labeled, in my gran's neat block handwriting, FAMILY PHOTOS.

"*Aha!*" I settled back into my seat and opened it. Lifting the lid revealed a messy stack of photographs, some having aged badly, the colors faded; others stuck to the thick backing paper used for shots taken by my gran's old instant camera.

"Ooh, I love pictures. Let me see." Emma all but leapt out of her seat. Moving aside a stack of boxes, she plopped down on the couch beside me.

Smiling, I started passing photos to her, explaining each one as I did. "This is my grandpa Peahi on his boat. He called it *The Dreamcatcher.* He always said he named it that because it's how he caught my grandma's attention, and it was where he proposed to her. He was out at sea on it, all alone, when he had the heart attack that killed him. Gran couldn't bear to look at the boat after that, so she sold it."

"So, is he the ancestor with the siren blood?"

"None other. I think it's why he loved the water so much." I set the picture aside. I'd see if my great-aunt Lopaka wanted a copy. She'd told me before that she and Grandpa were close before he left the siren islands.

The next shot was of Ivy, blowing out the candles on her fourth birthday cake. It was one of those cakes that had a doll in the middle so that the cake looked like the doll's poufy dress. It had been iced so that it looked quite a lot like Scarlett O'Hara from *Gone with the Wind*—a dark-haired woman in a big hoopskirt. Ivy had been so delighted. She'd played with that doll all day, every day after that, swiping clothes from my Barbie to dress her. Looking deeper in the box, I saw that same battered doll, dressed in a faded orange swimsuit and buried in photos. I shuffled through more pictures and spotted several of me in my ballet clothes. There were even a couple of shots of me on stage at one of my performances.

Every photo held a memory, most of them good. There were few images of my father. My mother had thrown most of them out in the great purge after he left. I had grabbed a few and hidden them under my mattress, unable to bear losing that last bit of the past. I still had them; they were in the drawer of my nightstand. I never looked at them anymore, but they were still there.

Em and I flipped through the box of memories, chatting happily. My psychiatrist had tasked me with finding pictures of myself and my baby sister from shortly before Ivy died. I picked out a few, but discovering that box put an end to the cleaning for the day. Emma and I just sat, drinking and talking, until it was time for her to leave and meet Matty for dinner.

I was sorry to see her go.

I returned most of the photos to the box and closed it reluctantly, leaving only a pair of photos out on the coffee table to take to my appointment tomorrow.

I wasn't hungry, but I fixed myself some food anyway. I have more control over my vampire nature than I used to, in part because I've learned not to go too long between meals. Tonight's menu was from the assortment of baby food I had stocked up on: squash, plus pureed chicken and noodles, warmed in the microwave, with a bit of organic applesauce for dessert. Not exactly haute cuisine, but so much better than the full liquid diet I'd started out on after the bite that I wasn't about to complain.

I ate at the kitchen counter, then rinsed the dirty dishes and put them in the dishwasher. It was nearly full, so I went ahead and started the cycle. On impulse, I fixed myself another drink before heading back into the living room.

The place was a wreck. Just looking at it was depressing. I knew I should finish going through the boxes, but I *so* wasn't in the mood. Nor was I willing to put them back as is. After some internal debate I decided that I would deal with them tomorrow, and on impulse I sat down in front of the computer.

I scolded myself for being stupid and indulging my idle curiosity. I had plenty of real work to do. Abigail Andrews had very definitely not hired me. Nobody was going to pay me for what I was about to do. But something about our meeting just kept bugging me. I couldn't seem to let it go. So to satisfy my very unprofitable and probably unhealthy curiosity, I brought up my favorite search engine and began doing a little research. I felt a momentary flash of annoyance with Dawna again—this was work she should have done.

There was nothing on Harry Jacobs. Well, not quite nothing. There was a Harry Jacobs who owned a used-car lot in Tulsa; I found links to videos of a couple of seriously bad commercials he'd made. But they were recent, and he was not in prison, so I was willing to bet that he wasn't the right Harry. There were other Harry Jacobses, but nowhere near Santa Maria.

So I tried Abigail Andrews. Again, nothing useful.

Now, I know not everybody lives a newsworthy life. I'm sure there are plenty of people who have no identity online at all. But Abby had some seriously interesting scars. There would normally be some record of anyone or anything that had caused them—even a simple car wreck. But I was getting nada. In my head I heard that ancient childhood taunt: *Liar, liar, pants on fire, your nose is as long as a telephone wire.*

As an experiment, I typed in Emma's name. In seconds I was looking at a whole history of her achievements, including all her gymnastics titles and her second-place finish in the tristate spelling bee back in grade school.

Similarly helpful results popped up when I searched Dawna's name.

But nothing on Harry, and nothing on Abby.

I wasn't even a little bit surprised. Feeling distinctly grateful that I hadn't been hired, I shut down the computer. Taking my drink with me into the bathroom, I ran a hot bubble bath. The combination of alcohol and hot water might just relax me enough to get to sleep.

Friday morning came too soon to suit me. I know a lot of "morning people." I am not one of them. Still, I managed to haul my sorry butt out of bed and stumble into the kitchen, where I proceeded to pour myself a cup of coffee and took up a position by the French doors to see what the weather had to offer. It was beautiful. The sun was shining, not a cloud marred the perfect blue of the summer sky. Later in the day I expected it would be miserably hot, but now it was perfect. Setting down my coffee, I reached for the bottle of sunscreen I keep by the door. I slathered high-SPF lotion over every inch of skin not covered by the sweatpants and T-shirt that were my usual nightwear and pulled on my favorite picture hat. On impulse I detoured into the living room to snag the pair of photographs from the coffee table. I stuffed them into my pants pocket on the way out the door.

A strip of private beach came with the guesthouse. It's a little rocky, and the currents are tricky, but I swim there anyway when the water isn't too cold. When it is, I just sit on the rocks or under a beach umbrella and watch the gulls and the waves.

I'm part siren—the ocean soothes me. But I've seen plenty of humans who do the same exact thing when they can. There's just something about the sea.

Today I needed some soothing. This afternoon I was due at the therapist for a preteleconference therapy session. I needed it. I so didn't want to have to deal with my mother and her issues. I'd rather be doing anything else. Seriously, *anything*. Demons, vampires, zombies—I've faced them all. And I'd rather do any of that again than deal with my family history. But there you go. You do what you have to do.

I clambered up on the rough surface of my favorite rock and stared out to sea. When I thought I was calm enough to handle it, I pulled the first photo from my pocket. Old and faded, it had been taken with a technology that no longer even existed. I remembered that day so clearly. It had been my birthday. My father had grabbed the Polaroid and snapped a shot of me right out of bed, blonde hair tangled and sticking up as I stood there in my Barbie pj's. Ivy was in the background, looking small and adorable, her wide blue eyes staring at the cartoons playing on the television, completely oblivious of everything else going on in the house.

I'd also brought the shot of Ivy with her cake. I hadn't said anything to Emma, but this was the last picture of my sister. Gran had taken it just about a week before three of my mother's male "friends" had kidnapped my sister and me. They'd hoped to get Ivy to use her gift of speaking with the dead to find treasure—they'd seen something in the news about a kid in Florida who had done that. They tortured me to get her to cooperate. Instead, she'd called up zombies from a nearby cemetery. She was powerful enough to call them but didn't have the knowledge or experience to control them. The thugs died a gruesome death. My sister did, too. The only reason I lived was that I'd been tied to a table and couldn't move. Movement draws zombies like honey draws flies.

I sat on the rock, tears flowing so hard I couldn't see the picture in my hand.

For years, my memories of those horrible events had been magically suppressed, my emotions blunted so that I could function, if not heal. Unfortunately, the magic that had suppressed them had been negated by something that had happened to me a few months ago. And I got to experience my feelings for the first time in years. So though these wounds were old, they were still raw.

I blame myself. I always have. They call it survivor's guilt. Why did I survive when she didn't? She was my baby sister. I was supposed to protect her.

An icy breeze blew against my face, freezing the tears on my cheeks.

"Ivy."

My sister's ghost was here. She comes to me often. Well, less often lately. In the eighteen months or so since my mother went to prison, Ivy's spent a lot of time there instead. But she seems to sense when I'm most upset, and then I can count on seeing her.

Ghosts are the spirits of the dead who remain tied to something or someone until they can achieve some specific purpose and move on to their eternal reward. It's pretty typical, for example, for ghosts of murder victims to stick around until the murderer is caught and convicted.

I don't know why Ivy's ghost is tied to me. I suspect that she's waiting for me to forgive my mother. If that's the case, she may be with me until I die. Because try as I might, I can't seem to let go of the past. I love my mom. But the guys who took us were her *friends.* They wouldn't have known about Ivy and me if she hadn't blabbed about us at the bar; wouldn't have been able to kidnap us if she hadn't been fucking passed out from booze and drugs in some dive somewhere, leaving us home alone. They'd even used her keys to get into our apartment.

No, I was not ready to forgive my mother. Not now, maybe not ever. I just don't want that to cost me my relationship with my grandmother. Gran has always been there for me. But she refuses to see or hear anything negative about my mother. She's a classic enabler. Our conflicting attitudes about my mom have come way too close to destroying our relationship. The only reason I agreed to family therapy was to try to save my relationship with Gran.

The cold wind that marked my sister's presence blew my hair back from my face and made the fabric of the beach umbrella flap loudly. I held out the photograph. "Do you remember this? It was your birthday."

The wind stilled, the air around me growing so cold that goose bumps covered my flesh and my breath misted the air. A hint of frost appeared on one corner of the photo. A moment later the cold vanished. Ivy was gone. Where to or why, I had no idea. She'd be back eventually. We were tied to each other until I could figure out a way to free her. In the meantime, I needed to get inside and get cleaned up. Sitting here brooding was not going to make things any better and would only make my mood worse.

3

"So, how have you been sleeping?" Gwen asked.

Gwen Talbot is my psychiatrist. She's a trauma specialist. I first worked with her when I was a kid, after the kidnapping. I've gone back to seeing her because my life has overflowed with trauma in the last few years. Gwen's the administrator of Birchwoods, a very high-end mental health and addiction treatment facility, so she has limited time available to see patients, but she always manages to fit me in.

We were seated in her office, a large, beautiful space decorated in colors that matched the beach that could be seen through the wide bank of windows: sand browns and the blue-greens of the ocean. As I took in the view, I realized that there were storm clouds gathering on the far horizon. Gwen's suit was the same gray as the clouds, a color that looked good with her silvering hair and olive complexion.

"Better, but not great," I admitted. I have recurring nightmares, in part from what happened when I was a kid, in part from my up-close-and-personal meeting with a bat, and more recently from an encounter with a demon who told me he'd see me in my dreams. All of this makes sleep a very tricky proposition.

"Did you have a priest come bless the house as I suggested?"

"Yep." Matty had been happy to do it. In fact, he did such a good job that it stung *me* every time I crossed the threshold of my bedroom. I'd also hung dream catchers that had been decorated with crosses and sprayed with holy water: one in the bedroom doorway, in every window, even on the mirror of my dresser. It looked more than a little odd, but the demon hadn't actually manifested in my dreams in the week since I'd installed them.

"And has it helped?"

"It has," I answered. "But I've been a little stressed out about the whole family therapy thing."

"Ah. I see. It's reasonable to feel apprehensive under the circumstances. But our goal is for you to be ready. Is there something in particular that's bothering you?"

I looked from the windows back to Gwen and seriously considered her question before answering. "Not really."

"We could reschedule," she offered.

"No point." I sighed. "I'm never going to be ready. I'll just have to do it anyway."

Never one to let me wallow in self-pity, Gwen grew stern. "That's not quite true. You don't *have* to. You have a choice, Celia. You need to recognize that fact. It is your decision to make. Your mother's therapist thinks this would be useful for her. But I'm your doctor, my concern is *you*."

I smiled at her. "Thanks. I appreciate that." I did. But it didn't change anything. No matter what I thought about my mother and whether or not I believed she could get well, I needed to do this if I had any hope of salvaging my relationship with my gran. And I wanted that, badly. Not long ago, the terrorists had tried to kidnap her to use against me. They'd failed, but it was a close enough call to make me realize that we really needed to work on the issues standing between us before it was too late.

I reached into my purse and took out the pair of pictures I'd been carrying around all day, setting them gently onto the desk where Gwen could see them.

Gwen looked at the pictures carefully. She seemed more interested in the one from Ivy's birthday, so I said, "That was taken about a week before Ivy died."

She nodded. I watched as she gathered herself, preparing for something. But when she spoke, it was to ask a surprisingly innocuous question. "Is that you in the background?" She pointed a manicured finger at a figure in the background, leaning forward so that I could get a clear view of the image.

I found myself giving her an odd look. Gwen had to know that was me—she'd treated me when I was that age. She knew what I'd looked like. So she must be trying to make a point—leading the horse to water, as it were.

I looked from the picture to her face. Her expression gave nothing away.

"Yes."

"How much do you think you weighed, looking at this picture?"

I'd been young enough not to have reached my full height and was still pretty skinny. "Probably ninety pounds, less than a hundred, anyway. Why?"

"You've recovered all your memories of the kidnapping, is that right?"

"Yes."

"So tell me, how much do you suppose your attackers weighed?"

I closed my eyes and actually thought about it for a moment.

The biggest of the guys had probably been six two, and he'd been heavy, with a beer gut, and muscular, with the kind of calluses you get working construction. If I was describing him to the police, I'd put him at around 250. The others were both smaller, say, five ten and 180 pounds.

"Celia, I want you to look at this picture again. Do you really think that any girl that size, no matter how tough, could fight off three full-grown men?"

I opened my eyes and really looked at the girl in the picture. I knew it was me, but for the first time I looked at the girl in the image as if she were a separate person. Damn, she was tiny. She probably weighed half of the smallest of the three guys who had attacked her and her sister. She was a tough little thing, a fighter—you could see that in her eyes and the slant of her jaw. But there was no way she'd be able to fight off even one of those men, let alone three.

My eyes blurred. I couldn't breathe. The realization hit me like a club to the brain or a semi doing ninety. It was just so obvious. That little girl hadn't stood a chance in hell of stopping what happened or protecting her sister. *I* hadn't stood a chance.

It wasn't my fault.

For the first time I really felt that, really believed it.

Gwen moved the tissue box to where I could reach it but remained silent, letting me release the torrent of painful emotions. I'd blamed myself for so long—allowed my mother to blame me. These wounds never healed; the pain was raw, always just beneath the surface. Now I saw everything differently, but the adjustment was agonizing.

It took a fair amount of time, and most of the box of tissues, for me to pull myself together. Eventually, however, I blew my nose noisily a couple of times and began to get my breathing back to normal. As I regained control of myself, I felt the temperature in the room start to drop, a sure sign of a ghostly presence.

"Ivy, is that you?" I whispered. The light flickered once. It was a code we'd worked out the first time she'd manifested after death: once for yes, twice for no. Since ghosts cannot lie, it was Ivy.

I spoke to the air, to the ghost of the baby sister I love and had failed to save. "I tried. I tried so hard. I just couldn't stop them." I'd swear I felt small arms holding me, hugging me close.

"I did everything I could. But it wasn't enough." I turned to Gwen then, barely seeing her through the blur of the tears that were threatening to start again. "It wasn't my fault."

She looked at me, her expression gentle and compassionate, but said nothing.

"Mom blames me. I always blamed myself. But it really wasn't my fault." I was repeating myself. Over and over. I had to. It was the only way I could wrap my mind around a concept that was so huge and so fundamental to who I was.

The air swirled around me, making my hair float away from my face, drying cheeks still wet with tears.

I felt a surge of power—not magic, something different, more pure, strong enough to steal my breath. A slit opened, becoming a doorway hovering in the empty air six inches off the floor in the middle of the office. It was filled with light so bright I couldn't look at it directly. I felt the ghostly arms of my sister tighten around me again and somehow knew it would be the last time I felt her touch. Then she released me. In my mind, I heard the echo of laughter. I saw the shape of my sister outlined against that brilliant white light. She turned back, her familiar features beaming. She waved once, then turned away, extending her hand upward as if taking the hand of some being of light. She walked into the opening and it closed behind her, leaving no evidence that it had ever existed.

My sister was gone. I knew that this time it was forever.

Gwen and I sat together in silence for a very long time, well after the bell had rung to end the session. I didn't know if she had seen what I had. Awestruck, I was not coherent enough to ask. It was too much for me to process—the personal revelation that it really hadn't been my fault combined with the certain knowledge that Ivy was gone. Ivy, who hadn't wanted me to forgive our mom but had needed me to forgive myself.

Finally I pulled myself together. "Did you see that?"

Gwen nodded. "Yes. It's not common, but I'm not surprised. After what you told me you experienced in the circle with Okalani, it seemed likely you'd be given the chance to tell Ivy goodbye."

My "experience" with Okalani had included an actual angel, a spirit of light, fighting a demon who had taken the shape of a dragon. "Do you mean I can see angels now?"

"Only when they let you, I suspect," Gwen said. "But you needed to see this, to know that Ivy would be well and happy, that she was moving on to a better place. To heaven, as it were."

She said the word "heaven" as if it were in quotes. Obviously, despite what she'd just seen, Gwen was not a true believer. Then again, neither am I. Although, I have to admit, having been party to quite a lot of religious-based supernatural shit, I was beginning to wonder if my gran had it right.

"You've had a real breakthrough today. There's a lot for you to assimilate. But there's one more thing I want you to consider before the family therapy session."

I resented that a little. I mean, something else? Seriously?

Didn't I have enough to digest? I didn't answer, so she continued, her voice firm.

"Ghosts *must* leave this realm when their purpose is fulfilled. I know that Ivy had left you to care for your mother. But that wasn't her purpose. Her purpose was to see you healed. Your healing was as necessary for her as it was for you. Ivy was not here for your mother. She was here for *you*."

I pulled myself together. Gwen had a big budget meeting scheduled, and I needed to go. I was exhausted when I left Gwen's office—physically, mentally, and emotionally wrung out. Still, I managed to drag my butt to my car. I tried to call Gran before I headed home, but she didn't answer the landline or her cell. I left a message asking her to call me, then drove back to my house. Once there, I went straight to bed. And even though it was the middle of the day, I slept soundly and dreamlessly for the first time in ages.

I woke up at midnight physically refreshed. I could literally feel that a huge emotional burden had been lifted from my shoulders. At the same time I was sad. Ivy's ghost had been with me for more years than Ivy had lived. She'd helped me through all sorts of trials and crises. She'd protected our mother from the other inmates in prison. Whenever I needed her most, she'd come.

I'd miss her.

I knew it was best for her. But that didn't change the fact that I felt well and truly alone. Even when she'd been with our mom, these last eighteen months, I'd known she was still around. She'd visited me often and every time I'd really needed her. But now, knowing that she was truly gone, her absence was different, a permanent void.

On the one hand, it was an odd, sad feeling, and I knew it was one that would take a lot of getting used to. On the other, a load of terrible guilt that I had been carrying for so long that I didn't really even think about it anymore was just . . . gone. I felt so light, like I might float away. I knew it was silly, but that didn't change how it felt. I'd miss Ivy and grieve for her. But this time, when the grieving was over, I'd finally be able to heal.

4

I went out on the beach for a while and stared at the waves. I felt very alone. Late as it was, I could've called Bruno or any of my friends, and they would've come. But I didn't want company, wasn't ready to talk about what had happened, not even to the people closest to me. Besides, it just seemed wrong telling someone else before I told Gran. Eventually, I went back inside and back to bed.

When morning came, I checked to see if Gran had called. She hadn't, so I tried to call her again. I wasn't going to call Mom. First off, I wasn't positive the prison hierarchy would let me talk to her. If I pulled rank and used the whole "princess" thing and said it was a family crisis, they might. Though I wasn't sure that what had happened qualified as a crisis. Ivy had, after all, been dead for years. Mostly, I just wasn't in the mood to deal with Mom and the inevitable fallout. I hadn't willingly spoken to my mom in a very, very long time, not since the day she'd tried to exorcise me as if I were a demon. She'd let loose with the kind of invective I wasn't capable of forgiving. I'd tell Gran about Ivy. Gran could tell Mom.

Of course to do that I needed to actually talk to Gran. I'd tried the telephone without success, maybe I should try telepathy.

Closing my eyes, I concentrated on an image of my grandmother's face—and tried to contact her. No luck. My thoughts hit a shield that was solid enough that I couldn't get through. That was . . . odd . . . and a little worrying. In the end I decided to call my great-aunt Lopaka's assistant and ask if she could get in touch with Gran and have her call me. It was a roundabout way of doing things and I really didn't have the authority to ask for that kind of favor. But Hiwahiwa didn't seem to mind, telling me cheerfully that she'd "get right on it."

I spent the rest of the day puttering around the house, putting boxes back in the closet, cleaning out the refrigerator, and waiting for the sun to go down. I could've put on sunscreen and used a beach umbrella, but the day was just too bright—too cheerful—for the mood I was in. Still, I longed for the ocean.

The hours passed slowly. I didn't cry. I was too numb. I didn't answer the phone either. When Lopaka, queen of the sirens, tried to reach me telepathically, I shielded her out. She probably could have forced the issue, but she didn't. I was glad. Lopaka was family, and I'm sure she was concerned—I'm sure her assistant had told her something was up. But I still wanted to talk to Gran before I spoke to anyone else, even mentally.

Eventually, the sun set and I gathered up a few things and went out onto the beach.

One of my favorite memories was sitting around a campfire on the beach—me, Ivy, and Grandpa Peahi, eating s'mores under the light of the stars. I couldn't eat them now, but I could light a fire in the portable firepit, sit on the beach, and watch the waves and the flames. So I did. Only after the tide had turned and the fire was long guttered out did I pack up my things and head indoors to bed. I'd kept my phone with me the whole time; my grandmother did not call. I was starting to worry.

At nine thirty the next morning I was awakened by the buzz of the intercom. Someone was at the front gate and wanted to be let in.

I stumbled out of bed, cursing, and shuffled over to hit the switch. "Yes?"

"Celia, it's me, Alex. Let me in. We need to talk."

Heather "Alex" Alexander was a detective at the Santa Maria de Luna Police Department. She had been the lover of my best friend, Vicki Cooper, until Vicki's death. We had been friendly acquaintances—we socialized well enough when we were with Vicki but never sought each other out otherwise. While we both loved Vicki dearly, mourning her hadn't brought us closer together. If Alex was here without an invitation, it wasn't a social call.

Crap.

I hit the button to turn on the camera. It was Alex, all right. She was alone and looking both businesslike and cranky. With a sigh, I hit the switch that sent the signal to open the security gate, then went back into the bedroom to throw a robe over the worn T-shirt and men's boxers I'd worn to bed.

By the time she reached my front door, I was decently if not glamorously covered.

I greeted her as pleasantly as I could manage, even offering her a cup of coffee.

"No, thanks." She brushed past me, taking a seat on the living room couch without being asked. I didn't mind. I'd have liked to be closer, but it just never seemed to work out, perhaps because we were both so strong-willed and stubborn. Those two qualities had helped Alex to rise to detective in the competitive boys' club atmosphere of the police department. They'd helped me make a success of my business, guarding other people. They probably also made us too much alike to ever be completely at ease with each other.

Alex was dressed for work in a black pantsuit with a faint pale blue pinstripe that matched her prim cotton blouse. The jacket didn't quite manage to conceal the weapons she carried. I suppose that was understandable. On a public servant's salary she wasn't likely to be able to afford special tailoring or concealing magics. She'd inherited a bit from Vicki, but I knew that money had gone into her retirement fund and to charity.

"You haven't been answering your phone." She fingered the anti-siren charm at her neck when she said it. The charm had been made using my own hair, giving her special protection from me personally as well as other sirens. She hadn't asked, but I'd had it made for her. She'd needed to be able to prove I wasn't influencing her on the job. It had taken a lot for me to give it to her. A person's hair can be used to do some pretty serious bad magic to her. I had to trust that Alex didn't wish me ill and wouldn't let anyone who did get hold of the charm. I had to trust that she'd destroy it before she'd let it be used against me. Vicki had trusted her like that. I still wasn't sure I did.

Had she tried to call? I must have slept through it. There was a hint of accusation in her voice, an edge to her voice that made it more than a simple observation.

"I've had a lot on my mind." I took a seat on the chair facing her. Looking into those intense blue eyes, I knew that something big was up. So it wasn't a surprise when she started grilling me.

"What do you know about a woman who called herself Abigail Andrews?"

"Look, Alex, I just woke up. Can we do this in the kitchen? I need some coffee, and I need to eat."

"Fine." She rose. "This could take awhile."

She followed me into the kitchen, pulling up a chair as I puttered around, starting a big pot of coffee and choosing my baby food breakfast. I didn't rush. There was no point. I knew Alex well enough to know that she wouldn't budge until she got the answers she was looking for.

"In answer to your question, I don't know Ms. Andrews well at all. I met her at La Cocina the other day. She was thinking of hiring me to guard her daughter, but we didn't hit it off. I thought she was lying through her teeth and hiding things from me. She thought I had an attitude problem."

Alex snorted, her mouth quirking in a grin she couldn't quite manage to suppress. "You? An attitude problem? Surely not."

I didn't argue. It was not, after all, an argument I could win and we both knew it.

"Then what?"

"She left. I ate lunch, had a drink, and left."

"That's it?"

"That's it. You can check with Barbara if you'd like. She'll confirm it."

Alex nodded. I got the impression that she'd known what I'd say, that I was just verifying information she already had. That was odd, and it made me worry, just a little. So I volunteered more information than I might otherwise have. "I did a little research on the Internet later, just from idle curiosity. Couldn't turn anything up on Andrews or the guy she said I'd be guarding her daughter from. I'm not surprised. Like I said before, I could tell she was lying. Then again, a lot of folks do."

Alex gave another amused snort. "Don't they just. Anything else?"

"No, why?"

"I take it you haven't turned on the television or checked out the news online?"

Uh-oh. That sounded ominous. "Not in a couple of days."

Alex looked at me as she said, "Abigail Andrews was abducted off the street in front of her apartment last night by a pair of masked men. We found the van they used a couple of blocks away. Ms. Andrews's handbag was in the back, near an empty syringe that contained traces of a sedative. Your card was in her bag."

Oh, hell and damnation. I hadn't liked the woman, but still I wouldn't wish that on anyone. "Do you want me to come down to the station and give an official statement?"

"No. Not yet, anyway. Neighbors and people on the street saw the abduction. The perps were two men and a driver, all in masks, all male. Nobody thinks you're involved, but we're hoping she may have told you something that can be of use."

"Okay. I'm glad to help, but it isn't much."

"I'll be the judge of that."

I started at the beginning. The story didn't take long to tell. After all, it had been a short meeting. "In all honesty, I got the impression that a lot, if not all, of what she told me was bullshit."

"So she didn't hire you," Alex said, bringing me back to where we'd started, going over familiar ground to see if something new might pop into my memory. I'd been questioned similarly before. While the technique can be annoying as hell, it does sometimes work.

"Nope. Like I said, she stormed out of the restaurant." Well, stormed as much as a woman in a wheelchair could. "If Barbara hadn't been able to cancel the order I would've had to pay for it." I paused, thinking about what Alex had . . . and hadn't said. The phrasing she'd used was curious. "You said she 'called herself' Abigail Andrews. That wasn't her real name?"

Alex's expression grew pained. "I was hoping you hadn't caught that."

"Sorry." I wasn't really, and she knew it. After giving me a long, level look, she apparently decided to tell me what I wanted to know.

"No. It wasn't her real name. She'd been using it for close to twenty-three years. But it was a fake."

Close to twenty-three years. That rang a bell. A loud one.

She gave me a hard look. "You've remembered something else. What is it?"

"The man . . . Jacobs, she said he'd been in prison a little over twenty-two years. I think she was lying about the name. But I got her pretty rattled with my questions. Maybe she didn't think to lie about the time line."

"We'll look into it."

"Do you want me to . . . ," I started to offer, but Alex was shaking her head before I could finish the sentence.

"No. Really, no." The expression on her face was stern and more than a little pained. "It's nothing personal, Celia, but every time you get involved in something, everything goes to hell in a handbasket. I know it's not your fault, but please, just let us handle it."

Ow. That hurt. Nothing personal, my lily-white ass.

My displeasure must have been written on my face, because Alex winced. "Look, I'm sorry. I didn't mean it to sound like that. But that curse mark of yours . . ."

Ah, yes, the curse mark. Damn Stefania. She'd been a queen of the sirens. Her psychic had seen something in my future she didn't like, so Stefania put a death curse on my baby sister, Ivy, and me when we were children, hoping we wouldn't live to cause her trouble. Ivy hadn't. I, on the other hand, managed to live to adulthood and helped send her on her way to hell. About once a week I wish I could do it again, just for grins. "Fine, let me know if you need anything else from me."

"I will." She started to rise, then seemed to reconsider. "Do you want to explain why you're avoiding the phone?" She settled back in her seat as if she was willing to wait until doomsday for an answer.

I hadn't been, really. But I didn't say that. Instead, I said, "It's not connected to the case."

"Don't care," she said, shaking her head. "You look like hell, Celia. I know we haven't been close, but I do care about you. If you're in the middle of another shit storm, I'd like to know. Maybe I can help. Even if I can't, I'd like to think you know you can talk to me about whatever it is."

I was touched and shocked in equal measure. Without Vicki as a buffer between us, Alex and I barely saw each other unless we were involved in a case together. Now she was extending an olive branch, or lifeline, without hesitation or reservation.

I'd wanted Gran to be the first to know. But Alex had lived through both Vicki's death and the passing of her spirit months later, when she'd completed the thing she'd stayed on this plane for. She was in a unique position to understand what I was going through.

"Ivy's gone."

Alex blinked at me for a second. Then her brain processed what I'd said. "Oh. Oh, Celia . . . Oh, God. I'm so sorry. What . . . how?" The hard professional veneer cracked a little, giving me a glimpse of the much more honest, and vulnerable, woman beneath.

"I had a breakthrough in therapy. I finally accepted that what happened wasn't my fault. Apparently that's what she was waiting for."

"You're sure?"

I nodded, suddenly unable to speak because of the lump in my throat. My vision blurred with tears. I closed my eyes, trying hard to breathe evenly, to not sob, and felt Alex's arms around me.

"I know you miss her, and how much it hurts. But it's better for her."

I nodded, unable to say a word, and took comfort from one of the toughest women I've ever known.

5

Gran called later that morning, before she went to church. When I told her about Ivy, she was thrilled. She's a true believer. It really bothered her that her sweet granddaughter hadn't been able to go to heaven when she'd died. Gran believed to the depths of her soul that Ivy was finally exactly where she should be. She had me repeat the details over and over again, reveling in the description, taking comfort in the fact that it supported her own beliefs.

I was glad she took it so well. Knowing that Gran really believed Ivy was in a better, happier place made the situation easier for me. I felt . . . not great, but much better. Right up until Gran asked the question I'd most been dreading.

"Have you told your mother?"

Oh, crap. "No."

For a long moment Gran didn't say anything. I knew she was still on the line only because I could hear her breathing. Then, "She deserves to know." There was no judgment or accusation in her tone, which surprised me.

Normally Gran vigorously leaps to Mom's defense if there's even a hint of a problem—a mama bear protecting her cub. Not this time. I wasn't sorry. But it wasn't normal, and I wondered what was wrong. "Gran, are you okay?"

There was a long pause, and I wished I could see her, especially because her voice didn't sound quite right when she spoke again. There was something false about her tone, though I knew she was speaking out of genuine concern.

"I'm fine, dear. How are you doing? You and your sister have always been close, even after she died."

"It's hard," I admitted, wondering why Gran hadn't pursued the topic of my mom. "I miss Ivy, but I know it's for the best." I sighed. I knew what I had to say next, even though I didn't want to. "I know I've got to tell Mom. I just thought it might be best to tell her tomorrow, during the session." I mentally crossed my fingers, hoping that my Gran would volunteer to talk to my mother.

She didn't.

"That makes sense," she said, still in that slightly fake voice. "It would be better in person, but a video conference is better than just a call, and her therapist will be right there if there's a problem."

Oh, there'd be a problem. I'd bet the bank on that. Gran was right about having the therapist handy, too. At least with Mom being in prison I wouldn't have to worry about her using this as an excuse to go on another bender. But hearing Gran say it, and hearing the way she said it, caused another little shiver of premonition. "Gran, are you sure you're okay?"

"I'm fine, dear," she said again. "I've just had a bit of a shock."

Well, I suppose my news was shocking. After all, Ivy had been a ghost for a very long time. "If you're sure."

"I'm sure. Don't you worry about me. You just take care of yourself."

Now she sounded more like her usual self. My gran always worried about everyone else and didn't take enough care of herself. "If you say so." My voice was clearly doubting.

"I do," she answered firmly.

We ended the conversation by telling each other "I love you." I hung up the phone feeling the odd mixture of relief and apprehension that was so familiar when I dealt with my family.

I shook my head. Gran said she was fine. And while she might lie to me about it over the phone, once I saw her in front of the camera, I'd be able to tell what was really going on. In the meantime, I needed to hustle and get ready for my brunch date with my boyfriend.

I'd been dating Bruno DeLuca exclusively for months. We had an extensive past; we'd even been engaged back in college, and we'd dated a lot, on and off, since then. He was smart, handsome, and one of the most talented mages around. When things were good between us, they were amazing. Unfortunately, things had been a little rocky lately. I hadn't seen Bruno in days, hadn't done more than text him a couple of times.

He was busy finishing his research and getting course materials ready for the classes he was teaching at the university in the fall, but that didn't keep me from feeling just a wee bit neglected. Stupid, really. I'd been too busy myself to spend much time with him. But I'm willing to admit that logic and emotion don't always coexist happily in my life. I wanted to talk to Bruno, to tell him about Ivy and to get his take on the situation with Chris and Dawna. Neither subject was exactly "text" material. I also wanted to be reassured about the upcoming family therapy session. I know it sounds needy, but everybody needs support sometimes, and I wanted his.

We had reservations at one of the nicest restaurants in the

area. Antoine's sits perched at the top of a steep cliff and has a wall of windows overlooking the ocean. The food is ridiculously expensive, but the view almost makes up for it.

It's next to impossible to get a reservation there, particularly for Sunday brunch. We managed only because I knew the owner and chef. Once upon a time he'd worked in the kitchen at Birchwoods. He'd considered my condition the ultimate challenge. The Belgian waffles he made—which he somehow designed to go through a blender while maintaining their identity—were one of the best things I've ever tasted. I'd experienced his cooking again when he'd worked at a restaurant in L.A. Now he had his own place, and I couldn't wait to see what he'd done with it.

I wanted to look my absolute best, so I spent a couple of minutes staring into my closet. There's a fine line between being overdressed and underdressed. I finally decided on a short burgundy dress with a sweetheart neckline. The color was dark as a fine wine and looked great against the paleness of my skin. A short black jacket, black pumps, and a black picture hat would complete the ensemble. I kept my makeup understated, pulled my hair into a tight bun, and finished with garnet stud earrings.

I looked good, really good—elegant yet not overdone. Yeah, the hat was a bit much, but I needed to keep my face out of the sun. With the big sunglasses it gave me some old-Hollywood glamour, or at least that's what I told myself.

So it's no surprise that I was hurt and just a little annoyed when Bruno barely glanced at me when he arrived.

He wore a charcoal gray suit with a silver shirt and a black-and-silver-striped tie. The suit was expensive and tailored to fit him perfectly, showing off his athletic build to the best advantage. He'd cut his hair again. It was a little shorter than I like it, with just a hint of curl and a tiny dusting of silver at the temples.

The only thing ruining his look was the sour expression on his face.

"What's wrong?" he asked as I let myself into the car. Normally he gets out and opens the car door for me. Not today.

"Nothing," I lied.

I'll give Bruno this, he's not stupid. He turned to give me the look that that particular comment deserved, and finally, *finally* noticed what I looked like. But instead of complimenting me, he sighed. "I'm sorry."

I raised an eyebrow at that, high enough he could even see it over the sunglasses, but didn't say a word.

"We need to talk."

Uh-oh. I knew that tone of voice. "What?" I hadn't meant to sound quite that suspicious, but there you go. The last time he used those words with that tone, he dumped me. Call me sensitive, but while I've forgiven him, I haven't forgotten.

"I need to know if you're deliberately insulting me or if you really are that clueless."

"Excuse me?" I was pissed. "What the hell are you talking about?"

"You really don't know?" His dark eyes were flashing, and I could feel the energy level rise to fill the enclosed space of the car.

"Not a clue."

"Right." His sarcastic tone left no doubt that he didn't believe me. Without another word, he started the engine with a roar and pulled out of the drive, gaze locked on the road ahead. Considering the speed he was driving, it was probably best that he was paying attention.

After several long minutes of silence, I decided to grab the bull by the horns. "What the hell is the matter with you?"

"We've been back together for a while now," he said, with that undercurrent of anger.

I nodded. "Yes."

"And I think I've proved myself *useful* once or twice."

"More than useful," I said honestly. "You've been amazing." He had been, which made this morning's attitude that much harder for me to comprehend. I am not any easy woman to live with. I know that. But we'd been doing really well. At least I thought we had.

"Then why"—he slammed his palm onto the steering wheel for emphasis—"did you ask Dawna to partner with you instead of me? Why am I hearing that you've *advertised for a mage* for your company? Why haven't we discussed one damned thing about your plans for the business?"

His face was rigid with barely controlled fury. And while it wasn't sensible, or even remotely smart for me to get into an argument with him, I was too damned stressed myself to deal with his temper.

"First," I snapped, "you made it clear that you don't want to work in the private sector. You want to teach." I met his gaze, completely unflinching. "Have you changed your mind?"

"No." He practically spat out the word.

"So forgive me if I took you at your word and made other plans."

There was a long moment of silence as he thought about that. He still wasn't happy, but the level of tension in the car ratcheted down significantly.

Bruno gave me a long, level look. "What's the other reason?" His voice was almost back to normal.

"What other reason?"

"You said 'First.'"

Shit. I had, and he'd noticed. I closed my eyes. I so didn't want to do this. "Bruno, I love you. But we're too much alike to work with each other all the time. It'd be a constant power struggle, and that wouldn't be good for our relationship or the company. I want my company to be *my* company."

He opened his mouth to protest, then closed it, his expression thoughtful.

I continued. "You made the decision to join the university all by yourself, without consulting me or getting my advice. And that's fine. You get to. But I'm going to be making my own career decisions, including who I'm going ask to be my business partner and who I'll be hiring. You can't ask me to butt out of your career and then expect to have input on mine. It's not fair."

He gave me a sour look but didn't argue.

"I love you, Bruno. But you've made it very clear that you run your own life, and I can respect that. I expect you to respect me enough to let me run my own life as well. The road goes both ways."

"And if I can't, as you say, 'butt out'?" He spoke quietly, but his face was flushed and he was so tense I could see the sinews in his neck.

"Oh, do not go there. Don't even," I snapped. "I have too damned much on my plate right now to play those kinds of games."

"You think I'm playing games?" His anger was coming back. Unfortunately, my own ire was rising pretty damned quickly. All the stress, the lack of sleep, my grief over losing Ivy—everything combined until I just couldn't handle it. I rounded on him, completely furious and totally heedless of any possible consequences.

"No, Bruno, I don't think you're playing games. I think you're being a monumental ass. I just lost my sister. I've got the family therapy session from hell coming up tomorrow, a woman got abducted right after she *didn't* hire me, and all you seem to care about is your wounded pride."

He hit the brakes hard, then downshifted and pulled off to the side of the road.

"You haven't told me any of this," he practically yelled, glaring at me.

"How could I? It's not like I see you every day, or even get a call, and this shit is not the kind of stuff you send a text about." I turned to look out the window. I was crying. Damn it! I didn't want to win the argument by crying.

Long minutes passed in silence. I stared stubbornly out the window. I might not be able to stop my tears, but I could keep from looking at him. He just sat there, his breathing slowly going back to normal. The only time I moved was to blot my eyes, hoping my makeup wasn't totally ruined.

"Why didn't you call me? You know I would have come." His voice was soft, but there was still an edge to it. He was trying to put aside his anger, but it wasn't gone. Not by a long shot.

"Days ago, I asked you if you could come by. You said no."

"You never said it was important. If you had, I would've dropped what I was doing in a heartbeat." The look he gave me held so many emotions it was hard to sort them all, exasperation and hurt were probably the dominant ones, but sympathy was in there, too. "You know that, right?"

"I know." I did know. He has always been good about being there when I need him. I don't expect him to read my mind . . . well, not often. "I was going to tell you at brunch." I hadn't wanted to fight. I'd wanted him to hold me, to listen to me, to help me heal. That wasn't likely to happen now, was it?

Bruno sighed and unfastened his seat belt. He scooted toward me as far as the gearshift knob would allow. "Come here."

I moved to meet him and was rewarded with the hug I needed so badly. His arms were strong, his muscled chest warm. Just the smell of him was comforting. I could feel his heartbeat slowing, his muscles unclenching as his anger faded. He spoke gently, his words not much above a whisper. "I'm sorry about Ivy. Even if it is for the best, it's going to be strange for you not having her around."

I nodded against his chest, unable to speak for the lump in my throat.

He sighed. "And you're probably right. I'm more of a leader than a follower." He said it grudgingly. "You okay now?"

I nodded again, pulling away a bit. He moved back into his seat and strapped in.

"I probably look like hell," I said as I rebuckled my own seat belt.

"Sweetheart, you always look beautiful to me." He meant it, it wasn't just another line of bullshit. Still, I pulled down the sun visor to check my makeup as he eased back onto the highway. This time he drove like a normal human being.

Neither of us said anything until he parked in the restaurant's lot. Then he turned to me and said, "I know you need your independence. But I need to be a part of your life. I'm not trying to be controlling, or an ass, but I'm not into being used, either."

Had I been using him? I didn't think so. But I might have been taking him for granted, and that was wrong.

"I'm sorry if I've been taking you for granted. I don't think I've been using you and I definitely have appreciated it when you've jumped in of your own free will. You've made all the difference in a couple of really tough spots. But we have to figure out what our boundaries are going to be, because I don't want to have this fight with you for real instead of just over a miscommunication."

I opened my door to get out of the car. The minute my shoes hit the pavement, the magical protections that had been spelled into the restaurant and the land around it sent a jolt through me that made me gasp in pain. Whoever had done the wards had put a lot of power in them. No vampire or other monster would be able to come near this place.

I am not quite a monster, but I am close enough that sometimes magic like this didn't much like me. I took a deep breath. Steeling myself, I rose slowly to my feet. Bruno had practically vaulted around the car to see what was wrong, but once he realized what I was reacting to he stood still and waited, letting me handle it. When I was ready, he took my hand and we walked together into Antoine's.

6

My alarm went off bright and early Monday morning. I felt like hell. I hadn't slept well. After clearing the air, Bruno and I had managed to have a pleasant meal, talking about our college days and my cousin's wedding the previous summer. Antoine had worked his usual magic and presented me with probably the world's best Belgian waffles and other goodies designed for my special needs. But even though things were better, there was still more than a little underlying tension between Bruno and me. I went to bed with a lot on my mind—not a good recipe for sound sleep. My thoughts had chased themselves like horses on a merry-go-round, only not nearly so pretty. When I finally did drop off, I had nightmares. Not the demon-stalking-me nightmares, thank God, but the old standbys: my father's abandonment; being attacked by zombies. Not exactly a restful night. I drank a couple of cups of strong black coffee along with a nutrition shake, then ate a jar of Gerber beef and noodles. I was running low on baby food. I'd need to stop by the store soon. In fact, I should probably grab something on the way to the library, just to be safe.

It didn't take long to shower and put on my makeup. I made sure to use concealer to cover the dark circles under my eyes. I wanted to look good but dignified, like the head of a successful company. Today was a big day. I'd reserved one of the small conference rooms in the university library for interviews. We'd scheduled them there because most of our potential recruits were recent university grads we'd found through the college placement office. It hadn't been difficult or expensive to book the room for most of the day, and it was certainly convenient.

I hoped Dawna would meet me there, but I wasn't counting on it. I texted her to confirm, but she didn't reply. So I got on the computer and printed out the e-mail she'd written setting out the plan for the day, along with its attachments—the schedule of appointments and the applicants' résumés. Then I stuck the packet in a file folder and drove into town.

Even early as it was, traffic was terrible. I was stuck for a long time on Oceanview, trapped by a multicar pileup up ahead. Frustrating. I barely had time to stop at PharMart for some baby food and nutrition shakes before I had to be at the library to get things set up for the interviews.

The wards around the building buzzed against my senses. They were a little painful to cross, but not nearly as bad as those at the restaurant had been. I was able to get through them and into the building with no real trouble and went immediately downstairs.

G-38 was a largish study/conference room. It was fairly boring: white walls, gray industrial-grade carpet, a big laminate table surrounded by cheap rolling chairs. The overhead fluorescent lights were the ecofriendly kind that turn themselves off if there isn't any movement in the room. They also wash out normal complexions. I probably looked like a corpse despite my very careful makeup job.

I was wearing a charcoal gray pantsuit with a dark rose blouse.

My silver jewelry went well with my storm-gray eyes. My gray shoes had minimal heels. I'd pulled my hair into a French braid. It was a very professional look but still feminine.

I stashed my groceries under the table at the far end. Then I picked seats for the interviews. I set down my folder plus a pen and pad I could use to take notes in front of my chair, put a bottle of water alongside them and two other bottles in front of two other seats—one beside mine, for Dawna, if she came, and one for the potential hire, opposite us. I sat down and flipped through résumés for three whole minutes before I got bored and decided to take a quick trip to the bathroom. After all, it could be hours before I got another chance. When I came back, Dawna was sitting at the chair next to mine. She looked gorgeous . . . and utterly miserable.

Dawna is Vietnamese, tiny and delicate, with gleaming dark hair and exotic features. She's a natural beauty who also knows the absolute best way to dress to play up her assets. Today she was wearing a hot pink skirt suit that nipped in at her tiny waist and was both long enough to be proper and short enough to show off a great pair of legs in three-inch heels. It was obvious she had been crying heavily, despite her perfectly applied makeup and the antitears eyedrops I could smell on her skin.

Crap. Apparently she was having an even worse morning than I was. "What's wrong?" I asked as I sat down next to her. She shook her head soundlessly, fighting back tears.

"Can't talk about it?"

"After the interviews," she whispered, her voice harsh and raw.

"Okay. I get that. But when we're done here, I'm taking you to La Cocina and we'll talk. You can tell me about whatever it is, and I'll bitch to you about Bruno."

She gave me a weak smile.

"You know I'll help any way I can, right?" I looked her straight in the eye, I needed her to know I meant it. I might be annoyed with her, but she was my friend, damn it.

She nodded. Rummaging in her purse, she found a tissue and used it to dry her tears and blow her nose. Then she pulled out a compact and made repairs to her makeup. She was just finishing when there was a light tap on the door. Our first interviewee was right on time.

Brian Carter was just about to graduate college and was looking for his first full-time job. That he was young was not a problem. That he was immature was. He kept staring very inappropriately at my chest and Dawna's everything and trying to make jokes, so I cut the conversation short. There was no chance in hell I was hiring that bozo. He left reluctantly, leaving the door open behind him.

Interview two came right on his heels. Talia Han stood five eight and was built like a tank. She was wearing a T-shirt so white it practically glowed, a visible anti-siren charm, and black dress pants. Her body fat ratio had to be under three percent and her musculature was impressive. I guessed that her trousers had to be specially tailored—her thighs were bigger around than Dawna's waist. Her upper body was equally impressive. Her skin was a lovely caramel color, her eyes a striking hazel and slightly tilted. Her hair had been shaved close to her head, but what there was of it was curly and medium brown.

"Hello, Dawna." She smiled, showing very white but slightly crooked teeth, and passed each of us a résumé with a folded paper attached. "Ms. Graves."

"Talia." Dawna was a little flabbergasted, but she recovered well. "Celia, this is my cousin, Talia. I haven't seen her in—"

"Fifteen years," Talia supplied. "Not since my father moved

us to Chicago. But I'm back, I need a job, and Grammie told me you were hiring." She took a seat, making herself comfortable while I looked over the résumé and its attachments again. It was a stall tactic. Dawna had obviously been thrown by her cousin's appearance. Evidently the name hadn't rung a bell when she'd scheduled the interview. I figured I'd give her a few seconds to recover. Besides, the résumé was worth another look.

Talia was former military, a marine, with experience in the military police. The attachments were a pair of targets from the range. The results were impressive. She was obviously skilled at handling both handguns and magic. She was only a level four, but I didn't doubt for a minute that the corps had trained her just as meticulously as the Catholic church trained its warrior-priests. I'd seen what a level four could do with proper training. The answer was: a lot.

I looked up from the paperwork. "So, what are your goals with regard to a position with our company?"

"May I speak freely?"

"I'd prefer it," I answered. Dawna nodded her agreement.

"I need a job. There aren't a lot of them available right now in the private sector, and some of the people with whom I've interviewed seem a bit"—she paused—"put off by my appearance. I didn't think you would be. And truthfully, I hoped that the family connection might help."

"You list several references on the résumé. Is it all right if I call them?"

"Please do."

We chatted a bit more. I asked most of the questions, exploring details of her training and specific examples of how she'd handled various situations. Dawna chipped in a little, but for the most part she let me take the lead. As we wrapped up, I told Talia I would call her in a few days, after I'd had the opportunity to check references.

She rose, shook hands with both Dawna and me, then left, closing the door behind her.

"Well?" I asked my partner.

"I . . . I don't know. Like she said, it's been fifteen years. She's changed."

I started ticking off positive points. "Well, I like to support the military. She seems to have credentials. I'm assuming she knows how to follow orders, and she was smart enough to come in wearing a charm. That earns her a few points. We need a mage. I was hoping for a six, but with enough training, a four can do pretty much everything we're likely to need, and she definitely has the intimidation factor that's important for a lot of the simple bodyguarding work."

"We do need another female bodyguard. You're going to be tied up in administrative stuff a good part of the time."

Oh, God, I hoped not. But she was probably right. Damn it.

"So what's the problem?"

"When we were kids she was kind of a bully, really aggressive and mean. I mean, she's probably outgrown it . . ." Her voice trailed off.

"But it may be her basic nature, which might make her too aggressive for what we need."

Dawna nodded.

"Okay. Why don't you do the calls? You're better at subtle than I am. See if you can find out if she's got it under control or if there's still a problem. Check around with the family, too, if you think you can without causing a problem. We'll hold off on a decision until we know more. Does that work?"

"It works fine."

We had a few minutes until the next scheduled interview. I cracked open the bottle of water in front of me and took a pull as I hastily racked my brain for something to talk about. Dawna's one of my best friends. It shouldn't have been difficult. But I heaved a huge sigh of relief when I was saved by a light knock on the conference room door. I called, "Come in," and the person outside opened the door.

"Kevin?" I was startled to see him. Kevin Landingham was Emma's brother and he'd worked at the university—until the day he gave the college president a shove. Happily, he hadn't killed President Lackley, and Lackley had decided not to press charges, since he knew about Kevin's PTSD. Post-traumatic stress disorder is a real bitch to deal with. People can have bouts of rage that are difficult to control.

Thankfully, Kevin hadn't totally lost it that day. If he had, Lackley would be maimed or dead. Werewolves are strong, with or without the full moon. President Lackley didn't know Kevin was a shifter—most people didn't—so he didn't realize just how lucky he'd been. In the end, Kevin still got fired. Since then, he's put in a lot of time remodeling his sister's new house, gotten himself a service animal, and is doing better. But he still has a haunted look in his eyes.

Standing in the doorway, Kevin looked uncertain but gorgeous in a navy suit that was just a hair too big for him. He was still big, blond, and strikingly good-looking, but despite working on Emma's house, he wasn't quite as ripped as he had been once upon a time. He was carrying a briefcase, and Paulie, his assistance dog, stood at his side, groomed to within an inch of her life, her work jacket strapped into place.

"What's up?" I asked.

"Emma told me you're hiring. I wanted to submit an application."

I blinked . . . twice, slowly. Wow. This . . . this was unexpected. "Well, come in. Sit down." He nodded and stepped into the room. Setting the case on the table, he withdrew two copies of his résumé, passing one to Dawna and one to me, before sitting down. Paulie settled onto the floor beside him.

It was an impressive résumé. Of course I knew it would be. Kevin has a background in both black ops and tech. More to the point, I'd worked with him before. He's a good man to have in your corner, smart, skilled. I'd love to have him on board. But I wasn't sure our company would be the best fit for him.

"What type of position are you looking for?" Dawna asked.

"I'm hoping to start out doing mostly tech support, but I'm capable of installing security systems and doing basic bodyguarding. I'm not up to going into military confrontations at this point. I may never be again." He said it calmly, but I thought I could see a little strain around his eyes.

"What would you consider a military confrontation?" Dawna asked.

"The situation Celia wound up in in Mexico would be a good example. There might not be a declared war going on down there, but it's still a war zone."

"Yes, it is," I agreed.

"I also am not certain how well I'd be able to handle anything demonic," he admitted, his expression haunted. "On the other hand, I know you're going to be setting up new offices. I could be a big asset with regard to the security systems and tech." He spoke with confidence, but his eyes were still dark from memories he'd rather not think too hard about. I understood that feeling all too well.

"There's no question in my mind that you have the skills," I assured him. "I'm only worried about one thing . . ."

"The thing with Lackley?" He sighed, his shoulders slumping a bit.

"No." I gave him a rueful grin. "I've wanted to pop him in the mouth more than once myself. I can totally understand the urge." Yes, his loss of control worried me. But I knew Kevin had gotten better in the past nine months. I was willing to give him a chance. "What worries me is this. In Mexico, I was working with an experienced crew that included some very alpha personalities. One of the men knew me personally. Even though I was in charge, he wasn't able to behave professionally and follow orders because of our prior relationship. That undermined my authority with the other men and made me look bad to the clients, to the point where I had to fire him. We've known each other a long time, Kevin. Can you follow my lead?"

To give him credit, he thought about the question before he answered. When he spoke, his voice was calm and confident. "There was a time when I couldn't have," he admitted, "but that was before I actually saw you in action, during the situation at the Zoo. You work hard. You're willing to invest in good equipment. You prepare as much as you can, you're good at strategy and tactics, and you're able to change your plans on the fly when things go wrong. You don't ask anything from anybody that you wouldn't do or haven't done yourself. I respect that, respect you. So yes, I believe I can."

"What are your salary requirements?" Dawna asked.

"I'm willing to negotiate," Kevin said. "I have extensive experience, but I also have a couple of black marks on my record."

I smiled at him as I sent a thought to Dawna. My siren telepathy still isn't perfect, but I keep working on it, and with the ring my cousin gave me, I'm much better than I used to be. *What do you think? I'm leaning toward hiring him.*

Dawna gave a minuscule shrug; apparently it was my choice.

"Assuming we can work out salary issues, I'd like to start with a ninety-day probationary period. Would that work for you? I know I've worked with you before, and I like and respect you. But I need to know that you're going to be able to handle the stress. You're free to bring Paulie to work with you."

He smiled and it was like the sun coming out from behind clouds. I heard Paulie's tail thump gently against the floor. She could sense he was happy.

"You won't regret this." He rose and leaned over to shake my hand and then Dawna's before gathering up his things and leaving, with Paulie at his side.

God, how I hoped he was right. Because if he wasn't, it was going to be such a mess.

Dawna waited until she was sure Kevin was gone, going to the door and peeking out to make sure before she said, "I guess you've finally forgiven him."

I knew what she was talking about. Some while back, Kevin and his father, Warren, had betrayed me. They'd done it to save Emma's life and soul. What had pissed me off was that I'd have willingly helped if they'd asked. I mean, *Hello,* they were saving *Emma's life and soul.*

But I'd trusted them—they were so important to me back then. Warren had been my teacher and my guide through all things supernatural; Emma was one of my closest friends; and Kevin . . . well, for a while, Kevin had been very much on my mind. Until Bruno had come along. And they'd betrayed me without an apparent second thought, offered me up as a sacrifice.

For a long time I couldn't get past it. Then someone threatened my gran. I discovered that I'd do pretty much anything to save her and I wouldn't be the least bit rational about it. In that moment, I forgave them both. I hadn't told Kevin or Warren about that, though—hadn't really had an opportunity, wasn't exactly sure how to bring it up. I knew I would, eventually. But right now I didn't want to go into the whole long story with Dawna, so I just said, "yeah."

"I'm glad." She smiled and came back to the table. "Do you think he'll be able to do it?"

"Yeah, I do. Particularly if we keep him on desk duty as much as we can. And wow, does he cover a lot of our needs. Pull out the list—other than a mage, what else do we still need?"

She pulled out the list, then gave me a long look. "I'm surprised that you don't have Bruno coming in as the mage."

I gave a pained sigh. I *so* didn't want to talk about this right now. Later, after a couple of stiff drinks, maybe. Still, Dawna was my business partner. She deserved an honest answer. So I started ticking reasons off on my fingers. "First, he doesn't want to work in the private sector anymore. He wants to teach. Second, there's no way in hell we could afford him."

She smiled, trying to take the sting out of what she was about to say. "And third, there's no way he'd follow orders any better than John Creede did." She shook her head. "You do pick such alpha men."

It was good to see her smiling. I wouldn't have expected it, as depressed as she'd been when she first got here. But I was still a little sensitive after what had happened yesterday, and I guess it showed.

"Uh-oh," Dawna said. "I know that look. What's up?"

"Bruno and I had a fight."

"Evidently there's a lot of that going around," she said wryly. "What was yours about?"

"He thinks I should have asked him to be my business partner, and that I take him for granted, and that I should consult him before I make 'major life decisions like this.'"

"Oh." Wisely, she didn't say anything more. Then again, what was there to say?

"Yours?" I asked.

"Chris doesn't want me working with you or hanging out with you. He says it's too dangerous."

Uh-oh.

"I told him that was rich, coming from a man who works for a paramilitary company."

I tried to think of anything I could say that wouldn't either make things worse or bite me in the ass later, and wound up empty.

Dawna took a deep breath. She met my eyes, her expression serious. "You're my friend, Celia—my best friend. I *like* working with you. I think what we do is important. I know I haven't exactly been holding up my end lately, and I'm sorry. But that's going to change."

"You're sure?"

She gave a firm nod. Her jaw was set in such a stubborn line that I decided not to press further. I changed the subject. "So, what do we still need?"

"Well, obviously a mage. It would also be good to have at least one other person to do basic bodyguard work. There are some other things that would be helpful, but we agreed that we didn't want to go overboard on hiring until we build up some business.

"Dottie has been calling. She's hoping we'll let her help out around the office. If not, we'll have to hire a clairvoyant or find one we can contract with."

Dawna was right on all counts. I had a fair amount of money on hand right now. The job for Adriana and Dahlmar had paid well, and the insurance money (be still my heart, they actually paid) for my old office building had come through. In fact, the city had offered to buy the land where the building had stood "as is," so they could expand their offices. The price wasn't great, but it wasn't bad. I was hoping that if I combined the insurance payout and the money from the sale, I could get or build a new building. And we needed a clairvoyant and a mage on staff. Neither came cheap. Oh, well, money always goes faster than you want it to.

"Does Dottie really still want to work part-time now that she's married?"

"Oh, yes. And she's hoping you find an office soon. Her super is starting to get suspicious about Minnie."

I grinned. I couldn't help it. I love the little fur ball. Minnie the Mouser had been Dottie's cat until Dottie had moved into government housing that didn't allow pets. For a while Minnie had been the office cat, and Dottie had worked for me part-time; that way she could spend time with her beloved cat and earn a little extra spending money. And it really was a little money. She didn't want to lose her benefits or her housing, so I got a high-level clairvoyant for practically a song.

"Tell you what," I said. "Check with Dottie; see if she's willing to work for us again, on the same terms as before. Tell her that Minnie can stay at my place until we get an office."

Dawna grinned and nodded. She loved Dottie like another grandma.

The next candidate knocked before we could say anything

further, and we dove back into the whirlwind of interviewing. Some applicants were better than others, but none were particularly outstanding. I was glad when we were finally finished at twelve thirty.

I turned to Dawna. There were so many things we really needed to talk about, but there just wasn't enough time. "I want to talk to you. I *need* to talk to you. But I have that big family conference call soon and I'm already cutting it close—I'll have to stick almost to the speed limit to get there on time. Do you maybe want to come by the house this evening and we can talk over a pitcher of margaritas?"

"Are you sure you're going to be up for a chat after dealing with your mother?"

I gave her a rueful look. "Girlfriend, after dealing with my mother I'm going to *need* margaritas. Say seven o'clock?"

"Sounds good. Do you need to eat something before you go?"

"I'll wolf down some baby food in the car."

"All right, just make sure you do. You don't want to go all vampity on a conference call with your mom."

She was right. The call was going to be bad enough without having to worry about that.

7

Birchwoods is a very exclusive mental health facility located on a huge swath of land outside the city. It has the kind of security required by rich and famous people who actually value their privacy. If you want your therapy or rehab to be showy and in the public eye, you go somewhere else. If you want secrecy to the grave and beyond, you go to Birchwoods.

In the decades the facility has been in business there has only ever been one security breach, and the bad guys had had to murder a guard and cut off his hand to accomplish it. My best friend, Vicki Cooper, had lived at Birchwoods for years. It had been the only place where she could control her clairvoyant abilities enough to be truly at peace.

Having been there so often, I knew the fastest and best routes to the place, but even with that advantage, I barely made it there on time. I twitched with impatience, my fingers tapping irritably against the steering wheel, as the guards put me through the security protocol: spray me with holy water, check my ID, make sure I had an appointment, have me sign in using a silver pen.

I drove up the winding road to the parking lot near Gwen's office faster than I was supposed to and smoothly pulled into one of the few open spots. I knew I should slather on some sunscreen, but I was about to be late, and it wasn't that far to the building's front door. So I just jumped out of my car and dashed across the pavement. I was happy to get under cover when I reached the entry—the sun, practically straight overhead, was plenty bright and hot.

Katy, the receptionist, knew that Gwen was expecting me and just waved me through the main doors. I hurried down the corridor, arriving in Gwen's office breathless and only a little sunburned.

Gwen smiled when she saw me, shaking her head slightly in exasperation. Still, she didn't scold me about my appearance or my last-second arrival.

"Good afternoon, Celia."

"Hi, Gwen." I didn't apologize. I had come. I wasn't even late.

Her smile broadened. She has a good smile, one that lights up her face. Without that smile, she's a very ordinary-looking older woman. With it, she's a knockout. "Before we get started, how have you been doing since our last visit?"

How had I been doing? I thought about how best to phrase it. "Okay, I guess. It's been . . . hard knowing Ivy's gone for good. I miss her a lot. I mean, I knew she was dead before. But she wasn't *gone*. And now she is."

"Are you going to be all right for this meeting? If not, we can cancel. You don't need to feel compelled."

Did I feel compelled? Not really. But, much as I dreaded it, I did feel this meeting was necessary. We needed to let Mom know about Ivy. And Mom, Gran, and I all needed to start dealing with our family issues. Our relationship wasn't a healthy one—hadn't been in years.

"I'm okay."

"If you're sure." Gwen's voice was neutral, but I got the niggling feeling that, while she would honor my decision, she wasn't sure it was the right one.

Gwen had originally suggested we use Skype or one of the many other available video-chat programs, but she ran into an issue. The magical barrier around the prison where my mother was an inmate caused interference on regular networks, so we were stuck using specialized equipment.

That had meant rearranging Gwen's office to make room. The large, comfortable couch had been placed facing the camera, with its back to the bank of windows. Gwen and I would sit there, close but without crowding each other. The video screen was already live, and one part of it showed my gran, who was sitting on her own couch in her new home. When she'd first moved to Serenity, Gran had rented a real rattrap of a place, but after the attempt on her life, I'd promised myself I'd get her out of there.

I'd needed the help of Helen Baker, a member of the Siren Secret Service who had worked with me a number of times. Helen's mother had been a friend of my gran's, and Helen had talked Gran into renting her mom's house, which was part of the Queen's compound. It's very nice and very secure, which makes me feel a lot less worried. And Gran liked the place and was comfortable there. Still, I was surprised to see her at home today. I'd expected her to be with Mom at the prison.

"Hi, Gran. You're looking good." That was both true and not. Physically, she looked much better than she had the last time I'd seen her, shortly after she had been attacked on Serenity. Gran is a tiny woman and has always been wiry. She keeps her white hair cut close to her head and carefully curled. Looking at her today, in her pretty lavender church suit, I could see that she was tan and that she seemed more vital. I was glad to see that she'd regained some of her energy, that she was closer to the little whirlwind I'd grown up around. But while she looked better physically, it was easy to see that she was in emotional turmoil. Her expression was both angry and sad, and her jaw was set in that familiar oh-shit-now-we're-in-for-it line. "How come you're not with Mom?"

"Hello, Celie." Gran smiled and her face lit up. "This is so much better than a phone call. I get to actually see you." Then her eyes narrowed as she inspected me and I knew I was about to be scolded. "You have a burn! You know better than to go out without sunscreen." Being chastised was so familiar, so right, that I found myself smiling. During our last visit, she'd thrown me out of her hospital room. We'd said things to each other that could have damaged or even ended our relationship, and for months we'd barely talked and were excruciatingly polite with each other when we did. But the call last night had felt so different, almost normal, and today it seemed that the old wound had healed.

"I didn't want to be late. Besides, it was just a dash across the parking lot. It'll heal in a couple minutes." In the meantime, it hurt. But I wasn't going to say that.

She harrumphed. "You need to take better care of yourself."

Talk about your pot calling the kettle black, I thought, but I forced myself to be diplomatic. I didn't want to ruin the new accord between us. "I'll try."

"Do that." She grinned at me and I couldn't help but grin back.

Then, with a flicker, my mom and her shrink, Dr. Thomason, joined us via split screen.

Dr. Thomason was a big man, probably a good six six, built

like a linebacker, and obviously Polynesian. He was dressed in a dove gray suit with a white shirt and blue-and-silver-striped tie. His smile of greeting was warm but professional. My mother sat next to him, wearing prison orange, on a long couch not much different from the one Gwen and I were seated on.

My mother, Lana Graves, had once been a beautiful woman, and you can still see the echoes of that beauty in her bone structure. But years of heavy drinking and drugging have put a lot of rough miles on her. Even now, clean and sober, she looked hard, brittle, and angry at the world. Her hair needed a good cut and a dye job, to make the two inches of dark roots match the yellow blonde of the rest of her hair. The bright orange jumpsuit washed out her skin and hung limply on a frame that was moving past thin and on to skeletal. Honestly, she looked older than my gran, and not nearly as nice.

She didn't bother greeting either me or Gran. Instead, she glared at the screen and said, "What have you done with Ivy? Where's my baby? For days now she hasn't come when I called. What have you *done*?" She spat the words at me.

"Lana . . ." Dr. Thomason's voice was calm but firm.

Shit. Well, wasn't this getting us off to a fine start. "Hey, Mom. Good to see you, too."

At my sarcasm, Gran's expression darkened. "That's enough! Both of you." She looked directly into the screen, but I could tell it was my mother she was addressing. "Lana, baby, Ivy's in heaven. She found her way home."

"*No!*" my mother shrieked, launching herself to her feet. She pointed at the screen, at me. "*You* did this. *You.* You're nothing but trouble. Well, you're not taking her away from me again. I won't let you. *You're not taking my baby from me again!*"

"Lana, stop," Gran ordered. But Mom wasn't listening to her. She wasn't listening to Dr. Thomason either as he tried to get her to sit down and calm down. Instead, she started calling my sister's name, shouting for her the way she had when we were little, when she called us in from playing outdoors—to no avail. When she finally realized that Gran and I were telling the truth, that Ivy was never coming back, she started sobbing hysterically. Dr. Thomason called a halt to the proceedings so that he could deal with her privately.

Half the screen went dark. I stared at it for a long moment, trying to decide what I was feeling. I knew I should care that my mother was distraught, but I didn't. That lack of feeling was so cold it scared me. But it was the truth. "Well, hell. That was useless." The words popped out of my mouth, unbidden.

"Celia Kalino Graves!" Gran snapped.

I sighed and decided an apology and a change of subject were probably in order. "Sorry, Gran. So, um, how are you doing? How are you liking your new place?" Yeah, I was re-covering old ground, but it was the best I could think of under the circumstances.

She gave me a level look, to let me know that she absolutely knew what I was doing before letting me get away with it. "Yes, I am. Quite a lot. It's so beautiful and peaceful. The view is magnificent."

"The stairs are a pain in the butt, though."

She laughed in spite of herself. "Yes, they are. But there's a trail. It's longer but less steep. I tend to take that instead. It's easier on my knees." She paused, her eyes going a little distant, her expression wistful. "It's hard to believe Ivy's really gone."

"Yes, Gran." My vision blurred. I hadn't expected to cry. I didn't want to. But the tears were very close to the surface. It wouldn't take much to push me over the edge.

"What was holding her here?"

I swallowed hard. Talking about this, even to Gran, wasn't easy, but she deserved to know. I forced myself to form the words, my voice soft and rough. "It was me. I blamed myself for what happened, felt guilty because I didn't protect her. She died trying to save me, when I was the one who was supposed to take care of her."

"Oh, honey, no. *No*. You can't believe that! It wasn't your fault at all!" Gran leaned forward, her expression earnest. "You mustn't blame yourself. You were a child, a victim of those horrible men." She was crying, tears sliding down her cheeks silvered by the light of the cameras. She pulled a cloth handkerchief from the bag next to her and wiped her eyes and nose.

I felt my throat tightening, and I had to fight to make the words sound normal as I said, "I finally figured that out and forgave myself for surviving."

"That's all that was holding her here—your guilt?"

I nodded. My vision was so blurry I couldn't see the screen. Gwen passed me a box of tissues. I used a couple to wipe my eyes, then blew my nose noisily.

"I'm so proud of you, Celia."

I looked at the screen, startled.

Gran continued, "And I'm so sorry. I was so blind." She shook her head. She was still crying, wringing her hands around the old-fashioned handkerchief. "I did what you said. I went to a seer." She stopped talking abruptly as her tiny body was racked with sobs. "I'm so sorry. I didn't know. I should've known. I didn't believe . . ."

Oh, *hell.* During that last fight, I'd been angry enough to tell her to go to a clairvoyant and look at the past, to see for herself what had actually happened. It had been a cruel jab and I hadn't actually expected her to do it. There were things she hadn't known about that were beyond hurtful. "Gran, stop. You can't beat yourself up over this. You were *always* there for us. You made sure we got by. You didn't do anything wrong."

"I should've known. You tried to tell me. I should've listened to you."

I stopped, thinking hard. She was right—she should have known, and I *had* tried to tell her. But she hadn't believed me, hadn't been willing to believe that her daughter could sink so low. Still, saying that would only hurt her more. She didn't need more hurt, didn't deserve it. I didn't want her to spend the rest of her life racked with guilt, thinking "what-if?" I wanted her happy and whole. In that moment, it was very important that I say just the right thing.

If only I knew what it was.

Then something occurred to me, something she had said to me not that long ago. "Gran, do you remember the night after you sold me your house? Do you remember what you said to me when we were sitting on the porch drinking margaritas?"

She blotted tears from her eyes with the wadded-up handkerchief in her hands and, though she didn't say anything, I thought I saw a small nod. So I continued, "You told me that 'people aren't perfect. You have to forgive them. And you need to forgive yourself.' Well, I forgive you. And you need to forgive yourself.

We can't undo the past, and I don't want what happened to ruin our future."

"I don't know if I can," she whispered.

"You have to try. Please, for me?"

I waited for a long moment until finally I saw her nod.

8

Gwen had blocked out enough time for a double session, figuring that we would need time after the family therapy conference to go over anything I needed help dealing with. Even though family therapy had been a bust, we needed the time anyway.

There was a lot to discuss. We talked about my mother a little, but not for long. I'd hashed out those issues again and again over the years. I'd made peace with my decision to cut my mother from my life until she became less toxic. I love my mom. I can't seem to stop. But I've decided I don't have to participate in her drama, don't have to accept the blame she keeps shoving in my direction. And I won't. So while her histrionics were upsetting and made me frustrated and angry, they weren't the huge problem they could have been.

No, my big worry was the problem with my gran. She was in so much pain. For good or for ill, she loved my mother with her whole heart—sometimes to the exclusion of her whole mind. Again and again over the years, Gran had done stupid things that had enabled my mom's bad behaviors. But she'd done those things for the right reasons, truly believing Mom was a better person than she actually was. I felt bad, knowing how much it must have hurt Gran to have that illusion shattered. I told Gwen that I wished I hadn't suggested she see a psychic to find out the truth.

"But you did. Why?"

"Because I was tired of being the bad guy. It was always my fault. I was always the problem."

Gwen nodded. "And now you're not."

"But I hurt her."

"No. The truth hurt her."

"But I'm the one who forced her to see it."

"No. That was her choice. She could have ignored your suggestion. Instead, she found a psychic and had that person show her the truth. Now that she has that knowledge, she can make informed choices. That's not necessarily a bad thing."

Gwen was right. The Bible says that the truth will set you free. I'm not sure I agree, but I hoped that in this case it would lead to much more honest relationships among the three of us in the future. But oh, getting through the present was going to be hard.

By the time I left Gwen's office, I was better, though I still felt like I'd been put through the wringer. Intellectually, I knew that we'd made huge progress, but I was emotionally shaky. That always brought the vampire in me closer to the surface. So before I did anything else, I made sure to drink a nutrition shake and chow down on some baby food. I wasn't hungry, but I ate anyway, and was rewarded by feeling the beast settle back down.

I stuffed the trash into the garbage sack I keep on the passenger-side floorboards and tried to think of what I wanted to do with the rest of my day. I wasn't due to see Dawna for hours yet. I really didn't feel up to looking at office space again, but I wasn't ready to go home either. Bruno was at work at the university and probably way too busy for me to stop by.

So I locked the doors, cranked up the air conditioner and the stereo, and went for a drive along Oceanview. I wished I could have the top down, but that would have to wait until the sun set. For now, it was enough to just drive. Eventually, I even felt up to singing along with the stereo. I'm not in the least bit musical. But nobody was there to hear me, so I sang my heart out.

I should have been paying attention, but my mind was elsewhere. I didn't notice the vehicles boxing me in until it was too late.

My doors were locked, but my Miata is a ragtop convertible, and while I have reinforcing spells in place, it'd been awhile since I renewed them. Stupid and careless. Not my usual style, but everyone makes mistakes. I just had to hope this one didn't cost me my life.

I hit the button to make a cell phone call as the car beside me started moving into my lane, trying to force me off the road. No signal. The tow truck in front of me was slowing, the SUV behind tailgating. All I needed was a tiny opening for the Miata to get through, but they weren't giving me anything. I tried using my psychic ability to reach out to Bruno—to anyone—for help. Amped up by the ring Adriana had given me, that should have worked. Instead, my thoughts rammed into a barrier as smooth and white as an eggshell but hard as titanium. The effort of trying to break through gave me an instant intense headache that brought tears to my eyes. Water streamed, unheeded, down my cheeks as I tried to come up with some plan for escape.

Oceanview is a beautiful stretch of road, but it is not an easy drive. It twists and turns, and there are many areas where the drop-off is steep and rocky. Lots of folks have died going off this road—I didn't want to be one of them. The thing was, every one of the surrounding vehicles was bigger and more powerful than my little roadster. They could've crushed me, or sent me off one of the cliffs easily enough. But they didn't. They were just very deliberately forcing me to stop on the shoulder.

That was pretty damned scary, because I knew full well that there are worse things than dying—maybe not as permanent but definitely worse.

I pulled onto the shoulder and stopped, putting the car in neutral but leaving the engine running. I got my gun out and laid it in my lap, then set a couple of spell disks on the dashboard as backup.

I was about to be attacked by three men. I grabbed my phone, again trying to dial 911, but the signal was still blocked. But hey, my cell has a really good camera. So I snapped quick shots of the three of them and the license plates of their vehicles, then shoved the phone under my seat.

Ready as I would ever bc, I waited. The two who went to the passenger side of my car had the look of hired muscle: big, brawny, with attitude and prison tats. One was black, the other white, but other than that they were interchangeable, both wearing jeans and battered band T-shirts that had seen better days. The white guy held a classic Louisville Slugger in his left hand, its tip resting gently against the rough gravel of the road's shoulder.

The man on my side was cut from a different cloth. He wore a hand-tailored suit that was obviously expensive. The fit was as good as Isaac's, but the spell work wasn't—I could see a slight bulge where he wore his weapons. He stopped about a yard from my door, making no aggressive moves, doing nothing overtly threatening.

He was of average height and not particularly built, but that meant nothing. He was tough. You could see it in how he held himself, the thin veneer of polish over the hard reality of violence. There were old scars on his face near those icy blue eyes, and his nose had been broken more than once. But his reddish hair was perfectly styled and his face had been shaved as smooth as a baby's bottom.

When he reached into his pocket, I tensed, readying myself to fight. But he simply drew out his wallet and removed a spell disk. He set it gently onto the ground between us, then rose to his full height, and with one stomp of his well-shod foot, he broke the disk.

A fine mist formed a full-color, three-dimensional, holographic image of the head and bare shoulders of a man who appeared to be an older, harder version of the guy in the suit. He was clearly a relative—probably his father, and despite the fact that he wasn't actually present, I would've sworn he was looking right at me, across who knew how many miles and through the car window.

"Hello, Ms. Graves." He didn't give his name, which was no surprise, but otherwise he spoke quite civilly. I could live with civil. Maybe literally. So I played along.

"Hi. What's up?"

"I have a problem, Ms. Graves . . . Celia." He stared at me long and hard, taking my measure, much as Abigail Andrews had done the other day.

"Oh?"

His smile was chilling. There was very little sanity in his eyes, certainly no warmth or empathy. He was a stone-cold killer. I knew, *knew* that if he said the word, the men surrounding my car would do everything in their power to kill me. If they failed, he'd send someone else, and would keep sending people until the job was done. I had to fight not to shudder, to keep my expression and body language impassive.

He watched me, his smile broadening, with a little sparkle in his eyes. Apparently I amused him. "I have a . . . project I've been working on. It's taken most of my life. Now, when it's nearly completed, my clairvoyant friends tell me there's a problem."

He didn't expect me to say anything, so I didn't. I sat, waiting for the other boot to drop.

"You're that problem. I was hoping that I could buy you off. After all, you're a bit of a mercenary or you wouldn't work as a bodyguard." He paused, waiting for me to deny it. "But I see now that that won't be possible. So I'm left with a dilemma. I'm told that if you become part of this, there will be trouble—but if I kill you, it will be even worse. The possibility of failure has been mentioned.

"I could tell you to stop. But you won't. I can see that. You're too tough." He shook his head in mock sadness, but his eyes were avid. "So I'm just going to have to prove to you that I'm tougher." The image turned to the suited man. "Do it."

At the sound of his command, several things happened at once. I grabbed the nearest spell disk, the suited man broke a disk he'd palmed while I was listening to the hologram, and the thug with the bat smashed my windshield. Thug number two . . . walked away?

I didn't have time to worry about him. I had worse problems. While the spell disk the guy in the suit had broken didn't seem to have done anything, I could feel the magic of it filling my car. And *my* spell disk, my very reliable, guaranteed by the manufacturer shield spell, failed. I felt the magic start to build, but then it hit what was already in the car and just *died*.

Oh, shit.

I grabbed my gun, switching off the safety as Slugger continued to rain blows on my windshield. Safety glass began to crumble and a small hole appeared. Suit tossed a spell ball to the Slugger, then dived for cover. In the instant it took me to turn and take aim through the broken windshield, the thug with the bat managed to crack the ball open and drop it through the hole.

I froze, victim of a variation of the full-body binding spell that my ex-boyfriend had developed at my request.

Irony blows.

I got to sit there, completely motionless, barely able to breathe, watching as thug two returned and nimbly broke into my car. He hauled my unresponsive ass out like a sack of groceries, then set me down on the gurney he'd brought from one of their vehicles.

At that point Suit started disarming me, then cutting my clothes off—in full sunlight, with no sunscreen. With exquisite care and a little sound of admiration, he set aside my knives and their sheaths, along with my Colt. My ring, too, was set aside as if it were a weapon. It was infuriating and humiliating to be so utterly helpless. The man could have done anything he wanted to me and we all knew it. But this was just business to him, and he was careful and respectful: no leering, no wandering hands. I might as well have been a mannequin in a store window for all the interest he showed.

When he had me down to my lacy pink bra and panties, he muttered another spell, which loosened the binding a little. Not enough for me to move, but enough for me to be moved. Then Suit pushed, pulled, and prodded my body until I was lying on the gurney. Done, he walked away, leaving the thugs to wheel me down to the beach. I couldn't turn my head to see him climb into his SUV, but I heard the engine start up and the crunch of gravel as the vehicle pulled onto the highway.

I wondered what was to come next.

9

Down on the beach, the black thug busied himself laying out a cheap beach towel and various accoutrements that would make it look like I was just another girl sunbathing on the rocks by the ocean. Slugger had left his bat up by the car and was taking advantage of his colleague's distraction to steal the diamond studs from my ears before copping a gratuitous feel. I couldn't do a thing to stop him. He was just beginning to slide his hand up my thigh toward the lace edge of my bikini underwear when his buddy, who was coming back to the gurney by then, caught a glimpse of what was happening. He struck like a snake, slapping away the offending hand.

"Don't even think about it," he growled. "Our orders were clear. Nothing sexual, nothing that would leave DNA or trace evidence, and no stealing her stuff."

"What they don't know—"

"Will get your ass killed," he snarled. "And maybe me with you. Hands off!"

"Oh, yeah? How're they going to find out? You plannin' on rattin' me out?" Slugger glared at the other man, his hands tightening into fists.

With a derisive snort, the first guy said, "I won't have to. Trust me. You do not want to cross this man. We got our money. We're finished here. We need to take off before somebody comes along and calls the cops."

Slugger didn't argue, but I could hear him muttering "waste of a fine piece of ass" and "never had a princess before" as he slipped my jewelry into his jeans pocket.

Shuddering inwardly at the thought of having that piece of scum touching, let alone raping me, I was hugely relieved when they passed out of sight. Soon I heard sounds that could only be the tow truck attaching to my vehicle. Moments later, the two thugs drove off.

I wasn't paying too much attention by then because my skin was starting to burn.

Vampires are flammable. While I'm not fully a bat, I'm more than halfway there. Smoke was literally rising from my skin as it blackened and blistered, a smell like meat on the barbeque filling the air. I kept trying to scream, but the magic bound me so tight that I couldn't draw enough air into my lungs to manage it. Only a weak, agonized wheeze passed my lips as overhead the seagulls that are my near-constant companions circled and swooped, cawing in agitation.

I couldn't blink; my vision blurred as my eyes began to burn. My healing abilities were struggling against a tidal wave of injury, and they were losing.

I had to do something. I tried desperately to think around the agony that was spreading over me. Telepathy was my best bet. I tried to focus my thoughts, to use my desperation to boost my meager talent's range and power. I put every ounce of strength I could muster into a psychic call to Alex, and Dom Rizzoli at the FBI, and any and all of my friends.

Nothing.

Despair, rage, and overwhelming pain swept over me.

Sirens are attracted to water, and vice versa. Even my little bit of siren power was enough to call the ocean; spray splattered over me. The tiny, wet drops of cool water felt wonderful—until the instant after they struck, when the salt in the water hit my wounds and sent me into more spasms.

I was going to die, alone and in torment, burning to death, if I didn't think of something.

Then I heard the flap of nearby wings, felt the faintest of breezes against my face, and it struck me.

The gulls. They're always around me, whether or not I want them. Well, I wanted them now—needed them. I concentrated on summoning them. Dozens, maybe hundreds of birds were likely to be in range of this thin strip of abandoned beach. They couldn't understand words, but they understood intent. I needed them to shade me, to cover me. I heard the rush of hundreds of wings. The cawing of angry birds overwhelmed the sound of the surf. At my mental urging, some birds landed on me, shielding me beneath their wings as others flew in waves above me, blocking the burning sunlight. The birds' sharp claws and their weight were a new misery, but the shade they created was a blissful relief. I could actually feel my body trying to heal the hideous damage that had been done to it.

But better even than the respite from torture was the surge of hope. I was going to survive.

Pain and rage had driven the human part of my consciousness into a small corner of my mind. Far more powerful were the aggression and naked hunger of the vampire. The binding spell had eased a little, though not enough to allow full movement. Now that I could, I closed my eyes, letting my body heal them as I used my other senses to search for prey.

There, in the distance. Faint, beneath the roar of the waves and the sounds of the gulls . . . human voices.

"She should be here somewhere. Wait, over there. Oh, no! The birds! Oh, God, are they eating . . ." I heard the woman gag, retching, obviously unable to finish her sentence. In the dim recesses of my mind I recognized her voice, but it took me a minute to place it: Dottie. Her name was Dottie. The image of an old woman, slow, weak, came into my mind.

"It's all right, honey. I don't think they're hurting her," the man—Fred—answered. "It almost looks like they're protecting her." He took a breath, then added, softly, "That smell . . ."

I heard the pair of them struggling to hurry across the wet sand. They stopped, too far away for me to attack without dislodging the birds. It was so frustrating! I could hear the rapid beat of her heart, could smell her fear even over the scent of my own burnt flesh. I knew that she would taste *wonderful* and that fresh blood would help my body heal faster, ending the maddening torment that roiled the entire upper surface of my body.

"Stop, Fred. Don't go any closer. She's in too much pain. She won't be able to control herself." Dottie's voice was commanding. "Celia, we've brought you food. I'm going to toss it over to you. You'll feel better once you've eaten."

Yes, I would. If they would only come a teeny bit closer—either of them. Despite the pain, I flexed my toes—the binding spell was gone. They were old and slow. Even hurt as I was, I could take them. Then I would feel so much better. I waited, keeping still. Perhaps if they believed I was still frozen in place, they would come closer.

I heard the soft thud of something hitting the sand beside me. Whatever it was sloshed; it smelled of plastic and human food, and beneath that, blood. Before I could think, my hand shot out, grabbing the container in a blur of speed and bringing it to my mouth. I tore through the plastic with my teeth as dislodged gulls circled overhead, cawing.

The blood tasted glorious—hot, sweet, salty . . . but there was a faint aftertaste that I recognized from another time, years ago. I started to pull back, but it was too late. Powerful drugs laced with magic were already hitting my system. My pain vanished, and the world with it.

I woke with the sunset. I could feel it sinking below the horizon, feel my body tensing to rise. I felt the pull of the moon, the need to stalk prey, to hunt.

I opened my eyes. I was alone in a hospital room, my body pinned to the bed by metal restraints. I hissed in anger, pulling against the brackets. The metal groaned but did not give way.

There was a crackling noise above and behind me as a speaker was activated. A female voice, tinny sounding from the distortion, spoke to me. "Ms. Graves, I can see you're awake. How are you feeling?"

Ms. Graves. The name was familiar . . . it was *my* name. I was Celia Graves. Memories flooded over me. I remembered who I was. I remembered what had happened to me. I strained to look at myself, naked on the bed, without so much as a hospital gown to cover me.

My skin was whole again. Not scar tissue, whole, new, and as clear as if it had never been burned. Only one thing was different. Years ago, I'd gotten a tattoo to honor my baby sister; ivy twined up one leg from ankle to hip. Now, the back of my leg, where the skin had remained unburned, looked as it had ever since, covered with green leaves and vines. But the front of my leg, where the skin had burned completely off before the gulls covered me, was unmarked. It looked . . . strange.

"Ms. Graves?"

"I'm here. Give me a minute." My voice was a hoarse croak, harsh from disuse. "How long have I been out?"

"It's Thursday. We kept you unconscious with magic and drugs for two days while your body healed the worst of your injuries. We'd hoped to keep you under for another forty-eight hours, but now that you're mostly healed, your body is processing the drugs too quickly, and using magic alone wasn't deemed advisable."

I looked at the tubes and machines I was connected to: IVs, a catheter, a feeding tube. A heart monitor that beeped frantically in response to my racing pulse as I fought to suppress my fear, anger, and the vampire instincts that were as near the surface as they'd been the first night after the bite.

"Ms. Graves, I need to ask you a few questions. Answer as honestly as you can."

"Okay." I closed my eyes and took deep, cleansing breaths: in through the nose, out through the mouth. I could get a handle on this. I could control it. I'd done it before. I could do it now.

"Tell me about your family."

I recognized the question. It's the first question asked of vampire bite victims, to make sure they're still human, that they haven't been brought over. New bats are practically feral. They have no sense of identity, no self, until their master imprints one on them. So if you've been bit, EMTs and doctors routinely ask about your human life, questions they have the answers to, to make sure you're still you. The fact that they recognized how close I was to falling over that edge was terrifying. If I didn't answer well and quickly, they'd cut off my head while I was pinned to this bed, then stake my heart to finish me.

"My name is Celia Graves. My mother, Lana Graves, is in prison after multiple DUIs. My gran is living on the Isle of Serenity so that she can visit her. My sister, Ivy, died as a child, and my dad bugged out when we were both little." I paused, steeling myself to say the part that was still fresh enough to hurt. "My sister's ghost passed over just the other day."

"Ah. Good. You remember." There was a pause before the speaker crackled again and the tinny voice continued, "We need to send someone in to change your IV bags. Are you in control of yourself enough for us to do that?"

I was in restraints. Did she really think it was that much of a problem? Why? What had I done while unconscious? I wanted to know—and at the same time I didn't. A tight knot was forming in my stomach—pure nerves. I couldn't have done anything too bad. If I had, I'd be dead. At least that's what I told myself as I answered, "I'm fine."

"Very good. Stay very still, please."

I could do that. At least I told myself I could. But it wasn't easy. Not at all. As soon as I smelled the faint scents of human flesh with a fresh hint of soap, heard steady footsteps on the linoleum floor of my room, my body tensed, muscles coiling. The predator in me prepared to spring.

I am not *a fucking bat. I am not going to* be *a bat.* I clenched my jaw tight enough to hear my teeth grinding and feel my fangs biting into the flesh of my own lip. But I made myself lie still, kept myself under control. It wasn't easy. It wasn't pretty. But I did it.

The nurse who moved around me was older, thick-bodied, her short dark hair cut in a no-nonsense bob that was in stark contrast to her playful pale blue scrubs patterned with Sylvester stalking Tweety as the little bird quoted his usual line. The woman looked vaguely familiar, and I flogged my memory trying to come up with either her name or a reason why I would recognize her.

"I'm glad you're awake. We've been worried about you." She smiled down at me as she began switching the plastic fluid bags with practiced ease. "You probably don't remember me, but I was on duty when you and your friend helped us during the M. Necrose outbreak. The zombie you took down in the hall was coming right at me. If you hadn't stepped in that day, a lot of people would have died. I probably would've been one of them." Her blue eyes locked on mine, her expression serious. "A lot of the nurses were afraid to come in here with you. But I don't believe you're going to attack me. You're stronger than that. I've seen it."

My eyes filled with tears. "God, I hope so."

She gave me a reassuring smile beforc adjusting a knob. Fluid flowed freely through one of the tubes into my arm. As the fluid flowed in, consciousness flowed out.

I slept.

10

"Hello." I opened my eyes at the sound of Alex's voice. She was sitting in a chair next to my bed. "Up and at 'em, sleeping beauty. I don't have all day."

"Hey, Al."

"Celia."

"Not exactly beautiful," I grumbled as I tried to sit up. Of course I couldn't, because of the restraints, which I'd forgotten about until they brought me up short.

I was dressed now, if you call a hospital gown dressed. It was better than being buck naked, I suppose. Still, the skimpy gown didn't do much to ward off the chill, and the room was definitely on the cool side. Funny, I hadn't noticed that before.

I turned my head toward Alex, who looked tired. She was wearing her usual neatly tailored suit and her makeup was understated and perfect, but I could see the dark circles under her eyes and the slight slump to her shoulders.

"Honey, compared to what you looked like a couple of days ago, you're freaking *gorgeous*. Although I have to admit it's a little odd seeing you without eyebrows or lashes." She forced herself to smile, and while I didn't have Adriana's ring, I caught a flash of thought from her. She'd been worried about me, scared I'd be permanently blinded or hideously scarred. Of course she'd never say that out loud. It would violate the unwritten "tough broad" rules.

"I don't have any eyebrows?"

"Nope. The skin's grown back, but the hair's taking longer. You've also got a receding hairline."

"Oh, *hell.*" I felt tears sting my eyes. Stupid, I suppose. I was alive and not blind or maimed. I was also myself, in full possession of my memories, and not feeling the least bit like munching on my friend. All of these were good things. But my *hair.*

"Don't feel too bad. You can already see little spikes where the hair's growing back in. You'll probably look perfectly fine before long."

"When do you think I'll be out of here?" I hate hospitals. I know they have a benign purpose, but they make me feel trapped and they smell funny. Mostly I worry that if I'm confined for too long, somebody's going to come up with a way to keep me confined permanently. It's not paranoia if there really are people out to get you. Since the vampire bite, I've had ample proof that there are *lots* of people after me.

"I don't know," Alex admitted. "They've moved you out of the burn unit because you no longer have any open sores, but they want to be sure you're not a danger to anybody." She sighed. "You should know there are folks trying to get you declared a monster and put down."

I started swearing under my breath.

"Not to worry; it isn't going to happen. You've done good in the past and there are lots of people on your side because of that. Bruno's never farther away than the cafeteria. Your gran's here, and Queen Lopaka, King Dahlmar, and Queen Adriana have all called regularly. Still, what's made the most difference is that a bunch of doctors and nurses are on your side. They swear you're yourself and that you're going to be fine." She leaned closer and smiled. "I think so, too."

Knowing I had support was a huge relief, as was hearing that the medical staff thought I was going to be fine.

I was beyond grateful to the doctors and nurses for speaking up for me. I wasn't sure I would have if I were in their shoes. I felt better today, much more normal. The bat was there, but in the background. I could control it. But they couldn't have known that. They'd taken a terrible risk to save me.

"I'll update you on everything in a minute, but first, I'm here on business. Who did this to you and why? Are you strong enough to work with our sketch artist?"

"There were three males physically present, and another guy via some kind of hologram spell. Two of the ones with me were white, one black."

She sat up straighter in her chair. I wasn't surprised. She's smart enough to put two and two together. Or in this case three and three. Three men had snatched Abigail Andrews off of the street and three had attacked me. Coincidence? Not likely.

"What did they want?"

"To scare me off."

"Off what?"

"I haven't got a clue. The only potential client I've met with lately is Abigail Andrews. But she didn't hire me, and like I told you before, she was lying through her teeth the whole time she talked to me." So whatever that scary man thought I knew, I didn't.

"All right, we're going to investigate it thoroughly. There's a good chance the two incidents are connected, but we'll keep an open mind just in case they're not. In the meantime, if you're willing, I'd like you to work with an artist we've got on staff. She's a telepath—you can just think the images at her and she can draw them."

"Oh!" I suddenly remembered something else. "I took pictures of them with my cell phone. It's under the driver's seat of my car."

Alex grinned, her eyes actually twinkling a little. "That'll be great—when we find your car."

I sighed. "*If* you find it. It's probably just so many parts by now."

"Maybe," she admitted. "But we're still looking. Now, you get some rest. I'll send the artist over sometime later this afternoon."

She left and I dozed. My system might have burned through the drugs quickly, but the nurses kept them coming. The next time I opened my eyes, late afternoon sunlight was shining through the open window and my gran was sitting in the chair beside my bed, working at a book of crossword puzzles.

"Gran," I said hoarsely.

"Celie, you're awake." She gave me a huge smile, setting aside the puzzle book. "How're you feeling, honey?"

"Better than I was."

"I should think so." Her expression darkened. "We were all so worried. Your Bruno's been practically living here at the hospital. I told him to go home and get some rest, but he doesn't listen." She shook her head, but she was smiling. "That man really loves you."

That was quite an admission coming from Gran. She'd never been much of a Bruno fan, even before we broke up all those years ago and he went back to Jersey. Once John Creede had come along, she made it clear that she liked him better.

"John's stopped by a couple of times, too."

I nodded.

"Tomorrow they're transferring you to a regular room and

then you can have all the flowers and plants people have been sending. It looks like a regular jungle out at the nurses' desk."

She was trying to sound cheerful, but her clothes were rumpled, as if she'd slept in them, and there was a shadow in her eyes that spoke of worries she didn't want to burden me with.

"What's wrong, Gran?"

She shook her head. "Nothing. Not a thing now that you're going to be all right."

She was lying. I could tell. My gran doesn't lie often, and not at all well. But before I could pursue it, the police sketch artist came through the door and Gran used that as her excuse to take off like a scalded cat.

Officer Alyssa Rivera was small, stocky, and dark-haired, with large dark eyes that took in everything and a soft voice that had just a hint of a Southern drawl. Off duty, I suspected she was a ball of fire. Working, she was all business, and careful, as if she was afraid to hurt me. She set her briefcase on the floor next to the chair by my bed and sat down, taking time to get her equipment set up just so.

"I know it's going to be difficult, working with such raw memories, but I need you to think of each of the men in turn, in as much detail as you can."

I concentrated, thinking first of the man in the hologram, the brains behind it all. I felt Alyssa's mind brush mine carefully, saw her drawing a chalk outline. I was surprised. I'd expected her to use pencils or even charcoal. But she worked with pastels, in color. She had a quick hand and a surprisingly gentle mental touch. It didn't take her long at all to come up with all four, pictures so accurate they could be framed and used as portraits.

I gave an involuntary shudder, then gave myself a stern mental shake. They were just pictures. Useful pictures, which we would use to find the bastards who had done this to me. "Can I ask you a favor?"

Alyssa paused in returning her art supplies to their case. "What can I help you with?"

That she didn't know meant that she'd withdrawn from my mind. It was very ethical of her, and I appreciated it quite a bit. "Could you please send copies of those to me electronically? I'd like to have my business partner do an Internet search, see what she can come up with."

I expected her to say no, to give me a lecture about staying out of it, letting the police do their job. I could see it in her expression. Then she looked at me, her gaze lingering on my missing eyebrows, on the stubble that was all that was left of most of my hair. I could almost see the memories she'd touched in my mind affect her—her lips set in a hard line, eyes darkened to near black.

"I'll be happy to."

As she left, Bruno came in. He kissed me gently and told me how glad he was that I was awake and that I was going to be okay. I really wanted to talk with him, but I was worn out. Just the small effort of dealing with the sketch artist had completely exhausted me, and while Bruno was still saying loving things, I fell asleep.

When I woke again, I was in a regular hospital room with pale yellow walls and an actual window. Every flat surface was covered with lots and lots of flowers and plants. I was no longer restrained, thank God, but a security camera was mounted on the wall so they could keep track of me. Still, no restraints, *woot.* I could tell it was morning from the angle of the light and the smell of breakfast, which mingled with the floral scents that filled the room. Glancing around, I spotted what had to be the breakfast tray on the rolling cart near my bed. I was wondering how it had gotten there without anyone waking me when I heard the sound of familiar footsteps outside my door.

I could tell it was John Creede from the scent of his favorite cologne, not to mention the warmth of his magic as he tested the wards on the door before opening it.

When he came in he looked . . . controlled, everything held carefully in check, his handsome face nothing more than a pleasant mask. He wore an expensive business suit that spoke eloquently of Isaac's custom tailoring. I was willing to bet he was carrying plenty of weapons, hospital regulations be damned.

"John!" I didn't bother to keep the surprise and delight from my voice. Our breakup a few months ago had been more than a little bit bitter, but I'd missed him. I don't regret choosing Bruno, but I'll always care about John.

"Celia, you're up . . . and looking quite a lot better."

Oh, shit. Gran had said he'd been here, but I hadn't really thought about him having *seen* me like that. Damn it, damn it, damn it.

He must have sensed how stricken I was, because he sat down and started talking. His first question wasn't a question at all. It was more an order. "Tell me exactly what happened."

I told him. As I did, I could feel his anger building, filling the room like water fills a cup. Interestingly, while Bruno's rage is scalding hot, John's is icy. Still deadly, but different. Then again, they're very different men.

"John . . ." I paused, struggling to find the right words. "I'm sorry about Mexico." I wasn't sorry I'd fired him. He'd undermined me with the clients—which was totally unacceptable—and doubted my capabilities, which was hurtful as hell. But I could have handled it better, and I was damned sorry about some of the hateful things I'd said during our big fight.

He gave me a rueful grin and took my hand in his. "No. *I'm* sorry. I was out of line." He sighed. "I'm not used to being second banana. I'm not very good at it." His eyes met mine, his expression dead serious. "When I learned you'd missed the last flight out . . ." He didn't finish the sentence. He didn't have to. He'd been sure they'd killed me.

I wasn't insulted by that. My trip into the tunnels had been a last-ditch escape plan with maybe a five percent chance of success—success being survival. I'd made it out, with the last of the MagnaChem employees I'd gone down there to rescue. But it hadn't been easy or pretty, and the two people who'd been escorting us had died.

I was saved an answer by the sound of whispered voices arguing outside my door. My expression must have shown that I was listening to something, because John gave me a questioning look. My vampire hearing had given me advance notice.

"Company's coming," I said with a smile. "Dawna and Chris."

They were still in the hall, but I could hear every word. I held up a finger to stop John talking and eavesdropped shamelessly.

"You're being ridiculous, Chris," Dawna hissed.

His voice rose in both volume and pitch. "Ridiculous? Seriously? She nearly *died.* She could've been permanently maimed—would've been, if it weren't for those stupid gulls of hers. And *she's* supernatural. You're *not.* These people are playing for keeps."

Dawna was firm, her voice steady and calm. I knew her well enough to know that Chris was on dangerous ground. When she's irritated, Dawna will raise her voice and argue. When she gets quiet and calm, she's seriously angry. "I'm just going to be working in the office, sitting behind a computer and doing a few meetings. There's nothing dangerous about that."

"Her last office—*your* last office—was blown up, remember? No, I want you out of it. It's much too dangerous."

"No."

"*No?*" He kept his voice quiet, but his whisper was the equivalent of a shout.

"No," Dawna repeated. Then she turned the knob and opened the door, effectively ending the conversation. "John, you're here!"

"Just leaving," he said. He gave my hand a squeeze and rose. "I'm glad you're doing so much better, Graves." His voice was gruff. Then, to my exasperation, he ruined the moment by saying, "*Try* to stay out of trouble."

He was out the door before I could give the answer I thought he deserved.

Dawna took John's place beside the bed. She was smiling broadly enough to light up the room, the tension of her argument with Chris vanished as if nothing had happened. She's a great actress. I knew she was glad to see me and thrilled I was better. She was also probably glad to see that John and I were speaking again. She's a definite Creede fan.

Her problems with Chris were real and painful, but if she didn't want to share them, it wasn't my place to push. I had no clue what to say anyway.

She sank into the chair as Chris sullenly clunked a floral arrangement in with the others on the windowsill. He turned to me. "Glad you pulled through, Graves. I need some coffee. Either of you want anything from the cafeteria?" His voice was gruff and his face was flushed, but at least he was trying to be polite.

"I'd love a can of Pepsi. They won't bring me one before lunch no matter how nicely I ask." I knew that from my last visit. I smiled at him.

"That's 'cause it's bad for you." He snorted. "All right, one Pepsi coming up. Dawna?"

"Get me a Dr Pepper, please?"

"No problem." He leaned down to kiss her forehead. "Back in a few."

She sighed as the door closed behind him, her expression an odd mixture of frustration, anger, and deep sadness.

"You okay?" I asked.

She sighed again. "Not really. But I don't want to talk about it. Where's Bruno? He's practically been camped out here."

"I'm pretty sure he went home to shower and shave."

"Makes sense. He probably also has to arrange to have El Jefe cover a couple more of his classes."

"Warren's covering for him?"

"Yup, and Dr. Sloan and some of the others. Bruno said there were plenty of volunteers when everybody in the department heard what had happened."

That was so nice. "When did you talk to Bruno?"

"Oh, one of the times I came to visit. They wouldn't let anyone actually in to see you, but a lot of us came by anyway, to check on you. The desk nurse was talking about how many friends you have."

Aw, that made me feel so good. Not good enough to want to stay and soak up sympathy, but good. "Anybody give you a clue how soon I can get out of here?" I asked.

"Nope. Sorry."

"Damn it."

"Relax, Celie," Dawna ordered. "You need to heal. I can

take care of the work stuff. Your gran and Bruno will take care of the rest."

"Speaking of work, did you get a chance to check out your cousin?"

"Talia." She supplied the name for me and nodded. "Everything I could find checked out. She could be a real asset."

There was something in her tone of voice . . .

"But?"

"I just can't get past that whole thing when we were kids. I know it's stupid—"

I shook my head. "No, it's not. People are who they are. They can change . . . but only if they're willing to work at it and they really want to." I firmly believed that, which was why I had so little hope for my mother. She didn't want to change and she was practically allergic to hard work.

I shoved that thought away, focusing on the problem at hand. "Okay," I suggested, "what if we hire her on a probationary basis, the same as we're doing with Kevin? If she doesn't work out, I'll fire her. You can tell your family it's all my fault, so you won't get in hot water with them. I can take the heat."

"You'd do that?"

"Sure." I gave her a so-sweet-it'll-rot-your-teeth grin.

"What?" she asked, rightfully suspicious.

"But you get the honors if we have to fire Kevin."

"Oh . . . oh, *hell*."

"Agreed?"

She gave me a sour look, but agreed.

We chatted for quite a while. I took a look at the breakfast tray and sighed. Liquids. Not even thick liquids. No baby food. I drank it, but I wasn't thrilled. Still, by the time Chris returned, Dawna was in a great mood, laughing and telling me stories about office spaces she'd looked at and some of the new applicants, whose résumés were completely *not* what we needed on staff. We agreed that if we hadn't found the "perfect" office in another month, we'd rent something on an interim basis. Not having an official place of business was getting old.

Chris had put the time away from us to good use as well. He wasn't nearly as surly as he'd been when he'd left to get the drinks. Still, they didn't stay long after he came back.

As the door closed behind them, I wondered if they'd be able to work through their problems. I hoped so. But I wouldn't put money on it.

11

Two more days passed, *slowly*. I was getting better. I knew this not only because the doctors *finally* told me I was being released the following morning, but also because I was getting really, seriously, bored even though I had a steady stream of visitors.

Gran and Bruno took turns being with me. Gran and I spent a lot time reminiscing about Ivy, but we also talked about Gran's new life on Serenity and my plans for the future. It was great, but when Gran offered to reschedule her flight and stay longer, I turned her down. I could tell she wanted to get back to the island and check on Mom. My grandmother might be mad at my mother, but she still loved and worried about her.

Bruno snuck me in a Sunset Smoothie for dinner. I was grateful. It tasted awesome compared to the thin, bland liquids the hospital had been feeding me. We chatted for a bit, but he was looking pretty worn out, so I sent him home to get some rest. He promised to be back bright and early to take me home.

Home! I couldn't wait. I wanted out of there so badly, and I wasn't looking forward to the long, lonely evening that stretched ahead of me once Bruno left. Fortunately, Dawna arrived, bringing clothes for me to wear at checkout tomorrow, and a surprise: one of her sisters—the hairdresser.

Mae, like Dawna, is tiny and pretty. But where Dawna is a more traditional beauty, Mae is edgier. She wears her hair very short in back, almost in a buzz; the front is streaked with magenta, and long bangs sweep across her forehead and over one eye. I'd met Mae only once before—she lives in San Diego and doesn't visit the family much. I didn't ask, and they didn't say, but I suspected that Dawna had asked her to come up as a special favor. Mae took a long look at me, said, "It could be worse," and set to work.

The results, when she showed me my reflection in the mirror, were startling. My hair was all short and a little ragged. The style looked like one of the cuts you might see on a punk musician or an artist. It made my features look more striking than pretty, though just a little bit harsh.

"It'll be better in a few days, when it grows out a little," Mae told me.

"It's amazing, really!" I was so impressed. I wouldn't have thought she'd be able to do anything, as bad as it had looked. "How much do I owe you?"

"Nothing," she said firmly. "This is a gift."

"Are you sure?"

"Positive."

"Thank you so much!" I was so grateful I was almost in tears. Stupid, I suppose, but appearances matter. At least they matter to me. I'd felt like a freak. Now I didn't. The difference was huge.

Mae cleaned up the mess. Dawna hugged me. Then they left. When they were gone, I read a couple of magazines Gran had given me until I finally fell asleep.

In the morning I got up early, took a birdbath in the little bathroom sink, brushed my teeth, and got dressed. Dawna had brought me some of my most comfortable clothes: black jeans, a purple polo shirt, and one of my standard blazers. She'd removed the weapons—hospital regulations—but it felt good to pull on such familiar clothing. I did my makeup carefully. The new haircut changed the whole look of my face, and my stubby new eyebrows were a little hard to deal with. Still, after a bit of creative work with an eyebrow pencil, I didn't look too bad.

I was just putting away the last of my gear when I got a shock: Dottie and Fred arrived. That wasn't the shock; they'd visited before. The surprise was that they'd brought the Wadjeti. Fred was carrying it in its carved and warded box, but I could still feel the humming power of it, even from across the room.

The Wadjeti was an ancient Egyptian scrying tool that had been given to me by the late, unlamented Stefania and her daughter, Eirene. Since I'm not a seer, I had passed it to Dottie on kind of a permanent loan. It's tremendously valuable and when Dottie doesn't need it anymore, I'll probably donate it to a museum, but in the meantime, she makes use of it. That it was given to my by an enemy doesn't make it any less powerful a tool. Still, I was surprised to see it, and Dottie and Fred, in my hospital room. I knew they knew I was about to be discharged—Dawna had talked to them last night while Mae was doing my hair.

"Good morning, Celia. You look so much better than you did. Doesn't she, Fred?"

"Much better," he agreed as he wandered over to stand on the far side of the bed. He set the Wadjeti onto the bed beside me and left the visitor's chair available for Dottie, who was moving slowly across the room, her walker making a soft whumping sound each time she set it down on the tile floor. She didn't take the chair. Instead, she cleared the clutter off the top of the rolling tray table, obviously preparing a clear workspace.

"I'm glad we caught you before you left. I was afraid we wouldn't," Dottie said.

"Traffic." Fred made a disgusted noise.

"Not that I'm not glad to see you, but what's up that couldn't wait? I'm going to be leaving in a few minutes." I tried to sound nonchalant, but my nerves were jumping. Dottie was a seer and, to this day, I wasn't sure how powerful she was. Pretty strong, was my guess. That she didn't want to wait until I was discharged to give me a reading was the opposite of reassuring. That she wanted to use the Wadjeti to do the reading was worse.

"I know, dear." Dottie smiled up at me, but her expression was a little vacant. "And there are things you need to know before you go. Sit on the bed, please."

I sat.

"Three throws, to represent your past, present, and future."

"Okay," I answered. After all, it wasn't as if I had a whole lot of choice. Dottie looked absolutely determined, and when a powerful clairvoyant gets that look, it's really best to listen. Sighing, I lifted the Wadjeti's lid to reveal a stack of ceramic scarabs and a small cup of beaten gold set with alternating lapis and moonstone. We'd done this before, and though that had been some time ago, I hadn't forgotten what to do. I held the cup in one hand and dropped the scarabs into it one at a time. The power built with each stone added. When the last one hit, there was a flare of heat, and a blinding white light shone out through the moonstones.

Dottie shook the cup, then poured the stones out onto the tray table.

Glowing scarabs scurried across the metal and plastic like

live beetles, their claws making clicking noises. When they settled into place and became smooth ceramic once again, there was a large group to the left, while on the right, two scarabs stood alone: a bright blue-green one mounted atop the sole red stone—the death stone.

Dottie looked at me and smiled. "That"—she pointed at the two stones—"is life from death. It means rebirth. In this case, your past life is coming to a close, and you're experiencing a whole new beginning. You can plan on there being a lot of changes in the near future."

She extended the cup. I took it and repeated the process to fill it. This time, when the last scarab hit, blue lights shone from the lapis stones until Dottie emptied the cup onto the tray.

Once again the scarabs skittered around, this time organizing themselves into identical groups on either side of the death stone. Each group had four scarabs, one at each compass point, surrounded by a circle of stones facing outward.

Dottie stared at the scarabs, her expression confused. When she looked at me, her eyes were wide. I could tell she was upset. "I . . . I'm not sure what this means. There's a conflict, life and death. But other than that—"

"It's okay, Dottie. Really." I reached out to pat her hand.

"But you need to know! That's why I'm here. What good is a reading if I can't translate it for you?"

"Maybe it's one of those things that will make sense later, when we have more information," I suggested.

"If it were a reading for the future, that would make sense," she said. "But this is the *present.*" She shook her head, lips pursed in an expression of annoyance. Still, after a moment she held out the cup and we prepared for the third throw.

The power built again, this time thick enough that it burned along my sensitive skin and stole the breath from my lungs. The room seemed to dim, as if the only light came from those small glowing ceramic orbs, each shining with its own individual magic. The cup glittered as if it contained a rainbow.

Dottie spilled the scarabs a third time. As she did, her eyes rolled back in her head and her voice changed, becoming deeper and richer. She sounded eerily like an Egyptian deity I'd encountered not so long ago: Isis, whose magical collar had been misused by a villainous witch who was hungry for power.

That voice rang through the room, clear and pure as the tone of a bell. "Spare the pawn, save the girl. Save the girl, thwart the enemy."

"Isis?" I whispered. But if I'd hoped for acknowledgment, or guidance, I was doomed to be disappointed.

"Spare the *pawn*," the voice ordered, and Dottie collapsed across the bed.

12

Bruno arrived as the doctors were checking Dottie out. She was fine, she insisted. The doctors agreed, but they made her eat some carbs and protein and told her that she needed to take it easy and not use her magic for a few days to avoid straining herself. She didn't argue, which was proof enough that she had exhausted herself. Fred promised he'd take her home and put her right to bed.

"I take it I missed something?" The lilt in Bruno's voice made it a question. He sat on the edge of the bed next to me, looking particularly yummy in black jeans, a black dress shirt, and black leather boots, all of which suited his dark hair and eyes.

"Dottie did a reading for me."

"And pushed herself too hard," he said, without the question this time.

I sighed in answer.

"She's a grown woman, Celia, and knows what she's doing. Don't blame yourself."

That was so much easier to say than to do, but I didn't argue. There really wasn't any point. I just shook my head and got up, crossing to where the little redheaded nurse, in her pale blue scrubs, was waiting with a wheelchair.

Bruno got up, too, then knelt in front of my wheelchair. Taking my hand in his, he said, "I'm so glad you're coming home. I love you. You have no idea how badly you scared me." His eyes grew haunted, then hardened with anger. "I just wish I could get my hands on the bastards who did this to you."

I shuddered at the look on his face. I didn't often see a resemblance between him and his relatives on the East Coast—reputed organized crime kingpins—or the man a vision had told me Bruno would have been if he'd never met me. But at this moment, I saw it all too clearly.

I don't know what expression he saw on my face, but it affected him. As I watched, he swallowed all that rage, forcing himself to calm down. When he had himself under control, he leaned forward, kissing me gently on the forehead. "Let's blow this pop stand."

"Sounds good to me."

He rose and gathered up the plastic tote bags that held the stuff I'd accumulated during my stay—books, magazines, toiletries, and other bits of junk. Bruno promised the same nurse who'd remembered us from the M. Necrose attack that he'd come back for the flowers and plants—and she reluctantly agreed to let him, so long as he did it *soon.* She wheeled me to the main entrance, where Bruno's black SUV was waiting in the loading zone. The car has heavily tinted windows, and seats that are more comfortable than my bed. It's new enough to still smell like vinyl and leather.

We drove in silence until we got onto Oceanview. Something was bothering him. Rather than sit and brood about it, I decided to just ask him straight out.

"What's up?"

"I need to tell you something," he said.

"Then why aren't you talking?"

His mouth twitched. It wasn't really a smile, but his expression softened enough that I didn't think he'd be moving to Mount Rushmore.

"I've been trying to trace your knives using magic."

"Wow, um, thanks. Any luck?"

"No."

Okay, that was just weird. His blood was an essential part of their making. Logically, he should be able to find them anywhere on the planet.

"They haven't been destroyed. I'd know it if they had been. But they're being blocked from me."

I blinked a little stupidly at that. Bruno is a top-level mage. He's got world-class talent, excellent training, and plenty of experience. It would take somebody—or several somebodies of equal talent—to keep him from finding those blades. Of course, it had taken more than a hedge mage to put together that hologram spell.

I looked more closely at him. Bruno's handsome features showed worry and exhaustion, and I'd have sworn there was a fine tracing of lines at the corners of his mouth where none had been just a few days ago. I reached out and laid a hand on his arm, gently, so as not to interfere with his driving.

"I hate to lose them. But if some collector has them behind wards that powerful, there's not much we can do about it."

"There's more." He pulled the car onto the shoulder, cut the engine, and turned on the flashers. I decided that whatever he was about to say, I wasn't going to like.

"On my last attempt, I came *this* close." He held his thumb and forefinger a fraction apart. "I wasn't quite strong enough, so I called Matty. We made plans to work on it together this afternoon."

That was a good idea. Matty's only a level-six mage, but he knows how to make the most of his abilities. And he and Bruno are brothers. Being blood relations would make the bond between their magics that much stronger.

"So what's the problem?"

"I'm thinking maybe I should reschedule. You see, I got a call from Alex this morning while I was on the way to the hospital to get you."

"And?"

"She wants me to drop you off at the station. She wouldn't give me any details and she doesn't want me to stick around—said she'd give you a ride home when you were finished. I don't like it."

I can't say as I blamed him. After all, until very recently a group of police officers had made it their mission to see me behind bars. The primary instigator was gone, dead through no fault of my own, but that didn't mean there weren't others who'd be looking to take any advantage.

Bruno continued, "I don't like it. It feels . . . off. I'm thinking either it's a trap for you or they've discovered something about your attack that Alex doesn't want me to know about."

I thought about it for a minute and decided the latter was more likely. Alex didn't always like me, but I didn't think she'd set me up to be imprisoned or executed. And she was a cop. She knew all about Bruno's more . . . colorful relatives. She wouldn't trust Bruno not to do something drastic. After the way he'd looked in the hospital when I first woke up, I wasn't entirely sure

I blamed her. Still, better not to say that. So I went with, "Alex wouldn't trap me."

He shook his head as if surprised by my naïveté. "I wouldn't have thought Angelina would betray me either. People do what they think they have to, and the brass might not give Alex a lot of choice."

There was a hint of hurt in his voice. Angelina Bonetti had been his high school sweetheart. He'd loved her once, and he would never have believed that she'd turn state's evidence against his family. But she had.

I decided it would be best to avoid the conversational minefield Angelina presented and kept on point. "If push comes to shove, I've got diplomatic immunity," I pointed out. "But I'm thinking it's much more likely that they got a hit on one of the drawings."

I'd told him about the drawings during one of his hospital visits. I hadn't given him copies. But Dawna might have. She has some very strong feelings about justice and protecting her friends. As to what he'd do with the information . . .

"So, you want me to drop you off?" he asked, interrupting a train of thought I didn't really want to ride.

I smiled at him. Not because I was happy but because he wasn't trying to make the call for me. Maybe what I'd said to him the last time we were pulled over on the shoulder of a road had sunk in a little. "Yeah. I think so."

"All right. But call me when you're finished. If I don't hear from you by two, I'm calling Roberto." Roberto was my very expensive, top-of-the-line criminal defense attorney who had, thus far, managed to keep me from getting staked, beheaded, or permanently incarcerated. If I was . . . unnecessarily delayed . . .

at the police station, calling him would be a very good idea. I nodded, and Bruno got us back on the road.

"You'll have to expect to see an unfamiliar number when I call. My cell was in my car."

He shook his head, a hint of amusement coming into his expression. "You and cell phones."

"Tell me about it."

The humor drained from his face, leaving him looking sad and grim. I wasn't trying to read him, but I caught a glimpse of his thoughts. He was remembering what I'd looked like when they'd brought me in from the beach. He'd been absolutely terrified that he was going to lose me, either to death or to the vampire part of my nature.

"I'm fine," I said softly, trying not to spook him.

He looked at me, his expression haunted. "This time."

I couldn't think of a way to respond, so I stayed silent. Fortunately, we reached the police station shortly thereafter. Before jumping out, I gave him a quick kiss. "Thanks. And . . . I'm sorry."

"For what?"

"For everything. Love you."

"You too." He smiled when he said it; his eyes lit up and his dimples flashed. I've always loved those dimples. "I'll wait for your call."

"Right."

The Santa Maria de Luna Police Department has a pretty lobby—once you get through security. The atrium is airy and there is a lovely fountain and a display of plaques honoring officers injured or killed in the line of duty. I always stop there to say a quick prayer for lost friends.

I was looking at the small gold plaque that bore the name Karl Gibson when Alex came up beside me—the officer at reception had called to let her know I'd arrived. I'd met Karl right after the vampire had tried to turn me, and though we hadn't had long to get to know each other before Karl's death, I'd liked him. He'd been shot trying to stop a plot that involved a greater demon and a political coup.

"He was a good man," I said to Alex.

"And a good cop," she replied. "I still miss him."

I didn't know what to say to that, so I changed the subject. "So, why am I here?"

"Upstairs." She gestured with one arm toward the door, and while she wasn't exactly acting friendly, I didn't get any kind of a weird betrayal vibe either. So I went with her.

I hadn't been upstairs very often since the building had been redecorated and redesigned—the city was turning a lot of offices into open-plan workspaces, and the police department was no exception. Considered on its own merits, it wasn't bad. The small, grim, mostly windowless offices had been replaced by a huge, brightly lit open area that held a cubicle farm. The half-height cubicle walls were covered in nubby mauve fabric; plants in colorful pots were placed at intervals throughout the room; more plants hung from the ceiling. The carpet was orange and purple in a weird, abstract pattern. I thought it was hideously ugly, but it looked serviceable, wouldn't show stains, and would probably last until doomsday.

All that light and color was intended to make the place look cheerful and bright, which struck me as wrong on so many levels. I mean, seriously? It's a *police station*; it's full of people who are being questioned or arrested. Then again, I suppose cops are just as entitled to a nice workspace as anyone else.

The size of the open space made sound echo and carry despite the cubicle walls and acoustical tiles in the ceiling. There was no privacy, but at the same time it would be hard to distinguish any particular conversation in the overall din of ringing phones, whirring copiers and printers, other conversations, and the click of fingers on keyboards.

Alex's cubicle was in the far back corner of the room, near the fire escape and only three steps away from both the copier and the coffee machine. She'd personalized the space a little with a *Far Side* calendar and a framed photo of her with Vicki. The suit she wore, charcoal gray, with a red silk blouse, was the same in both the photo and real life. The woman, however, had changed. She looked older, grimmer, and much more tired. She gestured for me to take the visitor's chair and poured me a cup of black coffee without bothering to ask.

"Alex?" I made her name a question.

She lowered herself into her chair. Taking a sip of her coffee, she sighed. "So, do you want the good news, the bad news, or the seriously weird shit?"

"It's been a rough couple of days. Start with the good news."

She nodded and smiled. "Love your hair. That cut looks really good on you."

"Thanks." My tone was dry. Not that I didn't appreciate the compliment, but I was pretty sure we weren't here to discuss grooming.

"The bad news: we found what was left of your car." She opened the center drawer of her desk, pulled out a little metal plate, and tossed it onto the desk in front of me. "Sorry," she said as I stared at my Miata's VIN stamped into the ID plate.

"Damn it!" I wasn't surprised, but I was disappointed. I'd hoped . . . well, never mind what I'd hoped. I'd liked that car. I'd had it for years. Now I was going to have to find something else and probably have some huge car payment to deal with. And,

God help me, I was going to have to deal with yet another insurance claim. Tears stung my eyes, but I blinked them back. I was not going to cry, damn it. I was *not.* I was alive. I wasn't horribly scarred. I had my friends and my freedom. I'd get another car. "And the weird news?"

"I got an anonymous tip a few minutes ago. Someone said that if I wanted to find some stolen magical artifacts, I should go to this address." She pulled a slip of paper from the still-open drawer. "Now, while lots of artifacts go missing, I'm not the one to get calls about them. Not my department. But since you're missing a couple of things, I thought maybe I'd go check this out . . . and that you might like to ride along."

I jumped to my feet.

"Don't get your hopes up, Graves. It could be nothing."

Too late for the warning. I was hoping like crazy. My knives and my siren ring are my most prized possessions—and they are such heavy-duty magical artifacts that there was no way I could replace them. I don't have that kind of money.

Still, Alex was smiling as she rose from her chair. Leaning over the cubicle partition, she told the coworker in the next stall, "I'm taking my lunch break. I'll be back in an hour."

He gave a nod of acknowledgment and kept talking on the phone.

The address was down in the warehouse district. The area was familiar. It's off the beaten track, not well patrolled, and not all that busy. Most of the manufacturing has moved elsewhere, so there are a lot of vacant buildings; their For Lease signs are barely readable under the graffiti. The street was echoingly empty and bits of trash blew across the road like modern tumbleweeds.

More than one bad guy has established a home base in this warren, with the result that the whole neighborhood just had a bad vibe. Even in broad daylight a chill ran up my spine that had nothing to do with the AC in Alex's car.

Alex pulled her car to the curb. Unfastening her seat belt, she reached between the seats to retrieve her bulletproof vest. As she put it on, she asked me, "That jacket of yours spelled?"

"Yes." In fact, I was probably safer wearing my blazer than she would be in her vest. I don't cut corners on protection, and Isaac Levy does terrific work.

"Yeah, well, you still stay behind me," Alex ordered as we got out of the car.

"Gladly," I agreed. "But I don't suppose you have a spare gun?"

Grumbling, she reached down, pulled a Derringer from an ankle holster, and passed it to me.

She led the way up a set of cracked concrete steps up to a loading dock and a metal door marked DELIVERIES in peeling white paint. The door was unlocked and partially open. Alex stopped outside. She drew her weapon, holding it next to her right leg as she called, "Police. Open up!" and swung her arm to pound on the door.

When her fist made contact, the door swung easily back—too easily. Somebody had spelled it to open at a touch.

I smelled blood, sweat, piss, and fear. My vampire senses heightened and I could hear the squeals of rodents and soft gasping noises that reminded me of the way it sounded when someone tried to scream without drawing a deep breath. My teeth lengthened, saliva filling my mouth.

Now was so not the time to go to the bat side. I concentrated, beating down that part of my nature by pure force of will.

Alex gave a hiss of displeasure. "You can sense magic, right?" she asked me.

"Yeah."

"You feel any booby traps?"

"Nothing," I said. "But I didn't feel the spell on the door either."

"Wow, that's real helpful." She edged around the door, moving carefully so as to have the best possible cover while still getting a look inside.

I couldn't see anything but her back, but I was okay with that. If there was something worth seeing, she'd tell me.

Sure enough, she began swearing. Turning to me, eyes blazing, she said, "Go back to the car. Use the radio to call for backup and an ambulance."

13

Of course I didn't retreat straightaway. Instead, I leaned around Alex to get a look at what was inside—and immediately wished I hadn't. Slugger lay naked in the center of the room, his hands pinned to the wooden floor by my knives. The blood had attracted rats, and while he wasn't dead, he was a mess.

I threw up off the edge of the loading dock, then ran to the car to call for help as Alex went into the warehouse and started giving what first aid she could.

Slugger had been a thug and a potential rapist. He'd left me on the beach to burn. As I sat in Alex's car, shivering and nauseated, I told myself he'd made his bed. It didn't help. It had been obvious from my quick glance that Slugger had been there for hours before anyone had bothered to call Alex. The casual brutality of it was chilling. I thought of the man in the hologram—the one in charge. Presumably he was the one who had arranged to have this done.

"You okay?" I started—I hadn't heard Alex approach. Not good. I must be a little bit shocky. I'd need to take care of that.

"Not really," I admitted.

"Too much like what happened to you?"

"Yeah." I hated to admit it, but it was the truth. As if from a distance I heard the slam of the ambulance doors.

"Do I need to take you back to the hospital?"

"No. I want to go home." I wanted a hot bath. I felt like I'd never be clean again. I needed to brush my teeth. More important, even though food was the last thing I wanted, I needed to eat something. It must be close to lunchtime.

Oh, shit.

"What time is it?" I turned to Alex, a little panicked.

"Eleven fifty-three, why?"

"I have to call Bruno."

She didn't ask why, just retrieved the cell phone from her pocket and passed it to me. My fingers were shaking so badly that it took me three tries to dial the number.

He picked up on the first ring. "Celia, is that you?"

"Yeah." I couldn't say much more than that. All of a sudden my throat was tight. I wanted to be sick again, wanted to cry.

"Are you okay?" I could tell from his voice that he knew I wasn't.

I searched my brain for what to tell him, but my mind couldn't seem to focus. Finally I said, "You don't need to look for my knives anymore."

"Celie . . ." Alex grabbed the phone from my hand, so I didn't hear the rest of what he said.

"Bruno, it's Alex. Celia needs to go home now and get some rest. She probably shouldn't be alone either, she's a little shocky. I've got a crime scene to process. If I send her home with somebody, can you meet her there? If not, I'm sending her back to the hospital."

"Where are you? I can come get her."

"No, she needs to get away from here. The sooner the better. Can you meet her at her place in a half hour?"

"Yeah, I'm keyed into the security."

"Good."

I didn't exactly sleep through the ride home, but I wasn't alert enough to pay much attention to it. The cop, a guy I'd never met before and whose name I didn't remember, was very nice, taking me through the drive-through at PharMart to buy nutrition shakes on the way to my place, and then waiting to make sure that Bruno had arrived and I wasn't alone before leaving.

Bruno met me at the front door. He took one look at me, swept me up in his arms, and carried me off to bed. He tucked me in like you would a child, and went to run a hot bath. Only when I was in the tub and, finally, finally beginning to feel warm, did he ask what happened. I told him.

"Oh, fuck. Do you need me to call Gwen?"

"No. I'll be okay. It was just—"

"Too much like what happened to you." Gee, everybody was getting that. Of course it hadn't exactly been subtle.

I nodded.

"Fine. You finish your bath. I'll make you some tomato soup." He left, pulling the door shut behind him.

I rinsed off and climbed out of the tub. Patting myself dry, I padded naked over to the full-length mirror. This was my first chance to look at all of myself since the day I'd been stretched out on the beach.

I looked . . . odd. My skin was fine, except for that weird lack-of-tattoo thing on my leg. I had little stubby lashes coming in, maybe an eighth of an inch long, but my eyebrows were still just stubble. The combination made me look like some sort of exotic lizard, especially with my new hairstyle.

I brushed my teeth, then got dressed, choosing loose, gray sweats and one of Bruno's ratty Bayview T-shirts. I didn't bother with shoes or socks, preferring to go barefoot. I went to the living room, settling onto the couch as Bruno brought me a bowl of soup. I had to clear a space among the flowers on the coffee table to set down the bowl. There were flowers everywhere. Huge arrangements, small arrangements, plants, and every conceivable color and type of flower. The scent was thick enough to walk on.

"Can I ask you a favor?"

"Name it." He smiled.

"I hate to ask, but I'm going to be taking in Minnie the Mouser. Is there any chance you can do an aversion spell? I don't want her to get sick from gnawing on any of this." I gestured at the greenery.

"No problem."

He was as good as his word, working the spell as I slurped my soup. When I'd finished eating, I went to bed. He climbed in beside me, not saying a word, and held me till I fell into a dreamless sleep.

I woke at four in the afternoon, feeling much better. I padded out into the living room to find Bruno sitting on the couch, working on his laptop.

"Don't you have a meeting on campus this evening?" I asked.

"This is more important."

I was more important than the job he loved—that was so good to hear. His work meant as much to him as mine did to me. "I'm fine. Really," I assured him.

"Uh-huh." His sarcasm was evident.

"Sweetheart, you can go. I'll be fine. I promise I'm not going to do anything but lie around, maybe look through the mug shots Alex sent me."

"I'm not leaving you alone." It was a simple statement of fact and his tone of voice didn't invite argument.

I argued anyway. "Bruno, you just got this job and you've already spent days having people cover your classes. You can't afford to piss them off. I'll be *fine*."

He glared at me, his jaw set in a stubborn line. I knew that look, knew exactly what it meant.

I sighed. He wasn't going to bend on this. I knew it. It was annoying, but only a little bit. I really wasn't doing that well right now. But I also knew that he needed to be at that meeting. Getting started on the wrong foot could really hurt him when it came to campus politics. "All right, how about a compromise? Why don't you call Emma, see if she can come. Then you can go to your meeting and I'll have somebody to watch over me."

He waffled. "You're sure? I'll stay if you need me to."

"Go. If Emma can't make it, maybe Dawna can come."

He closed the laptop. Leaning over, I gave him a kiss. He whispered. "I love you. You're the best."

"I love you."

While he was making calls to line up my babysitter, I went over to my computer and got online. Following the link Alex had sent, I began searching for familiar faces. Slugger was there. His name: Rob Douglass. I found the second guy, too, but there was no sign of either Suit or the leader. Not that I got through all of the shots. Not hardly. There were far, far too many of them. It was downright depressing knowing just how many career criminals were at large here on the West Coast.

Bruno came up, sliding his arm around my waist. "Emma said they can be here by seven. Think you'll be all right until then?"

"I'll be fine. I really am feeling better."

"If you're sure."

"Go. Scoot. Git." I made a shooing motion with my hands.

He laughed at that. "Fine. I'm outta here. Call me if you need anything," he said as he ducked out of the door.

It was seven on the dot when I heard the sound of cars in the driveway and the buzz of the intercom. I pressed the button for the speaker at the same time as I pulled aside the curtains to take a look outside.

There were a pair of vehicles in the drive. Emma's little beater and Chris's das Humvee. Even from this distance I could see that Dawna had Dottie with her, and that the big SUV was completely packed with stuff.

"Come on, girlfriend, I know you're in there," Dawna called. "Open the gate already. No more moping."

I found myself smiling. She was right. I had been moping. I was alive. I had friends who cared enough to come to see me, to make sure I was okay. That was no small thing. So I hit the gate release and said, "Come on in," with as much gusto as I could muster. I'd barely made it across the room when the front door swung open, admitting the sounds of laughter and the smells of a dozen different kinds of food. Delicious aromas assaulted my nostrils from cartons of the spiced broth and drippings from one of my favorite restaurants, plastic containers filled with strained pho lovingly made by Dawna's grandma, and a Sunset Smoothie.

"Get out of the way," Dawna shouted. "It's a girls' night in."

"Barbara even sent some margaritas in a sealed container," Emma added.

I shook my head, smiling as I looked at the three of them. Dawna, still dressed for work in a designer suit and heels, was carrying a box filled with plastic shopping bags and take-out boxes. Emma wore jeans and a T; she held a large gray cat carrier with a mewing Minnie inside. Dottie, in her usual sensible shoes and a mint green track suit, brought up the rear with her walker.

Dawna breezed past me, heading straight into the kitchen. Dottie paused just long enough to give me a kiss on the cheek before following. Only Emma actually stopped. When she was sure the others were out of earshot, she spoke. "Are you okay?"

The hug I gave her was a little awkward because of the cat carrier, but I did it anyway. I'm not much of a hugger, but she deserved it. When Bruno called, she knew I was in trouble and brought the gang to the rescue. You don't get a better friend than that.

"Thanks, Em. I'll be fine. It's been a rough few days, but I'll get through it."

She waved away my thanks. I could see she was debating what she should tell me, what she could say without compromising the future and making things worse. Finally she said, "Celia, I looked in the mirror, tried to see what was coming up." I wasn't surprised. Emma wasn't a very powerful clairvoyant, but with the mirror she'd inherited from Vicki as a focus, she was getting much more accurate. "You need to be really, really careful. These people are smart and absolutely ruthless."

Did she really think I didn't know? I'd just spent days in the hospital with burns over most of my body because Hologram Guy wanted to make a point. I shuddered, remembering Slugger, my stomach roiling. "I know, Em, but I don't know what I can do that's going to make a difference."

"I know, I know."

I took the cat carrier from Emma. I set it on the floor but didn't open it. Knowing Dottie, there was an entire car load of cat accoutrements waiting in the SUV, and I didn't want to risk Minnie getting loose and running off. "Do we need to unload the car?" I asked.

"Oh, yes." Emma nodded vigorously. "Dawna said that Chris told her your inner bat had to pretty much take over to heal the burns, so you're probably going to be back at square one on things like eating solids and fighting against the bloodlust. Dad agreed. So we've brought you lots and lots of your favorite liquids to stock the fridge and freezer. Dottie brought all of Minnie's stuff, too."

I knew it. Where I'd put the cat condo, scratching tower, and velvet cat bed I had no clue. Not to mention the litter box. My place was already ridiculously overcrowded. I really needed to find an office sooner rather than later. I shook my head, laughing a little at the byplay between Dawna and Dottie in the kitchen as I followed Emma outside.

It took three trips to get everything. But by the time we'd finished there were drinks and food waiting on the coffee table.

The combination of a Sunset Smoothie and a perfect margarita began working its magic. I felt myself start to unwind and was able to hold my own in a vigorous debate about who was the World's Sexiest Man and which superhero was likely to be the best lover. Now out of her carrier, Minnie the Mouser began cautiously exploring her new digs.

We ate, we drank, we made merry, each of us determined to set aside her problems. Dawna was still upset with Chris. It was obvious that Emma had something heavy on her mind she didn't want to talk about. So Dottie rose to the occasion, regaling us with tales of the things she and Fred had been forced to do to avoid getting caught with Minnie on the premises.

"I'm so glad you agreed to take her. I really think the landlord was getting suspicious. We could've moved to Fred's place out at the lake if we had to. But it's so far from everything, and with his heart the way it is . . . besides, he only has a life estate in it, and Mickey is pushing to sell, so that wouldn't have worked long-term either."

Apparently Mickey wasn't too bright. In the currently depressed real estate market, they weren't likely to get a fraction of what the place was worth. Of course, if he was out of work and strapped for cash, he might not have a lot of choice. Still, that he'd even consider putting his own father out of his home didn't impress me even a little bit.

"It really has gotten a lot more urgent now that he's come for a visit. Minnie hates him." She looked over to where the cat was pawing intently at a box in the corner. "I don't know what's wrong. He walks in the room and she just arches up and hisses. She even took a swipe at his ankles when he walked by."

I turned to look at the little orange-and-white fur ball, who had moved on and was now happily grooming herself by the French doors. She'd been our office cat for quite a while. I'd never seen her react badly to anyone—not even Ron, and he was a jerk. It made me wonder about Mickey, especially on top of everything else.

When the sun sank toward the horizon, the vampire side of me began to rise. Even though I'd finished my smoothie and some broth besides, I could feel the need to hunt stirring within me. My friends' bodies began glowing, my hearing becoming so acute that their laughter hurt my ears, and the beating of their hearts was like so many drums.

When I caught myself starting to drool, I made my excuses and dragged myself out to the beach, away from temptation. I walked until I reached my favorite perch, a huge flat-topped rock at the very edge of the ocean. Sinking onto the rough stone, I stared at the water. I fought to master the beast within me, my body shuddering from the effort not to chase, *not* to kill. It wasn't easy, and it wasn't pretty. But eventually, when the moon rose and the last traces of orange and red left the horizon, I was able to think human thoughts again and I started back toward the house.

Apparently I'd been gone too long for Dawna's comfort. I heard the scrape of metal on metal as the French doors slid open. In the background Emma was saying how she and Matty were waiting for word from the Vatican on his transfer. There was the soft sound of footsteps on the deck and Dawna called, quietly, "Celia?"

"I'm fine," I called back.

We both knew I was lying.

14

We'd all had a few drinks. None of us was okay to drive. So sometime after midnight Dottie called Fred. He showed up with Mickey a few minutes later, and they chauffeured everyone and their various vehicles home.

It was the first time I'd met Fred's son. He hadn't "been able" to attend Dottie and Fred's wedding.

I didn't like him. In fact, if I were a cat I'd be reacting pretty much the way Minnie did, all raised fur and hissing. It wasn't anything specific he did; it was just him. He dressed like central casting's version of a low-level street hood. His body language was both sneaky and aggressive. So, while he looked perfectly ordinary, with medium brown hair of medium length and hazel eyes, I caught myself watching him. It wasn't quite to the level of counting the silver when he left, but it was damned close, and I found myself thinking that maybe it was time to update the wards around the estate.

It was close to two by the time I fell into bed, expecting to have my usual fight with nightmare-induced insomnia. Instead, I was treated to a soft purring bundle of fur who somehow managed to take up almost half of my bed. I wound up curled in a somewhat unnatural position. But I slept like a rock, and if I dreamed, I didn't know it.

I woke up to just a hint of sharp little claws and imperious meowing that demanded food *now.* I shambled grumbling into the bathroom, dealt with the necessities, and started making the coffee before feeding the vigorously complaining fur ball. I love that cat. But five o'clock in the freaking morning? Seriously?

While the coffee brewed, I cleared a spot in the middle of the living room and started my warm-up, all the while making a mental list of what I needed to do that day: get a new cell phone, file the insurance claim on the Miata, rent or buy a new car.

In a few minutes I was as limber as I was going to get and began my kata: focusing body and mind, breathing deeply. Even before the hospital stay, I'd fallen out of the habit of exercising. It felt wonderful to be moving in the old familiar patterns. The cat stared at me the whole time, her expression saying as clearly as words that she thought I'd lost my mind.

Feeling virtuous, I wandered into the kitchen and poured a huge mug of coffee as I evaluated my breakfast choices. In the end I settled on leftover meat drippings from last night, reheated in the microwave. After breakfast, I debated what top to wear with my favorite jeans. In the end I put on an old Pantera T-shirt and my Frankenstein boots. The look was a little aggressive, but it worked with the hair. I set out my armaments, choosing a waistband holster for my Colt so that it would fit in the small of my back. It felt odd sliding ordinary knives into my wrist sheaths, odd and wrong. I'd been using the knives Bruno made for me pretty exclusively for years now, but they were locked up in evidence for the time being.

Just thinking about how those knives had last been used made me shudder. *Don't think about it. It's over and done. You can't change it. It wasn't your fault. The knives are just knives—tools for whatever hand wields them.*

I told myself that. Even though I knew it was true, it didn't change the visceral fear and loathing that rose in me every time I thought about what we'd found in that warehouse. I needed a distraction pronto. Luckily for me, there were plenty of them at hand. I spent the rest of the morning doing errands via my laptop. The rental car company promised to deliver my SUV "sometime between ten and noon." The car insurance people said they'd process my claim "right away." I searched online real estate listings for office space and the database of felons for any sign of my enemies, both with negative results.

At eleven fifty-five, just as the rental car guys were pulling in the drive, my landline rang. Caller ID said it was the Santa Maria Police Department.

"Hello, can you hang on a minute? I've got to deal with the rental car guys."

Alex's voice on the other end of the line was martyred. "Fine. I'll hold."

"Thanks." I set the phone on the counter and went to the door, where a skinny guy with big glasses and freckles, wearing a green polo shirt, handed me a set of car keys and held out a clipboard with half a ream of paperwork. Even though it was expensive, I opted for the full coverage. It's possible I wouldn't need it. But the way my luck had been running, did I really want to take the chance? Oh, hell, no. I signed here, there, and everywhere else as he tried not to stare. When it was done, he thanked me politely and left. I was glad to see him go. I practically ran back to the phone, hoping Alex hadn't hung up.

"Okay, Al, I'm back. Before I forget, I found two of the guys in the mug shots. Is that why you called?"

"Actually, no. But I'm glad to hear it. I wanted to check and see if you were feeling better, and if you were up to driving."

"I'm okay today. Why? Do you need me to come downtown?"

"Yes. Please come get your knives and ring."

"What?" That made no sense at all. They were evidence.

"Rob Douglass refused to give a statement or press charges. One of our best detectives tried to push him, but it backfired. Douglass killed himself in the hospital last night."

"He *what*?"

"Suicided. There's no case. The brass decided that we don't have enough security to hang on to artifacts like yours unless we absolutely have to, and they don't want to risk a diplomatic incident. So, if you want your things, you can come get them."

"Wait—he had the ring too?"

"Yes." She didn't elaborate, and her tone let me know that she didn't want to say anything more about it. So I dropped it and asked something else instead. "Do I get them from you?" It wasn't as stupid a question as it sounded. The police brass tended to use Alex as a liaison with me—sort of a siren filter. It was very handy for them, though that didn't keep them from bitching mightily about our "connection."

"Nah, the property department. But don't come until afternoon. They're still working on the paperwork. In the meantime, I'm going to be out at a crime scene. Someone found a body. Female.

"The coroner's guessing she's in her midforties. She's been beaten and tortured extensively, so facial recognition is a no go." Alex's voice was icy calm, but I could sense an underlying rage.

Whatever had been done to the woman was bad enough that it was getting to her, but she was enough of a professional to hide it. I could understand that. I've done the same thing, more than once.

She continued, "There were signs of old injuries, quite severe. She would've been paralyzed from the waist down."

"You're thinking it's Abigail Andrews?"

"Yeah. We're sending the DNA out to see if it matches anything on record, but that'll take a few days. In the meantime, I wanted to warn you to be careful. Things have escalated."

"I sure wish I'd been able to find the suited guy or the guy in the hologram." I had a brainstorm. "Maybe I should call Bruno and John. There can't be that many people capable of that kind of spell. I mean, I've never even heard of anything like it. Bet they'd know who to talk to."

"I already did. They don't know of anyone, and no one they checked with does either."

"Oh." Okay, I felt dumb. Of course she'd thought of that. She was a detective, and a good one.

"Celia, are you okay? You sound . . . odd."

My temper started to rise. "I just got out of the hospital, Alex. Those guys deliberately left me to burn. You saw what they did to one of their own people. Now you're telling me they tortured a disabled woman to death. So, no, I'm not all right. Not even close." I was snarling at her. I didn't mean to. It wasn't even her I was mad at. I was mad at the car rental guy for staring, at the bastards who did this to me, and at myself for still being so shaky—so damned *scared.*

"Sorry."

"No. I'm sorry." I sighed. "I shouldn't take it out on you. It's just these guys are so—"

"Brutal, vicious?" Alex suggested.

"Exactly. I don't scare easily, Al, but these guys scare me."

"Good," she said firmly. "They should. They're seriously bad news, and I intend to see that they're taken off of the streets for a very, very long time."

Her words gave me an idea, one that might make me sound like a complete nutcase. But now that the thought had come to me, I had to ask. "Alex, the link you gave me only has photos of criminals who aren't currently incarcerated, right?"

"That's right. There's no point in having you wade through thousands of people who couldn't have done it because they're locked up."

"But I spoke to a hologram. The boss wasn't actually there. Maybe there's a reason why."

She made no reply, but I could tell she was thinking about it. I pressed on.

"I know, if he's a mage and he's incarcerated, he shouldn't be able to work magic. That might explain why nobody's heard of this hologram spell. He can't advertise it without getting caught."

"I'll run Alyssa's sketch through the system, see what comes up." She sounded doubtful, and tired, but I knew she'd do it.

"Thanks, Alex."

"You're welcome." She paused. "And Celia, seriously, be careful."

Everyone seemed to be telling me that. You'd think I was disaster-prone or something. Still, it was good advice. "I plan to."

After we hung up, I thought about what I'd just learned. I hadn't liked Abigail Andrews, but I wouldn't have wished a death like hers on my worst enemy.

Most of what she'd told me had been a lie. I knew that. But most really good liars base their tales on the truth. Alex would check the prisons as I suggested. But would she tell me if she found Hologram Guy? Maybe—then again, maybe not.

Twenty-two years. Abigail had said the man had been in prison for twenty-two years. She'd also said that he'd been the one who'd injured her in the first place.

Rising, I slathered on sunscreen and armed up. I debated whether or not to take along a pair of one-shots filled with holy water. Bats only come out at night and I didn't think I'd be gone that long, but holy water is useful for a lot of things, like checking for demons, shattering illusions, and cleaning away corruption. Better to have it and not need it than the other way around. I slid the little squirt guns into their loops inside my jacket, grabbed my purse, sunglasses, and keys to the rental car. It was time to go to work.

The SUV was cherry red with tinted windows. It drove like a tank but I couldn't fault the visibility. I felt like I was a mile above the ground and had the pleasure of looking down on just about every other vehicle on the road. It had a killer sound system, built-in GPS, and that chemical and leather new-car smell. I turned the radio to my favorite station, cranked up the sound and the AC, and was on my way.

Errands: they breed like rabbits, always take longer than you want them to, and are generally annoying as hell. Still, it was nice enough to be up and around that I didn't feel too annoyed.

I started by picking up a phone—with Bluetooth. That way I could drive whatever new car I bought and use the phone hands-free. I didn't need the earpiece for this beast—it had a built-in system. Good thing, too: I could understand now what Dawna meant when she said that driving the Hummer took her full concentration. Once I had the phone I began checking the rest of the items off my list.

I needed research done—more than Dawna could do in a limited amount of time—but I knew Anna wouldn't let me into the university library in my current state. Been there. Done that. Wasn't fun the first time. So I called her. She grumbled but agreed to look up the information I wanted and send it to me in an e-mail. Said to check my box in about two hours.

My next stop, Santa Maria de Luna PD's property department.

Alex had said the police did not want to keep my knives or ring. That might be true, but they were not going to part with them easily, and not without lots and lots of paperwork: boring, tedious, meticulous paperwork.

That one stop killed most of my two hours of waiting time. I was *so* glad to get out of there with my little bag of goodies.

I was very tempted to just slip on the ring and strap on the knives. But I didn't. They needed to be checked for trap spells, then cleaned, blessed, and generally made safe before I could use them again. I knew just the guy to do it, too.

I found myself smiling, I had a perfectly legitimate reason to go see Bruno. And hey, it was lunchtime. Maybe we could head over to La Cocina for a bite to eat. (Okay, in my case, not a bite, but at least a smoothie, which counts, right?)

The good news: I got to see him and he agreed to make sure my stuff was usable.

The bad news: he had a big faculty luncheon. He offered to ditch it, but I turned him down and gave him a good-bye/thank you kiss to remember.

As I was walking out the door he called out, "Celie, *try* to stay out of trouble."

It was an exact echo of John's words. I turned, intending to say something in response, then stopped. I am disaster-prone. I don't look for trouble, but it finds me. Nothing I could say would change that.

15

There was a line of people waiting for tables at La Cocina. I settled down on the bench under the awning and used my new phone to call Dawna. I figured I could catch up on messages while I waited.

"Hello?" Dawna's voice was pleasant but questioning, not exactly a surprise since she wouldn't recognize this number on caller ID.

"It's me. Sorry I didn't call sooner. I had to get a new phone and run a couple of errands. What's up?"

"That's right, you lost your phone! I forgot." Now she sounded like her bright and bubbly self. "You've got like a dozen e-mails and several messages. And we have a problem."

What else is new? "What is it this time?"

"Well, I got a frantic call on the business line from a woman who said she was Abigail Andrews's daughter, Michelle. She said that her mom was supposed to meet her at the airport and didn't show up. Michelle got really scared and checked with the police, who told her that Abigail was dead and then asked her all kinds of what she said were 'strange questions.'

"Apparently the cops also told Michelle that the last person to talk to Abigail was a local bodyguard. Evidently Michelle has been going through the phone book. She found us by process of elimination and is desperate to meet with you. She's grieving and angry and really, seriously confused. I told her I couldn't tell her anything and she just lost it. Started crying really hard and then hung up on me."

"I don't suppose she gave you a number at any point?"

"No, but I got it from caller ID. Do you want it?"

"E-mail it to me?"

"Sure. Are you going to call her?"

I thought about it. I wasn't thrilled with the idea. For one thing, it was ethically squishy. Yes, Michelle's mother hadn't actually hired me, but confidentiality is important in my business. On the other hand, Abigail Andrews was dead and Michelle Andrews might be in danger. After all, Abigail had wanted to hire someone to protect her daughter, not herself. If something happened to Michelle because I wasn't willing to talk with her, I'd blame myself. Decisions, decisions.

"Celia?" Apparently I was taking too long to answer.

"Just thinking. I'll probably call. Not that I actually know anything." That wasn't quite true. I knew that the people we were dealing with were lethally dangerous and highly creative—masters of mayhem, as it were. I didn't have a clue what they wanted or why, other than me out of the picture. Which meant that meeting with Michelle was a seriously bad idea.

"Well, be ready to get an earful," Dawna warned.

"Like mother, like daughter," I answered sourly.

"Sorry."

"Not your fault."

"Actually, it kind of is." Dawna sighed. "I was the one who was supposed to meet with Abigail Andrews in the first place."

"Yeah, well, it's better you didn't." Painful as the burns had been, I'd survived. I'd healed. I could survive more damage than Dawna. I didn't say that out loud, though. That would be too close to admitting Chris was right, that she wasn't safe working with me.

"Still. Sorry."

"Apology accepted."

We exchanged good-byes and ended the call. I was glad to see that I had nearly reached the front of the line, because I needed food. When I first got turned, several years earlier, I'd had to drink something nourishing every four hours without fail or risk all kinds of bloodlusty madness. If I really was back at square one on the bat control, I was past due.

None of the coeds looked like lunch, which was good. But I was getting grumpy, which was not. Finally it was my turn. Barbara greeted me with a huge hug. "You're back! You're okay!" She held me at arm's length, looking me up and down, her eyes narrowing as she took in the hair and the drawn-on eyebrows that showed above my sunglasses. "You *are* okay, right? Did you get the flowers?"

"Getting there." I smiled, to take any sting out of the words. "And yes, they're gorgeous. Thank you so much."

"You're welcome. Are you by yourself or meeting someone?"

"By myself. I need to catch up on some reading, but I'm starving."

"One Sunset Smoothie coming up. And, I assume, a margarita?" I nodded. Barbara knows me *so* well. She led me through the cheerfully noisy main dining area, asking over her shoulder where I'd like to sit. As we passed through the room, I overheard discussions about upcoming parties, past dates, work, and classes.

I didn't hear any comments about my appearance. Of course I wasn't the most oddly dressed person in the restaurant, not by a long shot, even with the hair.

I chose a table in the corner near the patio doors. It was out of direct sunlight, but there was enough ambient light that I could read the screen of my phone without straining or resorting to vampire vision.

Setting the phone on the table, I opened my e-mail. Sure enough, Anna had come through, sending an e-mail with a large attached file. I settled in and started to read.

I'd managed to cover most of the basics when she entered.

There are people who can change the nature of a room just by walking into it. She was one of them. Every eye in the place turned to her when she stepped through the door—including mine. She was probably in her late teens or early twenties and an absolute knockout. Petite, her black hair hung in natural curls almost to her waist. Her eyes were large, dark, and doelike, framed by thick black lashes. She had the warm brown skin of a Latina and curves that weren't concealed by the rather dowdy dress she wore. Conversations that had paused at her entrance stuttered back to life as she scanned the room, looking for someone.

An instant later she began striding purposefully toward my table, her face taking on lines of grim determination.

Oh, crap.

She stopped a few inches away from me. This close I could see she'd been crying. I could also see her body was actually quivering, with nerves, anger, or some other emotion.

"You're Celia Graves."

There was no point denying the fact. I'm pretty recognizable, what with the über-pale skin and the fangs. I'd thought the new 'do and Goth-style clothing might confuse the issue a little, but apparently not. "Yes. Can I help you?"

She pulled out the chair and sat down without an invitation. Barbara gave me a quizzical look from where she stood by a nearby table. I just shrugged. I didn't know who my guest was, but she didn't seem the type to start trouble.

"My mother met with you the other day. I want to know why."

Ah. This had to be Michelle Andrews. I shouldn't have been surprised to see her after my conversation with Dawna, but I'd hoped to have a bit of time to figure out what the hell I intended to do before I actually had to speak with the woman. I kept my expression calm and pleasant. My insides, however, were shaking nearly as badly as she was. La Cocina is very public, and I'm known to hang out here. If the bad guys were watching the place . . .

When I spoke, I made my voice sound ever-so-slightly bored. Which I wasn't. At all. I was pretty much terrified. Hologram Guy had made his point, loud and clear. I decided to play dumb. If I let her take the lead I might learn something useful. "Really? Why don't you ask your mother?"

"My mother was supposed to meet my plane this morning. When she didn't, I went to the police station. They told me she'd been abducted.

"They found a body they think is hers. They even asked me for the name of her dentist so that they can check dental records." Tears trailed gracefully down her perfect cheeks. Her voice quavered.

"I can't believe it. It can't be." She hid her face in her hands, her body jerking with the sobs she couldn't hold back any longer. It took her several minutes to regain her composure. All the while, the restaurant's customers either stared openly or tried desperately to pretend nothing was wrong.

Michelle dropped her hands onto the table and pleaded with me. "Please. *Please.* You have to help me. The police were kind, but they didn't tell me anything. They mostly asked questions, and the few things they did say didn't make any sense. But I overheard someone saying that my mother had tried to hire a bodyguard. I've been calling everyone in the book from here to L.A."

"What makes you think I'm the right bodyguard?" It was neither an admission nor a denial.

"I met with a man at Miller and Creede. He suggested I speak with you. Please. You have to tell me. Why did my mother want protection? What was she afraid of?"

I closed my eyes, trying to decide what to tell her. If Abigail had been alive, I couldn't have said anything due to ethical considerations. But damn it, she'd wanted to hire someone to protect *this* woman, the one sitting across from me. Michelle was in very real danger and she didn't have a freaking *clue.*

God, I wanted that drink.

As if on cue, Barbara came to the table with a tray containing a pair of water glasses, the smoothie, and a great big beautiful glass of frozen alcoholic goodness. I swear I wanted to kiss her. I took the margarita glass from her hand and drank most of it in a single pull as she set the little paper napkins on the table, followed by the water glasses. Then I took polite sips of the smoothie—I didn't want Michelle to think I was a barbarian.

Barbara gave me a wide-eyed look, her brows climbing high enough to disappear beneath her bangs. But she didn't say anything to me; instead, she turned to my guest. "Can I get you something, miss?"

The young woman toyed with her water glass, then picked up her napkin and wiped her eyes and nose. Speaking in a voice that was soft and a little hoarse, she asked for the special of the day and a Coke.

Barbara moved off to fill the order and I set about sipping my smoothie before the alcohol from the margarita kicked in.

Michelle Andrews sat there, waiting silently for me to make up my mind about what to do with her. She didn't seem to have anything personal against me, just seemed to be generally upset. Still, if I was going to speak with her for more than a few minutes, I'd better check to make sure she was protected.

"Are you wearing an anti-siren charm?"

"Yes. Mr. Creede gave it to me. He said that I'd need it if I was going to meet with you."

"You spoke with John personally?"

She nodded. "He was very . . . kind."

Yeah, he was that kind of guy. It was one of the many reasons I missed him. I took a long drink of my smoothie, using it as an excuse to not speak while I gathered my thoughts. "All right, Michelle," I went ahead and used her name. She hadn't introduced herself, but in her state I don't think she'd realized it. I said, forcing myself to smile—but not too much; no fang. "Your mother didn't come to me for protection for herself. She wanted someone to guard her daughter." It was a stretch to say what I did next, but it was something that had occurred to me just that morning. "I wonder if it had something to do with your adoption, with your birth parents?"

"My what? No." Michelle shook her head. "That's impossible." She reached into her bag, pulling out her cell phone. After a couple of quick strokes, she passed me the phone.

The screen showed a photo. It was a cute picture. Michelle

was kneeling beside her mother's wheelchair, hugging her. Michelle was wearing a cap and gown—I assumed from her college graduation, given how she looked now—and Abigail was beaming with joy and pride as she held her daughter's diploma in her lap.

"Is this the woman you met with?"

"Yes."

Michelle shook her head in vigorous denial. "But I'm not adopted. I'm *not*."

"Look—" I started to speak, but she interrupted me.

"*No!* Damn it, no. I refuse to believe my entire life is a lie. She's my mother. My *real* mother. Do you understand? She wouldn't lie to me. Not about something this important."

Actually, I suspected she would, if it would keep Michelle safe. Abigail Andrews had appeared to me to be a tough, pragmatic woman. Kids talk. Oh, they swear each other to secrecy . . . and sometimes, not often, they even keep the secrets. But mostly, they talk. Adults do, too. If you truly want to keep a secret, you don't tell anyone.

"Did she ask you to come here? Say the two of you needed to talk?" That was a shot in the dark, but it made sense.

I'll give her this, Michelle Andrews wasn't stupid. She caught my drift immediately. It pissed her off, and she reacted pretty much the same way her mother had a few days earlier.

She stood, shaking and with tears of rage in her eyes. "You bitch." She turned on her heel, then shoved her way through the crowd and out the door.

Sighing, I brought the last of the smoothie to my lips, determined to enjoy it before it got too cold and became inedible. I was sipping it when I heard the crack of a rifle.

16

People often tell themselves a gunshot is just fireworks or a car backfiring. The sound is similar and the lies are reassuring. But there've been enough nut jobs on shooting sprees in the news recently that people don't simply assume the sound is harmless anymore. When they hear it, they look around. And when they see a woman fall to the ground, bloody and screaming in agony, they react—badly.

People began trampling each other to get away from the restaurant's glass doors. Some dived under tables, seeking cover. Nearly everyone was screaming. I could see a few people on their phones and hoped they were dialing 911. The smell of fear filled the air and despite the fact that my stomach was full, the predator within me began rising to the surface. My vision sharpened to hyperfocus as my body took on a sepulchral glow.

I needed out of there now, before I did something irretrievable. Drawing my Colt, I flipped off the safety. Holding it at my side, I stepped through the patio doors, moving quickly among the knocked-over tables that shielded the crouching restaurant workers and patrons.

Amid their sobs and prayers, I moved to cover, a corner formed by the awning post and wall. Peering out, I scanned for sniper spots. There were one or two, empty. No gunmen were in sight.

Michelle Andrews lay in the middle of the parking lot in a spreading pool of blood.

Taking a chance, I slid my gun back in its holster, vaulted the patio railing, and dashed across the lot.

No one shot at me. In fact, everything outside La Cocina was perfectly normal—other than the body on the ground. Traffic flowed by on the street, people were walking along the sidewalk. There were sirens in the distance, growing closer. But that was it. Eerie. I knelt beside the injured woman. The shot had hit her in the right shoulder, creating a mess of shattered bone and torn flesh.

The smell of blood and meat made my mouth water. I closed my eyes, willing the beast within me under control. I was winning when Michelle whimpered.

My body swayed from the effort it took to fight down primal instincts roused by the sound of wounded prey. I wasn't hungry. She wasn't food. Damn it, she *wasn't food.*

Shaking with effort, I managed to open my eyes and found her staring at me, her own eyes wide with fear and pain.

"Help me. Please, help me," Michelle pleaded weakly.

I couldn't speak—I knew if I tried, I'd hiss, and that would only terrify her more—so I nodded. Swallowing hard, I stripped off my jacket and T-shirt. She shrieked in agony when I pressed the quickly folded shirt against the wound and put pressure on it, to try to slow the bleeding. I knew it wouldn't stop—the injury was too severe. But slowing the blood loss might keep her alive long enough for the medics to arrive.

They were coming. The sirens were very close now. I just had to hold on. I closed my eyes, blocking out everything but keeping pressure on the wound. Sights, sounds, smells—anything that might bring the bat that fraction closer to the surface was a threat. I was in control, but only by the thinnest of threads. I knew that anything at all could push me over that edge.

"Celia." I recognized Barbara's voice. She spoke softly and clearly. "You need to go. If they see you over the body like this . . ."

"Pressure, blood loss." I couldn't seem to manage a full sentence, and there was a definite lisp to my *s* sounds.

"I've got it. Go. You're burning and glowing. They'll shoot you on sight if they see you like this."

I nodded. Staggering to my feet, I lurched over to my nearby rental SUV. I prayed I hadn't locked the doors—and I hadn't. I hauled myself inside, slamming the door behind me.

The relief was instantaneous. I hadn't consciously acknowledged the pain of the sun burning my skin, but now tears of relief poured unheeded down my cheeks as I lay panting, curled in the fetal position, on the smooth leather seats.

The back of my mind heard the ambulance and police cars arrive, but I didn't move. I lay still in the hot, dim interior of the SUV, too weak to move, whether from post-traumatic shock or reaction to the fight with my inner vampire, I couldn't say. Either way, I was going nowhere and was grateful to be left alone. Footsteps, voices, the sound of vehicles pulling out of the parking lot—I ignored them all.

Eventually there was a soft tap on the driver's-side window. I groaned, raising myself onto one elbow just as the door opened.

Sunlight hit me like a club. I threw my arm in front of my face and hissed. Just like in the movies.

"Whoa. Easy, Celia. Easy." Alex's voice was both gentle and stern. It's an unusual combination, but it works for her.

I swallowed hard. Lowering my arm, I turned so I could sit up. "Ssssorry. What are you doing here?" I knew it was her day off, so I was surprised she'd caught this case.

"Barbara called me. She said you saved the victim and that you were in a bad way. She was afraid if any of the other cops saw you they'd shoot you, stake you, and take off your head."

Thank God for Barbara and her quick thinking.

"Do you want my statement?" I spoke carefully so that I wouldn't lisp or hiss.

"I'll send Charles over in a minute. I wanted to give you your jacket and make sure you were capable of giving a statement before I let him talk to you."

"Thanks." I took the jacket from her hand. I was wearing a pretty lacy bra, and it felt wrong not having a top over it in public. I shifted in my seat and shrugged into the jacket, wincing a little as the fabric touched my quickly healing sunburn. Buttoned, it made me look like a Frederick's of Hollywood model, but I felt better. I'd take all the help I could get. "Alex, do me a favor."

"What?" She sounded suspicious.

"Grab me a piece of gravel from the parking lot."

She blinked a couple of times before bending down and doing what I asked. As she reached out to hand it to me, she said, "Mind telling me why?"

"It's for Dottie. I figured I might have her take a look to see what actually happened."

Alex let out a low whistle. "It takes some serious chops for a clairvoyant to do that sort of thing. We don't have anybody on staff with that much power."

"Yeah, well, it takes a lot out of her, so I don't ask her to do it too often. In fact, the way she strained herself yesterday, I'm thinking she won't be able to do it at all. Still, it doesn't hurt to pick up a piece. Just in case."

Alex sighed. "Yeah. Though the judge might not admit the evidence or testimony anyway." There had been a lot of rulings recently against the use of magic in police investigations. The theory was that magic was too easy to manipulate with illusion—which is true, up to a point. It was tying the hands of the cops who were just trying to do their jobs.

Alex shook her head ruefully. "I bet it's something to see."

I fought not to shudder. The first time I'd seen Dottie do this particular trick, I'd gotten to witness my own murder. Not exactly a pleasant memory. "If we wind up doing it, I'll give you a call."

"I might just take you up on that. But first, you need to give a statement. You okay to do that now?"

I took a deep breath. I felt better, more like myself than I had a few minutes earlier. "Yeah."

She gave a brisk nod, then stood up and stepped away from the SUV, shutting the door.

She was back in less than a minute, accompanied by another detective. I assumed that meant he'd been waiting nearby for the all clear. Smart move. Everyone was being careful around me, but at the same time they were giving me the chance to control myself, to show that I was not a monster. I appreciated that, quite a lot. At one time a large number of cops in the department had been actively seeking an excuse to execute me. Times and things had changed for the better. I wanted to keep them that way.

When the car door opened again, I was ready and didn't react to the sunlight. Instead, I smiled, careful not to show fangs, and said, "Hello."

"Hello, Ms. Graves. I'm Charles Andrulis." The man in the doorway stood back just a bit, holding up the gold badge of a detective. He was a small man, probably barely made the minimum height requirements for the force. His features reminded me of a pet ferret one of my former clients had doted on—sharp features, bright dark eyes, and just a hint of sharp teeth. Not that I actually saw his teeth. But the impression was there just the same.

He looked me over appraisingly, taking in everything from the perspiration coating my skin to the drying blood on my hands. "I understand you were the first one out of the building and that you gave first aid to the victim. Is that correct?"

"Yes. We'd been talking inside. She got upset and left. I heard the shot. People inside the restaurant were diving for cover, so I went out the patio doors to see if I could help." I looked at Alex, who was standing behind Andrulis. "Any chance you could get me my purse from inside? I'd really like to turn on the AC. I'm roasting."

Alex nodded and left. Andrulis watched her go, then turned back to me. "Is there something you wanted to say to me without her here?" He pulled a little handheld recorder out of his jacket pocket. It was the tape kind, not digital, and I could see the little wheels turning when he pressed the button to start the machine.

"No. I'm just hot. I'd take off my jacket, but . . ."

"But you used your shirt to help stop the bleeding." He smiled at me. It was a good smile.

"How is Michelle? Is she going to make it?"

"The victim's name is Michelle?"

It occurred to me that the girl hadn't officially introduced herself. "Michelle Andrews, I think. Her mother's name was Abigail Andrews, so I'm guessing her last name is Andrews, too."

He nodded, and although he didn't write it down, I could tell he was committing the information to memory. "You're a bodyguard. Did Ms. Andrews tell you why she was in danger or who might be after her?"

"Actually, no. She came looking for me because I'd met with her mother before Abigail's death. When I told her what we'd discussed, she didn't believe me.

"I can understand why it was a shock. Apparently Abigail never told Michelle she might be in danger and also never told her that she was adopted. Michelle was pretty much in denial about everything—being in danger, being adopted, and that the woman whose body was found was her mother. She stormed off. Then she got shot."

He nodded in acknowledgment as Alex arrived and handed me my purse. I found the keys to the SUV and stuck them in the ignition. "Do you want to get in? The air conditioner will work better if the door's closed."

Charles climbed into the passenger seat while Alex got in the back. The detective raised his brows a bit but didn't argue. Neither did I.

I started the vehicle, and soon blessedly cool air was blasting out of the vents. I felt better immediately and gave a little sigh of appreciation.

Andrulis resumed his questioning. "You said Abigail Andrews hired you to protect Michelle."

"No. I said we met. She didn't hire me. She didn't like me. Part of that was because she wasn't wearing a charm against siren influence. But it was also because I pushed her. She didn't give me a straight story and I didn't want to take a job blind. So she left. That was the last I saw of her."

"Yet you say she's dead."

"A woman matching Abigail Andrews's description was kidnapped. A couple of days later, a body was found that could be her. I know that because I was questioned after the police found out she'd met with me."

"I see." He cast a brief but meaningful look over the back of the seat. Alex gave him her sweetest smile in return.

"Ms. Graves, I understand that you were attacked recently and wound up hospitalized as a result. Is that correct?"

"Yes."

"Do you think that attack was connected to this incident or to the kidnapping and possible murder of Abigail Andrews?"

He meant it to be an aggressive question, but I wasn't thrown. I mean, seriously, he had to ask. Too, I had nothing to hide.

"Yes. I do. The attack was supposed to scare me away from taking the assignment. I told them that I hadn't been hired, but that didn't matter. The man in the hologram wanted me scared and he wanted to hurt me."

"The man in the *hologram*?"

"It's in my report, Charles," Alex growled.

"Of course."

"The man in the hologram was the one in charge. I don't know his name. I've been going through mug shots, but I haven't had a lot of luck."

"We had a hit on the artist's rendering in the prison database," Alex said.

"Who was it?" Andrulis asked before I could.

"Connor Finn."

Oh, fuck a duck.

17

In college, I majored in paranormal studies. As part of my classwork, I took two semesters of the history of magic. One semester dealt primarily with the mage wars. The second included an eight-week session on the Finn/Garza feud.

The Finns and the Garzas were families of mages. They'd been good friends at first. The originators of the feud had even gone into business together, developing spells and artifacts that were still in general use today. One of my favorite spell disks, the Mudder, a handy little spell that turns solid ground into deep, wet mud, was a Finn patent. They made money hand over fist.

Until something went wrong.

The textbooks said it was a dispute over a patent, and maybe it was. But I doubted it. Business disputes generate lawsuits. Feuds are more . . . personal.

Whatever the initial reason, the two clans set to killing each other.

Connor Finn was one of the last two surviving members of his family. The other was his son, Jack, who'd been born during his father's trial for having loosed a blood curse on the Garza family. Anyone else would have been executed for that crime, but because of his "value" as a mage, Connor had been granted clemency in exchange for providing our government with the spells needed to keep us from losing our last war. He was serving a life sentence—with no possibility of parole—in the Needle, the high-security supermax prison in the middle of Death Valley. The Needle had been created to house mass murderers, terrorists, certain serial killers—the worst of the worst.

My professor had been completely obsessed with the creativity with which each family had wreaked havoc on the other. I had been treated to detailed descriptions of each and every spell used by either side: Connor's curse that burned people alive, Juan Garza's spell that tore them into pieces no bigger than a dime.

Connor Finn had unleashed his curse at the wedding of Juan Garza and a pregnant Maria Santiago. Every single person present with Garza blood in his or her veins was destroyed. The baby in Maria's womb was saved only because Maria killed herself as the spell struck. The baby was delivered by postmortem C-section. The child, Lucia Santiago Garza, disappeared from the hospital shortly after her birth, never to appear again.

Until now.

Because if Connor Finn was somehow behind these attacks, I'd bet my last dime that the intended victim was a Garza, and Suit—Suit was probably his son, Jack. Like father, like son.

"You look sick. Are you okay?" Charles asked.

I felt sick. Remembered images from photographs of the carnage flashed through my mind. The man who'd done that was the man who was threatening me.

I'd been scared before.

Now I was freaking terrified.

"I'm fine," I croaked.

"Liar." Alex made the accusation sound kind.

Charles shook his head. "Connor Finn is in the Needle, in solitary. There's no way in hell he's responsible for this."

"Pretty to think so," Alex said.

"Have you *seen* that place, Heather?" he snarled. "I have. It's impossible. Maybe Connor's son is behind it, or some copycat who's obsessed with the feud. But it isn't Connor. It can't be."

He was so certain. I wasn't. Connor Finn has one of the most brilliant minds of all time. His IQ scores are off the chart. His magical ability and creativity are infamous. And he is a psychopath, a murderer with double-digit kills to his credit.

Charles sighed. "Look. I've got at least a dozen witnesses who saw you in the restaurant when the shot was fired. I've got your statement of what happened. Why don't you go home and get some rest? I'll check back with you later."

He opened the car door and started to climb out. Heather, however, didn't move. "Are you okay to drive?" she asked me.

"Yeah. I guess so." I looked down at my hands. The blood on them, Michelle's blood, was drying and starting to flake. It looked so gross.

"You know what, you look a little shocky. Why don't I drive you home?"

I wasn't up to an argument, so I agreed, though I was getting tired of being in situations where Alex had to look after me. "Okay. But first I need to wash my hands." She reached into her purse, retrieved a small package of diaper wipes, and passed them over the seat.

"Here, use these. Now scoot over."

I climbed over the gearshift to the passenger side while she moved from the back to the driver's seat. As she pulled out of the parking lot, I began using wipe after wipe to clean the mess on my hands. Soon I had a dozen filthy wipes and nowhere to put them, so I stuffed them into the cup holder in the passenger door, promising myself I wouldn't forget to take them out later.

I slept, or passed out, or whatever. One minute I was fastening my seat belt, the next thing I knew we were pulling into the driveway. I rolled down the passenger-side window to lay my palm against the reader and line my eye up with the retinal scanner, glad there were security checkpoints on both sides of the entrance. I said my name and the gate swung open. We drove through, and before we'd gone more than twenty feet, the gate closed and locked with a clang.

We parked in the usual spot. I grabbed the wipes and hurried into the house, since I'd already been burned once that day and hadn't reapplied sunscreen since. It was a real relief when I stepped through my front door and into the living room.

Minnie mewed a greeting but didn't leave her sunbeam. I was fine with that.

"Wow, that's a lot of flowers," Alex said, sounding mildly awed.

She was right. Yesterday I'd been too preoccupied to really take it in. Now, looking around, I was seriously impressed. The living room, kitchen, and part of the hallway looked as if a florist's shop had invaded. There was a riot of color and the scents were nearly overpowering. Every flat surface was covered, as was most of the floor. There were small arrangements, large arrangements, and two that were so spectacularly huge they nearly blocked access to the kitchen.

I remembered those. The yellow and peach one was from Queen Lopaka and Gunnar Thorsen; the purple and gold was from King Dahlmar and Queen Adriana. There were live plants, too. I love flowers and plants, but this was ridiculous. Maybe I could call David and Yolanda and see if they wanted to take some of them up to the main house.

"Come close to dying and they really hit up the florists for you," I joked.

"Not funny, Graves." Alex's face sobered. "These people are playing for keeps."

I dropped the wipes into the nearest wastebasket. "Alex, please. Do you really think I don't know that? After what they did?" She opened her mouth to argue, but I kept talking. "I have to joke about it. If I don't, I'll lose my nerve. I can't afford to do that. My job isn't just what I do, it's who I *am.* I believe in it. I'm good at it. And I am *not* letting these bastards take that away from me."

18

Michelle Andrews was not my client. Nobody was paying me to take care of her, and some very scary people had made it abundantly clear that they wanted me to stay away from her. They'd let me know that I could be absolutely certain that my safety depended on it. There was no logical reason for me to protect her.

I'm not always logical.

She was a kid. Yeah, I know, she was in her twenties and I'm not all that much older. But I've lived a harder life than Michelle Andrews and it showed. I'd been less of a kid at twelve than she was at twenty-three. If I didn't protect her, she was going to die. It was that simple. Besides, these guys had seriously pissed me off.

So I made what might, admittedly, be a stupid, self-destructive decision and called Kevin. After I filled him in, his first words were, "What do you want me to do?"

"Find out what hospital she's in. Make sure the police have someone on her door. If they don't—"

"I can stand guard until morning. But if it's a magical attack, there's not a lot I'm going to be able to do. Have you hired a mage yet?"

"Yeah, I did. Look, if we're doing this, there needs to be a team and some organization. E-mail or text Dawna and me when you get the information. I'm going to be working on the other end of things, trying to neutralize the threat at the source. I'm putting you in charge of the team." I still had to figure out who the hell was on the team, but hey, one thing at a time, right? "Dawna will coordinate things between us. Expect her to get in touch with the details after a bit."

My next call was to Dawna. "Get your cousin up to speed and put her in touch with Kevin. He's in charge of the team protecting Michelle Andrews."

"We took the case? Michelle's the client?"

"Not exactly," I admitted. "Michelle got shot in the chest in front of La Cocina. I expect it's all over the news. Kevin's going to the hospital to make sure the cops are guarding her door. If they're not, he'll stay. We're going to need to set up a team in shifts. I'm putting him in charge of it."

"For a woman who's not a client."

"For a twenty-three-year-old kid whose mother was murdered and who just got shot by a sniper."

She sighed, then said, "I'll take care of it."

"Thanks."

"We'll need more than two people—particularly since you're not going to be working a shift. You're *not* working a shift, right? You just got out of the hospital."

I grunted. I didn't like admitting I wasn't up to taking a shift, but I really wasn't. Damn it. "I'll deal with that tomorrow. I need to get some sleep."

"All right. You rest up. I'll take care of things."

"Thanks."

"You're welcome."

We hung up. I fed Minnie and threw a plastic bowl filled with beef juices into the microwave for dinner. When it was ready, I drank it, then used a double chocolate diet shake to wash down a pair of sleeping pills. It was still early, but I was exhausted. Too much had happened. I needed rest. So while I normally avoid taking pills, I gave in to the temptation in the hope that I might have a night of deep, dreamless sleep.

It was a wasted effort.

I knew I was dreaming. But I was too deeply asleep to control or change what was happening. So I had no choice but to go along when I found myself with my eye to the scope of a rifle pointed at the exit of La Cocina. I waited for my target, smiling in satisfaction when she . . . also me, stepped out into the light.

I aimed between the victim's eyes, enjoying seeing the cheery little cherry red light dance over my forehead. Then I moved the sight to aim at my heart, knowing I could take either shot and have a perfectly clean kill. But that was not my objective. My job was to injure, not kill. So I lined the sight up with the victim's right shoulder, an injury that would be painful and debilitating but not fatal. I pulled the trigger, waking with a scream as I heard the shot ring out.

I sat bolt upright in bed, panting, my heart pounding as I grasped at the right shoulder of the T-shirt I'd worn to bed with my left hand.

Holy crap, that had felt real. "It was just a dream, a nightmare. No biggie," I told myself. But as I threw aside the tangled sheets and shambled down the hall to the bathroom, I couldn't put the image out of my mind.

The more I thought about it, the more it seemed likely that my subconscious was trying to tell me something. So I slid on my shoes and went for a walk on my beach. I sat on my favorite rock, staring at the moonlight and starlight reflecting off of the ocean, letting the sound of the waves lapping the shore soothe me as I tried to figure out what was bothering me.

Michelle had been shot in the right shoulder with a rifle. The only spots suitable for a sniper had been close enough that even an amateur could have made the shot.

So why wasn't she dead? Had it been, as my subconscious was telling me, a deliberate choice? The more I thought about it, the more I believed I shouldn't ask Dottie to scry about it. It would be the easy solution, but it wouldn't be right to risk her health. Maybe I could have Emma give it a try. Now that she had the mirror to use as a focus, she was able to do a lot more than most people with her level of talent. And she was young and healthy. Yeah, maybe in the morning I could ask Emma to take a look. But for now, I'd see where logic got me.

Okay, say the sniper had deliberately missed. Why would somebody shoot if not to kill? If he wanted Michelle dead, why not just kill her?

Bio samples can be used in a lot of negative magic. DNA can be determined from a blood sample as well. So I started asking myself what-ifs. What if the bad guys weren't positive she was the right target and needed to make sure? What if they wanted a DNA sample so that they could do a spell that affected an entire family (as had been done to the Garza family at the wedding)? It would make sense. If they used what they thought was her blood to target the spell and got it wrong, the effort would be wasted. I wasn't sure they'd care, but innocents would be wiped out. And in either case, the police would be on their trail.

Too, the type of spell that would target a family would take a lot of juice. Most individual mages couldn't pull it off once without draining themselves dry and possibly dying. That was one of the main reasons spells like this were so uncommon. Self-preservation is a basic instinct. Fortunately for humanity, there haven't been too many groups of homicidal mages willing to work together.

If I was right and Connor Finn was behind this whole thing . . . well, it seemed he liked things messy, liked inflicting pain. The spells he'd used against the Garzas before going to prison twenty-three years ago had been hideously violent. Leaving me in the sunlight had been truly effective torture. Abigail's death hadn't been clean. Slugger's punishment had been torture as well, capped by his death. Just shooting Michelle wouldn't be enough for someone like that. He'd want her to suffer.

Michelle was just a kid. She didn't know about Connor Finn. She didn't know about the feud, hadn't done a damned thing to deserve being shot. But right now she was in the hospital, afraid and in pain. The only mother she'd ever known was dead.

It was wrong.

I'm no saint. I've done things I'm not proud of, made choices that I don't like thinking too hard about. But if I let my fear keep me from protecting this young woman, whether she hired me or not—if she died because I didn't shield her from the monster who was stalking her—I wouldn't be able to live with myself.

Knowing what I was going to do didn't make the possible consequences any less terrifying. But I'd face that when the time came.

Staring at the ocean, I confirmed the choice my subconscious had already made when I'd called Kevin. I was going to stop Connor Finn.

The question was how.

I needed advice from somebody I trusted who could be objective about things. One name sprung to mind: Isaac Levy. I knew just where to find him, too. He'd be at his shop at ten o'clock sharp.

I dressed conservatively, choosing a nice blue suit with a plain white silk top. My good sheaths had disappeared with the knives, so I strapped on a backup set. They were just a little less comfortable, and the stiff leather chafed slightly. Still, once the jacket was on you'd never know they were there. And even with the chafing, I was glad because, hey, I had my favorite weapons back. Sad to admit, I felt really naked without them.

I was waiting in front of Isaac's shop, reading Kevin's text, when Isaac arrived. He strode up to the SUV, his expression curious. His face broke into a genuine smile when I opened the door and he saw it was me.

Isaac stood a step or so back, giving me room to climb down. "Celia, so good to see you. Have you been waiting long?"

"No, just a couple of minutes." I smiled at him. Isaac and his wife, Gilda, are dear friends of mine. They're old enough to be my grandparents, and sometimes they act like the set I lost when my father abandoned us. Isaac was wearing his usual dark gray suit, but instead of his usual snow-white shirt, he'd chosen one in dove gray with silver striping. It looked very good on him.

"You're looking very spiffy today," I said. "Something special going on?"

"Gilda's birthday. We have reservations at her favorite restaurant for lunch." He smiled. "I've got her gift in the safe inside. Would you like to see it?"

"Does it sparkle?" I was teasing him a little. Gilda loves jewelry and Isaac loves to indulge her.

We both laughed fondly as Isaac began disarming the complex web of spells that protected his shop. Once that was done, he disarmed the more traditional alarm system. This might seem like a lot of security for one store—even though it was a triple storefront—but Levy's was a high-end place. They stocked a lot of valuables and weapons, so they were always very careful. I'd even helped them pick out the firm and system they used.

When all was well, Isaac held open the door for me. I stepped in and flicked on the lights.

I felt like a kid in a candy store.

Levy's had started out as a small place, tucked in beside a dry cleaning shop in a neighborhood that was just a bit off of the beaten path. They hadn't moved, but they'd expanded into the spaces on either side and the shop was now fairly large, bright, and airy. It carries all my favorite stuff, and it's of the highest possible quality. I've purchased all of my weapons and had all of my professional tailoring done here since I first went into business. Not only that, I've gladly referred everyone I know with similar needs, which is why Isaac and Gilda Levy are now responsible for outfitting the security services for both Rusland and the Isle of Serenity, the staff of Miller & Creede, employees of several other businesses, and more than a few "general contractors" like myself.

A part of me wanted to roam the aisles, see what was new, and pick up a few goodies. But no, I was here on business.

Isaac is the best at what he does. If anyone could give me the straight scoop, it would be him.

"So, what are you in the market for today?" Isaac asked as he walked past me. He inserted a key into the control box for the retractable metal gates, like those that protect the doors of stores in the airports or malls, that covered the shop's windows.

"I know you're busy, but do you have a couple of minutes to talk? I could really use some information."

"Of course. Go on back into the workroom. I'll join you in a minute. We can chat while I work. Gilda's at the hairdresser this morning, but Edna will be in soon to cover the front."

Edna was a widow from the neighborhood. They'd given her a part-time job after her husband died, to give her "something to do." It had worked out well for both sides. Business at the shop had grown so much that the Levys had really needed the extra help. Still, I was sorry I wouldn't be seeing Gilda.

At Isaac's gesture, I made my way to the back room. Isaac's workroom is a very personal space that is centered on a silver casting circle eight feet in diameter. Inside the circle are three daises of various heights that always remind me of the prize stands at the Olympics. If clients stand on the low dais, most of them are at the perfect height for Isaac to pin the hem of and do the tailoring on a jacket. The "second place" dais is great for hemming skirts. The highest stand is just right for hemming pant legs and tailoring them to perfectly to disguise an ankle holster. I remember how excited Isaac was when he had them designed and installed. No more crawling around while he performed either mundane tailoring or complex spell work.

Along the walls outside the circle are cube-style shelves in unfinished oak. They hold books in multiple languages, various spell components, thread, and sewing equipment. In one corner a wooden, roll-top desk and a pair of chairs sit next to a beautiful old sewing machine. A high-definition television hangs from a mounting attached to the ceiling. It could be rotated to face anywhere in the room and was helpful to keep clients from getting bored during long fittings.

I spent a few minutes scanning the book cubicles while I waited for Edna to arrive, freeing Isaac.

"So, you have a problem?" he said, right behind me. I hadn't heard him approach, which was startling. I jumped a little; he laughed and I smiled. There was no danger here. Isaac continued, "Come sit down. Tell me all about it."

We went over to his desk, where we sat down and I told him the story from the very beginning. Every once in a while he would stop me to ask specific questions. He was particularly interested in the hologram disk and the failure of my shield spell. As I was going over that for the third time, he opened his desk drawer to retrieve a pad and pen and took notes.

I told him about the research I'd had Anna perform and shared my theory about the reason for the shooting. I finished with, "My guy sent me a text a few minutes ago. He's found out what hospital she's in and is guarding the room. But I'm really not sure how much good it will do—particularly against a spell. And if we could find out where she is, I'm sure they can, too."

Isaac tapped his pen against the desk in an irregular rhythm, then rose abruptly and strode over to a section of shelving that was filled with worn and dusty hardbacks. Reaching up, he pulled down one, flipped through it, and put it back before bringing a second volume back to the desk.

He set down the book and flipped it open somewhere just past the middle. Flipping a couple more pages, he found what he was looking for and turned the book so I could see the page clearly. "Is this the man in your hologram?"

The man in the picture was much younger, his features softer and less wrinkled, his hair a darker red. But there was no mistaking that it was Hologram Guy. I was not at all surprised to see the name associated with the photograph: Connor Finn. The two-page spread was fascinating: in addition to the photo, it contained biographical information on Connor, his family tree, a detailed summary of all of his mage test scores from grade school on, and a list of the spells he designed and executed.

"That's him, all right. I don't suppose you have a picture of his son, Jack?"

Isaac rose and retrieved another file. Sure enough, Jack Finn was the guy I'd called Suit. Damn it.

"Where did you get all this?"

Isaac smiled. "You didn't know? I'm surprised. I would have thought Bruno or Isabella would have told you."

I gave a bitter little laugh. Bruno doesn't talk mage business with me. As for Isabella—Bruno's mother—I wasn't positive she'd spit on me if I were on fire. Sadly, this was an improvement on my relationship with her from a couple of years earlier.

Isaac's expression softened. He's my friend and he doesn't like to see me unhappy. But he also knows me well enough to understand that I wouldn't discuss my relationships with my lover and his mother. So he didn't address it, just answered the implied question. "You know that Isabella DeLuca is the Grand Hag of the East Coast?"

"Yes. Back when she was first appointed, Bruno explained that it's a really big deal."

Isaac smiled benignly. "He's right, it is. Well, I am her counterpart on this side of the country. I am the Interim Grand Master of the West Coast. I am also Head Chronicler."

Holy crap! Go, Isaac. I'd always known he was a terrific mage, but I hadn't had any idea he had a place in their hierarchy. "Wow. Congrats."

"Thank you." His expression sobered. "Connor Finn is in a maximum-security facility. He should not be able to work magic of any kind. Are you absolutely *certain* it was him?"

"I am, It was."

Isaac drummed his fingers against the desk, his expression pensive. "I will need to check into this. I very much hope you are wrong, but I fear you are not. Connor had—has—one of the finest minds I've ever encountered and power no less than that of your Bruno." He sighed. "But he lacks any conscience or sense of empathy. There are those born physically handicapped or mentally disabled. Connor Finn was born spiritually stunted."

"He's capable of anything." I stated it as a fact because I believed it was one. Isaac nodded in agreement. Then he stood, and I rose as well, realizing my audience—which is what it had turned into—was over.

"If you will excuse me, Celia, there are things I need to do now. Thank you for bringing this to my attention."

I paused in the doorway. "Isaac, can he do another spell like the one he used on the Garza family to kill Michelle Andrews?"

"Until I spoke with you, I'd have said no. Now I am not sure. But even if that is his intent, he will need the power of the full moon to do it. So we have some time to prepare.

"Thank you. Good-bye, Isaac."

"Good-bye, Celia." He raised his hand and made an odd gesture. I felt the warm wash of magic flow over me like a blessing. "Take care."

19

I went from Isaac's shop straight to the hospital where Michelle was being treated. I wanted to check in with Kevin and see what Michelle's prognosis was. Watching her in the hospital didn't worry me too much. The risk of injury to one of my people would be minimized. Not gone. People like Finn were too dangerous to be discounted completely, even in a secure setting. But it would lessen the risk. That was the best I could hope for. And hey, the magical wards around the building would do half the work for us, and there were security guards to help if things went south.

I pulled the SUV into the parking garage and into the first slot I could find. I'd still have to walk about half a block to the actual hospital building, with the sun beating down, so I slathered myself with sunscreen. I was annoyed with myself for not having replaced the hat and umbrella I'd lost along with my car. Not thinking about them was beyond careless; it was stupid, and being distracted was no excuse. I'd check the hospital gift shop. They might have something.

I walked briskly, covering as much ground as I could without actually running or alarming people. Despite the liberal application of sunblock, it was a relief when I finally made it to the awning that shielded the main hospital entrance.

I stopped in the gift shop and bought a little collapsible umbrella and a Mickey Mouse ball cap. On impulse, I decided to get some flowers for Michelle. The arrangement of pink and white carnations I chose was cheery and not terribly expensive, but I figured she could use a little cheering up, especially since it wasn't likely that any of her friends knew she was here. I went from the gift shop to the main elevator bank, then up to the third floor—Kevin had said that Michelle was in room 305. A small sign across from the elevators directed me down a hall to the right.

I saw Kevin the minute I stepped around the corner. He was wearing brown dress trousers and a silk dress shirt the color of melted caramel. He wasn't obviously armed—no one other than the police and hospital security was supposed to carry guns in the hospital. But I knew Kevin; he was perfectly capable of turning something perfectly innocuous into a weapon if the need arose. Or, like me, he might have chosen to ignore the rules and afterward deal with whatever fallout resulted. After all, no one would know, or care, unless something went wrong.

I spotted him sitting in a chrome-and-vinyl chair outside room 305. Paulie, his golden retriever, lay at his feet, wearing the navy blue–and-white vest of a trained assistance animal. Her tail started thumping against the linoleum when she caught sight of me.

Kevin stood as I approached. "Hey, boss. Nothing much has happened so far. Heather Alexander was here earlier. I heard her talking to Michelle through the door. They confirmed the ID on the body. The kid's been crying ever since."

"Damn it." It wasn't a surprise, but it was still bad news. "Did Alex say anything to you on the way out?"

"She just told me to be careful."

"Always good advice."

He grinned, flashing deep dimples. That smile took a good ten years off his age, reminding me of the crush I had on him when I was younger. He's a handsome man, but the past few years have been hard on him.

"The kid's going to be here another twenty-four hours. Who should I expect to relieve me at the end of my shift?"

"I'm hoping it will be a new hire. But, honestly, it'll probably be me. I'll call and let you know for sure."

"You sure it's okay for you here? Sometimes hospitals aren't the best place for you."

He was right about that. Fortunately, at the moment I was well fed and not feeling the least bit bloodlusty. Still, it was something to think about. If I came back to relieve him, I'd need to take sensible precautions ahead of time. "When's your shift end?"

He smiled again. "When do you want it to?"

"Six work for you?"

"Works fine. You do realize it'd be better if we had two people on the door."

I sighed. He was right, of course. With two, there'd always be someone on guard, with no worries about food or bathroom breaks. Kevin was good, but he was human—mostly—and Paulie had needs, too.

I sighed. I like being in charge most of the time. But sometimes responsibility sucks. "I know. I'm working on it."

Kevin nodded. "If I need to go, I can use the bathroom inside the room, and Paulie has a cast-iron bladder."

"Good to know. But I'm still going to get you some backup soonest." I knocked on Michelle's door and was rewarded by her inviting me in.

Even though it was a private room, so there was only one bed, there was barely a foot of space to walk around in. The television mounted high on the wall wasn't turned on, so the soft whoosh of the air conditioner and the beeping of the equipment at the head of the bed were the loudest sounds in the room. I spotted a second door, which I assumed led to the bathroom Kevin had mentioned.

Michelle's bed had been raised so she was sitting upright. She looked at me with red-rimmed eyes.

"Hello, Michelle." I looked around, trying to decide where to set my flowers. There were plenty of options, since there was only one flower arrangement in the room. Nearly identical to mine, the carnations yellow rather than pink, it sat on the counter by the window. The lack of cards and arrangements made the room feel bleak. I set my flowers on the windowsill.

The young woman in the bed looked like hell. Tubes coming from bags of blood and something clear that I was betting held antibiotics on an IV stand ran to her arms. She was hooked up to a pain medication pump as well as to various monitors. Her right shoulder was heavily bandaged. Her hair had been pulled back into a ponytail tied at the base of her neck, a look that didn't flatter. The hospital gown, faded and shapeless, didn't do her any favors either, even though most of her was covered by a thin blue hospital blanket. When I'd seen her in the restaurant, her complexion had been warm, with a rose tint to her light brown skin. Now she looked unnaturally pale.

"You were right." Michelle's voice cracked when she said the words. "She is dead and she wasn't really my mother."

I looked her straight in the eyes and said, "Bullshit." I kept talking, making sure that every word was emphatic as I could make it. It wasn't hard. "You may have been adopted. But she *was* your mother. She raised you. She loved you. And she died protecting you." There's a damned sight more to being a mother than giving birth. And I was sure that Abigail Andrews had been a mother every minute of her life since Michelle had come into it.

"You don't know that." Michelle wouldn't look at me. Instead, she stared out the window and the singularly unimpressive view—a few treetops, the landing pad for flight-for-life, nothing interesting.

"The hell I don't," I said with enough heat that she turned to glare at me. "Listen to me, kid. You would never have made it out of the airport if your mother had told them you were coming. She didn't." I moved to stand by the window, looking out so that I didn't have to meet her gaze. "They probably would never have found you if you hadn't come looking for me. They'd seen your mother meet with me. They were probably watching to see if you'd make contact. And you did."

"You don't understand."

"Oh, really?" I turned to face her. "Let me guess. You think your whole life was a lie. That you can't trust any of it."

She flushed, giving her skin the first hint of real color. The machine monitoring her heart rate reacted to the change in her pulse. She glared at me, too angry for words.

I backed down. "Look, I'm very sorry for your loss. I truly am."

"You didn't even know her."

"No. But I respect what she did."

"Lying to me? Pretending that I was something, someone I'm not?" It was the outburst of a wounded child. Physically Michelle was an adult, but emotionally she wasn't there yet, certainly not when under this kind of stress.

"Did you ever think to ask yourself why?"

"The detective said it's because of my bloodline. That I'm the last member of a clan that was wiped out in some stupid feud." Michelle's gaze locked with mine. "It's insane. I'm not even a mage. I'm a channeler. That's it.

"I do ghosts, and I'm not even particularly good at that. I can't control it enough to stay myself when they use me." She started sobbing.

I grabbed the tissue box and went over to sit on the edge of the bed. She cried hard, but not for long. When she was done, she took a couple of tissues, wiped her eyes and blew her nose.

I embraced the chance for a change of subject. "Personally, I've always thought channeling was pretty cool. My sister was a ghost. I would've loved to be able to talk with her. Instead we worked out a code with her turning the lights on and off. One was yes. Two was no."

"I could help you talk to her if you want," Michelle said. "You saved my life. It's the least I could do."

I smiled at her. "Thanks. I really appreciate the offer, but Ivy finally moved on not too long ago." I took a tissue from the box where she'd set it on the wheeled tray that fit over the bed. I wasn't actually crying, but I did seem to have the sniffles all of the sudden.

Michelle's next words were so sad. "Did you get to say good-bye?" She looked at me, her wide brown eyes swimming with tears. "I can't believe my mom is dead and I didn't even get to tell her good-bye, didn't get to say 'I love you' or anything."

I was about to say something trite and reassuring when the temperature in the room dropped like a stone. Michelle stiffened, her eyes rolling back in her head. For a second the machines connected to her body went nuts, then settled back to a normal rhythm.

"Ms. Graves."

I recognized the voice, even though I'd only heard it once, for a few minutes. More than that, I recognized the body language. It was so weird, it was Michelle's body in the bed, but it obviously wasn't her using it. "Abigail Andrews."

"Elena Santiago, actually. My birth name was Elena Santiago. The girl you know as Michelle was my sister's daughter, Lucia. I was privileged to raise her as my own."

"Ah."

"She needs protection from both Connor and Jack Finn. The son is a mere pawn who will do nothing without the consent of his father, but he is still dangerous. They seek to wipe out the last of the Garzas. Their sources have told them that there are three remaining members of the bloodline."

"Three?" I blinked at that. "But the spell killed everyone. Lucia only lived because she was born postmortem, after the spell was over."

"It killed all but Lucia, the man who cast it, and the child his wife conceived days later."

"Wait . . . Connor Finn . . ."

"Has Garza blood in his veins. The feud between the families started when Sherry Garza went to Edmond Finn with proof that their spouses were having an affair. What neither of them knew was that the affair had been going on for years. Two of the elder Finn children were actually sired by Julio Garza. Connor Finn is the descendant of one of them."

"Holy crap."

Michelle's mouth turned up in a bitter smile. *"I must go. Lucia is tiring. But as of now I am hiring you to protect her. There is plenty of money. You will be paid."*

"And if I say no?"

She was as firm as ever in her response. *"You won't. Other-*

wise your werewolf wouldn't be standing guard outside her door." With that, Michelle's body thrashed once abruptly and fell back against the bed.

Well, hell.

I leaned over to check on the patient. I could easily see that I was looking at Michelle, who was gasping in pain. She ignored me completely as she fumbled around a bit before finding and hitting the button on the pump that controlled her pain meds. Her body didn't relax until the spelled morphine actually hit her system. When it did, Michelle's eyes fluttered shut.

I left the room as the nurse came in to check on her.

Ghosts don't lie; they can't. Connor Finn hated the Garzas more than anything in this world . . . and he was one. The irony of that was bitter enough to choke on. I had more knowledge than when I'd come in. I just wasn't sure what to do with it.

"Celia, are you okay? You look . . . strange." Kevin's voice brought me back to the present.

He rose and guided me to his chair, where I tried to gather my scattered thoughts. After a moment, I said, "Michelle Andrews channeled the ghost of her mother while I was in there. Abigail hired us to protect Michelle from Connor Finn."

"A *ghost* hired us." He shook his head, bemused. "Really?"

"Yup."

He chortled, his eyes sparkling with real mirth. "Well, one thing about working for you. It isn't boring."

I found myself snickering. It was a little funny, now that I thought about it. I asked Kevin if he wanted to take a quick break, maybe take Paulie outside, then grab something from the cafeteria.

He agreed and left just as the nurse came out of the room. I settled farther into the chair, using the quiet time to think.

Kevin needed backup. It was tempting to stay here and help stand guard. It was familiar duty and I was good at it. But I remembered those pictures from my college textbooks. Standing watch at a door wasn't going to protect the woman in the room from that kind of attack. It wouldn't keep her alive.

Connor Finn had taken drastic preemptive measures to keep me from taking this case. Clairvoyants had seen the possibility of my stopping whatever the hell he was doing. That meant I could.

That was encouraging. I needed encouragement at the moment. I was feeling particularly stupid and frustrated.

All right, one thing at a time. One of the reasons for my success at my job—even though until relatively recently I had been fully human, even though I'm a woman in a male-dominated field—is my ability to plan, and plan well. Good planning is flexible and thorough, taking into account many likely contingencies.

The attack that had put me in the hospital had spooked me, thrown me off my game. I'd been running frantically around in reaction ever since. Now that I had a minute, I needed to take a deep breath and logically and calmly think things through.

What were my strengths? I'm good at tactics and I'm great in a crisis. I know weapons. I can do violence and physical mayhem as well as anyone I know. I can be physically intimidating.

I'm *not* good at investigating things. I'm not nearly patient enough. Dawna is. In fact, I'm blessed in having surrounded myself with people who are some of the best in the world at what they do.

"*So, Graves,*" I asked myself, "*why aren't you using them?*"

Okay, the first thing I needed to do was get someone here to relieve Kevin, a couple of people, actually. If we were going to cover Michelle 24/7, it would be better to have a minimum of three people, each on an eight-hour shift. Six—two on each shift—would be better, but I didn't think I had the personnel resources for that just yet.

Dawna could do research, see what she could find about blocking blood curses. In the meantime, I could start figuring out what we were going to do with our client once she got out of the hospital.

Kevin came back to find me writing notes on a scrap of paper I'd begged from the duty nurse. Both he and Paulie looked relieved as they resumed their positions.

Signs all through the hospital let me know that cell phone use was forbidden, so I had to wait until I was walking into the parking garage to call Dawna. She picked up on the first ring. "Graves Personal Protection. Can I help you?"

"Hey, Dawna, it's me."

"Oh, hi! I've got the business phones forwarded to my cell while I look at some of the office space we talked about. One place looked pretty good, but when they heard it was us, they said no."

Damn it, that was frustrating. These landlords weren't the first and, sadly, probably wouldn't be the last to turn us down. I needed a real office soonest, but after the destruction of my last place played multiple times on every news channel, nobody seemed to want to let me rent from them. I couldn't blame them. In their shoes I'd have felt the same way, but it sucked. I fumed silently for a few seconds, wondering what, if anything, I was going to be able to do about it.

"So," Dawna asked, "you obviously called for a reason. What's up?"

"We need more people to cover Michelle in the hospital. Did you get a chance to check out your cousin's references?"

"Yeah, they were all good."

"Cool. Call her. Tell her that her eight-hour shift starts tonight at six. She can meet up with you to do the official paperwork tomorrow sometime. And if you've got Bubba's number, give him a call. See if he wants to do some pickup work. If he does, his shift starts when Talia's ends. The client's in room 305 at St. Joe's."

"We're hiring Bubba?" Dawna didn't even try to hide her delight. Bubba had been a friend of ours for years. We'd met when he moved his bail bonding office into the third floor of our office building, just down the hall from my office. He'd had to close his doors awhile back when his wife had been diagnosed with cancer. I'd wanted to stay in touch, but somehow I'd lost track of him. He's big, tough, smart, and utterly loyal. I've trusted him with my back more than once and never regretted it. I could only hope he didn't.

"If he'll take the job. I don't know that he will."

"He might," Dawna answered. "He's been working as a bouncer and as a roadie for his brother-in-law's band. I'm sure he'd rather have something that pays better. They had to sell the house to pay Mona's medical bills so he's living with Mona and Sherry on the boat King Dahlmar bought him to replace *Mona's Rival.* I've got the number."

I'd known about the house, had even offered to lend Bubba some money. I'd have given it to him outright, but I knew he wouldn't take it. He was much too proud. As it happened, he wouldn't even accept a loan. "Dahlmar replaced his boat?" I hadn't known that. I was really, really glad. One of the things that had weighed on my conscience was the fact that Bubba's precious boat had been destroyed during one of our previous adventures.

"I told you that. I know I did."

"Nope. All you said was that Mona was better."

"Oh. Oops. Well, he did and she is. Full remission. No sign of the cancer returning so far."

I smiled. That was the best news of all. I knew that Bubba wouldn't begrudge having lost his business, the house, or anything else, as long as Mona was going to be okay. I've known a lot of couples. Very few are as crazy about each other as Mona and Bubba. They've been together more than fifteen years and they still act like newlyweds.

"Awesome. I may just head down to the marina."

"Oh, can I call, please? I'd love to be the one to offer him the job—and Mona likes me better."

That was so true it wasn't even funny. "Fine, you do the honors. Call me and let me know whether he takes it."

"I hope he does. It would be awesome, having Kevin and Bubba both on staff."

"Then all we'd need is Ron," I teased her. Ron, an attorney, had had an office on the first floor of our old building. He was a monumental ass and he'd treated Dawna like slave labor.

Her voice grew hard. "Not funny, Celia. Don't even joke about it."

"Aw, come on, Dawna. You know you miss him," I teased.

"About as much as a case of the clap," she snapped.

I decided not to push it, mostly because she wasn't taking it well. I wasn't sure what had happened between the two of them, but obviously something had. It was time to change the subject. "So, any good prospects for office space?"

"Nada. It's getting depressing. I'm beginning to wonder if it would be better to build something from scratch."

"Too expensive," I assured her.

"I know. I know. Uh-oh. Call waiting just beeped. Could be a client. Before I forget, Dottie wants you to call her. Talk to you later."

"Later," I agreed.

20

I swung by PharMart to pick up supplies, including more sunscreen and a big, floppy picture hat. When I first became an Abomination—the official term for my half-vampire condition—a doctor had given me a huge list of things I could drink to keep me healthy and keep things under control until I learned to manage my inner bat. I didn't have the list anymore, but PharMart's records are computerized. If I was lucky, they'd be able to tell me everything I needed to buy to get back on track. It would be expensive. I still had painful memories of the credit card bills from before. But anything that kept me human was worth the price, and then some.

I lucked out. The pharmacy did have the records. They printed out the list for me and I set about loading up my cart with dehydrated beef and chicken broth, the liquid form of a multivitamin and mineral supplement, flavored shakes from a popular liquid fast program, and more. I also stocked up on lots of sunscreen and picked up another hat and a couple of umbrellas to use as sunshades. My favorite employee had been promoted to night manager, so he wasn't on duty, but I asked the pharmacist to let him know I'd been by and that I said hi.

Though I'd grown tired of drinking nutrition shakes over the course of the past couple years, they were the quickest and easiest way to take the edge off of my hunger. I popped one open and drained it as I loaded my groceries into the back of the SUV. I hadn't had any bloodlust yet that day, even though I'd been in a hospital, and I wanted to keep it that way. Besides, I think better on a full stomach.

Michelle would be discharged tomorrow. She'd need a place to stay. Someplace safe, where no one would think to look for her, preferably far away from innocent bystanders in case the defecational matter hit the rotary oscillator. In short, a safe house.

I didn't have a safe house. Hell, I didn't even have an office. She certainly couldn't come to my place—Connor Finn's goons would undoubtedly look there first. Besides, I barely had room for the cat. Just bringing home these groceries would put me at risk of starring in the next episode of *Hoarders*.

Climbing into the car, I strapped in, turned on the engine, and let the air-conditioning bring the temperature down to something close to bearable. Digging in my purse, I pulled out my cell phone and typed in Dottie's number.

She picked up on the third ring, right before it would have gone to voice mail. "Hello."

"Hi, Dottie. How are you feeling?" I was kicking myself a bit for not having checked on her earlier. Yeah, I'd been busy, but straining your magic is a big deal. The doctors had said she'd be okay, and I knew Fred would take good care of her, but *still*.

"I'm fine. Really. And I have the solution to your problem."

She knew. "Dottie, the doctors said—" I started to scold her, but she interrupted.

"Hmpf." She sounded completely disgusted. "Like I was telling Fred, it's not as if I can just turn it off like a tap. But I am trying *very* hard not to use my gift."

Judging from her tone of voice, she'd been telling him repeatedly. I was betting he wasn't buying it. Still, it might be true. Psychic ability is notoriously difficult to control, particularly for someone with as powerful a gift as Dottie's.

"Which problem are you solving for me this time?" I put a smile in my voice.

"Fred and I have discussed it, and we think we have the perfect safe house for you. And while I know the answer to your office problem, I'm not telling."

"Dottie—"

"I don't want to ruin the surprise."

She was using the same tone of voice my gran always used when she'd locked the Christmas presents in the front closet when I was a kid. So while I was frustrated—I *hate* not knowing things—I was also amused. "Fine, have it your way."

"I fully intend to," she said smugly. "Now, if you'll come to our apartment, I'll get everything ready for you."

"I'll be there in a few minutes."

It was a quick drive. Dottie and Fred live in government subsidized housing on the east edge of Santa Maria. The complex is composed of six one-story brick duplexes connected to each other by a web of sidewalks with a central courtyard. There's a two-story office and "clubhouse" on the north end of the property, with parking for guests. Residents have numbered parking spots on the surrounding streets. It is a pretty place and very well kept. Dottie told me her only complaint was that they didn't allow pets. It was so nice, in fact, that when she and Fred married, they decided to share her apartment rather than the house he had lived in with his previous wife, out by Edwards Lake.

I pulled into a guest spot under a shady tree next to the office building, slathered on sunscreen, plopped a hat on my head, and stepped out of the SUV—just in time to see Mickey drive past in a black Dodge Charger so new it still had temporary tags. Okay, a Charger isn't the most expensive car around, but it's not the cheapest, either. I wondered how a man with no job and supposed money troubles could afford a brand-new car of any kind. Something definitely wasn't adding up.

I could tell he didn't see me. That was good.

Fred met me at the front door with a hug. Leaning close he whispered in my ear, "She's been blaming herself for not being able to interpret the stones."

I gave a tiny nod to let him know I understood. According to the sirens, Dottie is my personal prophet. Her job is to be sort of an advance-warning system, to help keep me safe. I don't know what my great-aunt Lopaka said to her when they met, but it made Dottie, who was already protective, absolutely ferocious in performing her duties.

I smiled as Dottie came in. The ice in the pitcher of lemonade she was carrying on the tray of her walker clinked against the glass with every step she took. I stepped forward, intending to help, and she gave me a *look*.

Uh-oh, she was in one of her I-can-do-it-myself moods. Definitely time to change the subject. "I saw Mickey as I was driving in. Where was he headed off to?"

Fred looked pained and I knew I'd stepped into it again. Apparently this was just going to be one of those days when tact abandoned me.

Dottie smiled up at her husband. "Fred, could you go get us some glasses from the kitchen? I couldn't manage them and the pitcher both."

"Of course, dear." Fred made his escape. Dottie gestured me into a seat. As I passed, she whispered to me, "Please don't bring up Mickey today, dear. He and Fred got into another argument about those people he's been hanging around with, down at that pool hall—and how he's been getting the money he's been spending since he lost his job." She sighed.

"It wouldn't be so bad if Fred wasn't a telepath. He knows that Mickey's lying, even if he's too ethical to dig for more." She might have continued, but Fred appeared with the glasses just then so Dottie busied herself playing hostess, pouring drinks and making small talk. Only when everybody was settled did she bring up the subject that had brought me here.

"I didn't use my gift to see this." She said it like it was a warning. Almost like the "Don't try this at home" warning you see on television. Then again, perhaps that's how she felt. If she couldn't peek at the future, she couldn't know whether or not a particular idea would work out. She'd just be taking her chances like the rest of us.

She continued. "You need a safe house for the client—and an out-of-the-way place to get away from things. Fred needs to rent out the house at the lake."

Fred had a life estate in the house, but it was technically Mickey's, left to him by Fred's first wife.

"If it's producing income, Mickey won't have any excuse to keep nagging me to sell." Fred's voice held a combination of sadness and bitterness I recognized all too well—from dealing with my mother. "I thought if you had some time this afternoon, maybe I could drive you out there and we could look at the place. I'll cut you a good deal on it."

I thought about it. I didn't really have any firm plans for the day, and they were right that this might just be the answer to the problem of where to stow Michelle.

Edwards Lake is a man-made lake in a valley forty miles

northeast of Santa Maria de Luna. It was created in the nineties to provide a secluded little getaway spot for Silicon Valley types and successful dot-com investors.

The fact that the lake house was secluded meant it wouldn't easy to get to—which would be perfect for my purposes. Even better, there wouldn't be a lot of nosy neighbors around. "Sure, why not." I smiled at them and was rewarded with twin looks of such relief I wanted to throttle Mickey just on principle. How badly had he been hounding these people?

"I've got some groceries out in the car I need to take by the house, and I'll need to grab something to eat."

"Why don't I follow you to your place, then we can drive out to the lake in my truck?" Fred suggested.

"Sounds like a plan," I agreed.

Secluded was an understatement. Isolated would be more accurate. The only way to reach the lake house was via the dam road, a little two-lane highway with no shoulder. All that stood between a vehicle and a sheer drop was a simple guardrail. Oh, it was probably spelled, but who knew how often they renewed the mage work out here? Fred's truck was a big old GM that took up most of the road. I felt my stomach flutter more than once as we snaked along that narrow stretch of highway.

By the time he turned into the house's gravel driveway, I was more than ready to be out of a vehicle. It had been a long, mostly silent drive. Fred was lost in his own thoughts, and I could tell they were not happy ones. I was tired. Vampire healing was great—injuries disappeared quickly and usually without scarring, but I'd had a couple of truly hellish days. I was emotionally drained. I was glad to climb out of the truck and into the fresh air to use the key Fred gave me to unlock the old-fashioned padlock on the chain that held the gate closed.

What the place lacked in security it more than made up for with visibility. The house sat on a peninsula that jutted out into the big, open lake. We'd come in on the only road and it was clearly visible. No one would be able to sneak up on this place.

Michelle might be hiding, but at least she'd be doing it in style. The home was long and low, just one story, with lots of windows facing all that water. When Fred entered the security code and opened the door, I found out that the interior was even better.

I roamed around at will while Fred called Dottie to let her know we'd arrived in one piece. The place was freaking gorgeous. Every room was bright and airy and designed so well that it was comfortably cool despite all the sunlight. The rooms were mostly painted off-white, with bright rugs scattered on the hardwood floors and matching pillows on the Arts and Crafts–style furniture. The bathroom was actually a minispa, with towels big enough to use as bedsheets and a walk-in tub fitted with whirlpool jets. One wall of the bathroom was made of glass blocks that let in light while preserving privacy. Every other room had lots and lots of large picture windows.

Sighing, I returned to the living room and pulled the vertical blinds partially closed, shutting off a clear view of a private dock with an aluminum canoe stowed beneath it. I wanted warning of approaching cars, but this much sunlight was not good for me.

As Fred hung up the phone, I turned to him, preparing to dicker. "How much are you going to want for this?

"I'm willing to be reasonable." He smiled, but there was a twinkle in his eye that let me know that he would relish negotiating for the best possible price. He'd been a high-powered businessman for a lot of years before his heart problems forced him into retirement. I wondered if he missed it or was glad to be out from under the stress.

Before I could ask him, or even make an initial offer, my cell phone rang.

"Graves here."

"It's Bubba," said a wonderfully familiar voice. "I'm calling from the hospital. We've got a problem."

21

"You're sure it was him?" I wasn't doubting him. If Bubba said he'd spotted one of the guys from the pictures Dawna had given him of the men who'd attacked me, he'd spotted him. I was stalling for time. I needed to come up with a plan—fast.

"Positive."

"All right. Who's with you?"

"Talia. Kevin went off duty at six."

I thought furiously. I'd have preferred Kevin, if for no other reason than that I know him better—probably not fair to Talia, but it was the truth. Still, having a mage handy might just be an advantage—if I could just think of the right way to use her.

"Do you think he knows you spotted him?"

"No."

"How long ago was this?"

"As long as it took me to hit speed dial."

Good. "Okay, is Michelle still hooked up to any machinery?"

"Nah, they disconnected everything after the last round of spells. They're going to release her tomorrow morning."

I took a deep breath. Moving Michelle would be chancy, but as it was, she was a sitting duck. Now that they knew where she was and that she was under guard, they'd plan accordingly. Which meant it was more risky—to her and to my people—leaving her in place.

"All right. Ask Talia if she's capable of doing an illusion of you sitting in the chair outside the door."

I heart muffled sounds as Bubba covered the phone and did what I'd asked. A second later he was back. "She said yes, but she won't be able to hold it long."

"All right. Does Michelle have any street clothes?"

"Yeah, since she was due to check out tomorrow, Kevin had Talia bring her some sweats."

Way to go, Kevin, thinking ahead! "Good. Have Michelle get dressed. When the nurse is distracted, you take Michelle down to the cafeteria. There's an exit right there that leads into a staff parking lot. Once you're out of view, Talia should put the spell on the chair, then talk to it, say something about going to get herself a snack, that she'll bring you back a sandwich. Tell her to make sure that the nurse hears her. Then she leaves, gets the car, drives around to the cafeteria exit, and picks you up there."

"Right," he agreed. "I'll call you back when we're on the road."

He hung up and I started pacing. Damn it, damn it, damn it. I should *be* there. I knew Bubba was good. I was pretty sure Talia was. But *damn it*.

"Something's gone wrong." Fred didn't have to read my mind to know that. He'd heard me talking on the phone.

"Yeah. The bad guys are at the hospital."

My phone rang again. Before I could even say hello, Bubba said, "They hit the room with magic just after we left. I'm thinking it was a fire spell."

I could hear the alarm sounding in the background, along with a calm voice announcing the code for the evacuation protocol.

If he wasn't in the room, I wondered how he knew it had been a direct hit, but I didn't ask. Maybe Talia had felt it and said something. She might have done the wards when she came on duty. It really didn't matter. "Where are you now?"

He started to answer, but the cell signal cut out. I wasn't surprised. There was a lot of magic flying around, and some of the regular equipment at a hospital could interfere with cell transmission. But damn it! What I wouldn't give to have my siren ring back from Bruno. My telepathy just wasn't strong enough to connect clearly with Bubba without it.

"I didn't hear that. Repeat," I said.

"The pantry off the kitchen. There was a guy in the hall by the cafeteria exit."

"Shit."

The call dropped again. So frustrating! I started focusing, trying to picture Bubba in my mind. I could *almost* do it, but damn, it was hard. I was panting from the effort when I felt Fred's gentle touch on my arm.

With a jolt, Bubba popped into focus, as clear as if he was standing in front of my face. I could even see the room around him and Michelle in her plain gray sweats. It was almost as if I was actually there. Bubba was whispering softly into his phone. "Do we have a plan, or do I improvise?"

Bubba, close the phone. We're going to do it this way. He jerked, startled, then slid the phone into his pocket.

Someone is searching the kitchen, he thought.

How many?

Just one.

One meant they didn't have a bead on Michelle. Magical tracking is tricky, and the same things that were wreaking havoc with cell calls would make it hard for them to find her. Still, if they were smart, they'd have people watching all the exits, and Bubba isn't exactly unnoticeable.

Want me to deal with him?

Yes. Then put on an apron and a hairnet and take Michelle out the cafeteria door.

It wouldn't be much of a disguise, but it was something—maybe enough to make a watcher overlook him. Maybe. I hoped.

Fred and I watched as Bubba signaled for Michelle to stay in place, then slipped out of the pantry, moving in utter silence. Straining, using his ears, I could hear the soft shuffle of steps, harsh breathing. There was the crackle of a radio, and a metallic-sounding voice said, "Have you found them yet?"

"No. But I swear I saw them come in here, and they haven't gone out the fire exit. I've been keeping it in my line of sight."

"Fine. I'm sending Ted down to back you up. But we need to hurry. We only have a two-minute window left." I shuddered. Even with the radio distortion I recognized that voice. It was Suit. Finn.

"I know."

Bubba waited beside some metal shelving stacked with pots and pans until the hunter stepped forward. With brutal speed and zero hesitation, Bubba swept one arm down, knocking the thug's gun to the floor as he threw a hard punch into the man's throat with the other. The enemy was a big guy, built like a bodybuilder, but he fell like a sack of grain, too busy struggling to breathe around the swelling in his throat to worry about anything else.

DUCK! Fred's voice shouted in both our minds. Bubba dropped to the floor, diving for the gun he'd knocked from his opponent's hand, as a spell ball exploded against a pan right behind where his head had been. Acid ate through the steel in less time than it took to draw a breath.

Bubba didn't spare time or thought to watch. Grabbing the dropped gun, he turned, aimed, and pulled the trigger three times in rapid succession. Only one slug hit, but it was enough to put the skinny little spell slinger down.

Bubba called to Michelle, who rushed out of the pantry to join him. The two of them looked around quickly. It took a few precious seconds, but they found a pair of aprons that had headgear in the pockets. They had just gotten dressed when the radios the thugs wore crackled and Finn's imperious voice said, "Jon, Ted, report."

The crackle of the static that followed that last word echoed behind Michelle and Bubba as they hurried out of the kitchen toward the cafeteria exit.

Then my connection with them vanished.

22

I supported most of Fred's weight as I guided him over to the couch. His skin was grayish and clammy. He'd pushed himself too hard. He wasn't having a heart attack—I could hear it beating steadily in his chest. But he'd badly overstrained his magic. I'd been so worried about Bubba and Michelle I hadn't really thought about how hard what Fred was doing would be on him.

"Damn it, Fred!"

"You needed me. It was important." He stretched out on the couch, looking terrifyingly frail. "Don't tell Dottie."

"You think she won't notice?" I snapped as I looked around. I tried to remember exactly what the first aid was for this sort of thing. In the hospital with Dottie they'd given her fluids and carbohydrates. I ran into the kitchen. It was echoingly empty. Not a glass for water, no food in the cupboards. Shit! No, wait. There was a nutrition shake in my purse. I'd packed it because this was a fairly long trip and I didn't want to risk getting vampity on the way. I ran out to the truck fetch it.

Fred was already breathing easier when I got back. Once he'd drained the shake, his color began to improve.

"Promise me you won't tell Dottie. After the trouble I gave

her the other day, she'll never let me live it down. And I'll be fine, I just need to rest."

I scowled at him and didn't answer. Chances were good that she'd hauled out her bowl and was watching us right now. So I said the only thing I could think of that would make him happy without getting me in trouble with his wife. "I try not to get caught between married people when they're arguing."

He gave a snort of acknowledgment tinged with wry humor.

"So, back to where we were before we got interrupted. What are your terms for leasing this place?"

He smiled, and for an instant, energy and animation filled his face. When he spoke, his voice was weary. "Six-month lease, going rate, and you cover the homeowner's insurance. I don't want to risk having this place uninsured with you using it."

I didn't argue. My record with insurance companies was a joke. I pay my premiums—very high premiums, mind you—but it's reached the point where they consider me just too much of a risk. Go figure.

"Fine. Call your attorney. We'll sign the paperwork as soon as he has it ready."

My phone rang. Bubba's number showed on the screen. "Graves."

"Hey, boss. Everybody's good. Tell Fred I owe him a beer. We're in the car. Where are we going?"

I gave him the address of our brand-new safe house and told him to call Kevin, fill him in, and ask him to pick up groceries for the next several days.

"Done," Bubba said. He hung up without saying good-bye. I was okay with that. I had another call to make, and it wasn't one I was particularly excited about.

She picked up on the fourth ring. "Heather Alexander."

"Alex, it's me. They made a run for Michelle at the hospital. We got her out. She's safe. But there are a couple of injured thugs in the kitchen. I can come in and give you a statement in a couple of hours."

"A couple of *hours*?" She was pissed. "They had to evacuate the hospital, Graves. Get your ass in here now!"

"Can't. I'm at least two hours out—and that's if I drive like a maniac. I only saw what happened telepathically."

"Then who . . . no. Never mind. Just get your ass in here. I'll tell the guy in charge you're on your way. You can tell us everything when you get here."

"Okay, let me get this right." The man speaking was FBI Special Agent Shawn Shea. He was six one and had black curly hair and the bluest eyes I'd ever seen. His skin had that porcelain quality with just a hint of freckles that told me of his Irish blood. His voice, however, was pure Midwestern. Shea was all business at the moment, and none too happy with yours truly. The interrogation room was a little crowded, I must admit, with Shea, me, my attorney, and two other law enforcement officers who were obviously friendly with me. I wasn't sure how he did it, but Dom Rizzoli managed to loom while leaning against the wall, and Alex's stony expression spoke volumes. Still, Shea plowed on. "You were out of town and you got a call from one of your employees telling you he'd spotted one of the guys who attacked you."

"That's right."

"And he didn't bother calling the cops."

"I'm sure he would have, if there'd been time. But there wasn't. The first priority is always to get the client to safety."

"So why isn't he here instead of you?"

"As soon as my client and her protectors reach the safe house and his relief arrives, he'll come down and give you his statement." He would, too. It was standard protocol. Bubba knew that.

"So you called it in instead."

"Yes. I was a witness. And I figured if you moved quickly, you could pick up the guys in the kitchen and question them."

The police hadn't been quick enough. Jon and Ted were dead. Each had been shot once in the head with a .45, a different caliber from the .38 Bubba had taken from Jon. But that didn't mean Shawn wasn't going to try to pin the murder on him. I wasn't going to allow that.

"And you know everything that happened."

"The part in the kitchen, yes. The telepath who was working with me does, too." I smiled sweetly. I knew Fred was in another room giving his own statement. We hadn't coached each other or worked out a story, but I was pretty sure Shawn would accuse me of it. After all, Fred and I had made a long drive all by ourselves. "And I'm sure that the hospital security cameras probably caught the whole thing." That last was a guess. I didn't *know* that there were cameras in the kitchen, but I was betting there were. I have friends who own a restaurant. They had to install security to keep their meat and produce from walking out the back door with less than honest staff. It's a common problem, and one I suspected the hospital had been forced to deal with.

Shea gave me a sour look. I forced myself to smile, though I didn't feel like it. Just look at me, the good-natured businesswoman, cooperating her little heart out with the nice officers.

Alex said, "Cameras show Bubba and the girl leaving and a different guy coming in and offing the wounded."

"One of yours, no doubt." Shea was trying to provoke me.

I answered calmly. "Had to be one of the bad guys tying up loose ends. I don't have that many people. I had a man and a woman with the protectee. My other guy was off duty and long gone. The woman was getting the car while Bubba got Michelle out of the building."

"We have video of Bubba relieving Kevin at six o'clock, and of Kevin leaving the building with Paulie. And the guy in the kitchen is too short and dark to be Kevin." The way Alex said it, I could tell she'd told him before—and probably more than once.

What was his problem? I used telepathy to ask Dom and Alex simultaneously. I probably shouldn't have done it, but he really was starting to get on my nerves. It was a good thing Fred and I had stopped for food for me on the way in or I might be getting really irritable.

"My *problem*," Shea said, "is that every time you get involved in a case, bodies start stacking up like cord wood."

I sighed. He was right. But it wasn't my fault. It was my line of work and the level of bad guys I was going up against. This particular batch seemed to think that their people were as disposable as tissues. Somebody needed to stop them. I knew the police were trying, and now the feds were involved. But somehow I couldn't bring myself to have faith in them. Besides, the bad guys had singled me out for their attention from the start. Call it intuition, or paranoia, or whatever the hell else you want, but I had this sinking feeling that I was going to be involved in this to the bitter end.

I spoke clearly, enunciating enough that the answer wasn't *quite* insulting. "Not . . . my . . . fault."

Roberto, my attorney, spoke up. "I think we're done here. My client has been most cooperative. She's given a statement. She was not physically present at the scene, and you have nothing that could connect her to any crime." He rose. I rose.

"We're not finished until I say so," Shea snarled and gestured for me to sit back down. I didn't and he took a threatening step toward me.

Dom straightened up. That's all. He didn't say anything, didn't do anything other than move away from the wall. But Shea subsided.

Roberto opened the door and we left, walking along a wide hall that led to the fire stairs at one end and the cubicle farm at the other. We hadn't quite reached the cubicles when Dom's voice stopped me.

"Yo, Graves, hang on a minute." I turned back as he stepped out of the interrogation room and started walking toward me; we met in the middle of the hall. Roberto waited nearby, still within earshot, ready to do his duty if need be but giving me at least the illusion of privacy if the conversation with Dom wasn't business.

"What's up?" I asked.

"Glad to see you looking so much better."

"Thanks. I got the flowers. They were great."

"Yeah, the wife picked them out." He shifted his weight a little uncomfortably. In the better light of the hallway I saw he looked tired, and while his suit was still crisp, it fit loosely, like he'd lost a little weight. He sighed. "Look, Shea's an ass, but he isn't wrong. The body count is climbing and we're no closer to solving this than we were when we started. These guys have no limits. They attacked a freaking *hospital*, for Christ's sake."

"I know. I know." I met his gaze. "I have some ideas, but nothing solid. What I'd really like to do is change things up—go on the offense. Because, frankly, playing defense just isn't working."

"No shit," Alex agreed, joining us in the hall.

"What do you have in mind?" Dom asked.

I told him.

"You don't ask much," he said sourly. "Give me your number. I'll let you know what I find out."

23

When Gilda Levy hadn't been able to reach me by phone or e-mail, she'd contacted Dawna. Isaac was missing. I called Gilda right away. She said Isaac had been terribly upset since I'd spoken to him. He'd left the shop abruptly, shortly after noon yesterday, telling Gilda he had urgent business to take care of. No one had heard from him since.

Did I know where he'd gone? No. But I had a sneaking suspicion it had something to do with our meeting—and with Connor Finn. I was worried. Isaac is a skilled mage and he's a tough old coot. He'd taken the news that something might be going on in the territory he was responsible for very seriously. I just hoped he hadn't done something foolish as a result. Because tough as he was, and powerful as he was, he was still an old man. He'd never told me his age, but he had to be close to eighty.

I felt physically ill from worry and stress by the time I reached the Furnace Creek exit.

Isaac, where the hell are you? I thought hard, trying to picture him in my head. Nothing. Nada. Zilch. *Please don't let him be dead.* It wasn't like him to disappear without a word. He would never have missed Gilda's birthday lunch. He wouldn't worry Gilda like that.

I wished there was something I could do, but there wasn't.

I was meeting Dom Rizzoli for breakfast at Irma's Diner, a little place just off the expressway, nestled between diesel pumps and a car wash sized to accommodate semis. It had taken Dom some time to get things arranged, but he'd managed it.

Irma's had the design of a classic fifties diner: a long narrow building with rounded windows and lots of chrome. Three different colors of neon chased around the upper trim and lit the big sign that showed a waitress holding a full tray. I pulled into the only empty spot in a large parking lot, slathered myself with sunscreen, and steeled myself for a dash through the sunshine.

The inside of the building was just what I'd expected. There was a long counter, with seats at fixed intervals. Booths lined the outside wall. The seating was all covered in bright turquoise vinyl; the low ceiling and walls were made of bright white plastic that shone in the light from the windows.

Rizzoli occupied a booth just steps away from the emergency exit, near the narrow hall that led to the restrooms—the only shady spot in the place. He wore jeans, a leather bomber jacket, and a sour expression. On the table in front of him was a white ceramic cup filled with coffee and a saucer with a half-eaten piece of cherry pie smothered in whipped cream.

"Hi, Dom." I slid into the booth across from him.

"Celia."

The waitress came over, an older black woman with broad hips and a ready smile. She set down a steaming cup of coffee and a little metal carrier filled with plastic tubs of cream and packets of sweetener. Dom raised his eyebrows when I ordered, but I ignored him. When the waitress left, he spoke.

"Explain to me again why we're doing this?" Dom looked

across the table at me, his expression more serious than I'd ever seen it. Since we've been through some hellish times together, it hit me hard that I had pushed him to his limits.

"Connor Finn has found a way to work magic from inside the Needle."

Rizzoli shook his head. "Not possible."

"He's done it, Dom. I don't know how, but he has. And he's planning a big curse to wipe out the last of the Garzas. My source says he has to do it on the full moon."

"So, Monday night. Your client is the Garza girl?"

"Yes, but she's not the only person with Garza bloodlines." I took a sip of my coffee. It was almost too hot to drink and strong enough to stand on its own without the cup. Perfect.

"Our records indicate she's the last." Dom quirked an eyebrow at me.

I dropped the bomb. "Connor Finn and his son, Jack, have Garza blood. They just don't know it."

His eyes went wide. For a long moment he just stared at me. Finally, he spoke. "You're sure?"

"A ghost told me."

"And ghosts can't lie." He took a bite of pie. His expression was thoughtful. "Connor won't believe you. It'll just piss him off if you tell him."

"Maybe, but I've got to give it a shot. Lives are at stake. And while I couldn't care less whether or not he survives"—in fact, I'd soooooo much rather he didn't, but I wasn't about to say that out loud—"Michelle's just a kid. And then there's his son."

"What do you know about Jack Finn?"

"Not much, but I've met him. He's one of the men who left me on the beach to burn."

Rizzoli's eyes darkened to almost black, his expression hardening to stone. "Sounds to me like the world might be better off without him."

I certainly wouldn't miss him. But I wasn't the one we needed to worry about. "I'm hoping his father doesn't agree with you."

Dom was saved from framing a response to that by the arrival of my order, a heaping bowl of vanilla ice cream with chocolate syrup. He gave a snort as I dug in. "I still can't believe you ordered that."

"Hey, it's comfort food. I need comfort."

"Well, when you're finished being comforted, we'd better get moving. I had to pull a hell of a lot of strings to arrange this. We don't want to be late."

I took a couple more bites before shoving the bowl aside.

Rizzoli reached into his wallet, withdrawing a twenty. Slipping it under the edge of his saucer, he rose. "Let's do this."

The Needle is in the middle of nowhere. It's surrounded by inhospitable desert, where the temperature rises into the triple digits. The heat is brutal, the landscape sere. There is only one road to the tall, narrow tower that rises from the heat shimmers. Made from smooth concrete, its construction had been no ordinary feat. Magic had been combined with skilled workmanship to make it an inescapable fortress. The tower gleamed silver in the blinding light of the morning sun. It was thirty stories tall, with a row of windows every ten floors.

I expected to feel the protective magics woven around the Needle from miles away, and I did. But it was not the burning pain that it should have been. The spells I felt were weak, like delicate spiderwebs brushing against my senses.

That was very bad. I turned to Dom. "Something's wrong."

Rizzoli glanced at me. The dark sunglasses he wore made it

hard to read his expression, but at a guess he was worried. He should be. There were supposed to be concentric rings of wards surrounding the prison, stretching out for miles.

"Can you be more specific? What exactly is the matter?"

I answered his question with one of my own. "How far out is the first perimeter?"

"We passed it a couple of miles ago."

I'd thought so, but I'd hoped I was wrong. "I didn't feel it, Dom. I'm only now getting any sense of barrier magics, and they're so weak as to be useless. The wards around PharMart are stronger."

He swore softly. I figured that summed up the situation pretty well. After a long moment, Dom pressed the button for the car phone link and said, "Call supervisor."

A pleasant computerized female voice responded through the car's speakers. "Dialing supervisor now."

The phone was answered after only one ring. "Anderson here," said the man at the other end.

"Jason, it's Dom. We may have a problem."

"The girl?"

"No, she's fine. She's with me. We're headed to see Finn now. But she tells me the outer perimeter's down, that something's wrong with the Needle's magical defenses."

"How the hell would she know?"

I spoke, hoping the microphone would pick up my voice. "There's enough bat in me that I can feel protective wards. The strong ones hurt like a bad sunburn."

I heard the clicking of keys of a keyboard, then Anderson said, "The records say they were just checked a week ago."

"Bullshit."

"I'll make a couple of calls, see if I can get someone out there.

In the meantime, you might consider aborting. If the barriers have been lowered, something big may be going down."

I shook my head.

"I think it might be better if I go on in and speak to the warden in person." Dom didn't put any particular emphasis on his words, but they made Anderson pause. With good reason—Dom Rizzoli is a high-level intuitive. I've seen him in action. Intuition is a subtle gift but an incredibly useful one. Dom was giving his boss a big, fat hint that we needed to visit the prison.

"If you say so. But be careful, Dom. I don't like this."

Him and me both.

The second perimeter was no stronger than the first. It made my skin crawl, but there was no buzz to it, no pain. This was so bad. As he drove, Dom had been watching me out of the corner of his eyes. When he saw that I didn't flinch at the second barrier, his eyes darkened.

"Where's the minefield from here?" I asked. It had been a long time since I read about the prison, but that detail had stuck in my head.

"It's between the second and third rings," Dom answered, "so we're driving past it right now. Despite all the protests, it's still unmarked."

I remembered reading about the protests in the news. They happened from time to time, with the protesters saying that the minefield was a menace and should be fenced in and marked with warning signs. The last round of pickets had taken place shortly before the most recent election. The governor had made a public statement about it, basically saying, "Yeah, it's a menace. It's supposed to be. Get over it." He was reelected by a landslide.

Shortly before we reached the third ring, the SUV hit a bumpy patch of road about twelve feet long—a section where sensors had been put in place to scan approaching vehicles for magic and weapons. This time I actually felt the power wash over me. It *hurt*. I gasped in pain as tears filled my eyes.

"That's what you were expecting from the perimeters?" Dom asked tensely.

"At *least*," I said.

He grunted in response as we neared the outer fence and the first guard post.

The fence itself was impressive. Built of sand-colored concrete, the base stood fourteen feet high and three feet thick. Triple rows of razor wire spooled above the concrete barrier in dizzying helixes, dangerous and beautiful in the bright sunlight. Motion sensors and video surveillance cameras were set every few feet, pointing in every direction so that not an inch of the area inside the wall was out of view. I assumed there were a number of guards assigned to view the camera feeds at all times.

The prison's parking lot was outside the wall, for additional security. As Rizzoli turned into the lot, I studied the entryway. Two small guard posts flanked the heavy metal gate, which was just wide enough for two people to walk through abreast. The narrow space between the buildings was filled by a built-in full-body security scanner like the ones used at airports. The twin guard stations were made of tan brick, with white trim around the thick bulletproof glass of the windows and doors. The whole setup was spelled so heavily I could feel it, even from this distance and in the protective confines of Rizzoli's SUV.

We pulled into one of the six marked visitors' spaces. A pair of armed guards approached, wearing the Needle's standard security uniforms: navy DETENTION CENTER ball caps, bright white starched shirts, and navy dress slacks. They hadn't drawn their weapons, but the snaps on their holsters were undone. Their tinted aviator sunglasses hid their eyes, and their mouths were set in identical grim lines.

As we waited for the guards to scan the vehicle with technology and magic, Rizzoli turned to look at me. "You're sure about this?"

Actually, I wasn't. I hated the sight of this place. It reminded me of the Zoo, the prison for preternatural creatures that used to exist in the desert near Santa Maria de Luna. Bad things had happened there. I'd seen some of them. This place had the same feel to it. I so didn't want to go in there. But I needed to. "I'm okay," I said, lying as I slathered on sunblock from a little tube I'd tucked into my jacket pocket earlier.

"Yeah, right." He snorted, then pressed the button to open the back hatch. "You're going to have to leave your weapons here."

"Fine." I'd known they wouldn't allow me to carry weapons inside in the facility. I wasn't positive they'd let Rizzoli keep his; even though he's law enforcement, the Needle was an ultra-max facility.

Gathering my courage, I opened the car door and hopped out. The heat slapped against me with almost physical force. I could taste the dusty grit of sand in my mouth.

The guard on my side of the SUV took a step back, giving me room to move but staying out of reach. He didn't bother greeting me. That was fine. I wasn't feeling all that social.

Rizzoli chatted with the other guard as I strode around behind the vehicle and started disarming. My jacket came off first, then the knives and sheaths. After that I removed the gun and holster at my waistband. Finally I shucked off the Derringer and my little ankle holster.

As the weaponry stacked up, the guard's eyebrows started rising until I could see them, blond and bushy, above the rims of the sunglasses.

"I believe in being prepared." I smiled when I said it.

"No shit." He laughed, the first crack in his professional tough guy persona.

"Is that everything?" Dom asked as he joined me.

"Yup."

"All right." Choosing a small key from his ring, he turned the lock placed discreetly on the far left corner of the back compartment. I heard a soft popping sound and Rizzoli slid the tips of his fingers beneath something I couldn't see—nice illusion spell at work there—and flipped up a section of false floor.

This revealed a weapons safe with digital and bio controls not unlike the one I had back home. It was very nice. I guessed that it was also very expensive, since it looked as if it had been built into the car. My tax dollars had evidently been put to very good use.

"Sweet." The guard beside me said what I was thinking.

"This is my personal vehicle. The ones in the staff cars aren't nearly as nice."

Aha. So much for the tax dollars.

If we'd been alone I would've had him tell me all about it. I love tech toys and weapons and everything connected with them. We could've had a wonderful discussion about all the details. But the guard on Rizzoli's side of the vehicle was practically twitching with impatience, so now was not the time.

"Remind me to ask you about this later. I have to get a new vehicle anyway. I may decide to have one of these put in."

"Sure," Dom agreed as he went through the multiple security steps to get the safe open. When the door finally swung up, he stepped aside, giving me room to stack my gear on top of the things he already had stored inside. Little things like stacks of spell disks, ammo, a double-barreled shotgun, a riot gun, and a pair of Glock 9mms.

Glancing over my shoulder at "my" guard, I said in a mock whisper, "He likes to be prepared, too."

It won me a snicker from him and a glare from his partner.

Dom locked the safe and the trunk, and the four of us took the short walk to the gate.

"Ladies first." The guard next to Dom made it sound like a threat. Rizzoli turned, giving the man an unfriendly look.

"No. I think I'll go first." Dom opened the gate and stepped through. I waited as the machine did its thing. When it finished, the guards locked inside the guardhouse waved him through. Then it was my turn.

It wasn't pleasant, but it wasn't as bad as I expected. The guards took their time, far longer than they had with Dom, but I'd expected that. I stood patiently as I could, waiting for the all clear, and eventually they waved me through. I joined Dom on the other side of the gate, where the vehicle stood that would take us the rest of the way into the complex.

It was the ugliest ATV I'd ever set eyes on. It had four wheels with tank treads on each side. The passenger compartment had been built to carry six on a pair of bench seats and was covered by a spelled canvas top with plastic windows. The whole thing was painted olive drab, with the prison logo emblazoned on the only bit of metal that showed—the hood.

Dom held the door open for me and I climbed in.

The vehicle was loud and the ride was rough. The bench seat might have been as comfortable as sitting on a splintered board, but I doubted it. Conversation wouldn't have been easy even if we'd wanted to talk. I didn't. I was checking out the security. There were guards set at frequent intervals, and yet more cameras.

It was damned impressive. No one had ever escaped from the Needle. Now I could see why.

We came to a stop at the stairs that led up to the front door. As we mounted the steps, the ATV drove off. I felt a chill run down my spine as it left us stranded.

There was a man waiting for us at the door. Tall and thin, his hair was cut short and was the same steel gray of the fabric of his suit and a couple of shades darker than the color of his eyes.

"Special Agent Rizzoli." He shook Dom's hand, ignoring me completely. "I see you brought us a guest."

The inflection he put on the word "guest" made it clear he meant "prisoner." I fought to swallow my anger. I had done absolutely nothing wrong, but this asshole wanted to lock me up. Gritting my teeth, I counted silently to ten before turning to look over at Dom.

Dom's expression darkened dangerously, but when he spoke, his voice was level. "A *visitor*, Eric. Princess Celia is here to see Connor Finn regarding a case she's working on. Warden Davis has approved it. And you might want to be a little more polite. You keep insulting her and we're liable to have an international incident on our hands." He turned to me.

"Princess Celia, allow me to introduce a former coworker of mine, Eric Zorn. Eric, her Grace, Princess Celia Kalino Graves of the Pacific line of sirens."

"Oh, I know who she is." Zorn's eyes flicked over me dismissively. "I know all about her. We do our homework around here."

He finally looked straight at me, his gaze locking with mine in a direct challenge. "I don't like you, *Princess*. I think you use the press, your looks, and your rank to get away with things you shouldn't. I've heard you have diplomatic immunity along with that royal blood. But you should know that that only goes so far. You may not be staying here today, but you'll wind up here eventually. I'd bet my life on it."

"Eric." A new voice spoke like the crack of a whip. Zorn jumped, just a little, and turned to face the man who'd joined us so silently.

The newcomer wasn't tall or particularly imposing. His features were as average as his coloring. His black suit was off the rack but well tailored, and his white dress shirt was crisp with starch. His red-and-black-striped tie was held in place by a silver-and-onyx tie tack. But while his appearance was ordinary, the man himself wasn't. There was a strength, a presence to him that Zorn couldn't match.

"Princess," he said, bowing slightly, "it's a pleasure to meet you. I'm Warden Bob Davis. I don't believe you remember me, but I was at the demon rift. You saved me and God knows how many others that day. It's an honor to have you here."

"Thank you. I hope my being here isn't causing too much trouble?" I put a lilt in my voice to make it a question.

"Of course not." Davis turned to Dom. "Special Agent Rizzoli. I just got off of the line with your superior. If what he tells me is true, we need to talk. Eric, why don't you show Dom to my office? I'm sure you want to catch up on things. Princess, if you will follow me?"

I didn't smile, snicker, or give any indication that I felt smug as the warden and I walked away, but it wasn't easy. Dom, however, felt no such reservations. He was grinning from ear to ear as a scowling Eric led him down a narrow hall that branched off to the right of the huge atrium Davis and I were crossing.

I stopped, looking around the place for a second. It was . . . imposing, with dark green marble veined with black and white, taking up a full two stories. The light fixtures and all of the building details were Art Deco, giving an otherwise cold and functional space just a bit of style.

The warden stopped, waiting for me to catch up before speaking quietly so that only I would hear. "I apologize for Eric's behavior. He's a good man, but for good or ill, he believes that high-class criminals do not get the same justice as the poor."

That really wasn't a good excuse for his behavior, but I decided I'd try to be gracious anyway. After all, I was a guest at the Needle . . . and truthfully, I wasn't positive that Zorn wasn't right. I'd read about studies done of prison populations—both regular prisons and the special places like the Needle and the Zoo. The inmates were predominantly poor and members of minority groups. What kind of minority depended on what part of the world the prison was in. But the percentages were nearly identical across the board.

Warden Davis changed the subject to my reason for visiting. "Connor Finn is on the twenty-ninth floor in one of our four most secure cells. The wards on that floor are supposed to be checked daily by our in-house mage." He paused and waited for me to look at him.

"I hope it's a coincidence that Mage Barton went home sick right after Special Agent Rizzoli called to arrange for your visit. But just in case, I'm sending you up there with a pair of armed escorts, both of them with mage gifts.

"Please be very careful. Connor Finn is an incredibly dangerous man."

We'd reached a bank of four elevators. Waiting in front of the brushed metal doors were two guards who wore the same uniform as those I'd met at the front gate—but these guys were carrying a lot more hardware, including holstered wands. They were big and strong and looked reassuringly competent. I really hoped that nothing would happen that required their expertise, that they were just going to be intimidating decoration, but it felt good to have them there. Just in case.

"Thank you." I smiled at Davis. He didn't smile back.

"I just hope we aren't both making a terrible mistake."

Going through the prison was creepy. It wasn't like on television or in the movies, where guys in jumpsuits behind bars catcall the people walking by. There were no bars, for one thing. Every person in the Needle was in permanent solitary confinement. There was nothing to see but sterile white concrete walls, gleaming polished floors, and the evenly spaced steel doors. Each door had a four-by-six-inch window of wire-and-magic-reinforced glass and was sealed by four separate locks that were evenly spaced down the side away from the hinges.

Video cameras were placed at ten-foot intervals on opposite sides of the hall, angled so that there was overlapping coverage. I doubted there was one inch of space that wasn't covered by the cameras. There were no dropped ceilings. Instead the lights, wiring, and ductwork were out in the open, clearly visible above our heads. That area, too, was full of surveillance cameras.

It was all very quiet, very impressive, and very depressing.

My escorts took me to a circular meeting room that seemed to be in the center of the twenty-ninth floor. As I stepped over the threshold, I gasped in pain. The room had been built on a powerful magic circle and was ringed with major protection magics.

The room was bisected by a wall that was divided horizontally. The bottom half was cinder block; the top was made of what I assumed was a very thick layer of the kind of glass used to protect the audience at hockey games. There was a chair on my side of the room and one on the other side, each centered within a magical protective circle. Matching microphones and speakers hung overhead. The only entrances were two doors—one behind me and one directly opposite, in the other half of the room. All the walls, including the cinder-block portion of the divider, were painted a cheerful lemon yellow. I doubted anyone on either side of this room ever felt all that cheerful.

The guards with me took positions on either side of the visitor's chair. I sat down and felt the circle spring to life; the power washed over me in a rush.

I tried to be patient and calm while I waited for them to bring Finn into the room on the opposite side of the glass. Then the door opened and everything changed.

I knew what Connor Finn looked like. I'd seen him in the hologram, after all. But seeing him in person, I was still surprised by his sheer *presence.* Even wearing the trappings of a prisoner—standard-issue orange coveralls and green rubber flip-flops—he held himself like a king.

The silver circle that glowed around his seat was much more elaborate than the one on my side. It was engraved with symbols meant to block magical power so that no spell of any kind could be worked from inside. His hands and feet were bound in silver-and-steel shackles, and he sat calm and patient as the guards locked the connecting chains to a ring bolted to the floor. Connor Finn smiled, and I fought not to shudder as I remembered the last time I had seen that smile. Then he spoke, and I heard anew the voice that had haunted me as I lay burning on the beach.

"Well, well, Celia Graves, as I live and breathe. I thought you were smarter than this." He pretended bonhomie, but there was no warmth in his expression.

My return smile could've given the man frostbite. "Evidently not."

He laughed at that. "So, not so smart. But brave. You'd have to be, to come here when you know that so many people would love to make the Needle your permanent home. One wrong move and you'll be joining me."

I shrugged, trying to look impassive, as if his words hadn't hit a nerve.

"I really hoped you would learn your lesson from our previous encounter. Burns are painful enough that they usually make a very effective teaching tool."

He said it so very casually. I knew then that I'd made a mistake. I'd thought a man who'd been obsessed with a family feud would be obsessed with family, that he'd care what happened to the son who was the last of his line. But Connor Finn wasn't capable of caring about other people for any reason. It simply wasn't in his nature. I wondered why he'd killed the Garzas. It certainly wasn't about the blood feud.

He stared at me, waiting for an answer. "Sometimes I can be a little bit stubborn," I admitted. He smiled again, looking self-satisfied. I hated that smile.

"You've gone to quite a bit of trouble to see me, and now that we're together, you're very quiet. What would you like to talk about?"

What did I want to say? My insight of a moment ago changed everything and nothing. So I plowed ahead, hoping that if we kept talking I might stumble onto something important. "You've got Garza blood in your veins. If you do this curse of yours, you'll not only kill Michelle, you'll be killing yourself and your son as well."

He gave a snort of what appeared to be real amusement. "You

went to all this trouble . . ." He laughed. "Celia, sweetheart, you're so cute." He was feeling superior and oh so smug. It showed in his posture and in the condescending tone of his voice. "Don't forget I've done a bloodline curse against the Garza family before. I didn't die that time. *If* I was planning to do another curse like that again, don't you think I'd take the same precautions?

"Really, how stupid do you think I am?" He shook his head, mocking me by pretending my stupidity was making him sad. "You have one piece of the puzzle and you think you see the whole picture.

"You're delusional."

I smiled. It wasn't a pleasant or happy smile. It was a fuck-you-buddy smile that flashed just a bit of fang. I don't like condescension. "I may only have one piece of the puzzle, but without it, you won't get your picture."

Connor's amusement disappeared as if it had been cut off with a switch, replaced instantly by ugly rage. His blue eyes blazed with anger. "You think you can stop me? Better than you have tried. They're all dead . . . or dying." He sneered, an honest-to-God movie-villain sneer. I wanted to laugh, it was so over the top. I knew he was dangerous, deadly, even. But I didn't care, because in that moment, he was a cartoon.

Apparently, my amusement showed. A slow flush spread from his neck upward; his jaw clenched so hard I could hear his teeth grind. "You are going to die."

My smile widened. I knew that provoking him was stupid, but I couldn't seem to help myself. He'd pissed me off so mightily that reason had left the building. "We all die eventually. But if you don't stop what you're doing, you'll go sooner rather than later."

He snorted in derision. "I will survive. Just as I did before."

"And what about your son? Will he?"

"Hard choices have to be made. Children die every day." He spread his hands.

I shook my head. I wasn't shocked. I know better than most that not all parents love their children, and I was fairly certain that Connor wasn't capable of loving anyone or anything other than himself. "Bet he'll just love hearing that."

Another derisive laugh. "Tell Jack if you like. He won't believe you. He's as delusional as you are. Now if you'll excuse me, I think we're done here."

I rose. "I think you're right," I said and turned my back to Connor Finn. Despite the protective circles and the thick glass between us, my shoulders were clenched in anticipation of a blow until I walked out the door.

My guards fell silently in beside me. We walked down the hall and into the elevator; the only sound was of our footfalls echoing through the empty corridor.

As I rode down to the main floor, I replayed Finn's words in my head. He was so damned arrogant—and not without reason. He was brilliant and hugely talented as a mage. He'd accomplished things magically that other men had never even dreamed of. But he was not invincible, and his disdain for others meant that he wasn't careful about what he said.

"They're all dead . . . or dying" was the phrase that stuck in my mind. I thought about my last meeting with Isaac Levy, the man whom I now knew was the Grand Master of the West Coast. I'd brought him a problem that fell into his area of authority. He'd consider it his responsibility to check things out, and he wouldn't have thought twice about it. Finn was a mage, but Isaac was a mage, too, and, I was guessing, a pretty strong one if he was Isabella's opposite number. He'd think he could face whatever Connor Finn dished out.

I hoped I was wrong, but every instinct I possessed screamed otherwise. Closing my eyes, I said a silent, desperate prayer. "Please, God. Not Isaac. Please."

24

We stepped out of the elevator into frantic but well-organized activity. There were probably a hundred guards grouped in a semicircle around Warden Davis, Dom Rizzoli, and Eric Zorn, who was holding a tablet computer.

"What's going on?" one of my escorts asked the nearest man. He was rewarded with only a glare, so he shut up and we stood still, trying to be inconspicuous.

The warden spoke without a bullhorn, but his voice rang out clearly; I wondered if there was a spell helping him or if he was a natural at projecting. "Listen up, people. We've had a major security breach. We have a missing civilian. There's no time to waste. Break into teams of four. You'll get your assignments from Assistant Warden Zorn." Zorn nodded and moved to stand by the exit door.

Davis gestured to a supply clerk who was standing next to a rack loaded with a large number of what looked like the kinds of poles routinely used to check the efficacy of the magic perimeters that surrounded many public buildings. "One member of each team takes a pulse check stick."

His arm swept to the other side of the atrium, where three women in street clothes—I guessed they were the warden's office staff—were organizing more racks, this time of body armor and helmets. "Everybody wears full protection. No arguments, no exceptions. Six teams will go to the outer ring. Four to the second."

He pointed to a small group of men in the equivalent of SWAT gear. "Specialists will be checking the minefield. Everyone else will be going through the building, room by room, floor by floor. We're checking for *anything* out of the ordinary, and particularly for any flaws in either physical or magical protections. And everybody keep your eyes open.

"The missing man is a mage, Isaac Levy. Levy arrived yesterday as a visitor and was last seen walking out the inner gate with Mage Barton. There's no record of him actually leaving the site. Any questions? All right. *Move,* people."

They moved. So did I, forcing my way through the milling mass until I reached Dom Rizzoli. My two guards disappeared somewhere along the way. "What happened?"

"Celia. You're all right?" He looked so relieved to see me that I wondered just what was going on and what he'd thought might have happened to me.

I nodded.

"I told Warden Davis what you'd said about the outer rings. He decided we should check it out in person. So Davis, Zorn, and I took a couple of pulse sticks and an ATV and rode out to check the outer ring. It's down. So's the second ring. And when we came back, one of the gate guards asked about a visitor who'd come in yesterday to meet with the staff mage. Apparently Isaac seemed pretty agitated when he arrived but was calm and relaxed when he left. Not a big deal, by any means, but the guard overheard Isaac saying there were problems with the wards. The gate guy says he reported it, but when he tried to show us, we found that there's no record in the computer. So now the place is on full lockdown and red alert until they figure out the full extent of the problem and get it fixed."

"Isaac is missing, Dom," I said, and filled him in on my call from Gilda. "Are they sure he left?" I realized I was shaking. Damn Finn. Damn him anyway.

"The guard says he left under his own steam, and there's video to prove it." Then Dom thought about it some more and sighed. "They don't spray people leaving the facility. After all, it's a prison for mages, not spawn. And besides, no spawn should be able to get in through the wards."

But the wards were down, I thought. I didn't say anything. There was no point—and besides, Dom was already thinking it, too.

"Look, nobody knows anything for sure, Celia. I'm sorry, I know it doesn't look good, and I know he's your friend."

"Dom, Finn is involved in this."

"Celia, that's just not possible."

"He told me. I said I'd stop him, and he said, 'Better than you have tried. They're all dead . . . or dying.'"

Dom gave me a long look. "There's no way to be sure that he was talking about Isaac."

I glared at him and he sighed again.

"Fine. Maybe you're right. But there's no way to prove it."

My answer was colorful and unprintable. Dom didn't argue, just hustled me down the hall to the reception area outside Warden Davis's office.

I had rarely felt more helpless in my life. Using my vampire abilities, I could hear the radio behind the closed door of the warden's office. Most of the information being relayed back was bad: perimeters down everywhere, the minefield completely disabled—both physical and metaphysical defenses down.

When I heard they'd discovered Isaac, I jumped to my feet and started pacing. Dom shot me a startled look but said nothing. The security team was bringing Isaac to the infirmary; he was in bad shape according to their reports. Once the lockdown was lifted, if Isaac was stable enough, they'd attempt a helicopter evacuation.

The sweep of the lower floors was complete by the time they brought him in from the minefield, so Warden Davis let Dom and me go to the infirmary—with an armed escort, of course. I didn't care that we were under guard; I'd be there when Isaac arrived and could see for myself how he was and hear anything he might have to say.

The infirmary was a large rectangular room with white walls and an acoustical tile ceiling. It held only four beds, two on each of the long walls. Each sat in its own spell circle and was equipped with full metal restraints. Surrounding the beds were a variety of machines, large and small, only some of which looked familiar from my own hospital stays, as well as the expected cabinets for medical supplies and other equipment.

At one end of the room was a large table equipped with computers as well as a large interactive clear plastic touch screen.

The man in charge was Dr. Halston. Middle-aged, tall, and slender, he had thinning dark hair that he wore in an oiled combover. The skin of his face and hands was smooth and baby soft, with no sign that he'd ever needed to shave or that he'd used his hands for anything as mundane as physical labor. His white lab coat was pristine, and it was clear from the first moment that our entrance into his domain was an unwelcome invasion.

"This is unacceptable." He glared at me and Dom. Before either of us could say anything, Halston flicked one hand, dismissing us. "There is no waiting room, but my office is through that door." He pointed a manicured finger. "Go."

I could tell that there was no point in arguing with him.

Halston's office was spartan, physically and psychically cold, without a single picture or personal item in view. The screen saver on his computer was the standard factory-installed image. I found the whole effect disturbingly impersonal.

Time passed slowly. We waited without talking for hours. I could hear things going on, the guards standing outside the office door wore radios, but there was nothing worth discussing with Dom.

Finally the door opened and the doctor stepped wearily through. He stripped off his jacket, dropping it into a plastic bin that opened with a foot pedal, and said, "I've got him stable enough to travel. I've set up a magical barrier that will protect his wounds from any further contamination. He needs surgery as soon as possible, so I've arranged to fly him to UCLA Medical Center. The medevac chopper will arrive in five minutes." I opened my mouth to speak but Halston held up one hand, forestalling me.

"The complete lockdown is being lifted, but special safety protocols are still in place, so under normal circumstances, neither of you would be allowed to leave yet. However, I've checked with the warden and he says that one of you can fly out with Mr. Levy if there's room in the helicopter and the pilot agrees to take you."

"You go," Dom said to me. "There are some things I want to check into before I leave. And you should be with Isaac."

I nodded, hoping Dom knew what he was doing. Halston slid

on another jacket, then opened the door and escorted me into the main room and to Isaac's bedside.

Isaac looked like hell. He'd been beaten and left to die in the middle of the minefield. Despite a severe concussion and multiple broken bones, including an open fracture of his right thigh, he'd somehow managed to drag himself into the shade of a large rock. Had the mines been active, that movement would have killed him. But I knew from the reports I'd overheard from outside Warden Davis's office that the mines had all been deactivated. Every single one.

Despite that fragment of luck, he had nearly died from a combination of shock, the effects of his injuries, and dehydration. I wasn't sure what Halston had done, but Isaac was hooked up to several machines and had more than one IV running. I assumed he was heavily sedated, but even so, he kept making small, desperate sounds that hurt to hear.

I closed my eyes, concentrating, trying to speak to Isaac mind-to-mind. He was too far gone, his thoughts totally incoherent. That was terrifying. "Has anyone called his wife?"

"I did." I hadn't noticed the woman in scrubs before. I'm usually more observant than that, and it bothered me that I'd missed her. "Mrs. Levy is on her way to Los Angeles."

"Good."

I don't remember much about the flight from the Needle to UCLA Medical Center. I was too worried about Isaac to notice anything else. There was a close call—his heart stopped and I was shoved aside so they could lower the magical barrier and use the paddles on him. We were greeted on the medevac landing pad by ER doctors and nurses with a gurney. They wheeled him off, already working on him, as I climbed carefully out of the helicopter. I stayed low even though the rotors were set well above my height. Sometimes you have to listen to your instincts.

Waving my thanks to the pilot and the EMTs, I hurried out of the way. As soon as I was clear, the chopper rose from the pad and roared out of sight.

By the time I reached the lobby, Isaac was being prepped for surgery even while other medical personnel worked to stabilize his less-urgent injuries.

I sat in the waiting room blaming myself for what happened to Isaac and dreading seeing Gilda. Just as they were wheeling him out of the ER Gilda arrived with John Creede. I was surprised to see her—it usually takes at least two hours to get to Los Angeles from Santa Maria.

Gilda ran to me, taking me in her arms and holding me so tight I thought my ribs might break. She looked like hell—her hair a mess, eyes red, makeup smeared from tears. For the first time she looked old, her features gray with worry and exhaustion. Her only jewelry was her wedding set.

I tried to be reassuring and realistic, even though I didn't have a lot to tell her. "He's tough, Gilda. He's hurt, and the leg was pretty bad . . ."

"They found him because of you. If you hadn't gone there . . ." She choked up, unable to finish the sentence.

I eased her into a chair, gently breaking her panic-tight grasp, then took the chair beside her. She held one of my hands in both of hers. John Creede took the seat on her other side, giving me a nod of acknowledgment. While Gilda composed herself, John explained that she had called him and begged him to fly her north on his corporate plane. He hadn't hesitated.

I gave him a grateful smile. It had been incredibly kind of him to bring her—though since Isaac was the Grand Master of the West Coast, it was probably important that John stay on his good side—and it was considerate of him to stay in the background, letting Gilda get the comfort she so desperately needed.

I wasn't surprised at his kindness and tact. John is a good man. It was that, as much as his good looks and charm, that had drawn me to him, and that kindness was what I'd missed most about him since our relationship had ended.

We sent in word that Isaac's wife had arrived, and after a little while one of the doctors came out and asked for a private word with Gilda. John and I made ourselves scarce, heading for the cafeteria. As we walked down the hall, I took a good look at him. It looked as if Gilda had caught him at the office—he was dressed for business, wearing a medium gray suit with a pale blue shirt and navy tie. He didn't look rumpled, despite the flight. He'd cut his hair quite short since I'd last seen him, close enough to his head to keep it from curling, and there wasn't a hint of stubble on his cheeks. It was a very formal look, and I knew him well enough to know that while he did formal well, he preferred not to. So I was pretty sure he'd interrupted important business—perhaps even a meeting or client appointment—to help.

"Thanks so much for bringing Gilda," I said as we entered the cafeteria. I got in line ahead of him, picking up a yellow plastic tray and prepacked silverware.

"Don't be ridiculous." John slid a tray onto the counter beside mine. "You've known them longer, but Isaac and Gilda are my friends, too. In fact, I'm technically his apprentice."

"Really?" I hadn't realized that. I couldn't quite wrap my mind around it. John was an adept-class mage, how could he possibly be an apprentice?

"He's training me to replace him. That way if he retires, or dies, I'll be ready to take over his position." John looked seriously at me. "So I need to know what we are dealing with." It wasn't really a request.

"I'll tell you, but not here. And before I do, I need to eat." I hadn't eaten since my bowl of ice cream that morning with Dom. I wasn't hungry, in fact I felt a little queasy. But I remembered from painful experience that it was only a matter of time before bloodlust would hit, and hit hard, if I didn't get some nutrition into my body.

John reached in front of me to pick up a small saucer filled with a small stack of orange Jell-O squares.

I love orange Jell-O and this was plain, without any chunks of fruit in it. Maybe if I let the squares melt in my mouth, I'd be able to eat it. It was worth a try anyway. I put a similar saucer onto my tray and moved forward. The soup of the day was tomato, so I asked for two bowls, then got a couple of cans of soda. I'd drink one with my meal and save the other for later. It had already been a long day and I suspected it was going to be an even longer night.

John insisted on paying for our dinner. I didn't argue. I followed him to a table in the far corner of the room, away from most of the few doctors and nurses who were scattered at tables around the room. We didn't have much privacy, but we wouldn't be overheard if we spoke softly.

"So, what is going on?" John asked. "Gilda told me that you came to see Isaac and that he left almost immediately after you did. He said it was 'business' but wouldn't tell her anything more. Then he disappears, and nobody knows what's become of him, until he's found at the Needle, beaten half to death."

I cringed at his tidy summation of the facts. This situation was at least partly my fault and I felt more than a little guilty about it. I'd been the one to drag Isaac into this. I'd gone to him for advice, brought the problem to his attention. If I hadn't, he wouldn't have gone to the Needle, wouldn't be in critical condition right now. Yes, it had been his choice to go . . . and to go alone. But that didn't make me feel any better about it.

Did I really want to risk anyone else? No. On the other hand, John is a big boy, and despite our disagreements, I value his opinion. So I decided to give him an edited version of what was going on.

I hadn't gotten very far in describing what had gone down at the Needle when he started shaking his head. He didn't interrupt, but he was obviously having trouble believing me.

"John," I said, looking him straight in the eyes—and for a second I felt the pull of the old attraction between us. His magic had always had a deep, frequently sexual, pull for me. I shook *my* head, to clear it. "I know. Everyone keeps telling me that Connor Finn can't possibly be working magic, that there are protections built into the prison that make it impossible. And yet, it happened. I saw that hologram. Damn it, it was *him,* talking to me, ordering his men to leave me to burn in the sun. It was *him.*"

John reached over and took my hand. We both jumped at the tingle of electricity that passed between us. Magic, mine and his, mingled for just an instant. I forced myself to set aside the memories, both good and bad, of the time we'd shared. There was a flicker of sadness in his eyes, quickly suppressed.

"Celia, the Needle is built on a node—a nexus of lines of magical power. Its protections tap into the node. It takes four mages—working together—and a death to access the power, and it would take another death to break it. The warden would know if there'd been a death at the Needle. Every inch is under constant surveillance."

I sighed, leaning forward so that we were very close and no one could possibly overhear. "This isn't for public consumption, John, but the outer perimeters had both been broken and the minefield was disabled. That's where they found Isaac."

He pulled back, startled beyond calmness. "Fuck!"

Everyone in the room turned to look.

I grimaced. John had the grace to blush. "Sorry, sorry." He looked around. Eventually people went back to their food, but they were keeping an eye on us now.

"So you told Isaac there was a problem and he went to check it out."

"Yes."

"And somebody did this to him."

I nodded. "The mage on duty disappeared. At first I thought he might be responsible for the protections being down and for what happened to Isaac, but I'm not so sure now."

John's gaze intensified. "Why not?"

"You said they'd need to kill someone to disrupt the protections. Who better than the mage who's supposed to be checking them every day and doing the renewal spells?"

He looked a little sick. "That makes sense . . . but the only way someone could pass for the duty mage, even for a little while, is if he was a spawn."

Ah, yes, spawn, the child of a demon by a human. There weren't a lot of them, so far as anyone knew, but it was hard to be certain. Most of them could shape-shift to look like anyone, and they lived much, much longer than normal humans. They weren't immortal, but they were very hard to kill. Fortunately, for the most part, they were subject to the same weaknesses as all demons: holy water, holy artifacts, and the like.

My eyes locked with John's. I barely spoke above a whisper.

"Nobody sprayed me with holy water at the Needle and there wasn't a single artifact to be seen. I've gone through tighter security at Birchwoods."

Now he looked horrified. "That's not right. I consulted with the architects on the magical parts of the design. I know what the procedures are supposed to be."

"Well, I don't know what they're supposed to be. I can only tell you what I ran into when I was there yesterday, and I wasn't impressed."

I brought a spoonful of soup to my mouth. It had cooled to the perfect temperature. As the food hit my stomach, I felt a tension inside of me ease. I hadn't realized how hard I'd been clamping down on my inner bat. I'd just done it. Now that I was away from the immediate crisis, and eating, my control loosened just a fraction.

Letting go even that little bit was a huge mistake. Quick as a snap of the fingers, my vision shifted to hyperfocus. I became very aware of the scent of John's flesh, the strong, steady beat of the pulse in his neck.

"Celia?"

"Ssssorry." I closed my eyes; it helped not to look. But I could hear his heartbeat speed up—and the smell of him . . . God, it was wonderful. I *wanted.* The need to hunt made my entire body ache.

"Celia, I'm going to go get you some beef juices. Can you hold on while I do that?"

"Yessss."

I kept my eyes closed, taking deep, slow breaths. My hands clutched the edge of the table. From a distance, I could feel the brushed steel of the tabletop giving, bending. It made a soft groaning sound. Or maybe that was me.

I smelled John as he returned—his skin, his cologne, the fabric softener on his clothes. I also smelled what he carried. Meat juices. There was the clink of metal against metal as he set a large pitcher in front of me, then slowly backed away.

He didn't leave the cafeteria. He stood, out of my reach, between me and the rest of the patrons. They had no idea what was going on, but he did. I knew what was in his mind. He was waiting to see. He thought I could regain control of myself. He was almost sure of it. But if I went feral, he'd shoot me. If he had to, he'd stake me, kill me. He didn't want to. It would kill a piece of him to do it. But he would. If he could. If I made him.

I breathed deeply, taking in the scent of the juices. Grabbing the pitcher in both hands, I raised it to my lips, gulping down the contents, feeling the bat in me recede with every swallow. I groaned in pure pleasure as tears of mingled grief and relief streamed from my eyes.

We didn't go back upstairs. Instead, John led me out to the rental car he'd picked up at the airport. He called Gilda and explained what had happened. She told him she would be fine, to take me home. So he did.

25

I didn't lose control. Ten points to me. John stuck with me the whole time, on the drive to the strip where he'd left his plane, on the flight back to Santa Maria, and on the drive home. He was by my side, a strong, calming influence, not judging but making sure that I wouldn't hurt anyone else if I lost control. Ten bazillion points to him.

He left me, reluctantly, at the door to my house. "Are you *sure* you'll be all right?"

"I'll be fine," I assured him. "I'll eat again, then I'll get some rest. You don't need to worry."

He might not need to, but he'd do it anyway. He might even park outside and watch the house, just to make sure I didn't sneak out to hunt.

Whatever. That was his choice, and his business. I just needed some time alone. So I told him good-bye on the doorstep, then went in, shutting the door gently but firmly behind me.

Minnie came to greet me. She stared at me intently. I knew that look from when she'd been our office cat. It meant, *Where have you been? My cat box is filthy and disgusting.* I was pleased that I could tell the difference between that and the only marginally different glare that meant, *You do realize that my food was supposed to be served two point eight minutes ago?*

I checked anyway, just to be sure. Minnie's plate was empty. Her box was full. I remedied both situations, in that order. Then I took a shower, fixed myself some chicken broth, put some watered-down mashed potatoes and gravy through the blender and sucked them down, then went to bed.

I woke up at nine thirty. My mouth tasted dry and furry, in part because I'd been snoring and the cat had apparently shed on my pillow. Gargh.

I got up, brushed my teeth, and grabbed the phone. I tried calling Bruno, but it went straight to voice mail. Dawna, however, answered on the first ring.

"Celia, you're home."

Ah, caller ID, lets everyone know where you're calling from. "I called to see if everybody's gotten to the safe house, and if Bubba's given his statement to the police."

"They did and he has. He called me after, said it went as well as those things can go. Fred called. His attorney has the lease ready. And while I don't mean to be a party pooper, how are you planning on paying the rent? We've got money in the bank, but we're blowing through it like water."

Dawna was right. We were spending like mad, hiring staff, insuring them, buying weapons and spell disks, and more. But I wasn't worried. "Just keep track of expenditures. Michelle Andrews is actually the last living member of the Garza clan. All the profits from all of the patents they own are hers outright. I don't think we need to worry about the bill."

"You're sure?"

"Trust me."

I heard her give a snort of what might have been laughter.

"Fine, whatever. I saw on the news about Isaac being hurt out at the Needle. They made a big deal about him being medivaced out, but they didn't really give a lot of solid information. Is he going to be okay?"

I sighed. "I don't know. It was bad, but the doctors at UCLA were pretty encouraging. I'm going to call and check again first thing in the morning. By the way, can you pick me up around eight o'clock? I'm stuck here without a vehicle."

"Make it nine. I'm going to see Fred's attorney at eight to sign the lease and drop off the first check."

"Nine it is."

I tried Bruno again. This time he answered on the first ring. "Hi, honey, I'm home."

He snorted—well, at least I was amusing my friends tonight. "Good. I was worried. I heard about Isaac from John. He told me what you think we're up against."

"We?"

He sighed. "Sweetheart, it's Connor freaking Finn. And it's mage business. Those protections need to be restored *now.* Please don't tell me you're going to get all territorial about this."

"No, of course not." I totally wasn't. In fact, it was kind of a relief knowing that Bruno and John were going to be involved. I might not want either of them on staff, but as backup? Oh, hell, yeah. Was that wrong of me? Maybe. But it's how I felt. "Any word on my knives or the ring?"

"Almost finished. There were some seriously nasty curses on them, took awhile to untangle. But it'll be after midnight before I finish and I'll probably just fall into bed after. Would it be all right if I don't come over tonight?"

"You're wearing yourself out doing something nice for me.

It'd be pretty crappy of me to complain about you needing to rest. Stay home. Get some sleep. That's all I plan to do. It's been a rough day."

"Sounds like a plan." He sounded weary. "I love you, Celie."

"I love you too. See you tomorrow?"

"Tomorrow," he agreed.

I slept like a dead thing and, thankfully, Minnie didn't get me up at the crack of dawn. Of course, she might have tried and I might just have slept through it. I was really tired—tired enough that I didn't dream at all.

It was hard to drag my butt out of bed to get ready, but I did it, feeding the cat and calling to get my messages and check on Isaac before having breakfast. Bruno had called. My stuff was ready. He'd get it to me this morning.

I did an internal cheer as I headed into the bathroom to shower and get ready. I was getting my stuff back, clean and ready to use. *Woot!*

I was putting the finishing touches on my outfit when Dawna pulled up to my front gate and pressed the intercom button at nine o'clock sharp.

"I'll be right out," I announced and went to pull on my sneakers. I was wearing pale blue jeans and a white polo shirt. I'd left my best blazer in Rizzoli's truck with a bunch of my weapons. It was annoying but unavoidable. I have a couple of different backup jackets, but none that I like as well. Still, since I didn't have any business meetings planned for the day, I decided to go with a denim jacket that I'd had altered, adding loops for stakes and inside pockets that I used for spell disks and One-Shot brand holy water guns. The backup holster that fit in the small of my back wasn't quite as comfy as my usual, but it was adequate, as were my third-best wrist sheaths. I slathered on some sunscreen, grabbed my floppy hat, and went out to face the world.

Dawna was waiting in das Humvee. Given everything that had happened in the last few days, I was glad to see that she'd brought the tank, even though I knew she'd done it because Chris insisted. I'm not short, but I had to use the little chrome step Chris had installed on the passenger side to climb into the cab. And even with the help, it was a challenge.

"Hi, Dawna."

"Celia." Dawna reached across the seat to give me a huge hug. "I've been so worried about you. Are you all right? " Her beautiful features were drawn and there were dark circles under her eyes. More telling, she wasn't wearing a bit of makeup and was dressed in plain white T-shirt and jeans. We almost matched. Dawna doesn't do casual, and she never goes out without makeup. It was so unlike her that I found myself staring.

"I'm fine," I said, which was mostly the truth. Things weren't great. But I'd definitely been through worse. "How are you?"

"Been better," she admitted.

"What's up?"

"I don't even know where to start." She checked her mirrors, then pulled out of the driveway and onto the road. "Your knives and ring are in the backseat. I ran into Bruno at Starbucks. He was going to bring them himself, but when he found out I was headed here he asked me to deliver them. He's got a tight schedule this morning."

"Damn. Sorry I didn't get a chance to see him."

"Don't be. I'm not sure what's up, but I don't think I've ever seen anyone that angry before. He scared me."

I was shocked. Bruno has always liked Dawna. I couldn't

imagine him being mean to her for any reason. "What did he do?"

"Nothing. He was very quiet, very polite." She shuddered. "It scared the shit out of me."

"Oh." I knew exactly what she meant. His uncle Sal could do the same thing—be utterly cordial and freaking terrifying at the same time. Still, I felt like I should defend him. "I think it really shook him up seeing what those guys did to me—and who knows what kinds of spells they put on my stuff?"

We stopped at a sign and she turned, giving me wide eyes. "I mean, I always knew he was a tough guy, and he comes from that family . . . but I never really felt it before." She gave me a wide-eyed look. "You're a brave woman."

"You know he's not usually like that," I protested. "And you'd better believe that Chris can be that way if he needs to."

She chewed lightly on one lip for a moment, then changed the subject. "Where am I taking you?"

"I need to rent another car. I left the last one at a diner in Furnace Creek."

"I could drive you out to get it," she offered.

"Nah." I smiled at her. "Thanks, but we don't have time. We need to be local in case all hell breaks loose."

"Do you think it will?" she asked as she turned the corner and started down Oceanview.

"God, I hope not. But it's better to be careful, just in case."

She switched lanes, passing an old woman who was driving well below the speed limit. "That makes sense. And there really is a lot to do. First, before I forget, you need to sign some more checks. I used the last one for the lease on the safe house. Oh, and we may want to rethink the two signatures policy. When you're out of reach, it would be really handy for me to be able to sign on my own. Anyway, payday is tomorrow, and Bubba, Kevin, and Talia will want their money. I need some, too—reimbursement for money I had to advance Kevin out of my personal account so they could set up at the safe house. You know, groceries, that sort of thing. And I've got to pay the premium for the insurance.

"I went with group health, life, and disability. It's a special package that we qualify for. It's a little pricey but definitely worth it—especially if you're not going to stay enrolled at the university."

Holy crap. We qualified as a *group*. I suddenly felt very grown up, very responsible, and utterly terrified. I fought down a wave of panic that rivaled anything I felt while facing down bad guys and gave Dawna what was probably a fairly sickly attempt at a smile. "Fine. Where's the checkbook?"

"In the box with the knives."

"How's Michelle?"

"According to Kevin, now that they're out in the middle of nowhere, it's boring as hell. Just the way he likes it, he said. He is not at all sorry he missed out on the excitement at the hospital. He also suggested you might want to give Bubba a bonus, or at least cover his legal fees."

"Legal fees?"

"Bubba hired an attorney to go with him when he gave his statement. Oh, and Kevin asked me to remind you that the full moon is coming up."

"Full moon, check," I said—and realized it was good to be reminded that no matter what I had to deal with as a result of whatever Connor Finn was planning, I still had to make provisions for Kevin's needs as well. Then, "Cover the legal fees. They were a business-related expense."

"Okay. By the way, Bubba wants to know what's next. He said

they can't hide Michelle forever, and while he can use the money, eventually he'd like to get back to Mona and Sherry."

"How's Talia doing?"

"So far as I can tell, she's doing pretty well. Nobody's complaining, anyway."

"Good." I wasn't sure how to say what I had to tell Dawna, so I just did it. "There's more to this than just protecting Michelle, but I haven't been able to unwind just what yet." I didn't want to tell her about the problems at the Needle. Whatever she'd heard on the news would be enough; any more and she'd really be scared.

"So if Bubba and Kevin are expecting detailed information, well, I don't have it yet. I'm working on it, but—"

Dawna glanced away from the road long enough to roll her eyes at me. "And you don't want to have to explain that to the guys. Fine. I'll handle it." I could hear the frustration in her voice and guessed that it wasn't all due to having to take on more work than she'd expected.

"Dawna . . ." I started to ask specifically what was wrong, but she waved me to silence.

"I can't talk about it. I just can't. If I do, I'll start crying, and I don't want to do that. So don't ask."

"If you say so."

"I do."

"You know that if you need anything—" I said, but she interrupted me.

"I know. Emma said the same thing. But it's stuff I have to deal with by myself." She smiled, and it had almost her usual level of warmth. "Maybe soon we can have some peace and quiet. I'd love to go to the spa again. I need some girl time."

"Sounds like a plan. Make reservations for the three of us for next weekend."

"You think this will be over by next weekend?"

"It'll be over on the full moon. One way or another."

Put that way, it sounded ominous. She turned her head, giving me a look. "Celie?"

"I'm fine. Really." I was lying, and Dawna probably knew it, but there was no time to call me on it. We'd arrived at the car rental place. I jumped out of the vehicle—much easier than climbing up—then opened the back door to rummage through the box she'd stowed there. The checkbook was on top. I signed a bunch of checks. I trusted Dawna, and I had no idea how long we'd be in crisis mode. Better for her to have them on hand. That done, I stuck my siren ring back into place on my finger and slid the very special knives Bruno had made for me into the wrist sheaths. I had to suppress a shudder as I slid them home. The memory of how they'd last been used was horrible. I pulled my jacket back on a little hurriedly, wanting the knives out of sight.

"You have your phone?" Dawna asked, turning around in the seat so we could see each other's faces.

"Yeah."

"Well, keep it handy. I'll be staying in touch now that I've got the number—especially if something goes wrong."

"Right," I agreed. "And Dawna . . ." I paused, trying to find the right words. I wanted to thank her. But more than that, I really wanted to just talk with her. I could tell there was something going on with her. As a friend, I knew I should ask what. But there was so damned much on my plate right now.

Her smile was a little bit sad. "It's okay, Celia. I'll be fine. I'll make the reservations at the spa, we'll have plenty of time to talk then. But if I'm not driving you to Furnace Creek, I need to get the Humvee back to Chris before he blows a gasket."

She was right, of course. But that didn't make me feel better about it. I hesitated.

"Go!" she ordered, making a shooing gesture.

"Fine, I'm going." I waited a beat, then said, "Thank you for everything. I don't know what I'd do without you."

She grinned, and while it didn't have the wattage of her usual smile, it was still a real grin. "Believe me, I know."

Smiling, I slammed the door and stepped aside so that she'd have plenty of room to maneuver her way out of the parking lot. I watched her until she was out of sight.

It didn't take long to get a new rental—an SUV not unlike the last one, only in blue. Normally I'm more of a sports car kind of gal, but on the off chance I'd have to ferry people, I figured bigger was better. Like the previous vehicle, it was set up for a hands-free phone. Before I pulled out of the rental place's lot, I called the hospital.

Isaac had been moved to a regular private room after his surgery. He was listed as being in stable condition. Stable was good—especially since it wasn't "stable but critical." Given the shape he'd been in when he was found, it was very good indeed. His age worked against him, but I knew he was tough. I believed he'd pull through.

The nurse told me that Gilda had fallen asleep in the chair beside Isaac's bed and that Isaac was sedated, so I just asked her to leave word that I'd called and said I'd be in touch again later.

Then, before I could forget, I ordered flowers for him.

That done, I had the GPS do a search for Finn Billiards. In a matter of seconds I had directions.

Visiting Finn Senior hadn't been a rousing success, but I'd learned a few things and set the authorities onto a few more. Maybe I'd have even better luck talking to his son, Jack.

Assuming I survived.

26

On a good day, with the wind up your tailpipe, the drive between Santa Maria de Luna and Los Angeles is just under two hours. This was not that day. Sitting, unmoving, in bumper-to-bumper traffic, I turned on the radio just long enough to hear that there'd been a huge wreck somewhere up the line. Ugh. At least I would have plenty of time to finally finish reading all the material Anna had sent me while I waited for things to start moving again. And maybe figure out my next steps.

Bubba was right. We couldn't hide Michelle forever. From Anna's research and my conversation with Isaac, I knew that Finn would need to use the power of the full moon to pull off his curse. Being thorough (and knowing it would interest me), Anna had also sent some more esoteric information about how blood curses work.

First, the person laying the curse needs a bio sample, usually blood, from someone with a DNA link to all the prospective victims. Then you need power—natural talent and the full moon would cover that. Finn was a powerful mage to begin with, and he'd spent close to two decades behind bars: years of not having to expend magical energy on much of anything. He had a lot of banked power to draw on, I'd expect.

Unless you were totally sure you had the right bio sample, you probably would make a preemptive strike against your first target. That explained why Michelle had been shot but not killed. Once you were certain you had the right sample, you used it to send the curse through the chosen individual and from him or her to everyone linked biologically.

The only way to stop a blood curse is to remove the link. In other words, if I wanted to save the Finns, I could do that by killing Michelle.

So not my goal.

I had turned off the engine to conserve fuel, but the heat was getting to me, so I started the car, turned on the AC, and pondered while I crawled a whopping six feet before stopping again.

I needed to break the link without killing Michelle. Not because breaking the link would save Connor Finn or his son, but because breaking the link would save Michelle. If the curse couldn't "recognize" her from the bio sample, it couldn't affect her.

When I'd first been bitten, the bio controls of my office safe hadn't recognized me and I'd had to use the "pregnancy override" to get in—a convoluted process that the safe's builders had come up with which allowed the safe to recognize the change in my biology—for nine months. Obviously the answer was not to get Michelle preggers or have her attacked by bats! But maybe we should try coming up with something that would change her enough to make the blood sample identification fail.

As an idea, that had promise. But how?

On impulse, I called Chris at the Company, the huge, private paramilitary company with fingers in pies all over the world. He answered on the first ring. "Gaetano here."

"Hey, Chris."

"Oh, it's you." His voice went flat and cold.

Wow, talk about your warm welcomes. Could he be any less enthusiastic? "You know, once upon a time we were friends. What happened?"

"I got to know you better."

Ouch. Bastard.

"What do you want, Graves? I'm busy here."

"It's a business call. I want to hire you. Who do I talk to and what's the daily rate?"

He dropped the phone.

I couldn't help myself. I laughed.

"Yeah, yeah. Ha ha ha." He was practically snarling when he came back on the line. "What are you looking for?"

"A client is going to be attacked with a blood curse on the full moon. I know there has to be a way to duck the spell—I've met someone who survived one. But he won't tell me how he did it. I was wondering if a blood transfusion would work, make it so the bio sample wouldn't find her."

There was a long silence during which all I could hear was his breathing and the scratch of a pen on paper. Finally, he grudgingly admitted, "It might work."

"Would it have to be a full transfusion?"

"Not by my calculations, but more than half."

"How much would it cost?"

"I'll need to run some figures. I'll need to get blood from the patient so I can type and screen it and find a suitable match. Then rent the equipment and find enough blood—we'll need six or more pints, depending on the client's weight. It won't be cheap."

"The client was hospitalized recently. Can you get the blood type information from the hospital records?"

"Not unless you can get me a signed release."

"I can probably get one from the client." I wondered if Fred's house had a fax machine. If it did, I'd have Dawna fax over a release for Michelle to sign and fax back. Maybe get a written commitment to paying our bill while she was at it—Abigail had promised we'd be paid, but she was dead. Michelle had to be the one to sign the checks. And hiring the Company would not come cheap. I was hoping for a "friends and family" rate, but I wasn't family and apparently we were no longer friends. That hurt worse than expected. It also pissed me off.

"Fine. I'll check with the mages to be sure we're on the right track, run some figures, and get back to you. Now put Dawna on the line."

"I can't, she's not here."

"She's not with you?"

"Nope."

"Well, that's something, anyway," he replied and hung up.

I punched the button to end the conversation with more force than was really necessary.

Since I was already in a foul mood, I decided I might as well call Gwen. I'd missed a couple of appointments and I was sure she'd want to lecture me and talk to me about my family. That was bound to make my day. Not. After that, if I didn't feel bad enough, I could sit in traffic calling all the other people who were angry with me and liable to be nasty.

Stop it, Graves. People get mad. They also get over it. How pissed were you at Kevin a couple of years ago? Now you're his boss and the two of you are doing fine. Just give things time. Of course that was easier said than done, and it did absolutely nothing to help me deal with the present.

I talked to Gwen, who wasn't nearly as fierce as I'd expected her to be—then again, some of my flowers had come from her.

I figured that maybe she was cutting me some slack since it was obvious I was in the middle of yet another of my infamous shit storms.

By the time I reached Los Angeles, the phone needed a recharge and I was seething with rage. I forced myself to go through the drive-through at a local PharMart to pick up some nutrition shakes, swallowing two out of the six-pack while I waited for my change. I didn't trust myself to go inside.

On the other hand, this was the perfect mood to be in to go confront a bad guy. So, hey, not a total waste.

Only a few blocks farther and I was pulling up outside Finn Billiards. I'm not sure what I'd expected, but it wasn't what I found. Jack's place was in an upscale, mixed-use neighborhood. There were a couple of twelve-story office buildings across the way and a pub on the first floor directly below. It wasn't quite time for the happy hour rush, but there were plenty of patrons inside, most wearing business suits. I caught a whiff of fries and burgers cooking even inside my vehicle. It took me a minute or two to find a free parking space.

I slathered on sunscreen, which looked odd given the faint glow my skin was putting off. The smell of coconut and aloe mixed in with the scents of food reminding me of beach parties with Gran and Grandpa when I was little. That made me smile—right up until I caught a glimpse of fangs in the rearview mirror.

I did a quick weapons check. I wasn't completely happy with the result. I've got backup gear, and carrying it is better than going unarmed, but I wasn't nearly as comfortable with it. Still, it's all kept in good condition, so it was ready to use, just in case Jack wasn't any happier to see me than his daddy had been.

The stairs leading up to the pool hall—were they still called pool halls? I wondered—were steep and narrow, but the lighting was good and there were sturdy handrails. Even so, they were nothing I'd attempt drunk. Then again, most of the really serious pool sharks I've known don't drink much "on duty." It messes with their game.

The temperature started to drop when I reached the midway point on the stairs. A cold breeze ruffled what was left of my hair. Frost began forming on the metal fittings that held the railing in place. My breath misted the air in front of me, and each time I inhaled I felt the sharp sensation of cold air biting against freezing nose hair.

A ghost. I bet I even knew which ghost.

"Hello, Abby," I said cheerfully. "Glad you could join me." The overhead light blinked once.

The staircase opened into a large room. A long, polished bar and an accompanying string of the usual black vinyl stools ran most of the length of the interior wall. Most of the rest of the room was taken up by billiard tables of various vintages and sizes, spaced far enough apart to allow ease of play. I spotted an antique snooker table in one corner. A pair of lights hung above each table, casting clear light onto the green felt surfaces with no distracting shadows. There were seats and tables placed at intervals around the room so that spectators could watch and order food and drink.

The décor was pleasant and clean and included movie posters from films like *The Color of Money* and *The Hustler* along with large autographed photos of champion billiards players from various eras.

There weren't a lot of customers at this time of day, only a couple of die-hard types who looked like they'd been here awhile, judging by the backlog of glasses and half-eaten sandwiches on a table near where they played. They ignored me, intent on what was probably a high-stakes game.

Jack Finn stood behind the bar, drying a glass with a white towel. Instead of the suit he'd worn when we met the last time, he wore jeans and a polo shirt that was the exact color of the table felt, with an embroidered eight-ball rack on the left breast. He looked younger than he had in the suit but still older than the twentysomething I knew he must be.

"You," he said, his tone almost identical to the one Chris had used. If this kept up, I might develop a complex.

"Me." I smiled sunnily. I might have shown just a wee bit of fang. The temperature in the room dropped precipitously.

"What do you want?" He set down the glass, moving ever so casually to his left, wherc I assumed a weapon was concealed under the counter.

"Don't," I told him. "I'm not holding a grudge right now. I'm here to give you some advice."

"Yeah, right." But he stopped moving.

The guys at the pool table had looked up and were watching us very closely. They hadn't moved this way, but I made sure to keep them in my peripheral vision. I know from painful experience that billiard balls and cue sticks make nasty weapons.

Behind Jack's back a few of the glasses started levitating . . . just a little. I hoped Abby would give me a chance to talk to Jack before she went all poltergeist, but she might not. After all, odds were good he'd had all sorts of things to do with her getting tortured to death. She was probably just itching for a bit of payback.

"I spoke to your dad in person yesterday. He's planning on going ahead with the whole blood curse thing, even though he knows that the two of you both have Garza blood in the family tree.

"Bullshit." His voice was cold, but there was a flicker of something in his eyes. Not agreement, precisely, but he was listening. The pool players had settled back into their game, but I could tell they were still watching and wary.

"If you don't believe me, check. I'm sure you have a couple of bio samples left. Use your magic. Check her blood against yours. I think you'll be unpleasantly surprised."

I continued, "I don't know how, but Connor plans to survive the curse. Maybe he's let you in on the secret?"

Jack glared at me, murder in his eyes. If I wasn't so intrepid—and if Abby hadn't gotten all sorts of weapons ready—I might have been a little nervous.

"Apparently he hasn't," I said. "Look, you know what he's doing. You know his plans. If you work with me, we can stop him."

Jack leaned forward, planting both palms on the bar. His gaze locked with mine, cold, hard, and steady. When he spoke, he enunciated every word absolutely separately and with perfect clarity. "Get the fuck out of my bar."

"If you say so." I turned toward the exit. He went for his gun. Before I could react, a wall of cues flew up between the pool tables and the bar, cutting off reinforcements. Simultaneously, Abby began pummeling Jack Finn with glasses and bottles of alcohol, even going so far as to fling the knives he'd been using to slice limes at his chest.

I turned back to the door and kept walking, ignoring his swearing and grunts of pain.

A guy from the table called out, "Hey! You said you weren't holding a grudge."

"I'm not," I answered without looking back. "The ghost is. Nothing I can do about that."

It takes a serious amount of mojo for a ghost to manifest with that much power. I didn't figure Abigail would be able to keep it up for long, so once I got to the stairs, I dropped the whole casual thing and hustled. I was starting the SUV when the first police car arrived; an ambulance passed me, heading toward the building as I pulled out of the parking lot.

Nobody stopped me. Hell, nobody even noticed me. All eyes were on the hubbub at the door to the pool hall. I pulled onto the street behind some guy in a subcompact and drove away with no muss, no fuss.

Well, Graves, that was next to useless. It was a shame, really, but then again, the plan hadn't had a lot of promise to it to start with. After all, I already knew that Jack was a murderous thug. I should've known he wouldn't be frightened by what I'd told him. Still, I'd hoped.

I called the hospital again, figuring that as long as I was already in town, I should see Isaac. Checking at the desk, I was told that he was allowed to have visitors. I then followed the cashier's directions to room 320.

I tapped on the door and was rewarded by Gilda's voice calling, "Come in."

When I stepped into the room, the first thing I saw was Isaac himself, sitting up in bed. He was pale and half his face was still swollen and black with bruises. His right arm was hooked up to an IV and various machines. But his left hand held Gilda's.

She was looking great. She'd pulled herself together this morning and was radiant in an icy pink silk track suit that set off her coloring, and her trademark jewelry, platinum today. Best of all, though, was her smile. It lit up the room. That smile told me the doctors had given the two of them good news.

"Celia." Gilda beamed at me. "I was going to call you, but the doctor was just here."

Isaac spoke softly. "He says that, barring complications, I can expect a full recovery."

"That's wonderful!"

I saw him squeeze Gilda's hand. They exchanged a look and she rose. "Celia, come sit. I'm feeling a little peckish. I'm going to head down to the cafeteria and get myself a snack. Would either of you like anything?" She bent down to pick up a handbag that was bigger than some carry-on luggage.

"I'd love a can of soda," I admitted.

"I'm fine, sweetheart," Isaac said, "but close the door behind you?"

"Of course," she agreed.

I took my place in the chair next to the bed. Before Isaac could speak, I asked him one of the questions that had been simmering in the back of my mind.

"Isaac, I've been wondering. The demon rift occurred at a prison. Now this thing with Finn—at the Needle, also a prison. Do you think they're connected? I mean, two incidents aren't exactly a pattern . . ."

"It's definitely something that will need to be looked into." He tried to smile when he spoke, but the half of his face that was bruised and swollen didn't do it well. In fact, he winced a little from pain and I saw a drop of blood form where his lip split open again at the effort. "But that's not what we need to discuss."

"Isaac." I took his hand, giving it a small squeeze. "Whatever it is can wait until you're better."

"No, Celia, it really can't." He seemed to steel himself, and I heard a small sigh escape his lips. "Isabella DeLuca came to visit me yesterday."

Oh, hell.

"We discussed what needs to be done to restore the protections around the prison." He sighed. "It will take the energy of the full moon, a mage for each point of the compass, and access to the node."

Access to the node . . . I met Isaac's eyes. The one that wasn't swollen shut was infinitely sad and terribly weary. "Because of my injuries, I am not physically strong enough to do what is needed and the doctors won't allow me out of the hospital at any rate."

Neither would Gilda. Not a chance.

"So John Creede will take my spot on the south point. Isabella has performed node magic before and will take the north."

Mama DeLuca had used node magic? Scary, but at the same time I wasn't surprised. Then again, I'd had so many shocks in the last few days that I might have lost the ability to be surprised. Plus I was so damned tired, I just wanted to crawl in a hole and pull it closed behind me.

Isaac continued. "Isabella has had to choose strong mages with a powerful connection to cover the east and west. She will hold the spell together, so she will be protected by the others. But they would do that anyway." He waited, letting the realization of what he meant kick in.

A strong connection to Isabella and Creede . . . Bruno . . . and Matty. The other two mages would be Bruno and Matty.

Tears blurred my vision. I was having a hard time breathing. I wanted to shout my denial, scream at the unfairness. But it wouldn't do any good. They'd chosen this. I was as sure of it as I was of gravity. The fact that Bruno, Matteo, and Isabella were family would make the magic stronger. The fact that Bruno had shared his magic with John Creede, to give him back his abilities when he'd been drained nearly dry, connected the two of them, which further strengthened the foursome's power. It made perfect sense. And any one of them would be willing to do whatever was necessary—even sacrifice his or her own life—if it would keep the horrors in that prison locked away from humanity.

They were heroes.

And one of them was going to die tomorrow.

"No." It was a hoarse whisper, a visceral denial. Tears were pouring down my cheeks. I could barely breathe from the pain in my chest.

"Celia, it is going to happen. It must." Isaac squeezed my hand.

"There has to be a death, but it doesn't have to be one of them." My voice was odd, thick with tears, but it was gaining strength.

"It has to be a mage, and the mage must be killed by magic. You are not a mage."

He thought I was planning on sacrificing myself? I'm noble, but I'm not *that* noble. Although for one of them . . . but it wouldn't be necessary. I had an idea that might actually work. "What about Connor Finn. What if he dies?"

"Celia . . ." His voice was stern. I knew just from the way he said my name that he thought I was talking about human sacrifice.

"I'm not thinking murder, Isaac," I assured him.

"Then what?"

"Karma. Magical backlash. Finn plans to use a blood curse on Michelle tomorrow night." I paused, then said, "If he can't kill her—"

Isaac sat up a little straighter. "His own magic will double back on him."

"And while he might have figured out a way to shield himself from the blood connection—"

"He can't hide from his own magic." Isaac's smile was cold, hard, and just a little anticipatory. "It's simple and elegant. But can you do it?"

"Do I have a choice?"

27

The drive back was much faster than the trip up had been. When I got home, I called Kevin to make sure he had his laptop. He did. So I used Skype to contact Michelle at the safe house.

"No. I won't."

I counted to ten, slowly, trying to keep my temper in check. I'd expected Michelle to jump at the only chance she had for surviving the death curse. Instead, she was balking.

"Why the hell not?"

"This isn't a hospital. I am not going to have a major medical procedure in somebody's living room. I won't do it. Besides, how do you even know they're going to try a death curse? You don't. Not really. You're just assuming they will."

I stared at her image on the screen. She was still very pale, but her jaw thrust out stubbornly, and her eyes were flashing.

"You saw what happened at the hospital. If we hadn't gotten you out of there ahead of time, they'd have captured or killed you."

She flinched. "Yes."

"We're doing our very best to protect you."

"I know. And I appreciate it. But—"

"But *what?*" I didn't shout. I very carefully did *not* shout. But she flinched anyway.

"Michelle," I heard Kevin's voice come from off screen. She turned, looking off to the left. "You have to trust us. This is what we do. If Celia says they'll try it, they will. And I know the doctors Celia's hired. They're the best in the business. They'll take good care of you."

"You're sure?" Now that Kevin was talking to her, she was wavering. Irritating, but useful. Maybe it was that he was male. Or maybe it was just that she'd spent more time with him. Whatever the reason, I was grateful.

"I trust Celia absolutely." He said it without any hesitation. "She's saved my life before."

"If you're sure." She turned back to the screen. "I guess I'll do it."

"Good. I'll see you soon."

I ended the session mentally and emotionally exhausted. Not good. So I took a hot bath, drank some comfort food, fed Minnie, and tried to rest for a couple of hours. Chris would be calling sometime soon with prices and details regarding delivery of the equipment and supplies necessary to make Michelle not "herself," at least for a while. I needed to be ready when he did. A nap wasn't a lot of recovery considering the kind of life I'd been living lately, but it was better than nothing.

I really wanted to sleep, but unfortunately, my mind kept racing—and running into dead ends, like a rat in a maze. I was missing something obvious. I knew it. I just couldn't see it. I tossed and turned so much that the cat jumped off of the bed in disgust. I gave up the attempt after a half hour. Instead, I covered myself with sunscreen, put on my favorite jeans and a T-shirt, grabbed the beach umbrella, and went out to sit on my rock and stare at the ocean.

I was still sitting there when Emma stopped by on her way home from work. She stood on the deck and called my name. When I looked over, she waved at me with the hand that was holding a pair of wineglasses. A bottle of wine dangled from her other hand.

I waved back, beckoning her. Soon she was picking her way across the rocks and damp sand to where I was sitting.

I scooted a bit to one side, making room for her. She handed me the glasses and bottle, then sat.

"Inez buzzed me in." Emma answered the question I'd been about to ask. Inez and her husband live in the main house. They're dear friends and have known Emma for years, so they'd be comfortable buzzing her through.

"Cool. So, what's up?"

"I need to talk. And I need a drink—maybe several."

"Hope you thought to bring a corkscrew."

"Here." She pulled it out of her pocket and passed it over. "By the way, love the hair. I wouldn't have thought of that look for you, but it works."

"Thanks." My smile was more sincere this time. I reached over to pick up the wine. "Dawna's sister did it."

"Seriously?"

"Yup."

"Very cool. And hey, you've got eyebrows and lashes again."

"Thank God. I looked seriously creepy for a while there. I had no idea that eyebrows were so important." I peeled off the foil cork cover and set to work opening the bottle. I was thirsty. Besides, this was one of my favorite wines, a very special vintage that John Creede had been part of developing. It tasted different—fantastic, but different—to each person who drank it. It became the wine best suited to each drinker's taste.

Thinking about John made me falter a little. We weren't together anymore, and it had ended badly, but I didn't want to think about a world without him in it. The same was true for Bruno and Matty. Hell, I'd even miss Isabella . . . but I was less worried about her than the others. I knew that both her sons would protect her with their lives.

I needed a distraction even more than a drink. So as I worked the cork loose, I turned to Em and asked, "What do you need to talk about?"

"Well, there's good news, and there's bad news," she announced. I had the cork out, finally, so she picked up the wineglasses, holding them while I poured.

"Good news first; I could use the lift." I slid the cork partway into the bottle, setting it carefully beside me so that it wouldn't tip over. I did not want that bottle to break or spill. The wine was too good, and too expensive, to waste.

"The church approved Matty's transfer out of the militant order and into the regular priesthood. So we can get married." Emma grinned.

"Yes!" I did a fist pump with my left hand. Then we clinked glasses and took a celebratory drink.

I didn't want to hear the bad news. I figured I already knew what it would be. Damn Connor Finn anyway. Then Emma surprised me.

"But they're transferring him. There are no openings in the regular orders in California right now. So we'll be moving to either Seattle or Portland." She sighed. "I mean, I love him. Of course I'll go wherever he's posted. But damn it, I just got the house finished! It's awesome. It's perfect. And now I won't get to live in it."

"Oh, hell. That sucks." I almost stumbled over my words because what she'd said so wasn't what I'd expected to hear. "But Portland and Seattle are just a road trip away. I was afraid they'd send you guys somewhere on the other side of the world—if they approved the transfer at all."

"Me, too," she admitted. She sipped her wine. "That's not what you thought the bad news was going to be." She stared at me through narrowed eyes.

Oh, crap. If Matteo hadn't told her, it sure wasn't my place to. But damn it.

Before she could pursue it further, my phone rang. I just about broke my neck in my hurry to get it out of my pocket. I was absolutely desperate to avoid the inevitable grilling Emma was about to give me. "Hello?"

Rizzoli answered me with, "About freaking time, Graves."

"Sorry. Life's been crazy. What's up?"

"You owe me two hundred bucks," he growled.

"Huh?" Okay, not the most intelligent response, but he had me at a disadvantage. I had no clue why I would owe him any money.

"I figured that with everything going on you might not be able to go back to the diner to get the SUV for a couple of days, so I paid the owner of the truck stop next door to park it in an empty bay. That way it won't get stolen before you can pick it up. But it's only paid through Tuesday, so don't dawdle."

"Thanks, Rizzoli, I really appreciate it. I'll be sure to pick it up before then. And I'll give you the money next time I see you." I paused. "So, what happened at the Needle after I left?"

"A lot of paperwork. A lot of interviews. There'll be inspections and all sorts of crap going on for God alone knows how long. Zorn is having conniptions. So is the warden. You were lucky to miss it. They're trying to keep a lid on how bad the situation actually is, so the press is being given limited information. If any reporters contact you, don't tell them anything. We don't want to start a panic."

I agreed with that. Just so long as they fixed the problem. "And Connor Finn?"

"They've got him under special guard."

Maybe that was good enough. I hoped so. But I wouldn't bet the bank on it—in part because I suspected that someone high up in the prison hierarchy was helping Finn and that at least one spawn had been added to the staff while the barriers were down. So the "Connor Finn" in the Needle could be a spawn and the real man could be free to do whatever he wanted. I *thought* that the Connor Finn I spoke to was the real deal, but I couldn't be sure.

Just the thought of it chilled me to the bone.

Dom was talking, and I got the impression I'd missed something. "Sorry, could you repeat that?"

"I said, I've still got your jacket and weapons. How do you want me to get them to you?"

"Where are you?"

"Right now? I'm at the L.A. office. I probably won't be back in Santa Maria until sometime Wednesday."

"Any chance you could drop my stuff by the hospital and leave it with Isaac? I'll probably go see him again tomorrow."

"Fine. I need to ask him a couple of questions anyway."

"Thanks, Rizzoli. I owe you one."

"You owe me *several*," he said, without malice.

I hung up. Emma was waiting, her expression very serious, her eyes dark and fathomless. For a second I couldn't remember what we'd been talking about before Dom's call. Then she spoke.

"You know what Matty and Bruno are doing tomorrow, don't you?"

"Em . . ." I started.

"The four of them made me swear not to tell, but you already know," she said accusingly.

There was no point in denying it, so I just nodded. "I don't have a lot of specifics. But Isaac gave me an overview of what's probably going to happen. And I think I may have a way to keep everybody alive."

Her jaw dropped in shock and she very nearly dropped her wineglass, recovering after a bit of wine spilled onto her leg. She looked at me and I swear I could see the hope rise in her. "You do? How?"

"By keeping Michelle alive. She's the key. If he can't kill her, Finn's magic will backlash on him. If he dies, none of our guys have to."

"And how do you plan on keeping her alive? The top mages in the world haven't figured out a way to stop a bloodline curse." I could tell she didn't quite believe that what I was suggesting was possible.

I smiled, but it wasn't a happy expression. "Don't be too sure about that. Finn is related to the Garzas, but he survived the first curse he cast against those with Garza blood."

"How?"

I told her my theory and how I planned to save Michelle. "I had to go through Chris and hire the Company to do it, but it'll be worth the cost."

"The Company." There was bitterness in Emma's voice when she said the name. Kevin had been affiliated with them for a number of years. She knew more about the Company than was probably good for her.

"They're the only ones I know with the resources who'd be willing to take this kind of risk."

"For a price."

"Always," I admitted.

As if on cue, my cell rang again. "Hello?"

"Graves, where are you?" Chris sounded pissy.

"At home, why?"

"There's a private airstrip outside of town."

"I know it." I'd been there a few times, since John Creede kept Miller & Creede's corporate plane there. It wasn't a big place, but it was secure and well maintained, and the runway was just long enough for a small jet.

"Can you get there in a half hour?"

"Why?"

"We need to get the equipment out to wherever you've got my patient stashed, and I need to do some basic tests—typing, screening, the usual.

"Didn't Dawna get you the hospital records? I know Michelle signed a release."

"Do you have any idea how long it takes the average medical records department to process paperwork to outside providers? Trust me. This is faster. And this way I know it's accurate. So I need to see the patient. Sooner is better if you want me to be able to get matching blood in time for tomorrow's full moon."

Made sense to me. "It's quite a drive—" I began, but he interrupted me.

"We're not driving. Hence the *airstrip*." He hung up on me. Again. That particular bad habit of his was getting very old, very quickly.

28

Emma insisted on driving me. I didn't argue. I went into the house just long enough to arm up, use the bathroom, and finger-fluff my hair, then followed her to her car.

It was a quiet ride to the airstrip, but not uncomfortable. Both Emma and I had a lot to think about. Waiting on the tarmac was a military-style helicopter. I had no idea what kind it was; all I knew was that it was big, green, and aggressive looking, with two engines, four rotors, and a fairly large cargo bay.

I jumped out the second Emma's subcompact came to a full stop, then leaned back in just long enough to say thanks and grab my purse before slamming the door and hurrying away.

Chris was waiting inside the open cargo door of the helicopter, looking impatiently at his watch. "What took you so long?"

"Traffic."

He grunted with displeasure. "I have other things I want to do yet tonight, Graves. We need to get moving. What's our destination?"

"Edwards Lake."

"Did you hear that, Rob?" Chris called over his shoulder to the pilot.

"Got it. Do you have an address, or do you just plan to direct me when we get there?"

I told him the address. Then I clambered on board and took one of a pair of empty seats, strapping on my shoulder harness.

The bay was large but crowded with cartons and wooden crates. A lot of the boxes were labeled, so I could see that they contained medical equipment. I supposed the crates were probably for Chris's other client. I didn't need or want to know what might be in them.

My inspection of my ride was interrupted by an unexpected arrival at the cargo door.

"Emma, what are you doing here?" Chris was shouting to be heard over the sound of the engines and the *whup, whup* of the rotors.

"I'm coming." She pushed past him and climbed on board.

"Em," I shouted, "what the hell do you think you're doing?"

"I'm coming." Her eyes flashed, her chin jutting out aggressively. Chris didn't argue, just rolled his eyes and gestured for her to take the seat next to mine. Then he closed the door firmly, as if to ward off any other invaders.

"Did you get any details?" I asked, but Emma shook her head.

We didn't talk after that. It was too loud. Besides, there was nothing to say. Plenty of experience had taught me that her talent as a clairvoyant wasn't something to underestimate.

There was an abrupt, upward jerk, and we were airborne. I closed my eyes, concentrating on not giving in to panic and not tossing my cookies. Once upon a time I was very afraid of flying. I've worked on that with Gwen. Most of the time now, I do okay. But the jerky liftoff of a helicopter is always a problem, and it gets worse when I'm nervous—which I was. I forced myself to remain calm. I succeeded, but mostly because I just couldn't bear thinking about the amount of crap I'd have to put up with from Chris if I didn't.

Vanity? Oh, yeah. But this once, at least, it was useful.

Forty miles was a short hop for a bird as large as this one. I had no idea how fast we were traveling, but we slowed to a stop and landed after just fifteen minutes or so. I helped unload the equipment while Chris did his medical stuff with Michelle, who was perplexed but cooperative. I hadn't explained anything to her or any of my team; I'd barely had time during the helicopter flight to text them to let them know I was coming,.

In less than ten minutes Chris was finished and the chopper was lifting off. Kevin, Emma, and I watched it go, hands shielding our eyes against the glare of chopper lights. Bubba was inside cooking dinner with Michelle. Talia had gone off duty awhile back and was out of sight, somewhere else in the house. At least I assumed she was. I hadn't seen her.

Maybe it was the wind raised by the rotors, but I caught a scent on the air, faint at first but growing stronger quickly. Beside me, Kevin stiffened. In the house, I heard Paulie start barking frantically.

Emma sniffed delicately. "Does anyone else smell smoke?"

I turned, tracking the odor, and on the ridge saw a wall of fire. In the instant that I stood there with my mouth hanging open, it began to race toward us.

"Everybody into the vehicle. *Now!*" I shouted. "We're evacuating."

Kevin followed my gaze. He swore, then bellowed, "*Move*, people! It's time to *go*!" His voice carried better than mine had; through the windows, I could see movement inside the house. Digging in his jeans pocket Kevin drew out a set of car keys, and the three of us ran around the house to the garage, where his SUV was parked. He started the engine with a roar as Bubba rushed out of the house with his gun drawn, a terrified Michelle at his heels, and Talia and Paulie close behind. Talia was naked and sopping wet from the shower, but she carried the holster with her Glock in it.

By the time we roared out of the garage, the fire had reached the driveway. The air was thick with smoke and soot, and it was hard to see. It was hard to breathe, and what air I could suck into my lungs stank of burning. Everyone was coughing, even the dog.

We flew down the road; crackling flames reaching for the vehicle like greedy fingers. The car lurched and bucked as we tried to outrun the blaze. If we could reach the dam, we should be safe.

Bubba was swearing under his breath, generating an impressively steady stream of profanity.

The fire chased us. No kidding. The road wound, and the fire wound with it, always staying slightly to our rear. At last we burst out of the woods, out of the flames, and onto the road that led across the dam at the base of the lake. The smoke and soot cleared just in time for Kevin to see a semi parked sideways in the middle of the dam, completely blocking the road. Sunlight reflected off the barrel of the rifle that rested at the ready on the truck's hood. I couldn't make out the shooter's face.

"Shit!" Kevin downshifted and slammed on the brakes, pulling sharply on the wheel. His attempt at a tight bootlegger turn rocked the vehicle onto two wheels and killed the engine, leaving us sitting sideways across both lanes. I shoved Michelle to the floorboards and climbed awkwardly over her to open the door and get out. Using the vehicle as a shield, I aimed my backup Colt at the threat in front of us. The fire continued to move inexorably forward, though it was considerably slowed by the lack of fuel out on the concrete dam and by the presence of water on one side.

The first shot rang out—not from the rifleman ahead but from an unseen shooter somewhere behind. It was a miss, but a second shot, fired from the bigger weapon a few yards away, thunked heavily into the engine compartment of the SUV.

"We're sitting ducks." Bubba fired his big old .44 cannon at something behind me. My eyes were all for the rifleman. He was biding his time, waiting for the perfect shot. That wasn't going to be easy with all the swirling smoke. My eyes were streaming and everyone was having periodic coughing fits.

"All right. I'm going to create a diversion. Give me a five count, then here's what we're going to do. Kevin, you take Michelle, Emma, and Paulie down to the water's edge. If you have to, you can jump into the lake to escape the fire. See if you can make your way back to Fred's by sticking to the edge of the lake; I saw an aluminum canoe at the dock there. Take Michelle out onto the center of the lake and wait for my signal. She'll be safe from the fire there and it's too far for a clear shot." I reached down, took my backup Derringer from its ankle holster, and handed it to Emma. If things went really bad, it wouldn't help much, but it was better than nothing and Emma was a steady shot. "Bubba and Talia, you take out the shooters behind us. Try not to get killed. I don't want Mona pissed at me."

Bubba gave a short bark of laughter.

"All right, people. Good luck." I took a deep breath, checked my weapon, and dashed away from the SUV, running straight for the enemy in front of me. In that moment, I did something I rarely wanted to do: I embraced my inner monster. I called to it, pulled on the always-simmering bloodlust to give me everything it had: strength, speed, vampire hearing and vision, the works. I tore across the pavement toward the semi, the scenery blurring around me as I gave a primal yell that flashed fangs.

I didn't get a good look at the shooter until I was almost upon him. I'll give him this, Jack Finn was no coward. I could hear his pulse speed up, but he still tried to take aim at me. He didn't stand a chance; I was moving way too fast. I leapt over the hood of the vehicle, screaming in rage and grabbing for him, but I had too much momentum. I overshot my target and landed on the pavement a few feet away. I spun around in an instant.

I expected him to fight, but he surprised me. Dropping the rifle, Jack rolled completely under the truck and out the other side. Scrambling to his feet, he ran straight for the edge of the dam, hurdled the railing, and dived in. The spell he'd used to control the flames died before he hit the water, the fire flickering and guttering quickly out.

The human ran so slowly that I had plenty of time to raise the gun in my hand and aim at him. Then I stopped.

Spare the pawn.

I didn't want to spare him. I didn't want to spare *anyone.* I wanted blood, and I wanted it now. I heard the splash as he hit the water, out of my reach, watched as he swam toward the dock with its little aluminum canoe.

He was gone.

But there were others close at hand.

I turned. With my vampire vision I could clearly see the humans a few yards away, despite the swirling remains of smoke and ash, despite the thin metal shell that enclosed some of them. As one, they stared at me.

I stared back, holding my body perfectly still as I tried to remember why I should not feed on them. There was a reason. I knew there was. But I was so hungry I couldn't think of it.

They were so warm, so alive. I was so cold. Hunger cramped my belly.

Still, I held my ground and tried to think like a human. I had a name. What was my name?

"Celia?" One of them said, without moving. It was smart of the large human to stand still. But it was oh so frustrating. If he just came closer I could feed, ease the pain, the hunger, and the cold.

My hands tightened into fists, nails digging deep into my palms until they drew blood. *I* was Celia—Celia Graves. The large human was Bubba, my friend. He was *not* food. None of them were.

The glow of my skin faded. I was Celia. I would *not* feed on humans. Not now. Not ever. But I still did not trust myself to let them close. Turning my back on them, I walked away.

I sat on the edge of the dock, my bare feet underwater, kicking in an uneven rhythm. I stared out at the moon reflected on the nearly still water of the lake, taking deep breaths—in through my nose, out through my mouth. The lapping sound of the water combined with the acrid smell of smoke competing with the heavy scents of algae and fish drowned out other sounds and other scents, but I still knew when Kevin drew near.

"You okay?" he asked.

"No." What else could I say?

I'd managed to beat back my beast, but it had been a hard fight. And I hadn't been thrilled when the very people I was trying to avoid followed me off the bridge and down to Fred's neighbor's place.

Kevin dropped two small plastic bottles onto my lap. "Emma

bummed a couple of nutrition shakes from the lady who owns the house. I brought them with me."

"I take it you drew the short straw?" It sounded more bitter than I'd intended.

"I volunteered. I figured I knew best of all of us what you were going through." He squatted down beside me.

"You know what it's like to see your friends and only be able to think of them as big, warm juice boxes?"

He grinned, showing lots of sharp teeth. "Steak tartare."

I laughed so hard there were tears in my eyes. Cracking open the first bottle, I took a big slug: strawberry, a little too sweet and a little too cold. But I knew that in a few minutes it would help take the edge off.

He was grinning when he sank down onto the dock beside me. "Mona's on the way with the minivan. She's bringing food. She'll take us wherever we're headed, but she can't stay. She needs to get back to the boat. Her brother agreed to babysit, but I understand he wasn't happy about it. I'm hoping to talk Em into going back with her. Or maybe she can ride with you and Dawna.

"Dawna's coming?"

"Yeah. I figured you'd need someone nice and harmless looking to deal with the authorities, and a ride home after."

Damn, he was good at this. "Thanks."

"No problem."

"We should probably talk about something else," I suggested. "Distract me."

"What would you like to discuss?"

"How's the client holding up?"

"She's a little shell-shocked, but she's hanging in there. Paulie's staying close to her."

"Good." The last thing we needed was for her to flip out. Not that I'd blame her if she did. As a normal person, she would never have had to deal with this kind of crap. I was actually used to shit storms, and this one was bad even by my standards. "Did Talia and Bubba get their guys?"

"Nah. When your guy bailed, the other ones set off some spell disks. By the time Bubba and Talia got through, all the bad guys were gone. Why didn't you shoot your target?"

"That was Jack Finn. A clairvoyant told me to spare the pawn, and a ghost told me Jack was the pawn."

"Well, shit. Doesn't that just suck."

I couldn't argue with that sentiment, so I didn't even try. After a minute or two of quiet sipping, I asked, "How are you on magical theory?"

"I was raised by my father," he answered drily. "I picked up a bit."

"Good." I ignored his sarcasm. "I'm going to bounce ideas off you. But this is all hypothetical and confidential as hell. You didn't hear anything. I didn't say anything. Got it?"

"Got it."

"I think"—I looked over at him as I finished off the first bottle—"that I've been an idiot."

He raised an eyebrow at that but didn't answer. That was probably a wise choice. We're friends, but I was his boss now.

"It takes four mages to do the spell to control a node, right?"

"Yes," he agreed, "one for each compass point. And the power of a full moon."

I nodded. "And a mage has to die by magic to activate it."

He blinked, apparently surprised that I knew that. I guess it's not common knowledge among the unwashed masses. "Yes."

"Does it have to be one of the four who are stationed at the compass points?" Isaac had said my idea was good, but he was also a champion liar. If he thought that I might interfere with the plan in order to save one of my friends, he'd lie to me to keep me out of the way and not feel guilty about it in the least. So I asked Kevin, knowing that he'd give me the truth, no matter how unpleasant. It's just how he was.

"No. In fact, it's better if it isn't. If one of the four dies, the whole thing gets thrown off balance, and the other three have to work harder to keep things stable."

Cool. That was what I'd hoped, and it was very good news for our side. But then the thing that had been bothering me all along, the thing I hadn't been able to pinpoint, finally reared its ugly head. "Michelle isn't a mage."

"No," Kevin answered.

I cursed briefly under my breath. This was a big problem that I couldn't see a solution for. I kept talking, trying to work it out. "Since she's not a mage, killing Michelle isn't going to do Finn and his buddies any good at all as far as the node is concerned."

"Whoa . . . Connor Finn is trying to get control of a node?" Kevin's eyes widened. "Oh, fuck. That is bad. That is so bad." Kevin didn't say it was impossible or doubt my sanity. That was a really refreshing change.

"Yeah. Tell me about it. He and his buddies are going after the node beneath the Needle."

Kevin shook his head. "Not doable so long as the prison's up and running. The magical protections around it would put up too much interference."

I opened the second bottle, chocolate mint. Not bad at all. I was starting to feel better, more in control. And chocolate after strawberry put me in mind of Neapolitan ice cream—one of my favorites. So I didn't sound the least bit irritable or panicked when I said, "More than half the protections around the prison are already gone. Creede, Bruno, Matty, and Isabella DeLuca are headed out there to bring them back up."

Kevin leaned back, stretched out with his elbows propping up his upper body. I could see that he had lost weight and gained muscle over the last few months and looked more like the man I'd crushed on when Emma and I had been in college together. "Repairing them should be much easier than tearing them down. You can use the existing remnants as a base instead of starting from scratch or having to break things so they won't interfere with whatever bad stuff you were planning to do."

"What would it have taken to bring down the Needle's defenses?"

He answered without a second's hesitation and without flinching. "Blood magic. And it will take more to destroy the last of them."

So somebody had already died and the bad guys needed someone else to die in addition to the mage. Things were starting to make sense again. "What if Michelle's death isn't really about the old Finn-Garza feud? I mean, Connor Finn wants her dead because of the feud, and the curse is how he's going to do it . . . But the reason he's doing it *now* is so that her death will take down the last of the prison defenses. And because of their shared bloodline, Michelle is a link to Jack Finn, who *is* a mage. And *he's* supposed to die so Daddy and the others can do the whole node thing."

Kevin blew out a breath. "It scans, but it's a little complicated. After all, Connor's already got a direct link to Jack. He doesn't need Michelle. "

"Yeah. But if he uses himself as the link, he can't use blood magic to make the kill; it'd double back on him. And if he does something to block that, he breaks the link. And he still needs to kill someone else anyway. So to my way of thinking, Connor Finn's decided to kill two birds with one stone."

Kevin and I sat in silence for a bit after that, both of us thinking hard. Finally he said, "It makes sense. You may not be exactly right, but I think you're at least in the ballpark."

I didn't know whether to be glad or sad. I suppose it was good that I had some idea of what was happening; it might make it easier try to counter the bad guys' plans. But a little part of me had clung to the hope that there was a more benign explanation. Silly. I knew that Connor Finn was truly a *bad* guy; meeting him had confirmed that for me.

But I just have a hard time wrapping my head around the fact that there are people who have such little value for life. I looked at Kevin. "You know what pisses me off most?" I sighed. I felt so tired and so damned stupid. All of this should have occurred to me earlier. If it had . . .

"What?"

"I'm the idiot who tipped Jack off to what was going on. If I hadn't, we'd still be safe over at Fred's."

"Well, hell. That sucks." He shook his head. "Why'd you do that?"

"When I went to see Connor, he baited me, said I had no clue about the big picture. I figured Jack didn't know he had Garza blood and would die if his father went through with the curse. I thought I might be able to turn Jack and that he would help us. And if I couldn't, maybe he'd let something useful slip."

"Not a bad idea."

"Yeah." I looked across the lake at the charred ruins of Fred's home. "Didn't work out so hot."

"Nothing you can do about that now." He gave my shoulder a reassuring squeeze. "And hey, we all survived."

"Yeah, we did."

"So now that you've figured out what's going on, what's the plan? Do you have any brilliant ideas?"

"As a matter of fact, I do—but I'm not sure you're going to like them."

29

Michelle was on her way to Kevin's place out in the desert, where he always went for the full moon. It was secluded to the point of being damned near inaccessible, and it was the only place I could think to put her where no one could possibly find her. Kevin hadn't been thrilled with the idea, but he'd agreed to it—mostly because he liked Michelle, wanted to keep her safe, and also couldn't think of anything better. Of course we had to explain about Kevin's condition to Michelle, Bubba, and Talia, and swear them to secrecy. I wasn't happy about that development. The fewer people who knew, the safer Kevin would be. But I really didn't see that we had a lot of choice. I trust Bubba implicitly. Michelle and Talia? I *wanted* to trust them, but . . .

Dawna and Mona arrived within five minutes of each other. Dawna stayed with me. Everyone else left with Mona in the minivan. I waited for the tow truck to haul away Kevin's damaged SUV and then gave a statement to the local cops.

It was a long drive back to Santa Maria. Dawna and I hashed out our plans for the next day during the first part of the drive. She promised that she'd make sure everybody got where they needed to go. I was glad to let her handle it. It would probably take most of the rest of the night to arrange, and while she'd be able to take it easy for most of the day, I wouldn't. Besides, I wasn't positive I'd be able to pull an all-nighter right now. I was beat.

We finished the ride in silence. I hadn't killed anybody. Other than that, I had thought the day had gone pretty much as badly as it possibly could.

Silly me, I hadn't factored in my mother.

It was after one and I was home warming a bowl of pho in the microwave when I got the call. I answered and heard Helen Baker on the other end, and immediately began to worry. No one called at this hour with good news. Before I could ask, Baker told me my gran was fine. The problem, as usual, was my mother.

"I'm sorry, Princess . . . Celia. I hate to be the one to tell you bad news."

"It's okay, Helen. Just tell me. I can deal with whatever it is."

"Your mother didn't react well to the news that your sister had passed over."

I remembered the scene she'd made during the conference call. "I know."

"She threatened suicide, so the prison kept her under close observation. After a few days, she seemed to be doing better. But when they relaxed their guard—"

"Is she dead?" My voice was flat, not hinting at the maelstrom of emotions I was holding at bay.

"No. It wasn't a very serious attempt. Her doctor said it was a 'cry for help.' "

Emotions boiled within me: hurt, anger, fear, anger, despair, anger. I love my mother. I do. But I don't want to. If I could just hate her, life would be so much easier. If I hated her, it wouldn't rip my soul to shreds when she did things like this or went to jail, or when she said the kinds of brutal things she'd said during the therapy session. If I didn't care, she couldn't hurt me.

But I did, and she did.

"Was there a note?" Why did I even ask? If it was a cry for help she'd have to write a note. I could even guess what it said: something about being abandoned by everyone. No doubt she blamed me. She always did. Fortunately for me, I no longer blamed myself.

"Yes."

"What did it say?"

She didn't answer me directly. "Your mother isn't in her right mind, hasn't been for a long time." There was no pity in her voice. If anything, I thought I heard an underlying note of anger.

"I should probably hear it," I said.

"I don't think so. And certainly not from me." Baker was firm. "I'll send a copy to your therapist; your grandmother can give me the contact info. If your doctor thinks you should see it, she can give it to you."

It was obvious she wasn't going to bend on this, and in a way, I loved her for it. Baker and I had looked out for each other more than once. And really, I knew what my mother was likely to say, and I didn't need the distraction with a major op looming. The mess would still be there when the crisis was over. I'd deal with it then, with Gwen's help. Assuming, of course, I survived.

I'd been silent for too long.

"You're not going to argue?" Baker said, obviously surprised. She knows me well enough to know how pigheaded I can be.

"Not when you're obviously right," I answered. "Are you sure Gran's okay?"

"She's worried about your mother, but she's also worried about you. She wants to be sure that you don't blame yourself."

That was a reasonable fear, based on our history. But this time, it was unfounded. For the first time, I didn't feel that what had happened was my fault. I blamed Mom. Even forced into sobriety, she couldn't take responsibility for her actions and their consequences. She would forever believe it was someone else's fault that she'd been "forced" to lie, or caught in a lie, or caught stealing, or any of the other stupid, hurtful things she had done. Maybe it was cold and reprehensible of me, but I didn't believe for a minute she was really suicidal. I believed she was desperate for attention, desperate to regain control—but not suicidal.

I was angry and upset, but not at myself. For once, not at myself. Ivy had taught me well.

"I don't." I took a deep breath, trying to steady myself.

"Good," Baker said firmly. "Because this is *not* your fault. Not even a little. Your mother is a sick, sick woman to try to blame you for her problems." I heard both conviction and support in her voice and drew strength from that. It was good to hear other people voicing my own thoughts.

"Thanks, Baker."

"No problem, Princess. I do hope you're not planning on being alone tonight."

"I think Bruno's coming over later." Actually, I wasn't too sure about that, but saying it would get her off the line. I was suddenly very tired of this conversation.

"Just so long as you're not alone."

"Helen, I'm fine." My voice was stronger. "I've been dealing with my mother my whole life. This is lousy news, and the timing's just about as bad as it could possibly be, but there you go."

That got her attention. "Is there anything I can do to help?"

"No. But thank you."

"You're sure?"

"Positive. I've got really good people working on it with me. We've got things back under control. I just need to get some rest."

"Princess, I'm very sorry about your mother."

"Yeah, me, too."

We hung up, and despite my emotional turmoil I was able to curl up with Minnie on the bed and fall asleep.

I woke up at three in the morning to the sound of a key in the front door. I was surreptitiously wiping a bit of drool from my cheek when I heard Bruno call out, "Celie, it's me."

I shook myself, trying to clear my head. "I'm in here." I shambled out of the bedroom feeling muzzy headed and went into the living room.

"Hi." Bruno tossed his keys onto the coffee table, then looked at me as I reached the bottom of the stairs. "What's wrong?"

Bruno and I don't have a perfect relationship, but we know each other very well. And we do love each other. I was more angry than hurt at what my mother had done, but I still needed to feel loved.

He put his arms around me and held me close. It felt so good. I buried my head against his chest, taking in the scent that was so uniquely him. I'd been doing this a lot lately, but it never ceased to make me feel better.

And now I was crying. Damn it. I didn't want to cry for my mother. Not now. Not ever again. And maybe if it had only been her I wouldn't have started weeping. But it wasn't. Tonight this man, whom I loved, was going to risk his life, and the lives of his mother and brother as well as one of his and my closest friends. They were going to try to stop Connor Finn and to protect the rest of humanity from the terror the prisoners in the Needle would release if they managed to escape—which they would if all the wards went down.

I didn't want to lose him, didn't want to lose any of them. If I was wrong—if even one thing went wrong—somebody I cared about was going to die.

"My mom tried to kill herself. There was a note."

"Oh, shit. Honey, I can't even tell you how sorry I am."

"Thanks." I held him tight, listening to the strength of his heartbeat, taking in the scent of soap, shampoo, and him.

He didn't say another word, just held me, and that was exactly what I needed. After a couple of minutes, when I was ready, I pulled back and looked up, straight into his eyes.

"I know what you're going to do."

His expression, so gentle before, changed to shock, his eyes widening.

"You know." He whispered the words as his hand came up to cup my face. "Mom swore us to secrecy. But you know."

I nodded.

I saw thoughts racing across his face. "Isaac?" he guessed with sad smile. "He's the only one not intimidated by her." He wiped a tear from my face with his thumb, then leaned in to kiss me. At first it was gentle, barely a brush of the lips. Then he pressed his lips to mine, kissing me as if I was life, breath, everything he needed to survive. I kissed him back the same way. He pulled away first, his eyes dark with passion and pain. "I love you, Celie. And while I wouldn't admit it to anyone else, I'm afraid. I know what we have to do. And I'm willing to do it. But Matty . . . mom . . . someone's going to die. What if it's one of them?"

He looked so lost. Normally he's incredibly confident, and with good reason. He's a powerful man, both personally and magically. But his family means everything to him. "Mom and Sal have been trying to find a mage willing to suicide. That's usually what people do when they need to access a node—find somebody who wants to die, offer to take care of his or her family. It's ugly, but it happens. There's even a standard contract."

I hadn't known that. I was a little shocked, but only a little. Life is hard. A lot of people decide they don't want to go on. Some of them were bound to be mages. But although I could actually sympathize with someone wanting to give up in the abstract, I had a much harder time dealing with my mother's suicide attempt. Maybe because a not so small part of me didn't really believe she wanted to die—but rather thought it was just one more manipulation meant to hurt me. Unfair? Probably. But still true.

I shook my head, forcing my attention back to what Bruno was saying.

"So far, we're not having any luck finding someone who is ready to die."

Maybe what I was going to attempt held only a small hope for success, but it was hope. He needed that right now.

"I may have a solution."

I could tell from his expression that he doubted that was possible. I could understand that part of him didn't want to hope, didn't want to risk being disappointed. He swallowed hard. Taking me by the hand, he led me to the couch and sat, pulling me down beside him. "Tell me."

I told him everything I knew and everything I suspected. I finished with, "I don't know who else is involved other than Connor and Jack Finn. I don't know what they're planning. I just know that they're afraid of me. Connor Finn told me at the beginning that their seer had said that if I got involved it could spoil everything, but that killing me would make it worse. He said there was even the possibility of failure."

"The possibility of failure," Bruno repeated. He didn't sound reassured.

"When I talked with Connor Finn at the prison, he said I didn't have a clue about the big picture, and he's right. But when I told him that I had one piece of the puzzle and that without it, he wouldn't have his big picture, he didn't deny it. In fact, it made him really angry."

"And what's your piece of the puzzle?"

"Michelle Andrews. I've got to keep her safe. And I think I know how to do it." I told him my plan. There was a long, thoughtful silence. Finally, I couldn't bear it any longer. "What do you think?"

"I think you may be right," he admitted. "But even if you're right and Conner Finn dies, that doesn't mean we'll automatically win. If the three remaining mages are strong enough and skilled enough to balance the power, they can use the node. I've read about it. My mother experienced it." He paused, taking a deep breath. "Is that everything you know? I need to know it all. I've never seen my mother frightened of anything, and these people terrify her."

I closed my eyes so that I wouldn't have to look at his face, see his pain and worry. I couldn't do anything more to make things better, and it hurt to know that. "I'm sorry, Bruno. I wish I knew more. I wish I could say I was sure we'll succeed. But we have a chance. And we have to try."

"Yes. We do." He was as firm as I was in that.

It was very late—or very early—and although we had only a couple of hours before we needed to be up and moving, we did have those hours. So we went to bed, and while neither of us was feeling amorous, it felt good to be together, just holding each other for comfort.

30

Minnie got us up at seven. I wasn't thrilled, but there was no denying her. I answered nature's call, then started the coffee brewing while Bruno took a shower. I went back to bed, curling up under the sheets, trying to relax. At seven thirty, I called my gran. It was really too early, what with the time difference, but I called anyway. She answered on the first ring, sounding wide awake. It wasn't a surprise, really, she's always been a morning person. But it broke my heart that her usual cheer had been replaced with something very close to despair.

At times like this, I would cheerfully throttle my mother.

"Baker said that it was more a cry for help than a real attempt."

"Yes," Gran admitted. "The doctor said that, and I think he's probably right. But it just breaks my heart. I know she's done wrong by you and made mistakes. But she's my Lana. I can't bear knowing she's in so much pain, that she feels so alone. I don't expect you to understand."

"It's okay, Gran, I get it. You love her. Hell, I do, too. And I know it had to be a real blow that Ivy left for good without even saying good-bye to her."

"Ivy was her baby," Gran agreed. "And while parents shouldn't have favorites—" They shouldn't, but they often do. Mom did, and I wasn't the one. "I wonder sometimes if it's because you've always been so strong and self-sufficient. Lana needs to be needed. Just like I do." She sounded wistful.

Wow, that explained a lot. Not about Mom; I wasn't buying that for a second. We'd needed the heck out of her when we were little and she'd chosen drugs and booze over us. But for Gran, it made perfect sense. It explained why Gran had to rescue Mom every time she did something stupid. She honestly couldn't help herself.

"Look, I tell you what," I began, thinking furiously as I spoke. Tonight was the full moon. Tomorrow everything would be over, for good or ill. "Why don't I see if I can catch a flight out to Serenity midweek? I'll have my doctor check with Mom's, and if they okay it, the two of us will go to the prison for an in-person visit."

"You'd do that? After everything?" I heard the edge of hope in her voice and felt my heart lift.

For Gran, I would walk through fire. "Yes."

"Oh, honey, that means so much to me! I love you so much." Now she sounded more like herself and I was glad.

"I love you, too."

When we hung up, she was in a better frame of mind, and Bruno was standing in front of me wearing nothing but a bath towel.

"Was that your gran you were talking to?"

"Yup. About my mom, of course."

He stepped closer and gave me a kiss on the forehead. "I'm so sorry you have to go through this. I wish I could help. I know I can't, but I wish I could."

"Thanks. I appreciate that." I did, too.

"Look, why don't you go take your bath while I fix breakfast. Sound good?"

"I have a better idea." I gave him a slow smile. "Why don't the two of us take a shower."

His eyes widened and his body immediately began to react. "What a wonderful idea."

It was a *long* shower. I've seldom felt so clean or so satisfied. We didn't get out until the hot water gave out and we were both completely sated and famished for breakfast.

Bruno dried off quickly and headed for the kitchen while I put on some makeup. One thing about the new hair, it was definitely easier to manage. No muss, no fuss, ready to go. A girl like me could get used to that.

I was feeling pretty good by the time I was ready to get dressed. Back in my bedroom and wrapped in my fluffiest robe, I found a shopping bag on my bed. It hadn't been there before.

"Bruno?" I called.

As he so often did, he knew what I was asking from just a single word. He called back, "I was at the hospital with Isaac yesterday when Dom Rizzoli stopped by. He gave me your things. I meant to bring them in before; I just got sidetracked."

Yay, the rest of my best gear! Before I had a chance to put it on, Bruno yelled that breakfast was ready.

I raced down the stairs. Bruno had not only made food, he'd straightened up—a lot of the flowers, which had begun to die, were gone. I assumed he'd taken them out to the trash when he'd gone to get my gear from his car.

A huge chunk of sapphire sat in the middle of my kitchen table as we ate.

"What's that?" I asked. I thought I knew, from some reading I'd done back in college, but I wasn't sure.

"It's a vosta, a focus stone. You can use a good-quality crystal in a pinch, but unflawed gemstones are better. Diamonds are best but damned hard to come by and very expensive. This was the best I could come up with on short notice. And I wouldn't have been able to get my hands on this if Isaac hadn't made some calls for me."

"Do I even want to know how much that cost?"

He looked at me soberly. "More than my house."

Oh, hell.

"It'll be worth it," he promised. "Using the vosta we can combine our magics better, turning them into a single, flawless whole."

I didn't doubt he was right. But *more than his house*? Damn.

I steeled myself, looking from the rock to Bruno and back again. "Seriously, how hard is this going to be for you?"

"It's probably the hardest thing any of us will ever do," he said quietly. "Combining magic is never easy, even when there's a strong connection between the mages; controlling a node is so dangerous nobody sane does it if there's any other choice."

"But you're still going to do it."

"We have to. We can't let Connor Finn have access to the power of a node and we've got to get the prison sealed up again. I know I could die and that scares me shitless, but this is something worth dying for. I have to do it."

I'd risen from my seat without thinking about it. I moved around behind him and wrapped my arms around him as I kissed the top of his head.

"I know you're right. But I hate it."

"I hate it, too."

It was nine o'clock by the time Bruno left. But having him around had helped—I almost felt like my usual self.

I spread sunscreen over my skin then stood in front of the closet trying to decide what to wear. Ultimately, I went with my most comfortable black jeans, a sapphire blue blouse, and my beloved black blazer. I also wore a Colt in a shoulder holster, a Glock in the back of my waistband, and anything and everything else I thought I might possibly need tucked into the pockets, loops, and compartments of my jacket. I was a walking armory, and damn, I looked good.

I finished off with my black Nikes, the ones with the white swoosh and the blue layer in the sole. You never know when you're going to have to make a run for it, and I wanted to be prepared. That was my motto for the day. Me and the Scouts.

When I put on my ring, I could feel the power of it augmenting my meager natural siren abilities. Good. I'd need the advantage of telepathy. Which reminded me . . . I went back into the bedroom, opened the safe, and took out some other very special jewelry. Then I grabbed the sniper rifle I'd liberated from Jack Finn during the previous day's confrontation and went outside.

My timing was excellent—Dawna had just reached the gate. I was surprised that she wasn't driving das Humvee. As I climbed into the car I started to ask whether everyone was in place and everything ready . . . then I got a good look at her.

She looked grim. Her makeup was minimal, her hair pulled back severely and tucked into a simple bun. She was wearing all black—black jeans and a black silk shell under a black suit jacket not unlike my own. Her jewelry was tasteful, just earrings and a matching bracelet. She wasn't wearing a ring.

Oh, crap. *She wasn't wearing her engagement ring.*

"Dawna?" I turned to her, not sure what to say or how to say it.

Driving, she spoke without looking at me.

"Chris and I have broken up. I don't know if it's forever. I'm not sure, but I won't live with him or any man ordering me around. I'm an adult and his equal. If we're ever going to make it work, he has to treat me like one."

"Dawna, I'm so sorry." Funny, I didn't feel at all responsible for my mother's failed suicide attempt, but I blamed myself horribly for Dawna's breakup.

"It's not your fault." She stopped at a red light and turned to look me straight in the eyes. "He keeps trying to make it about you, but it really isn't. It's about me, and what I want, and what risks I consider worth taking. And the fact that he refuses to recognize that, and respect it, is one of our biggest issues." Her voice was tight with both anger and pain, and I could see the tears that filled her eyes, tears that she refused to let fall.

"I'm so sorry." I knew I was repeating myself, but I just couldn't think what else to say.

"I'm okay . . . I'll be okay. I will. I know it's better that we found out now, before we actually got married." Her words cut off as her throat tightened too much for her to speak. She took a ragged breath, trying to steady herself. The light changed and she drove on. We said nothing further, but I tried to project *I will support you in whatever you decide* at her.

She drove to the airstrip, dropping me off at the curb, not even willing to pull into the parking lot for fear that she'd run into Chris.

"Be careful, Celia," Dawna said as I climbed out of her car. "I need you to come back from this okay so that you, Emma, and I can have that trip to the spa."

"Don't worry. We will, I promise. Later."

"Later," she agreed.

I watched her drive away, then hurried across the lot.

Even though I'd arrived a few minutes early, Bubba and Talia were already waiting by the gate, in the shade. Talia was dressed in desert camo. Bubba was wearing khaki cargo pants and a matching polo. They waved in greeting and I hurried over to join them, grateful for a spot out of the burning sun.

I pulled a velvet jewelry box from my bag, then turned to my employees. "Talia, I want you to wear the bracelet and one of the earrings. Bubba, you get the other one."

Talia looked at the beautiful diamond bracelet I was handing her with a mixture of lust and horror. Lust, because it was just freaking gorgeous. Horror, because, seriously, with *camo*? The look she gave me as she reached for the ornaments said more plainly than words that she was fairly certain I'd completely lost my mind. I didn't blame her. It's not every day that your boss asks you to wear a tasteful diamond earring and a matching bracelet into a possible firefight.

As she and Bubba took the jewels, I explained. "The bracelet is a microphone. It's got good range, even without the reinforcing magics, so I should be able to hear what's going on at your end no matter what happens. The earrings are speakers, in case I need to give you orders. I know they're a little flashy, but they're what I already had on hand, and I haven't had time to pick up something more boring."

"Ah, okay then." Talia smiled, relieved that the boss wasn't a complete nut job after all.

"Can't you just use your telepathy?" Bubba asked. He looked at the delicate earring balanced on his palm the way I'd look at a cockroach.

"I don't want to count on it. Finn was able to block my telepathy when they dumped me on the beach. I don't want to risk us being out of contact."

Bubba sighed and gave me a look that let me know in no uncertain terms that we would be discussing this later. Then he took out the simple onyx stud he usually wore and put the new earring on in its place.

He kept glowering until I passed him the rifle. The sour look vanished immediately, replaced by a toothy grin. I'd known he'd be happy about the rifle. "Would you look at this," he purred, caressing it lovingly. "Isn't this the one you—"

"Took from Jack Finn? Yes, it is. Spoils of war. You may not need it. But if you do, feel free."

"Have you ever used a high-powered rifle, Bubba?" John Creede asked from behind me.

"Yes, I have."

"Celia?" John was questioning my abilities and decisions. Again. I didn't like it. Not even a little. But I didn't want to piss him off. Then he might not let my people in on the operation. So I managed to be mostly polite when I replied.

"Why yes, John, I have used a high-powered rifle. I've also used a flame thrower and a grenade launcher."

Talia's eyes went wide. Bubba just grinned and said, "Tell him about the tank."

I scowled at my longtime friend. The tank story was not one I cared to share. It was just too embarrassing. "That was a long time ago and we are *not* going to talk about it."

Bubba laughed. John just shook his head in amusement. "Fine, fine. I doubt you'll need it, but I've never regretted having extra weapons."

He extended his hand to Talia. "I'm afraid I didn't give Celia a chance to introduce us. I'm John Creede."

"Talia Han. And I've used similar rifles in the service. I've got the marksmanship medals to prove it." I wanted to grin; having Talia continue my theme did wonders for my sense of humor.

But I kept a straight face as I wondered if I'd given the rifle to the wrong employee. Then again, Bubba was no fool. If he thought she was a better shot, he'd give her the weapon.

"Celia, do you have a moment?" John asked. "I'd like to speak to you alone."

I nodded and said, "Guys, hang out here for a minute. I won't be long."

"Sure, boss," Bubba said while Talia agreed with a nod of her own.

John and I walked a few steps away.

"What's up?" I asked.

"I'm working security for today's little escapade. I want your opinion on what I've got planned and any suggestions you have that could help—anything at all."

I blinked at him a little stupidly. He was asking my opinion. After the way he'd behaved in Mexico, not to mention ten seconds ago, I wouldn't have expected that in a million years.

He sighed, his expression growing more than a little exasperated. "I said I was sorry. I was wrong to undermine you with the clients like that. It was stupid of me. I *do* respect your opinion."

I forced myself to smile a little ruefully back at him. "Sorry. I guess I'm still a bit touchy about it." Yes, he'd just questioned my abilities not two minutes ago, but calling him on it would just lead to problems and more tension, neither of which was needed at the outset of a big operation. Better to let it go. "Okay. Fine. Now that we have that out of the way . . ."

He quickly outlined his plans. He'd organized the entire thing like a military campaign using all of the assets and personnel at his disposal as head of Miller & Creede. I was absolutely amazed that he'd been able to pull it off on short notice but wondered how he'd gotten permission to mount an operation like this so close to the Needle.

When I told him so, he said, "I didn't get permission. Whoever we're up against has to be in a position of power or someone would've tumbled to the situation before now. If I went through channels, they'd know exactly what we're planning."

Oh, crap. He was taking one hell of a risk, then. Seriously, he could get jail time, major jail time, at the Needle. We all could.

"Celia, there's a good chance I won't survive to see tomorrow. I'll deal with the fallout if and when I have to."

I didn't know what to say to that. He expected to die. He was even being matter-of-fact about it. I couldn't be. I love Bruno, but that doesn't mean I don't care about John. So I swallowed hard and tried not to think too much about the risks he was taking, focusing instead on the plans he'd laid out. "I can't see any flaws, John." I really couldn't. "It might be a little excessive, but hey, better safe than sorry."

His answer made me wonder if he was reading my mind or if he just knew me too well. "When I heard you were going to be involved, I took what I had originally thought were adequate defenses, tripled them, and prayed for divine intervention." He grinned, but I could see that he was only partially joking.

"Ha, ha, ha." I hated that I was dangerous to my friends and allies, that my death curse tended to increase the odds that someone I knew would be hurt or killed.

"Now, what exactly did you have in mind for your dynamic duo back there?" John asked. "I need to know how to fit them into my plans."

"I want them as close to the center of the action as we can get them. Their only job is going to be to protect the four of you and keep me advised of what's happening."

He opened his mouth, as if to protest, question my choice, but I cut him off.

"They're good people, John. The best. You want them watching your back."

He sighed. "Fine. Look, we both need to get going." He smiled for real then, and for a second I thought he was going to kiss me good-bye. But the moment passed. Instead, he said, "Be careful."

"You, too." My throat was tight. I turned away so that he wouldn't see that my eyes had filled with tears. I squared my shoulders and said to Bubba and Talia, "Go with the nice man. Make sure he and the other three involved in the working stay safe. I'm off to guard the client."

"Good luck!" Bubba called.

"You, too." We'd all need it.

My ride was waiting on the opposite end of the tarmac, the cargo door propped open. Same chopper, same pilot. Even similar boxes. Evidently the equipment had all been replaced. Good. But oh, Lord, I was not going to enjoy seeing that bill. Here's hoping Abby paid up promptly.

Chris stood just inside the open doors. Dawna had looked grim, but Chris was expressionless, a blank slate, wearing desert camo, a sidearm, and an anti-siren charm prominently placed outside his shirt. His manner was one of utter professionalism. Frankly, I was surprised he hadn't passed the job to someone else, all things considered. Unless the Company didn't have a lot of medics, which would make it difficult to shift assignments like this one on short notice.

"What are the coordinates for our destination?" Chris asked.

I pulled a slip of paper from my jacket pocket and passed it to him. He took it to Rob, and I took my seat, strapping myself in for the ride without waiting to be told.

Chris came back, closing the cargo door as the chopper's engines started up. Then he disappeared again into the flight cabin without saying a word.

I was fine with that.

I had to adjust the fit of the little bits of electronic equipment I'd be wearing to keep in touch with Bubba and Talia. Gilda had been the one wearing them last, and she's a much smaller woman than I am. Still, it took only a couple of seconds to get everything comfortable, and I was able to listen to Creede's briefing as Rob flew the chopper out to Kevin's cabin.

"Listen up, people. To work this magic, we need to be where the node comes closest to the surface. So do our enemies. There are limited options and they're not far apart. It's very likely we'll be working very close to the enemy. We'll keep up a veil as long as we can, but once the node is tapped, the interference is going to take everything down. When that happens, you can expect things to get hairy. Under the cover of the veil, we'll be building concentric walls of sandbags around the circle where the magic will be worked. Bubba and Talia here, are our last line of defense. Your goal is to make sure they have nothing to do. Once I'm inside the circle, Chuck is in charge."

"Celia," Chris said as if he'd already repeated my name a couple of times. Maybe he had. I'd been concentrating hard on Creede. "We're here. We've landed."

"Sorry. I was listening to John Creede. I left some people with him."

Chris shook his head, a half smile on his face. For just a second a hint of our old friendship surfaced, but then his expression hardened, his eyes going dark. "You'd better go ahead to the house. I know Kevin's expecting us, but I'd rather not startle him."

Smart man. Startling a werewolf on the day of the full moon is not a healthy pastime. So I unfastened my safety harness and climbed out of the chopper.

Kevin's place was on the edge of the desert, near Death Valley. I'd seen pictures when he'd bought the place just after the Needle had been built. The previous owners hadn't been thrilled with the notion of having the most dangerous criminals in the world living that close to them—even with miles and miles of inhospitable desert between the cabin and the prison—so Kevin had gotten it for a song.

I remembered that when the house had first been built, it had been featured in *Mother Earth News* as a perfect example of a building designed using recycled tires. The seller had given a copy of the article to Kevin, who had proudly shown us all the photos. The cabin had a stucco surface, with a wide veranda shielding the windows from the sun on the south side. The north side had been built into an earthen berm. There were solar panels on the roof and a windmill elsewhere on the property. It was austere but beautiful, blending seamlessly into the sere beauty of the desert, like a jewel in a brooch. I suspected the place was completely off the grid.

Emma had told me Kevin had made some renovations in the last few years. I'm not sure what I had expected. New bathroom? New appliances? Not this.

The simple fence that had previously surrounded the property had been replaced by a wall that was at least seven feet tall, two to three feet thick, and covered in tan stucco. Access was through a steel gate as tall as the wall and just wide enough to let a single vehicle through. The gate's controls looked similar to the ones at my place. A sign was attached to the gate, black with yellow block letters: TRESPASSERS WILL BE SHOT. SURVIVORS WILL BE SHOT AGAIN.

I stood outside the gate and bellowed, "*Yo, Kevin! It's me!*" Not the most elegant of greetings, but effective. I saw the edge of one of the curtains flick aside. A moment later, Emma came out of the cabin and approached the gate. She had my Derringer in a holster on her belt and carried one of those big squirt guns with the extra tanks. I had no doubt that the reservoirs were filled with holy water. I also knew that Chris, Rob, and I were going to get a little wet if we wanted to get past Emma. It was the only way she and Kevin could be sure that the three of us were who we claimed to be.

"Em, what are you doing here?"

She sprayed me. When it was clear that I was, indeed, me, she answered. "Kevin was worried that if something went wrong and he needed to hunt before you guys got here, Michelle would be unprotected. So I left Paulie with Dad and came out here as backup."

I hadn't realized her dad was back. I was glad. I knew she and Kevin had both missed him badly, and this might just give me a chance to extend an olive branch, see if we could work out our differences.

Chris and the pilot came over, both carrying boxes of equipment and supplies. Emma sprayed them, and only when they had both passed inspection did she put her palm on the control pad and open the gate.

"Where do you want these?" Rob asked.

"Put them in the living room. We've cleared everything out to make room."

"Right."

True to her word, the large room was empty save for a single recliner. The curtains had been drawn on all of the windows so that it was dim. Michelle sat on the wide ledge of a stone fireplace. After greeting me, she sat quietly, watching Chris set up the equipment.

I couldn't blame her for being afraid. A few days ago she'd been living a normal life. Now her mother had been murdered and she was being hunted by a mage who wanted her dead. And it looked like her only option was to put her life in the hands of people she'd only just met and attempt what sure sounded like a harebrained scheme with no guarantee of success.

In the last few days she'd been shot, had surgery, had run for her life twice, and been part of a gun battle. All that would have been hard on me, and I was used to violence. How difficult must it have been for her? I walked over to her. "Hey, Michelle, how you holding up?"

"Truthfully? Not so hot. Kevin's acting strange. He keeps pacing and looking out the windows. He hardly talks to anyone. Emma's worried, but she won't say why, and it doesn't feel like she's worried about *me*." She took a breath. "And I'm scared. What if the transfusion doesn't work? I mean, you're just guessing."

"It's the day of the full moon. Kevin is feeling a little restless." In fact, he'd gone outside the minute we'd come in, preferring to keep a little distance between himself and so many people. "And Michelle, you need to trust me. I am not going to let you die. I'll do everything in my power, whatever it takes, to see to it that you make it to tomorrow. Do you believe me?"

Her answer was a barely audible whisper. "Yes."

"I can't promise that this will work. I think it will; I think it's our best bet. But if it doesn't, we'll do something else." Right then, I didn't know what that something else would be, but I knew I wouldn't give up. I did not want her to die, not just because her death would help Connor Finn, but for her own sake. She seemed like a good kid. She deserved the chance to have a full, happy life.

Chris said, "We're ready, and we should probably get started right away. The rapid infusion device was destroyed in the fire yesterday and I couldn't get a replacement. So it'll take longer than planned to get everything done well before sunset."

I turned to Michelle, who had gone pale. She began to shake her head no, over and over.

"Michelle, you need to do this."

She didn't answer, just kept shaking her head. Chris, Emma, and Rob were all looking at me like: *fix this.* But I didn't know what else to say, how to convince her to go through with it. I wondered if Chris had brought sedatives; I wondered how he'd feel about transfusing an unconscious person against her will.

Just then the temperature in the room started to drop. A cold breeze ruffled my hair and my breath misted the air.

"Mama?" Michelle's voice held awe and wonder. "It's you, isn't it?"

The sound of scratching on the frame of the picture above

the fireplace mantel drew our attention. There, written in frost, was a single word. *Yes*.

"I miss you so much. I'm so scared." Michelle was crying, her words almost childlike in their desperation and simplicity.

You have to do this. You MUST. The words appeared slowly, but they were unmistakable.

Michelle stood. Swallowing hard, she turned to me. "Will you hold my hand?"

It was a bad idea. I'm part vampire, and there was about to be a lot of blood in the immediate area. I should be as far away from the whole process as possible. But she was so scared and desperate that I found myself nodding mute assent. I heard Chris tell Rob to turn up the blood warmer.

Michelle was still strapped to the machine when the attack came, a wave of heat that hit like a wrecking ball, driving me to my knees. Michelle shrieked as her hair burst into flame and burns began crawling up her arms. Reacting almost inhumanly fast, Chris yanked out the needle and tubing that were draining her blood, flinging the apparatus away from him as it burst into blue-white flames, the plastic melting to stinking black liquid before our eyes. He clamped down, holding pressure to the wound even as Michelle's skin began to blister and blacken beneath his hands.

"*Do something!*" he screamed at me. "You have to do something or she's going to die!"

He was right.

We needed to change her biology to make her unrecognizable to the curse, and the blood transfusion wasn't enough. My thoughts spun: what changed people? Demon possession . . . vampire attacks . . . shape-shifter bites . . .

"*Kevin!*" I shouted, spinning to discover that he was already in the room, probably because of all the screaming. "You have to bite her. It's her only chance."

"Are you *insane*?" He growled at me; his teeth were already elongating. He was so close to the change, holding it at bay by sheer force of will.

"You have to. She's going to die if you don't."

He looked past me at Michelle. I could see what he saw—blackened, crisping skin, swathes of destruction that grew as the stench of cooking flesh filled the room.

"Everyone get out of here," Kevin ordered, "now!"

Rob didn't need to be told twice. He vanished. But Emma had to grab Chris by the arm and drag him away.

"Go," Kevin said firmly, in a voice that was barely human.

I so wanted to run. But first I had to ask, "Will you be able to control her?"

He threw back his head and howled, his eyes bleeding to red as golden fur poured out of every pore. I heard his bones breaking over the sound of Michelle's screams. As he dropped to all fours, I drew my knives and began backing out of the room. I was at the door when he bit her and at the gate when her howls joined his.

I made it through barely in time, slamming the heavy bars in a pair of furry faces—one golden, one black as night—as they snarled and snapped, long claws slashing at me through the gaps in the bars.

I backed away, saddened and horrified. Michelle was alive, but at what cost? Would she return to human form, to humanity, when the full moon passed? What had I done?

Behind me, I heard the helicopter engine starting. Combined

with the howls of the werewolves, it was almost loud enough to drown out the sound of Bubba's desperate voice in my ear. "Boss, the veil is down. We can see them. It's bad. Tell Mona I love her."

31

The Larger wolf, a golden male the size of a small horse, drew back from the gate, while the female continued to try to reach me through the bars. The male's eyes met mine and, I swear to God, he smiled, showing lots of vicious teeth. He gave a sharp bark; she immediately turned her shaggy black head to him and there was a moment of communion. Then she trotted after him, and a moment later the two of them bolted toward the north end of the property, where the cabin was built into the berm.

Oh, shit.

I ran. "Get this thing off the ground!" I shrieked as I dived through the chopper's open door.

The panic in my voice had the desired effect. Rob pulled on the controls and the chopper slowly started to rise from the ground—too slowly to suit me. In my ear, Talia was shouting that they were facing a force of approximately two hundred, probably half of them spawn. Through the still open door I watched the wolves race up the north wall of the house and leap, first to the top of the wall, then in an amazing, flowing motion, down to the ground. They were beautiful—and utterly terrifying.

Chris was swearing and straining against the door, which

had jammed open. I scrambled to my feet and drew my knives. Not my guns—I didn't want to kill either Kevin or Michelle unless I absolutely had to. But I wasn't going to let us be turned into dog chow either.

The helicopter was probably thirty feet in the air when the wolves reached us. Michelle circled under us, howling her rage and frustration. Kevin didn't even slow. Instead, he poured on the speed and hurled himself upward in a mighty leap that actually brought his front paws onto the skid. He was struggling to pull the bulk of his body up when I stepped to the opening. I met his gaze. This time I was the one who smiled. Showing my knives and flashing fang, I formed thoughts and projected them individually and distinctly, directly into his mind: *I. Don't. Think. So.*

He let go, landing with a thud and a yelp of pain. As we flew off, I saw him rise and shake himself before the wolves ran off to together to find other, easier prey.

I slid my knives back into their sheaths and waddled to the front of the chopper, leaning into the pilot's area "Take us to the Needle," I ordered.

"Are you nuts?" Rob answered. "That's a no-fly zone."

"My people are under attack. I need to be there yesterday."

Rob turned to look at Chris, who was shoving past me to take the copilot's seat. "Boss?"

Chris met my gaze. He got a strange look on his face, and I noticed that the charm he'd worn earlier was nowhere in sight. "Do it."

Had I influenced him? Maybe. Maybe not. If I had, it wasn't deliberate. "If you say so." Rob sounded doubtful, but he turned the chopper and hit the throttle hard enough that I had to grab a handhold to keep my balance. I don't know how fast we were going, but the scenery was a blur, and the engines were running loud. Rob shook his head and hit a yellow button on the console. Suddenly there was utter silence. I could hear our harsh breathing and the rapid beating of four pulses.

I looked at Chris, a silent question in my eyes.

"Stealth mode," he answered, looking more like himself. "They won't see or hear us. It's damned dangerous—we're risking a midair collision—but nobody else is supposed to be flying around there and we don't want to get shot at.

Very cool.

"I don't know how long it will work. They're tapping into a node, and that's going to disrupt any magic in the area."

Rob scowled. Chris sighed. "Nothing is ever easy with you, is it?"

Emma appeared in the doorway next to me. Her expression was distant, as if she were watching a movie inside her head. Then again, she probably was. I had no doubt her clairvoyant abilities were putting on quite a show. "We need holy water—lots of it."

Chris sighed again and unfastened his seat belt. He shoved roughly past Emma and me, moving steadily despite the jouncing ride and the wind coming in through the open cargo door. Squatting, he opened a cabinet beneath the seats where Emma and I should have been sitting and started drawing out weaponry, a full-auto Uzi with ammo, pistols, and finally two odd-looking pieces of equipment that I'd never seen before. They looked a bit like flame throwers, but the tanks were marked with a cross and labeled HOLY WATER. They were obviously meant to be worn strapped on the back.

I grabbed one and put it on, grunting with effort. It was much heavier than I'd expected from its size.

Chris said, "They've been spelled. The tank holds four times as much as it should. I have no idea how they'll hold up around the node."

There was only one way to find out.

He passed me a belt laden with hand grenades marked with a bright gold cross. He had holy hand grenades. I found myself grinning. "Tell me these are from Antioch."

"Not funny, Graves."

"Two minutes," Rob called over his shoulder. "We're going in hot. It's ugly down there."

Emma started to reach for the second tank, but Chris shook his head. "No way. You're strong, but you're not strong enough. And Dawna would murder me if I let you both get killed. I'm in enough trouble already. You're staying here." As he said it, he hefted the second tank, slipping his arms through the straps.

"My husband is down there," Emma retorted, but Chris just shook his head.

Her *husband*? I didn't say anything—there was no time for it—but if I lived through this, I'd be asking Emma some very pointed questions. I went to the door. Despite the long drop to the ground and the gusting winds, I was determined to see what we were in for. I was trying to take advantage of our position to get a sense of what was happening.

It was eerily familiar. Everything was laid out just as the Wedjeti stones had shown Dottie and me.

The two circles of power were less than a mile apart. To the west, I saw a smaller force in the middle of a ring surrounded by two parallel walls of sandbags. The first wall served as cover for the troops and vehicles. The inner wall protected the mages. From above, I couldn't make out their identities; all four wore shapeless gray, hooded robes. The magic they wielded was colorful enough to compensate; it glowed a beautiful sapphire blue, creating a blinding glare.

Our fighting force—fifty men and women—was arrayed in a full circle between the sandbag walls. I couldn't see individuals, but I knew Bubba and Talia were down there.

I turned to the east and my stomach dropped. The circle of power there was huge, glowing a vivid ruby red. Only three mages stood. The fourth—it had to have been Connor Finn—lay still on the ground. I hoped he was dead and that he had died painfully. Even with Connor gone, the enemy's magic glowed brighter than ours, and by that light I could see a force easily four times the size of ours moving inexorably westward like a single entity. As I watched, there was a flash and a missile flew into the western encampment.

I heard the deafening roar of the explosion, saw bodies blown to bits.

I didn't throw up. But I wanted to.

Closing my eyes, I concentrated on my siren telepathy, sending out a message to everyone I could reach in our encampment. *This is Celia Graves. We're in the chopper between you and the enemy. Hold your fire.*

I said the same thing out loud, ordering Bubba and Talia to make sure the people in charge knew it was me. If I got killed, I didn't want it to be from friendly fire.

Emma came up beside me. She was wearing the Uzi. With calm determination she wrapped her arm in a strap by the open door. "Half of them are spawn. They're not even trying to look human. The holy water will injure them enough that the bullets can kill them. Go for a wide arc. I'll be shooting behind where you spray."

I turned to look at her face as the chopper began its descent. This grim woman wasn't the Emma I knew. Then again, I shouldn't have been surprised. She'd been tormented by a demon once and she was fighting for the lives of people she loved. I nodded as the chopper's stealth spell failed and the sound of the engines returned with a deafening roar.

Chris tapped me on the shoulder. I turned to see that he'd clipped two lines of black rope to a bar just inside the door. He was handing me gloves like the ones he was already wearing. I pulled them on as Rob prepared to fly us into the center of the melee, a no-man's-land between the two forces.

I thought of the death stone, lying alone in the center of my hospital bed, and shouted, "Wait! Not here." I grabbed Chris's arm before he could throw cables out the open door.

"What the fuck!" Chris snarled at me. I flicked the switch to activate my gun, spraying holy water directly at a spot between the two circles, the spot we were flying toward at alarming speed.

The water hit a wall of magic. As we watched, horrified, the concealing veil fell, revealing a thing I could only describe as a monster.

It was strange, a shimmering thing, its appearance so affected by magic that it was hard to focus on it. I could tell it was huge; I got the impression of batlike wings and long tentacles lined with vicious hooks made of bone, but I couldn't actually see them. I could see the eyes. Its eyes were terrifying, gleaming with intelligence, endless malice, and a terrible hunger. It roared, the sound beating painfully against both my ears and my psyche.

"*Shit!*" Rob shouted, banking the chopper hard enough that I would've fallen out had Chris not grabbed me. We made the turn, but when the thing swiped at us with a hook-lined tentacle, it missed only by inches.

"Where to?" Rob shouted, his voice hoarse. "The magic's too thick to get near either encampment."

"Go behind that rise." I pointed to a clear spot and prayed that I wasn't being an idiot. We'd be in for a long, hard run, but it was the best we were going to do.

Emma grabbed me by the arm. "That thing is demonic. Has to be. I'm going to call the archbishop and have him send in reinforcements."

"Rob," Chris called, "get the chopper as close to the blue encampment as you safely can. But stay alert. Don't let yourself get overrun."

Rob gave him a vigorous thumbs-up without bothering to turn around and look at him.

I nodded, and as Chris threw the cables out the open door I looked down, fighting to master my fear.

I was jumping out of a helicopter. Oh, God, *I was jumping out of a freaking helicopter.* Could I do this? I bit my lip till I tasted blood. In my ear I heard barked orders as our force rallied to repair the hole the missile had created in our defenses.

I grabbed the line and jumped.

Even with the gloves on I felt the burn of the rope, like fire sliding through my hands, as the ground rushed up to meet me. I had to let go about ten feet from the ground, dropping into soft sand, easing some of the impact by bending my knees and allowing myself to fall forward onto my bent arms. I rose into a crouch. As I did, I pulled the nozzle of my water tank around, aiming with my right hand as my left hit the lever to release the water. A plume of water as thick as my wrist arced upward. I made sure to aim high; drops of holy water fell like a hard rain on the front ranks of the attacking army. Most dropped their weapons, screaming as if acid were pouring onto them from above. The ones who didn't brought weapons to bear on me and on the man beside me. But before a single enemy shot rang out, Chris went to work, mowing them down with blessed bullets before pulling the pin and throwing one of his holy hand grenades.

There were cheers from our side; I could hear them even over the gunfire. As if we'd choreographed it ahead of time, Chris and I started backing carefully away, always adjusting the spray to keep the pressure on them. The footing was awkward, loose sand mostly, but with the occasional rock or cactus that would throw you off balance if you weren't careful. I could feel the tank on my back getting lighter—much lighter, and much too quickly. I was going to run out of water before we reached safety. The enemy sensed it. I could see them holding back, watching the volume of the arcing water drop, waiting for the moment to rush us, to make us pay for the pain we'd meted out.

The late afternoon sun beat down on me. My skin heated and began to burn. Tears of pain sprang to my eyes. But I kept the water flowing, even as tears blurred my vision so that I could barely see to aim.

"The opening is ten yards back and about forty feet to your right," Talia said in my ear. "There's a large rock behind you. Watch your footing."

I adjusted my steps as the flow of water from the nozzle in my hands sputtered and died. Without hesitation, I dropped the nozzle and started in on my own belt of grenades. The enemy had hung back, but not far enough—they hadn't counted on my vampire strength. Explosions tore through them, killing God alone knew how many. But not enough. Not nearly enough. We were close now, but Chris and I were both out of grenades. I drew my Colt, switched off the safety, and moved to cover Chris. There were plenty of targets: too damned many targets, many of them bearing hideous acid burns and expressions of unholy rage. They waited, poised to charge, as Chris's tank sputtered and died.

"*Now!*" Chris shouted. Turning, he sprinted full out for safety. I was right at his heels, running a snake pattern, seeing the sand puff up as bullets tore into the ground all around me.

Suddenly, directly above me, there was a flare of light, blinding as a welding arc, bright as a magnesium flare. Talia's voice, strong and clear, spoke the words of the Lord's Prayer as she held up the symbol of her faith.

There were screams behind us. Not all the creatures were affected by the holy items, but enough were to slow the horde to a stop, enough to buy us those few instants we needed to make it through the gap in the wall of sandbags to safety.

Bubba helped me strip the water tank from my back even as he half dragged me away from the gap in the sandbags. We were in the shade. It felt glorious, heavenly. As the burning of my skin eased, I was able to take in what my friend was saying: ". . . expected anything to happen until dark. They're using the power of the full moon. We figured it would happen after moonrise."

It seemed logical. I'd assumed the same, and I should've known it wasn't necessary. It didn't really matter all that much that the moon was on the far side of the planet. It was still full. The power was still there. Oh, it was marginally more difficult to control—but that problem had been more than offset by the element of surprise that they'd gained. Damn it.

"Now what?" Chris asked. "I'm assuming you have a plan, that you didn't just drag me down here so that you could die beside your buddy here."

I glared at him and bludgeoned my weary brain. We needed to tip the balance in our favor. There had to be a way.

And then I had an idea, an absolutely wonderful, workable idea. I started smiling. "Bubba, where's my rifle?"

32

Talia has it. She's the better shot."

"And where's Talia?"

"Right here." Her voice came from behind me. She was smiling, miraculously uninjured after her stint atop the sandbag wall. She wore the rifle slung across her shoulder with an ease that spoke of plenty of experience.

"Set the weapon up on top of the wall, aim it toward the circle," I ordered. "I have a target for you."

"Right."

She clambered up onto the nearest truck, lying on her belly on the roof. I watched, shivering from a sudden chill that probably had more to do with nerves than the fact that the sun was rapidly sinking in the West. The enemy had given up a cautious approach in favor of an all-out charge. The gunfire was almost constant.

When the grenade dropped in front of me, I didn't have time to think. Acting on instinct, I grabbed it, turned, and flung it over the wall as hard and fast as I could. Judging from the screams, it exploded behind enemy lines.

A familiar figure strode up. I'd worked with Roger Thomas in Mexico. He was a handsome man, well built, with prematurely gray hair and penetrating blue eyes. Even at the end of what had to have been a really rough day, his trousers had a crisp crease and his posture was perfect. His entire attitude spoke of command.

"Graves, you really know how to make an entrance." He greeted me with a tired smile. Something about the expression bothered me, setting off alarm bells in the back of my head. The whole time we'd been in Mexico I'd never once seen him smile. Then again, there hadn't been a lot to smile about. There wasn't now either. I shivered again but kept my voice pleasant and neutral and watched him very closely.

"Hey, Thomas, where's Chuck? I need to brief him."

His features darkened, but it was odd, as if the muscles of his face were fighting against the expression, making what should have been a smooth, automatic change of expression look stilted and uncoordinated. "Chuck's down. Flanders is in charge. He sent me here to pull you and your people to cover the breach."

My people—all three of them—didn't move. They were watching me, waiting for me to make the call.

"Thomas, I hate to ask, but I need to check you out. They've got spawn on their side, and you came from the direction of the breach." I reached into my jacket to pull out one of my little squirt guns of holy water.

Thomas scowled at me but didn't move. I hadn't expected him to like it. But if it was really him, he was professional enough to respect the necessity. If it wasn't, well, I'd know in a minute.

I stepped forward, intending to spray a drop or two onto his palm. When I did, he lunged at me. "*Damn you, Graves.*" Connor Finn's voice came from Roger Thomas's lips as he drew his Ruger. Fuck, Connor Finn was dead, all right, and now he was a ghost. Had to be. And he'd taken over the nearest channeler.

He didn't have time to aim as I closed the distance between us and chopped down on his right forearm with my left hand as I fired holy water into his eyes with my right. The gun fired as his forearm broke; the bullet went wild.

He screamed in pain and rage, his right arm now practically useless. The water hadn't burned him, but he'd pulled back reflexively anyway, giving me the opening I needed. I dropped the little water pistol and slugged him hard in the jaw, sending him staggering backward.

Chris drew his gun. Bubba moved behind Thomas, putting him in a classic choke hold, cutting off his oxygen. Thomas's face turned red, then purple, as he struggled to loosen the muscular arms that held him, bucking and struggling, trying to get air. I knew he'd lose consciousness any second. I was glad. I didn't want him dead. Thomas wasn't the problem; Finn was. I was about to explain that to them when Talia screamed and I felt warm blood splatter down on me like rain.

I looked up as she rolled off the roof into the truck bed, screaming obscenities. Her right shoulder was a red ruin. As Bubba used his belt to tie Thomas up, Chris climbed onto the truck bed and began giving Talia emergency medical attention. I scrambled up behind him, heading for Talia's previous position.

To the left, where the wall had been breached, I heard screams and heavy fire. The enemy had arrived.

There was no time to wait for Bubba or anyone else. It would have to be me. I took Talia's place behind the rifle. Ignoring the noise and chaos boiling around me, I set my eye to the lens of the scope.

What I saw was astonishing, awe-inspiring, an image that I would take to my grave. The destructive power of the enemy mages had grown, and they were using it to create a force of pure devastation that would wipe out anything and everything in its path, our small resistance band and their own troops as well. It looked like a tornado made of fire. Flames flickered up from the base, forming a long, narrow rope of orange and red that threaded up the center of a whirlwind of gray and black smoke and fury. Through the lens I could see individual flickering flames. I said a quick prayer as, taking a deep breath, I adjusted my aim downward, looking for that small pinpoint of light beneath the flames and whirling smoke. There it was, their vosta, a ruby as big as my two closed fists. I focused on the faceted red stone. With a small, silent prayer that my instincts were right, that this was the best true target, I tightened my finger on the trigger.

The rifle kicked painfully into my shoulder.

I looked into the distance, ignoring the chaos that boiled around me.

There was the briefest of pauses—perhaps the space of a heartbeat—then an explosion. The stone, unable to withstand the impact of the bullet after being weakened by the titanic magics forced into it, shattered, sending a shock wave outward. The fiery tornado was blown out like a giant birthday candle. The ground lurched sickeningly beneath me, as the power behind me expanded without resistance, flowing over me in a burning wave. I closed my eyes against both pain and nausea, bracing myself as my body reacted to the conflicting magical powers. Pure energy swept outward from the enemy encampment, flattening everything outside our walls, squashing the enemy army like so many roaches before burning their bodies to dust in an instant. The power hit the sandbags with hurricane force, the ground itself rocking from an earthquake that probably scored high on the Richter scale. The truck I lay in bucked enough to drop me into the bed.

When the powers met in the air above me, there was a sound like the chime of a huge bell. I opened my eyes, turning to see the pure blue-white light change to a vivid neon purple that shone more brightly than the noonday sun. People dropped to the ground, burying their faces in their hands, turning away from the light. I tried to use my forearm to shield my eyes, but I cared too much about the people in that circle to turn away. My four mages were tiny black specks against the painful brightness. As I watched, three of them fell to their knees. The hood of the standing figure's cloak was thrown back by eldritch winds, revealing Isabella's face as she shrieked the final words of the spell. Power poured into and back out through her, rebuilding the Needle's defenses, renewing them, making them more powerful than they'd ever been. The pain of the magic ripped across my skin and I screamed, writhing in agony, for an endless instant until the world went dark.

I forced my eyes open to find Bubba kneeling next to me. He looked a little worse for wear; one arm was strapped to his body and he was covered with dirt and scratches, but he was alive. There was something weird about his eyes. They were blue—really, really blue, like lasers or the light sabers in that old sci-fi movie. His eyes hadn't been that color before. Had they?

"Graves, you're back."

"Jeez," I wheezed, "can't a girl even take a nap without everyone getting spooked?"

It was a weak joke, but he gave a snort of laughter anyway, settling himself cross-legged onto the ground beside me as I sat up. Chris dropped a blanket over me and handed me a bottle of water. The blanket was rough wool and army green. Looking around I saw a lot more people milling about than had been there when I'd passed out. Most of them were in uniform.

"Drink this. Stay warm. I've got other people with worse injuries to tend to, but shock is tricky. Bubba, keep an eye on her."

Bubba nodded his assent. When Chris walked off to his next patient, Bubba turned to me. "Before you ask, they're National Guard. The governor sent in a unit at the archbishop's request. There's a group of militant priests here, too, working to banish the thing in the middle of the battlefield. The guard's pretty much taken things over. Bruno's fine. So're John and Matty. Mrs. DeLuca is alive, but every hair on her body is white, even her eyelashes. And she's blind. Chris bandaged her eyes, but I'm pretty sure it's permanent."

I was pretty sure it would be, too. She'd been a conduit for too much powerful magic. She was lucky to have lived. I figured she probably knew that. She'd been prepared to die. Blindness would be hard, and I wouldn't wish it on anyone. But it was better than dying.

So was being a werewolf.

Apparently it was a night for tough choices and compromise.

"What's up with your eyes?"

"The magic did it. Everyone the magic hit has blue eyes. You do, too."

Really? Wow. How weird. No matter how much I learn about magic, I'm always startled by the odd, esoteric stuff that gets left out of the textbooks.

"I have blue eyes now?" I knew he'd just said that, but I seemed to be a little slow on the uptake. Besides, I'd wanted blue eyes like Ivy's since I was a little kid.

He nodded.

"Don't suppose you have a mirror?"

"Nope, sorry."

Oh, well, I could wait to see my face. At least the color change didn't seem to have affected my vision. I could see the bustle of cleanup activity easily thanks to the full moon and the huge fluorescent lights mounted atop four big National Guard equipment trucks.

I sat, sipping my water, feeling strength seeping slowly back into me. Soon I might even be up to standing. But there was no hurry. For the moment I was content to stay right where I was.

"How's Talia?"

"Chris says she'll make it. He used some pretty hefty magic on her, and that helped. Still, she's going to need a lot of physical therapy if she's going to get full use of that arm again. They've taken her to the staging area for the medical choppers."

She was going to be fine. That was such a relief that I closed my eyes, saying a quick prayer of thanks.

"You okay?"

"Hunky-dory." He gave me a long, steady look, then asked, "Did you shoot one of their mages?"

I shook my head. "Nope. Took out the focus stone. That's where all the power was."

"Smart move."

"Thanks."

We didn't say much after that, just sat in companionable silence. I wondered what had happened to Thomas. He wasn't tied up on the ground anymore. But I didn't wonder enough to ask.

I turned at the sound of footsteps some time later. "Ms. Graves." Zach Stone, one of the lower-ranking employees of Miller & Creede, stood at full parade rest, as if we were military and I was an officer. I was startled by that but didn't comment. His expression was too serious.

"Yes?"

"Your employee, Talia Han, gave me a message for you."

"Yeah?"

" 'If I wanted to be in a war zone, I'd have stayed in the army. I quit.' " He extended his hand; on his palm rested my jewelry.

I laughed. I couldn't help it. It was a little hysterical, but it felt really good. I took the bracelet and earring Zach offered, then the earring Bubba held out to me. Rather than risk losing them by tucking them in my pockets, I put them all on.

When I thought I was steady enough to stand without falling, I got to my feet. Turning to the nearest medic, I asked where I could find the injured mages. His directions led me right to three of them.

Emma and Matty were holding each other upright, standing silently over Isabella DeLuca. Bruno sat next to her on a rock, his body sagging with exhaustion. His head was nearly between his knees. A wool blanket much like the one I wore was wrapped loosely around his shoulders; beneath it, he wore an old Mets baseball jersey and faded jeans. His eyes were blue, his hair liberally laced with silver. It was so strange. Not unattractive, but not the Bruno I knew and loved. I felt a pang of sadness but shoved it forcibly aside. He was alive. It was practically a miracle.

"Celia." He sat up, smiling hugely. "You did it." He held out an arm and I ducked beneath it, letting him pull me close. I buried my face in his shoulder for a moment, taking in the familiar strength, the warmth, the scent of him that had been a part of my life for so long.

"*We* did it," I corrected him. "It was a group effort."

He gave me a weary squeeze. "Yeah, but we were losing until

you showed up. And I heard you were the one who made the big shot."

I couldn't deny it, so I didn't even try.

The smile faded, his expression sobering. "Even with Finn dead, and them having to fight against both us and the existing protections, we were losing. Who the hell *are* these guys?"

"I don't know," I answered honestly. "Wish I did." It occurred to me belatedly that he'd spoken of them in the present tense. "Do you think they're still alive?" I hoped not. The force of the explosion when I'd shot the vosta had been huge. It had wiped out close to two hundred spawn. Surely nobody close to the blast could have survived.

He gave a huge sigh. "Finn's dead. I felt that. Another of the mages was killed when you took out the vosta. But two of them survived. I'm sure of it."

I swore wearily. Two new enemies, enemies strong enough and smart enough to have survived the equivalent of a magical Hiroshima.

"Celia." Isabella's voice drew my focus. She looked so frail, with her eyes bandaged and her hair snow-white, but she sat rigidly upright, her spine as straight as if it was reinforced with a steel rod despite the exhaustion she had to be feeling. She still wore her robe, but it had been bleached a white so pure it was almost painful to look at.

"Yes, ma'am."

"You did well. You should be proud."

"Thank you, ma'am."

"You're welcome." She sighed. "I owe Isaac an apology. Apparently he was right about you. He will no doubt want to rub my nose in it."

Isabella DeLuca was admitting she was wrong. She was going

to *apologize*. Holy crap. I stood there blinking. I knew I should say something but couldn't seem to come up with anything to say that wouldn't be seriously tactless. Bruno gave me a weary grin, but it was Emma who threw me a lifeline.

"Before I forget," she said, "Kevin called. He and Michelle are both fine. They didn't eat anybody."

"Oh, good."

Bruno's eyebrows rose, but he didn't interrupt.

Emma continued. "He said they'll meet us for breakfast at Irma's Diner at nine—if you're okay with him."

"Why wouldn't you be okay with Kevin? What happened?" Bruno asked.

"It's a long story," I told him, "and not important."

He didn't believe me, but he was too tired to push for now.

Emma and I shared a look. What had happened at the cabin wasn't something Bruno ever needed to know about. And ultimately, it really wasn't that important. I'd known for years that Kevin Landingham was a werewolf. I just hadn't realized what it meant—not until I saw him smile at me through the bars of the gate, met his gaze as he tried to climb into the helicopter after me. I knew now that there were times when Kevin looked at other human beings as food.

I couldn't blame him. Not when I had the same problem.

33

I was late for breakfast. I'd been right. The authorities wanted their questions answered. Rizzoli had shown up somewhere along the way, so while the powers that be were insistent about getting information, they were pleasant and polite about it. I overheard one or two interesting bits of information while I was waiting around. Warden Davis had vanished from the prison, and his magic signature was one of the four at the other site.

The authorities weren't happy with me. They were even less happy with John. But the evidence was clear. The other guys had demons and spawn, and in the middle of the desert were two dead mages who were supposed to be locked up in maximum security on the upper floors of the Needle.

We'd saved the day. Again.

So eventually they cut me loose. The first thing I did was telepathically contact Queen Lopaka—my cell phone, like everyone else's, had been confiscated, both to contain the leaking of information to the Internet and as evidence of what happened. At my request, my aunt agreed to call King Dahlmar and to apply her own political pressure, along with the King's, to help John Creede.

Since I didn't have a car, I caught a ride with Bruno. He agreed to drop me off at the restaurant, but he wouldn't be staying. He was headed to UCLA Medical Center, where they'd taken his mom for treatment. Matty had flown there with her—as a fellow patient. He'd overstrained his magic and they wanted to keep him for observation.

We didn't talk much on the drive. We both had a lot on our minds, and it wasn't far from the Needle to Irma's.

I knew Bruno was thinking of his mother and his brother, and worrying about John. They'd been rivals for my affection, but they were also friends. If there was anything Bruno could do to help the other man out of his legal difficulties, I knew he'd do it.

My thoughts were about the guys who got away and what that might mean for my future. I was glad to set that aside when I got out of the car at Irma's and joined my friends for a victory celebration.

Emma and Kevin exchanged meaningful looks, but I ignored them, the same way Kevin ignored the adoring looks Michelle was casting his direction. She was young, she was smitten. I didn't worry about him doing anything inappropriate.

Michelle tore her gaze away from Kevin long enough to meet my eyes. "Ms. Graves, I want to thank you. Your quick thinking saved me. I'd be dead if you hadn't had Kevin do what he did." She was so earnest, it was ridiculous. She was only a few years younger than me, but somehow she managed to make me feel ancient.

"It's not going to be easy."

"No, of course not." She smiled when she said it, flashing white teeth and deep dimples. "But Kevin's agreed to mentor me until I get full control of my beast."

I turned to him, one eyebrow raised in inquiry. He ignored me in favor of taking a big bite of rare steak, juices dripping from his fork onto the plate. Then again, maybe that was an answer.

I finished before everyone else. There hadn't been a lot of suitable food choices on the menu, and I wanted to get on the road. Kevin came up as I was paying the bill. He walked me out to the parking lot to wait as the mechanic brought out my SUV but didn't say anything until he was sure we were alone.

"Are you okay?" he asked.

"No," I admitted. "But I will be."

He stared at me for a long moment. "Yeah, you will. You've changed, you know, these past couple of years. You've grown up. Before the vampire bite, you'd never have been able to make the hard choices."

"It sucks."

"Yeah, it does." His gaze locked with mine, his expression more serious than I'd ever seen it. "Emma tells me that two of the warlocks survived. And that they escaped."

I didn't want to think about that right now. I knew I needed to, but I just didn't have the heart for it. I knew he could hear it in my voice when I said, "So they tell me."

"Do you want me to track them?"

Once upon a time Kevin had been a field operative for the Company. His specialty was hunting "hard targets," the worst of the worst. He was offering to do that again, for me, despite the fact that his PTSD was severe enough to require an assistance dog. He'd do it, too.

I stared at him, dumbfounded. Was it friendship that prompted the offer? Or was it something else? My gran had told me that men will fulfill a siren's needs, even to their doom. Chris had flown me into the middle of a war zone and jumped out of that helicopter because I needed backup. Kevin was offering to do for me what he'd done for the Company. Maybe out of friendship. Then again, maybe not. My vampire side had intensified after being left on the beach. Had my siren side been affected as well? I couldn't know without checking with my great-aunt, or maybe El Jefe, Kevin's father, Warren. But I knew one thing for certain: I was a siren. Influencing men was something I could do—but only if I let myself.

"No, I don't think so. Not this time."

He shook his head sadly and his shaggy blond hair fell slightly over his blue eyes. It was a boyish look, but his words weren't boyish. They were deadly serious. "You screwed up their plans, Celia. You. Nobody else. They're not going to forget or forgive."

He was right. I knew it. That Davis and the other man had gotten away was most likely going to bite me in the ass hard somewhere down the line. But it didn't matter. Kevin was my friend. I was not sending him up against these people. Not now. Not ever. There had to be another way to stop them. I would just have to find it.

I climbed into the cab of the SUV, feeling old and tired. My whole body hurt. Worse, my heart ached. So much had happened in the past few days. I needed some time alone to think and absorb it all. I rolled down the window to ask Kevin one last question.

"Are you really going to mentor Michelle?"

He grimaced. "It's traditional. If you turn someone, you're responsible for training her until she can control herself. When she's ready, I'll introduce her to a friend of mine who's the leader of a pack." He could tell from the expression on my face how I was feeling. "Don't feel bad. It's all right. I don't mind. You made the right choice."

If I had, then why did I feel so crappy about it?

"You're just tired. Go home. Get some rest."

"Maybe you're right." I turned the key in the ignition and the truck's engine roared to life. "Good-bye, Kevin."

"Good-bye. Be careful driving home."

"I will."

He stood in the parking lot watching as I drove away.

I thought about Jack Finn. I'd let him live. Had it been a mistake? Maybe. I didn't know. I'd done it because I'd thought I needed to, but he was a bad man, a killer who was probably only slightly better than his father had been. I thought about Connor Finn. We'd had quite the dance, he and I. I lived, he died, but his ghost was out there, a powerful, violent shade. There is only so much harm a ghost could do, but I'd no doubt he'd manage every bit of it given the chance. And there wasn't one damned thing I could do about it.

Thinking of ghosts brought memories of my sister. I missed Ivy. On the drive home, it really hit me. Usually during a long drive she'd provide the air-conditioning, mess with the radio, and draw hearts in frost on the driver's-side window. That would never happen again. She might be better off. I wasn't sure I was.

I turned on the radio, determined not to wallow in self-pity anymore. We'd won, damn it. Michelle was alive. The prison wards were back up. The bad guys' plans were foiled. We'd won. I hit the search button. The first channel it found was a disco station. The classic notes of Donna Summer's "I Will Survive" blasted out of the speakers.

It made me laugh. There were tears in my eyes, but the laughter was real, too. Turning up the volume, I sang along, belting out the words I'd learned from listening to the punk version. After that I felt better, enough better that I had a brainstorm. I hit the button to make a couple of hands-free calls, first to Dawna and then Emma.

"Celia, I just left the restaurant," Emma said. "I'm on my way to visit Matty in the hospital. What's up?"

"You're moving to Seattle, right? With your *husband*."

If it was possible to hear someone blush, I did. There was a short, embarrassed pause. "You caught that, huh."

"Yup. What happened to all that pre-Cana stuff the Catholics do?"

"Since Matty was going to be risking death to work the magic, the bishop gave us a dispensation. He married us himself yesterday morning."

"Congratulations! That's awesome." It was. I was so happy for the two of them. They were perfect together.

"Yeah, well, we haven't told his mom yet."

My happiness stuttered a little. Isabella has very strong opinions about big church weddings; I knew that from my previous engagement to Bruno.

"Fingers crossed it will be all right."

"You betcha."

"Is that why you called?"

"Yes and no. I had an idea." I was smiling so big I was pretty sure she could hear it in my voice.

"Oh?"

"We'd have to clear the zoning, but what do you think about Dawna and me putting our offices in your place?"

"I think that would be wonderful! And I'm going to be the one who springs for our time at the spa with Dawna. No arguments."

"And here I thought that trip would be a good engagement present."

"Nope. You'll have to find something else. This one's on me."

EPILOGUE

I slept all the rest of that day and met with Gwen on Wednesday. We talked about a lot of things. I felt better after. Isaac would be fine soon. Fred and Dottie were both fine. The bad guys were thwarted. John and I were on speaking terms again. I was getting used to the idea of living without Ivy. The only dark spot was my mother. But I was starting to get a handle on that. Just in time, too. I caught a flight to Serenity on Thursday morning.

Gran had seen the news and the press releases about what had gone down at the Needle. Everything had been edited severely so as not to cause panic. They couldn't totally hush it up; after all, the light show once the veils had fallen had been visible for miles, and the quakes and aftershocks had affected millions of people.

When she saw me, Gran hugged me hard, holding me close and telling me she loved me and was proud of me. She said she liked my hair and that I looked great with blue eyes. I was glad I'd come. I'd needed this, needed her faith in me to help cleanse me of my guilt and self-doubt.

We had a lovely dinner together at her place. Queen Lopaka and Gunnar Thorsen stopped by. She was hugely pregnant. He was just huge. It made me smile to see how protective he was of her. In all, it was a great day, very healing. By the end of the night I was almost my old self again.

Friday—not so much.

My mother refused to see me.

I wasn't surprised that she turned me away, but I was surprised that it didn't hurt all that much. I was more resigned than angry about it. She'll do what she does. I can't control it, but I don't have to play along.

So while Gran was at the prison, Baker and I did a little exploring in the city. I found a great tattoo artist who thought he could fix the damage to my ivy tattoo.

Friday night I flew back to the mainland. I had the big spa weekend to attend.

I took a sip of my margarita and glanced down at my leg, stretched out on a chaise longue in the shade. The new tat looked great. I felt good about that. In fact, I felt pretty good in general.

There were more of us here than I had originally planned, but it was a good group. Dawna and Emma were splashing around in the pool. Dottie was with Gilda in the hot tub. Baker . . . well, Baker was sticking pretty close to me. I had a strong suspicion that there was a gun hidden in the towel next to her lounge chair. I was okay with that. I had one in my towel, too.

I know the bad guys are going to come after me. But I'll be ready when they do. And I won't be facing them alone. I have friends.